THE SPIRIT OF NELSON STREET

With the threat of World War II hovering over Nelson Street, family and friendship have never been more important. Rosie Forrest's grandmother always told her to 'live every minute' and that's exactly what she's doing. Rosie is both excited and terrified, and when Blyth Vine walks back into her life, he complicates things even further. Pearl Bunting finally breaks free of her violent brother Kenny to make a new life for herself, but freedom has its price... When the bombs start falling all who live on Nelson Street are determined to preserve the Portsea way of life.

THE SPIRIT OF
NELSON STREET

The Spirit Of Nelson Street

by

Julia Bryant

Magna Large Print Books
Long Preston, North Yorkshire,
BD23 4ND, England.

British Library Cataloguing in Publication Data.

Bryant, Julia
    The spirit of Nelson Street.

    A catalogue record of this book is
    available from the British Library

    ISBN   0-7505-2225-9

First published in Great Britain in 2003 by Hodder & Stoughton
A division of Hodder Headline

Published in Large Print 2004 by arrangement with
Hodder & Stoughton Ltd.

Magna Large Print is an imprint of Library Magna Books Ltd.

Printed and bound in Great Britain by
T.J. (International) Ltd., Cornwall, PL28 8RW

In loving memory of Jeffrey Ashford
a man of laughter and wisdom

ACKNOWLEDGEMENTS

I should like to thank the following people for their help in the writing of this book.

Explosion Museum of Naval Fire Power, Gosport:
Stella Edwards, Mike Hockin, Mrs A Johnson, Mrs L Langford, Mrs Ann Maleham, Mrs Joyce McCarten, Bill Mansfield, Mrs Vera Palmer, Mrs Ivy Preskett, Mrs D Ranson, Mrs Ethel Reeves, Bill Sainsbury, Mrs M Trail, Mrs D Vernon, Mrs Jane Varndall, Alison Walton

Fleet Air Arm:
Commander Dennis White OBE FRAES FMA
The staff of the Fleet Air Arm Museum, Yeovilton
Commander Brian Wood, Royal Navy Historic Flight

Portsmouth Fire Brigade:
Mr Kenneth Hampton and Mr Eddie Wallace

Portsmouth and Gosport Libraries, the Portsmouth Records Office, and their staff

WRNS Members:
Zanne Aram, E.J. Carter, Lucy Desert, Nora Drake, Joan Dinwoodie, Patricia Dix, Jane

Eldridge, Paddy Erskine, Mavis Forster, Betty Gale, Nancy Hammond, Nora Harris, Daphne John, Josephine Johnson, Rose Johnson, Elizabeth McGeorge, Gwyneth Lynam, Monica Madigan, Josephine Mees, Florence Miller, Kathleen Pickin, Pam Pope, Betty Stratton, Joan Tyson, Georgina Tuckett, Audrey Vinson, Betty Williams, Cora Williams.

Thanks also to:
John Mitchell, Peter Rogers, Lydie Rolph, Chris and Margaret Seal.

1

Beattie Pragnell wanted to go home. She wanted
to be back in Portsmouth with sailors passing by
and the sea on her doorstep. Three years in a
country town had only intensified her longing to
return. Now, in late September, she'd wheedled
her husband back for a visit. They were going to
drop in on her son and family in another part of
Portsmouth, but that was just a sprat to catch a
mackerel.

Over sixty years had been spent in Lemon
Street. In that time she had been a bride, a widow
and a bride again. The Jutland telegram had come
to that house. She had sat in her doorway on
summer evenings gossiping with her neighbours
until the light failed – giving up the key had felt
like treachery.

Albert brought the car to a halt. 'Are you ready
for what you will find?' he asked. 'Slum clearance
isn't pretty.'

Beattie took up her stick. 'Had my fill of prettiness,' she said. Not waiting for him to follow, she
hurried as fast as her eighty-two-year-old legs
would carry her.

'Christ Almighty!' Her hands flew to her
mouth. Gutted of windows and reeking of cat's
piss her home was barely recognisable. It lay

13

cruelly exposed, like a tart in sagging corsets. She stood in the rubble, her head full of voices:

'Granny turn the rope will ya? We wants ter skip.'

'Beattie, lend us half-a-crown? Gotta send fer the doctor.'

'Beatrice, will you be a bride again and make me the happiest of men?'

Sounds came without words. The wails of the women she had sat with during childbirth, the gasps of the dying. Terror, joy and grief, here she had felt them all. As Albert hurried towards her Beattie struggled to speak. Then with a rushing in her ears the darkness came.

In that other part of the city, Rosie Forrest brought her motor bike to a roaring halt outside the Nile Tavern. She chuckled – that would wake up Nelson Street. As she slid from the saddle her father erupted from the pub door.

'Shut that off, for Chrissake!' he whispered fiercely. Grabbing her arm, he dragged her indoors and up the stairs.

'Cripes Dad! What's up with ya? No, leave go, I'm coming.'

'In the kitchen, quick!' He pulled her along the passage.

Angrily she rubbed her arm. 'You're scaring me.'

Dad turned away, but not before Rosie had seen his eyes. Her stomach lurched. 'God! Dad, what is it? Say something.' She grabbed his arm.

He stared out of the window, his shoulders shaking. 'It's your grandmother.'

'Gran? What about Gran?'

'She's gone.'

'Gone where? She's coming here for tea. I've made the trifle. Put jam on the sponge like she–' Rosie pressed her knuckles to her mouth as the full implication of the word hit her. 'Gone? You mean? You can't.'

He turned and took her in his arms.

She burrowed her face into his chest, drawing in the familiar smells of wool and Lifebuoy soap.

'Your Gran made Albert take her back to Lemon Street on the way here – shock of seeing her old home knocked down was too much for her – all happened in a flash. Rushed on ahead of him, she did – by the time he'd caught up with her...' Her father shrugged his shoulders.

Rosie nerved herself to hear the words that would turn dread into reality.

'Albert caught up with her just as she fell – must have bin a stroke or something – both ended up in the rubble. Gone in a flash, she was. Poor old chap, place was deserted. He had to lift her into the car and bring her round here all on his own. By the time they got here he was done for.'

Rosie felt her father's heart beating against her ear. All the time she was in his arms she could delay the acceptance of Gran's death. Once he let go of her the fact would have to be faced. 'Poor, poor Uncle Albert.'

'Exhausted, he was. Fell asleep on the sofa by the fire. God knows how he'll manage without her.'

'So you mean Gran's here?' She combed her fingers through her hair. It was terrible enough to

15

hear the words, but to see her grandmother? Panic prowled in her belly. Dead was something she witnessed in butchers' shops with the fowls hanging on hooks at Christmas time. Dead was at the pictures in cowboy films. Now, death was in her home.

''Course she's here. Doctor's been and signed the certificate. Mum's seen him out.'

'How's she taken it?' Rosie whispered into his pullover.

'You know, quiet like she gets. Wants you to help her get Gran ready for...' He broke off and looked at her as if she would know the words he was looking for.

'Get her ready?'

'Put her straight – ready for the undertaker.'

Everything was moving too fast. She clung to her father, trying to draw courage from him.

'We're counting on you,' he said. 'Always bleating about not being treated like a grown-up. Well love, this is about the most grown-up thing you'll ever have to do.'

Rosie rubbed her sleeve across her eyes. 'Gotta get out of my stuff.' She fled from the kitchen into her bedroom and slammed the door. 'I can't do it,' she said to the picture of her grandmother on the wall. How clever of Uncle Albert to have captured that moment as Beattie threw back her head and laughed at her, a six-year-old Rosie, holding her strip of seaweed. Her yearly visits when they lived on the Isle of Wight were treasured – Gran had time. Mum and Dad, rushed off their feet at the Tennyson, drawing pints and cooking breakfasts, rarely had that luxury.

16

Rosie turned away. 'Oh Gran,' she whispered, 'you can't be gone, I'm not nearly ready.' They loved one another unreservedly. Gran was rock-solid behind her always. With shaking fingers she drew a packet of cigarettes out of her slacks pocket. How was she going to – get on with things, without her? 'Oh Gran.' The match flickered and went out. She struck another one and inhaled the smoke. How could she have been zooming along the sea-front at the same time as Gran was dying? How could she not have felt something, some nudge of intuition? For the first time she wished not to be twenty-one and grown-up. Why couldn't she just remember her as she was in the picture? What did 'getting her ready' mean?

'Can I come in?' It was Mum tapping on the door.

Rosie was afraid. Soon she would be face-to-face with death, smelling it, touching it. How could she do that? What would her grandmother have done had it been Rosie lying there? Gulping back her tears, she opened the door.

'Your Dad's told you, hasn't he?' said Mum, holding open her arms.

'Oh poor Gran,' Rosie sobbed as her mother held her. 'Where is she? Have I got to see her dead?'

'We're both going to have to be as brave as she was. Can't have strangers touching Beattie. We're her family. It's what she would have expected of us.'

Rosie combed her fingers through her hair. What was expected of her, and what would Gran think of her if she funked it? 'Never seen anyone

17

that's died. Don't know if I can touch her and...'

'I need you, Rosie, we'll help each other. She was more than my mother-in-law, much more. It's the least we can do for her. Come on, love,' she whispered, 'you're braver than you think. Everything's ready in the spare room.'

Rosie followed behind, staring at the threadbare strip of matting on the passage floor. She pulled at her fingers, making the knuckles crack.

The curtains were drawn. Through a gap between them a patch of sunlight caught the edge of the dressing-table mirror, making a rainbow stripe on the bed. Rosie studied the mat on the dressing-table, concentrating on the pink flowers with their French knot centres. She was terrified of looking down at the bed.

Mum poured water into a basin from an enamel jug, unwrapped a cake of soap and unfolded a towel. 'We'll take off her clothes, and parcel them up for the bin, except for her coat and hat. She's had a little accident.'

Rosie gulped.

'Your Gran considered it an honour to attend to the dying. Sending them clean and tidy to their maker. Neighbours couldn't pay her but they used to give her a handkerchief or a couple of new-laid eggs, even some boiled beetroot.'

Time had run out. Plunging her hands down into her pockets, Rosie turned round and looked at the figure lying on top of the bed. It was and it wasn't her grandmother. Beattie's hair was full of dust and a bruise covered half her face. Dust speckled the paper violets on her hat. It was one of her 'Sunday numbers'.

'Dressed to kill,' she would have said, 'and died of fashion.' Rosie wanted those dark eyes, so like her own, to snap open and for Gran to laugh at herself.

'Gran,' she whimpered, 'Gran.'

'This is a privilege. You and me have something we can do for her.'

Rosie willed herself to touch her grandmother. Her skin was still warm but her face was empty. The difficulty of undressing the unresponsive body had her teetering between sobs and hysterical laughter. All she had to do was remember to breathe. But when she breathed her nostrils were filled with the stink of urine.

Mum dropped the soiled dress onto a heap of newspapers along with Gran's petticoat and drawers. 'We'll hang the coat out in the air, then have them cleaned properly.'

'Won't you throw it away?'

'Your Gran would want her coat to go to the Salvation Army. It would please her to think someone else would have some use for it.' She took up a flannel and soaped it before washing her mother-in-law's face.

Rosie dried the dead hands, remembering how – like herself – Gran hated sticky fingers. Washing the cold pendulous breasts, her granddaughter gulped down her tears; it felt like a trespass. She remembered being washed by her: sitting on the draining-board with feet dangling in the sink as Gran lathered her special lavender soap, Gran singing to her and making dolls from wooden clothes-pegs.

'We should have known,' Mum said, breaking

into Rosie's thoughts. 'When the slum clearance started she went off to Romsey with Albert, calm as you like. Said she was pleased the neighbours would be getting somewhere decent to live. Yet, all the time she was pining for Lemon Street.' She turned away and drew a handkerchief from her sleeve.

'You mean she was dying bit by bit from the moment they left?'

'Who knows? We're all a mystery to each other.'

Rosie watched Mum gathering herself together again. She wanted to go to her, but was afraid to draw away from the bed in case she hadn't the courage to return.

'You hold her while I dry her back,' she said, 'then I'll seal off her privates with a bit of cotton-wool.'

Rosie held Gran on her side while Mum soaped and towelled her. When she picked up the tweezers and the cotton-wool she closed her eyes and gritted her teeth. It was too intimate. 'This isn't Gran, is it? It's just the shell she lived in. Where d'you think she is, now, the real bit of her?'

Mum smiled. 'Beattie'll be meeting everyone that she loved in life, and keeping a seat warm for Albert.'

Rosie dried her grandmother's gnarled toes. 'Can't see her being happy in heaven. Always busy bossing people and planning things.' She giggled. 'What if she's sat next to some whiney old soul?'

'She'll love her and the old whiner won't be able to bear it.' Mum searched the hangers in the wardrobe and pulled out a gaudy flowered dress

20

and began to undo the buttons.

'I thought she would wear a nightdress,' Rosie protested, not knowing why.

'Loved bright colours. I was making it for her, just had to turn up the hem. Thrilled with it she was. "If I don't live to wear it, you stick it on my corpse."' Again Mum turned away.

Rosie held her breath.

'Come on darling, let's put on your glad rags,' Mum smiled down at Gran. 'Good thing she kept a few things down here,' she said, as she laid a fresh petticoat and knickers on the bed.

Together they struggled with the uncooperative legs and arms. While Mum cleared away, Rosie took the pins from Gran's hair and brushed out the dust. She found herself saying 'sorry' when she tugged too hard. From her earliest memory Gran had had long grey hair that she wound around her head. There were pictures of her with dark hair peeping out beneath her hat when she had been a young woman. She had never been beautiful but her face was arresting. Her dark eyes challenged and her smile was irresistible.

Between them Rosie and her mother straightened up the bed. Mum slipped a pillow under Gran's head and arranged her hair around her face to cover most of the bandage keeping her jaw closed. For a moment she rested her hand on her daughter's shoulder. 'You're a good girl and I'm proud of you.'

'Oh! Mum,' Rosie cried, holding her tight and feeling the tears flooding down her face. 'I know she's gone but I can't let her go.'

Her mother kissed her then slipped out of her

21

grasp. 'You go and put the kettle on and have a cigarette. Chop, chop! Undertakers will be here soon with the coffin.'

Rosie stayed in the kitchen just long enough to make the tea, then grabbing her jacket hurried down the stairs and out of the pub. Pushing the motor bike to the end of the street she kicked it into life. With the engine roaring in her ears she raced out of Nelson Street, along the dockyard wall, past the harbour and on to Old Portsmouth. Leaving the bike by the town wall she walked onto the strip of beach at the Round Tower. Hunkering down, she picked up a handful of stones and skimmed them across the surface of the water. She could hear Gran's voice talking to her as she had when she was a child.

'The sea is a great wonder, Rosie. Look at it. One day green, one day blue, yet when I let it run through my fingers it has no colour at all. It washed me ashore as a tiny baby tucked in the jacket of an unknown sailor. Listen! Listen! Isn't it the sweetest music in the world? It's like the sound of our breathing or the beating of our hearts. The sea is alive and talking to us.'

Rosie watched the waves folding and dissolving as they lapped the shore. The flirtatious kiss and retreat of the water running up the beach, then drawing back on itself. Gran wasn't on that bed in the Nile Tavern, she – was here within her.

'You pick up a handful of stones. Run them through your fingers. See Rosie, every stone along this shore is different. They're in a constant state of motion dragged from one beach to another. Who knows but what there's a stone here that was touched by Nelson.'

Rosie dipped her hands in the water and sniffed her fingers; they had a secret female smell. Was the sea a woman? Who could she ask now that Gran was gone? No one else shared her sense of wonder, or took things back to their source as her grandmother had done. She had rejoiced with Rosie when she bought the motor bike after months of holding down two jobs, one at the sweet shop and the other in the pub.

'If I had new legs I'd come with you,' she'd said. 'Youth and speed! What a wonderful mixture.'

Rosie stood, stone-throwing until the light faded from the sky. It was dusk by the time she stopped the engine at the beginning of Nelson Street and pushed the bike back to the pub. A note was pinned to the front door.

'Pub closed due to family bereavement. Open tomorrow. Apologies Alec and Miriam Forrest.'

She went into the empty bar imagining Gran sitting by the piano, her toes tapping and face alight with enjoyment. On an impulse Rosie went behind the counter and helped herself to a bottle of stout. Creeping up the stairs, she tiptoed past the sitting-room, ignoring the light beneath the door. Stoking up her courage, she opened the door to the spare bedroom. Gran was now in her coffin, on the table beside her a flickering candle and a vase of roses from the trellis in the back yard. Rosie bent and kissed her face. She took a stone out of her pocket and slid it down beneath the folds of Gran's dress. Beside it she placed the bottle of stout. 'You share it with Jesus,' she whispered.

As she turned the handle to leave, a voice whispered. 'Better put in a bottle opener while you're about it.'

Rosie started in alarm. 'Whaaa!! Uncle Albert, you frightened me!' she cried, making out the shape of him, sitting by the other side of the coffin.

She knelt down beside the old man and held his hand in hers. Albert gave her a returning squeeze. Rosie swallowed. 'What are we going to do without her?'

'Get on with living,' he whispered. 'My darling, you mustn't waste a minute.'

The chapel in Kingston Cemetery was crammed with mourners. How many lives she'd touched, thought Rosie looking around her. Here were old neighbours, some settled in new flats around Portsmouth and others who'd gone to Wymering, just off Portsea Island. There was poor old Uncle George from Eastney, walking on two sticks, behind him members of the Labour party; there was Madge Diamond the librarian and, of course, lots of sailors.

How frail Uncle Albert looked, his Lieutenant-Commander's uniform hanging on his spare frame. Albert Pragnell, the young midshipman who had fallen in love with Beattie when she was his mother's scullery-maid all those years ago. He had waited for her half his life.

Rosie squeezed the hand of her brother and felt a returning squeeze. Gran always said he was the image of Joseph Forrest, her first husband, with his fiery hair and shouting laugh. And so Joseph

24

Forrest the second he had to be. Dad blinked away his tears and Mum stared straight ahead.

The last verse of 'Abide with me' died away and the pallbearers left their seats. Dad and Joe lined up beside each other, and then behind them came the two neighbours, neither of whom she recognised. The undertaker fussed about making sure the coffin was securely on their shoulders before preceding them out of church. It was the last Friday in September, and the leaves on the trees were beginning to drift down onto the grass. Late afternoon sun warmed her back as Rosie followed Mum and Uncle Albert down the path. The dying summer intensified her loss.

Behind her she heard two old men talking.

'The world's holding its breath. Neville Chamberlain's an old man. What chance has he against Hitler?'

'We gotta get in there and give him a dose of his own medicine. By Christ! If I was twenty years younger...'

'All this talk terrifies me,' her mother was saying fiercely to Albert. 'If the youngsters only knew a quarter of the pain and terror of war. 'Least Beattie'll be spared. I couldn't bear it if Joseph got swept up in all that madness. There's him eighteen and Rosie twenty-one.'

Albert said nothing.

What if war did come? thought Rosie. She would have a real job, in uniform. Anything would be better than weighing out Old Holborn tobacco or quarters of toffee. Looking at her mother's stricken face she felt ashamed.

Albert was crying.

Rosie turned her head and glared angrily at the two old warmongers and they fell silent.

Mum gave Albert a hankie. 'You made her so happy – said you were her compass.'

'And where is mine?' he asked, his grey eyes swimming with tears.

'Only another half-hour or so and you can come home with us and rest. You keep hold of us – not long – not long now.'

Each taking an arm, Rosie and her mother walked him up to the graveside.

As the vicar droned on, Rosie fell into a dream. Then her skin prickled. Across the grave stood a blond sailor holding his cap in his hand. His face, dappled by the leaves of a chestnut tree, was part in sunshine, part shadow. He winked at her. Startled, she tried to look shocked but found herself almost smiling. She looked at him again as he ran his tongue slowly over his lips.

Rosie blushed. Ooh! He was succulent – like the best cake in the window, oozing sweetness. She wanted to reach across the coffin and touch his mouth. Desire in a graveyard! She wanted to laugh and weep at the same time. Beattie would have chuckled at the thought of her grand-daughter flirting at her funeral. Mum nudged her. As the coffin was lowered into place there was the faintest clink of glass hitting stone. Was it the bottle of stout chinking against the little stone from Gran's beach, she wondered? After throwing a handful of earth on the grave Rosie looked up, but Mr Succulence had gone.

2

Miriam Forrest stood in the public bar of the Nile Tavern and looked about her. On the wall opposite, hung perilously near the dart board, was a painting entitled: *A View of Egypt*. Bilious palm trees towered over pyramids surrounding an impossibly blue river Nile. It was bold, cock-eyed and peppered with holes. Alec had wanted to consign it to the Gents but she had insisted on it staying where it was. The regulars loved it. To Miriam it symbolised the spirit of Pompey, as the locals called their city.

When the lease on their pub in the Isle of Wight had run out two years ago, she and Alec, Rosie and Joseph had moved to the heart of Portsmouth. They had taken on the down-at-heel Nile Tavern and made a go of it.

Landport consisted of row upon row of pinched-together houses running north from the Guildhall. They straddled Commercial Road and included the Unicorn Gate of the dockyard. The residents were stallholders at Charlotte Street, sailors, shop workers, dockyard maties, charladies and corset-makers.

Tonight, Friday the sixteenth of December, was pay-out night for the Nile Tavern Christmas club. Miriam knew her customers would be in a ferment of excitement.

Soon maties would pour out of the dockyard

and collect their bikes, anticipating the pints of beer waiting for them in the pub. Others would buy, 'something for the weekend' from the barber, in expectation that, after a couple of port and lemons, the missus might oblige. For her part, the missus would be totting up the entries in her Christmas club membership book. Fifty-two weeks of sixpences and shillings paid in, plus the interest, was bound to amount to a pound or so. As hubby's dinner heated on one burner of the cooker she set her curling tongs on the other. Girls, having stood at their stalls in the market, stamping their feet on the slushy pavement, ached for packing-up time. Soon they would paint their lips and put a dab of 'Evening in Paris' behind each ear. What would their blokes buy them in exchange for a cuddle, they wondered. Lads slicked down their hair with Brylcreem and calculated how far they could go without committing themselves.

Miriam looked up at the banner strung above the bar. In gold letters it proclaimed: *'The Forrest Family wish all their customers a Merry Christmas and Peaceful New Year.'* She meant every word.

Alec walked up behind her and, wrapping his arms round her waist, 'What you thinking?' he asked, kissing her neck.

She turned and smiled at him. 'Be a different Christmas without Ma sat by the piano. Wasn't anyone like her for celebrating, was there? Could make a banquet out of a crumb.'

'Used to get all secretive, always hiding things under her chair. It was never the price of anything Mother gave you it was the thought that

28

went into it: the pot of bulbs with your name painted on it, the "Be Prepared" boxes with a tin opener, screwdriver and sewing things inside.'

Miriam laughed. 'What about the First Aid Manual filled with poems and bits out of the Bible written out by hand? Must have taken her ages. Reckoned the right word at the right time could save your life.'

'There are patches of time when I scarcely think of her, then I hear a bit of gossip she would have relished or hear a tune she once loved and it stabs me afresh – that she's gone.'

'I asked Albert was he coming down, but he wants to stay put in Romsey with Uncle Sam and Auntie Olive. Says he'd like Rosie to go over on Boxing Day. He's got something special Beattie wanted her to have.' Miriam shivered. 'We must make this a good Christmas. Might be the last one we're all together.'

Alec's arms tightened around her. 'Can't believe it's happening again, after all the slaughter of the last war. I'm an air-raid warden for God's sake. Last week dishing out the gas masks, it was like a nightmare. Ugly smelly things, yet people were queuing for them. Two o'clock in the morning we finished, two o'clock. We'll be in the thick of it again. With our dockyard and the harbour we'll be a prime target – poor bloody Pompey.'

Miriam shuddered. 'At least, this time, I shan't have to wonder whether you're alive or dead, we'll be in it together. But it's Rosie and Joseph I worry about. Well, not him so much, now I know that the fire brigade's a reserved occupation. God knows what she'd sign up for though, given the chance. Rosie's the image of Gran – got such a hunger for life and new experiences. But she hasn't got her gift for reading a situation, and I don't know whether she's got her staying power.'

Alec drew her into his arms. 'Mirry, love, she's only twenty-one. What d'you expect? Remember the way she helped you get Ma ready for her coffin? She didn't want to, but she did it.'

Miriam squeezed his hand again. 'You're right. That's Beattie's legacy to her granddaughter – facing up to things.'

Alec smiled. 'She reminds me of a spinnaker billowing in the wind. Life will teach her how to trim her sails. Let's get tonight under way, sweetheart. Make the most of our kids while they're here. Tomorrow we'll search out one of Ma's books and find something life-saving.'

Hand-in-hand they walked up the stairs together. In their bedroom Rosie was studying herself by the full-length mirror. She turned towards them and gave an experimental twirl.

Miriam smiled, their daughter looked stunning. She wore a black snug-fitting wool dress with silver tinselly stripes woven through the bodice, and puffed sleeves. Her lips were painted scarlet and pinned to her brown curls was a silver bow.

'Do I look tarty? Watcha think?' She studied them anxiously.

Alec grinned at her. 'A real bobby-dazzler,' he said, kissing her on the cheek.

'You look lovely. Like a robin, bright and cheery,' smiled her mother.

'Sure?'

'Rosie, why do you do that?' Miriam asked her daughter.

'What?'

'Doubt yourself.' She kissed her on the forehead. 'You're a beautiful young woman. What did Dad just call you?'

Rosie blushed. 'A bobby-dazzler.'

'All you have to do is believe in yourself and it will show. Now, off you go and let me get ready in peace.'

Miriam drew a comb through her blonde hair, frowning at the white hairs beginning to show themselves. I shall be forty, soon, she thought. Yet, I can still draw men's eyes to me. But I'm not ready to relinquish that attention, not by a long chalk. I'm greedy and want life to stand still, at this moment, with my children on the brink of everything and Alec still wanting me.

He came and stood behind her at the dressing-table. Undoing the top button of her blouse he kissed her neck. 'Want to show a sailor a good time?'

Miriam chuckled. She stood up and turned towards him. Standing on tiptoe, she held his face between her hands and kissed him. They lingered together, sure of their mutual attraction, teasing and tasting one another.

Alec sighed, then disentangled himself. 'If I didn't have a pub to run, I'd give you more than kisses.'

She smiled. 'Well sailor, you'll just have to tie a knot in it.'

Laughing, they made their way downstairs again with half an hour to spare before opening time. In the public bar Joseph was preening himself in his new green waistcoat. Miriam congratulated herself on having produced a fine son. Tall, with blue eyes and red hair, he was attractive to women: she could see that. But it was more than good looks. He moved with the same grace as his father and had his way of listening to women – of making them confide in him. If they trusted him with their secrets, what else might they do?

Someone rapped impatiently on the back door and her son went to answer it.

'Hello, my chicks, ready for the off are we?' Bernice, the pub pianist, her voice husky from a lifetime of smoking Capstan Full Strength, teetered in. 'Hello, big boy,' she said, lunging at Joseph and pinching his bottom. 'When you gonna take me down the station and show me your hose?'

'When you play Tchaikovsky,' he laughed, dodging out of her way.

'Story of my life,' Bernice sighed, stroking a hand through her peroxide curls. She pulled out the piano stool and slipped her handbag underneath. 'Could teach you a thing or two. A young lad needs an experienced woman.' Wincing, she pulled off her high heels before easing her bunioned toes into her slippers. 'I don't want to set the world on fire,' she sang, rolling her eyes in Joe's direction.

Miriam laughed. Another rapping on the back door and she answered it this time.

Thelma the barmaid, a thin, frizzy-haired blonde, tip-tapped into the bar on high heels.

Behind her came Lionel, her seven-year-old son. Miriam sighed, knowing what was coming.

'Mum's gone out. I know it's a liberty, but can I bed him down upstairs 'til we've finished? Ta ever so much, Mrs Forrest,' she said, without waiting for a reply. 'Come on, Li,' she said, dragging the child down the passage.

'I wants some crisps,' he demanded.

Miriam held out a packet to him. 'What's the magic word?' she prompted.

'Abracadabra,' Lionel answered.

With any other child she would have laughed, but whiney, snot-nosed Lionel tested her patience. She couldn't take to him. Yet, she could not refuse Thelma. Memories of her own spell of being a mother on her own always tempered her irritation. She remembered standing outside Albert's house in Lemon Street with Rosie in the pram just after the war. His kindness, and that of Beattie, had saved their lives. 'Oh Mother,' Miriam breathed, 'I miss you. Not a day goes by that I don't wish you were with us.' Deep in thought, she almost shut the door in Wally Organ's face.

'Good evening, Mrs Forrest,' he purred, his breath laced with violet cachous.

There he stood, the treasurer of the Christmas Club, attaché case gripped in one hand, and trilby hat in the other. 'Everything ready?'

Gritting her teeth she led the way to the table, where two chairs were set in readiness. He was so smarmy, but he had never got the better of Alec. Wally'd been furious when Alec insisted on banking the money himself, and having two signatures to every transaction.

'Wally, it's my name over the pub door. If you can't work with me, then you're free to set up elsewhere.'

'Who does he remind you of,' Joseph had asked her, 'with that hair parted in the middle and the little black tash?' He'd goose-stepped around the room.

Miriam shook her head. Gran had called him a tripehound. 'He's creepy, Miriam, the way he looks at women's bosoms, like he's got x-ray eyes. The way he sidles up to Thelma. Give him the nod, he'd be there like a racing snake. She could do better than that old ponce.'

'Is everyone ready?' Alec took up his position with Joseph and Thelma in the saloon bar while Miriam joined Rosie in the lounge. 'Bernice,' he called, 'play them in, gal.'

Stubbing out her cigarette in the saucer, Bernice did his bidding. 'Happy days are here again,' she vamped away.

The locals poured in, faces flushed from the cold, women queuing at Wally Organ's table and men forming up at the bar.

Blyth Vine sidled into the pub, not wanting to draw attention to himself. Tonight he would be an onlooker until the moment was right. He'd cursed having to leave the funeral that day and dash back on duty. But now, he had a fortnight's leave, plenty of time to make his mark on the girl he'd found in the graveyard.

His sister Mary had told him who she was. 'It must have been Rosie Forrest, Beattie's grand-daughter. Dark-haired and skinny, was she?'

34

That hadn't begun to describe her, or the excitement he'd felt after that smile she'd flashed at him.

'Didn't they live in the Isle of Wight?'

'Came back a few years ago,' Mary had said. 'Dad runs a pub, somewhere in Landport, behind Commercial Road. Ain't smitten with her, are ya? Reckon you could do better than that for yourself.'

'Can do my own choosing, thank you.' Mary had never got over the habit of mothering him. His joining the Fleet Air Arm and training to be a pilot had thrilled her and the rest of the family. It meant eventually becoming a naval officer. Much as he wanted to achieve this goal he had some reservations. Joining the wardroom would leave him in a no-man's-land between his childhood friends and fellow sub-lieutenants. He supposed Mary expected him to be a social climber and hitch himself up with an admiral's daughter.

'If you're hell-bent on findin' her, you'll have to do some digging around. Look up her dad's name in the Kelly's.'

'The street directory, of course.' He laughed and surprised her with a kiss. 'With a brain like yours, you ought to be rich.'

'Oh bugger off. I gotta get to work,' she blustered, pulling on her coat.

'The Nile Tavern, Nelson Street, proprietor Alec Forrest,' Eureka! Once he had put a name to her, a distant memory flickered in his mind. She had been his playmate that summer before her family moved away. He had ridden down to the beach on her father's shoulders. Would she remember that?

It was one of the rare happy days of his childhood.

Blyth wanted to see Rosie again and test if the excitement was still there. Once inside the Nile, he was wrapped around in a familiar fug of beer, fag ash and cheap scent. He smiled – Dad would have been in his element. This was Dad's world: thumping pianos, darts fixtures, belly laughs and instant friendships. Blyth listened idly to the talk among the men, flowing around him.

'See my old neighbour's signed up to be an air-raid warden. Proper little Hitler he is.'

'He just wants a quiet little billet out of the firing-line. Proper windy is old Sid.'

'Peace in our time, my arse, that paper of old Neville Chamberlain's wasn't worth a light.'

'If the government's so sure of its facts why they talkin' about sendin' our nippers off to the country? Evacuation they're calling it.'

'See all them cap ribbons on them shelves: *Iron Duke, Illustrious, Royal Oak, Albion.* You tot up the number of blokes it takes to man each ship. Thousands will cop it if Jerry has his way. What with all his Heinkels and Dorniers, Pompey will be a bloomin' ruin.'

'Stow it, mate! Bloody Jonah, you are.'

'Let's just get one more Christmas in before the balloon goes up.'

Looking up, Blyth instantly recognised Rosie's father pulling a pint. Standing at the other side of the bar was a giant of a fellow. Could it be her brother, Joseph? I'll have to watch my step, he thought. He looked around him. Where was Rosie? He had laid his plans so carefully and now

36

it could all fall apart. Well, nothing ventured– He went up to the bar.

'Boilermaker, please,' he said. Alec Forrest poured him the local mixture of mild and bitter beer.

Carrying his glass to a corner table, Blyth sat drinking his beer. He looked about him; if things panned out he would soon be entering a different world. It would require him to make the leap from the newspaper tablecloths and chipped cups of his childhood home to starched napkins and the attentions of a steward. Academically he could outdistance most of his fellow trainees, but it was the little class differences that would soon become a minefield. Still, he must be a survivor to have got this far and all of life was a game of some sort or another. You just had to bone up on the rules.

He stood up and glanced through to the women behind the counter in the lounge bar. Was that Rosie in the black jumper? Blyth couldn't be sure. She moved away and for a moment was lost to view, then she was in front of him close enough to touch. 'Look at me, look at me,' he commanded her silently.

Instead she dipped down beneath the bar and picked up a tray, before lifting up the flap and stepping out beside him.

'Glasses everyone,' she called.

At any moment he could turn, put out his hand and touch her. No, he would stalk her over to the corner away from her father and brother.

The door into the street was pushed open and a group of sailors strode in, their eyes swivelling round the room.

Rosie smiled at one of them and his face lit up like a new battery.

'Remember me from last week, Toots?'

The sailor oozed confidence and Blyth wanted to smack him in the mouth for muscling in. But no, he would bide his time. This caution surprised him. His habit was to stake his claim early, relying on his looks and well-honed charm to get what he wanted.

'Remember you all right, fancied yourself,' Rosie snapped back at the sailor. 'A real chancer.'

'And do I?'

'Do you what?'

'Have a chance with you, Rosie?' he asked her, sliding his arm around her waist.

'Don't remember telling you my name.'

She pushed his arm away and yet she was still smiling. Was she teasing or keeping him sweet to avoid trouble? Her tray was now full of empty glasses. For the second time that evening she passed close enough for touching. What was wrong with him? He had wanted her ever since that afternoon in the graveyard, and he was certain the feeling had been mutual. She was not the most beautiful girl he had seen, but Rosie Forrest fizzed with life. One of the regulars said something to her, she threw back her head and laughed. Blyth wanted to make her laugh and hear again that rich chuckle. As she walked back, he watched the other men looking at her. The sailor and his pals staked out their territory on the stools in front of the bar. He knew he had the advantage over them – of having known Rosie

38

before. What in God's name was stopping him? He wanted that look again – the look that told him anything was possible. Blyth downed his beer and pushed his way towards the bar. Her brother was watching him, weighing him up. 'Fortune favours the brave.' Uncle Albert's words came to Blyth from their childhood chess games. But this was more than game playing. This was – what?

Someone nudged him – a slim blonde woman who looked vaguely familiar. 'Would you like some raffle tickets, five for a shilling? Lots of good prizes.'

It was Rosie's mother, he was sure of it. He reached in his pocket and gave her a florin. 'I'm feeling lucky tonight,' he said, smiling at her.

'Pink or blue, you choose.'

He took five of each. When he looked up Rosie was deep in conversation with her brother. Blyth cursed his timidity. This was the moment he'd planned for and now he'd got cold feet.

Her father rang a bell behind the bar and called out, 'Time for the raffle. First prize a turkey to be collected from Coopers on Christmas Eve; second prize a dozen bottles of stout; third prize a Christmas pudding. I shall call on Rosie to pick the tickets.'

All talk ceased and all eyes were on her as she dipped her hand into the beer glass full of tickets. 'Pink sixty-two,' she called.

'Ooh, it's me,' a woman called out, her face red with excitement. 'Got six round the table fer Christmas. We'll really fill our boots.'

As she came up to claim her winnings, Rosie

grinned at her.

'Connie, I'm so pleased,' she said, leaning over the bar and kissing her. Again she dipped her hand into the tankard. 'Blue, one hundred,' she called out.

'Shame I'm teetotal,' teased a man in a shiny suit as he waved his ticket in the air.

After kissing Rosie, he bore his crate of Guinness triumphantly away.

'Last one, pink thirty-seven, the Christmas pudding.'

Blyth tossed the rest of the tickets on the floor and flourished number thirty-seven.

'Here,' he called.

Looking up, Rosie smiled directly at him.

Never mind the pudding. He had won the only prize worth having.

3

Rosie stood at the sink in the stock-room washing out sweet jars. She had scraped out a few choice bits and assembled them on a saucer: corners of Everton Toffee, broken shards of barley-sugar, lumps of peanut brittle and her favourite liquorice whirls. Later while the jars were draining she would chew her way through her treasures. Soon her boss would get her to mind the shop while he went out to lunch with the commercial traveller from Hostlers' sweet factory. Always when Charlie Cawdrey came around she would be hustled out to the stock-room. He would regale chapel-going Claude with *risqué* tales of actresses and bishops. Finally, after a boozy hour in the Cambridge, Claude Treagus would weave his way behind the counter and Rosie would be free to dash home for lunch. Today was no exception.

'Hello, my little posy,' said the traveller, raising his trilby, whilst sliding his eyes down the buttons on her blouse.

Rosie glared at him. 'It's Dan, Dan, the dirty old man.'

Charlie glared back. 'You watch yourself, Miss. So sharp, you'll cut yourself one day.'

She gave him a withering look she'd borrowed from Bette Davis at the pictures last week. The two men sauntered down the road nudging and smirking.

Today she wasn't going home for dinner. Out in the stock-room was a packet of liver-sausage sandwiches and a piece of Swiss roll. Hanging on a hook behind the door were her best skirt and blouse. Today she was giving up her lunch hour so that she could leave early – she had a date with Mr Succulence! It had all happened so quickly she didn't even know his name. Just as she had called out the last number in the raffle he had come out of the crowd and held up his ticket. Almost closing time it had been, with everyone wanting a last drink.

'How about the pictures next Tuesday?' he'd whispered as she handed him his prize.

She had nodded.

'Pick you up from work, what time?'

'Half-five, sweetshop in Palmerston Road, Claude Treagus.'

What had been intriguing was that he had known her name.

'Goodbye, Rosie Forrest,' he'd said.

How did he know?

The afternoon dragged as she handed things in to Mr Treagus while he knelt at the entrance to the window, setting out the Christmas display. The shelves were covered with cotton-wool snow, and in one corner was a Hansel and Gretel house made out of painted cardboard. A Father Christmas was wedged in the chimney and the door was made of barley-sugar sticks. Liquorice allsorts served as roof tiles, and chocolate finger biscuits formed the garden fence.

'Tea I think, Miss Forrest,' said Claude, edging out of the window and treating her to a whiff of

42

sweaty socks.

While the kettle boiled, Rosie ate her sandwiches. While the tea brewed, she changed her clothes. She stared at herself between the gold letters spelling out *Cadbury's Milk Chocolates* on the speckled mirror. As a burst of bravado she applied a slick of red lipstick to her mouth. She pouted experimentally. Would he kiss her? As she set the teacups down on the counter flap a car drew up across the road. It was him, and in uniform. Rosie blushed. 'Can I go now, please, Mr Treagus? I'll come in early tomorrow.'

Claude looked across at Blyth as he walked towards the shop. 'Miss Forrest, I think this is your escort. Go and get your coat.'

She rushed out of the door, not wanting to waste a minute. 'Didn't know you had a car,' she said, as he held the passenger door open for her.

'Not mine, I've borrowed it.'

Rosie settled herself in the passenger seat beside him.

Before starting the engine, Blyth leaned over and kissed her on the cheek. 'Where are we going?'

'Nowhere 'til you tell me your name.'

'Blyth Vine.'

'I know that name, it's something to do with Gran.'

'You're getting warm.'

'You were her neighbours.' She stared at him in disbelief. He couldn't be one of the Vines. They were always rowing. There were three sisters – a bossy elder one and the twins. Pretty girls. She remembered when she had been ever so little not being able to tell them apart. Their dad had been a drinker, always lurching about and smiling. And the mother ended up in the madhouse. 'You can't be,' she said.

'They was all bare-arsed and snot-nosed,' he said in a rough Pompey voice. 'Mother was a loony and Dad a boozer.'

Rosie blushed. He had read her mind. 'But you're going to be a naval officer.' She was flustered.

'Your Gran and Uncle Albert weren't surprised. They expected it of me.'

Never ever judge a book by its cover, Gran always used to say. *People are not always what they seem. Many a diamond in rags and a knave in satin.*

'I'm sorry,' Rosie managed.

'Do you know we once slept together, before you went off to the Isle of Wight?'

She blushed. 'I wasn't even five.'

'Well, Rosie Forrest, I shall have to make a better impression this time.'

He turned the key in the ignition. 'Where are we off to?'

'There's Clark Gable in *Test Pilot*. It's on at the Shaftesbury, in Kingston Road.'

'I'd be picking holes in it all the time.'

'Why, you're not a pilot?'

'I'm in the Fleet Air Arm, and I'll be up in the air any day now.' He looked at her. 'Doesn't give us much time, does it?'

Rosie gulped. It wasn't fair. Just as she'd met the most exciting man ever he was being whisked away.

'How about the Plaza at Bradford Junction,

44

they've got double seats in the back row?'

She gulped. His directness excited her. 'I don't know what's on there.'

'Does it matter?'

Rosie had meant to be cool and distant, at least to start with, but Blyth cut through all that. She smiled and shook her head, wanting the evening to stretch on and on like an everlasting strip of toffee. Why was it good times flashed by, and boring patches dragged on endlessly? Each day had the same number of hours and minutes, it was just the feeling you brought to it she supposed. Rosie laughed. 'I remember you riding on my Dad's shoulders coming back from the beach.' She punched his arm. 'You trod on my egg sandwich,' she accused.

Blyth burst out laughing. Close up he was even more handsome.

As they drove towards the Plaza he said, 'How's old Albert Pragnell getting on? He looked really cut up. I hardly recognised him.'

'Got a letter from him today. Says he can't face coming down for Christmas on his own. I shall nip over to Romsey on the motor bike on Boxing Day.'

'Your brother take you?'

Again she punched him on the arm, 'It's my bike.'

'Should have known, bright spark like you.'

'Yes, you should.'

'Can I come with you?'

'Where?' she asked, the nearness of him addling her thoughts.

'To see Uncle Albert, we were real pals. I loved

going in next-door to them, playing chess and drawing.'

'You'd have to be invited first.'

'So,' he said, 'I shall have to ask nicely.'

'He might want me to himself.'

'He's not the only one.'

It was like a game of tennis. As fast as she hit the ball he returned it at even greater speed. 'I shall just have to see how you behave yourself at the Plaza.'

He laughed. 'I don't think you want me to behave myself, Rosie. We knew what we wanted from the start.'

Red-faced, she scrabbled to open the car door as they reached the cinema. At the foot of the steps he took hold of her hand.

'Ooh, Rosie Forrest,' he said, as they ran up the steps together, 'the sooner we're in the dark the better.'

'You're in the middle of the big picture,' said the girl in the kiosk, unrolling the tickets. 'Want to come back in half an hour for the full programme?'

'Oh I think we can catch up, thank you.' Blyth took Rosie's hand.

They followed the usherette's torch to the back row. Blyth helped her off with her coat and folded it inside his own, putting them on the next seat. In the black fug of cigarette smoke, orange peel and cheap scent they stared at the screen. For a long while nothing happened. Rosie ached for him to touch her.

And then Blyth held her hand, taking her fingers and pressing them against his mouth. He

46

stroked her face, outlining her lips before he kissed them again and again in little teasing kisses.

'Rosie, Rosie, Rosie,' he whispered against her throat.

The lights went up for the interval leaving them dazzled and confused. 'Fancy an ice-cream?' he asked.

'Not specially,' she said, combing her fingers through her hair.

'I could run to a treacle toffee.'

Rosie laughed. 'You Rockefeller or something?'

'They're only the hors d'oeuvre. You're the main course, and then I thought chestnuts and hot chocolate to top off the evening.'

'Be back soon,' she said, escaping to the queue for the Ladies. Rosie splashed her face with cold water and drank a mouthful between her hands. Her face looked back at her from the washbasin mirror, her cheeks scraped scarlet by Blyth's stubble and her eyes fever bright. She felt fizzy and didn't want that feeling to stop. The cinema darkened, and as she worked her way along the row he drew her back into his arms. In front of them, with clashes of swords and screams of terror, the film played itself out. They stood together in fuddled silence when finally the lights went up and the national anthem was played.

'What's next?' he asked, helping her on with her coat.

'I think it's the chestnuts. Let's get them down at the Hard.'

The night air stung her face after the warmth of the Plaza and they ran to the car hand-in-hand.

She sat inside shivering while Blyth scraped the ice from the windows with a knife. He climbed in and turned on the engine.

'It's brass monkeys out there. Let's get some warmth in here.' He turned to her and smiled. 'It's been the best time, Rosie. I'm not ready to let go of it yet, are you?'

Rosie smiled in the darkness. He had read her mind. There was no way that she wanted to let go of Blyth, not 'til they'd squeezed the last drop out of the evening. 'Not nearly,' she echoed. They drove down to the Hard, which was alive with sailors lurching back through the dockyard gates to their ships. Couples hurried over the pontoon bridge to get the ferry across the harbour to Gosport.

She and Blyth stood in the queue for chestnuts. He drew her close and kissed her on the cheek. 'It's going to be a white Christmas,' he said.

The chestnuts were shovelled into newspaper cones and sprinkled with salt. They crunched over the snow-covered shingle on the strip of beach beyond the Hard and sat together on an upturned rowing-boat. It was a cold night. The stars shivered high above them. The sea was calm and dark with only the occasional streak of white from an incoming wave. 'Love the sound, don't you? Better than any music,' Rosie said, dipping her fingers into the paper cone. The chestnut was salty and sweet. 'If you're born by it like us, it casts a spell on you.'

'Perhaps there's a memory deep inside us of our ancestors: great scaly creatures who struggled up onto dry land ages and ages ago. And all our lives we long to return. Perhaps you're really a mermaid.'

'Yes,' she laughed. 'At the stroke of midnight you'll have to go down to the jetty and chuck me back in the sea.'

He looked at his watch. 'We've an hour left.'

'Blyth, how come you want to be a flyer if you love the sea so much?'

He chewed thoughtfully then said, 'In the Fleet Air Arm, you get the best of both worlds, the sea and the sky. Always fancied myself as Icarus flying up to the sun.'

'It's known as getting above yourself. Have you got any plans for fireproofing your wings?'

'I like risk. You must, too, with your motor bike.'

'Just like the rush of air, and the speed; but what's it really like – flying?'

'To begin with you're afraid of getting it wrong. There are lots of calculations, making the right moves, getting the plane to respond and reading the weather. You're like a bird, you take off into the wind and rise up and up. The earth drops away and you climb higher and higher. Then it's you and the plane and the sky.'

'I saw one of those aerial circus shows once. You know, with wing-walkers. That's what I fancy.'

'Won't be much chance of that if our Adolf gets his way.'

'Well, you'll have to give up swanning about in the clouds on your own. There'll be Messerschmitts and Dorniers leaping out at you.'

'What will you do when the war comes?'

'What d'you mean?' Up until recently she had

49

been an ostrich in her response to the gathering threat of war – dreading the thought of anyone she loved being killed. Yet she wanted to fling herself into something different to test herself in some way.

'The men will get called up and there'll be jobs for women in transport, driving lorries, or being a despatch rider. You might even be a Wren.'

'Thought they'd been shut down.'

'Everything will be opened up again. You should get in quick, that way you'll have more choice. You know the war's certain? What with your Dad having been a sailor, the navy would be bound to snap you up, and you've a driving licence.'

'Dad, Grandad and my stepbrother Andrew were sailors. Though I never met him.'

'Died at Jutland, didn't he?'

'Yes,' said Rosie. 'War's not all *Boy's Own Paper*. Lily and Gran never forgot the day the telegram arrived saying Andrew was killed. It was Lily's twelfth birthday. There were all the people crying in the street, and the hundreds and hundreds of names in the death columns in the papers.'

'I remember Lily,' said Blyth. 'She was your step-sister, wasn't she?'

'Yes, she and Andrew were Dad's first family. Lily married Michael Rowan from Lemon Street and they went off to Canada, years ago.'

'But even so,' Blyth was suddenly serious, 'you can't let Hitler get away with crushing everyone. All it takes for evil to flourish is that good men do nothing.'

'Funny, I was in the shop this afternoon,

50

wondering if anyone had ever died of boredom. Don't expect that'll be a problem anymore.'

'Always been a leaper, desperate to make things happen. I think there are people who say yes to life, and others where it's always maybe. Looking at you in the cemetery, Rosie, I knew you were like that, too.'

'How?'

'You were sad that your Gran had gone. I could see that, yet you weren't mournful. You could still see what was going on around you.'

Rosie smiled. 'And what was that?'

'It was me, sending out signals. I stared at you so long before you looked at me, thought your brother would punch me.'

As she laughed up at him, Rosie heard the chimes from the Guildhall beyond Victoria Park.

'Right, Rosie Forrest,' Blyth helped her to her feet. 'Your Dad will be loading his shotgun. I'd better get you home.'

They sat together in a dark corner not far from Nelson Street. Rosie kissed his hair and his eyelids and stroked his face.

'Are we going to Romsey on Boxing Day?' he asked.

'Ten sharp by the Air Balloon,' she said. Standing waving to him as he drew away from the kerb, her cool sophistication was in shreds. With Blyth Vine she had really burnt her boats.

4

In Hardway, across the harbour, Pearl Bunting's life was unravelling. There was no pattern to her days beyond yelling and hitting. If only her brother Kenny would stop. She longed for a warm home and a sliver of looking after. There was never any money – what she earned from her cleaning job was snatched by her brother; and even the allotment, for them, sent by her father from Singapore went into Kenny's pocket. He waited for her outside the post office each week and demanded that she hand it over. The boss at Fleetlands' Naval Yard had dismissed him from his apprenticeship, and now, Kenny ran with a gang that terrified her with their wildness.

Pearl had wanted to stay with Auntie Daisy down the road in Elson. It was what Mum would have wanted for her.

'Ain't having you blabbing to that nosy cow,' Kenny raged. 'We're fixed all right as we are. Christ! You're sixteen now, ain't a baby no more.'

Then Daisy and Uncle Frank went to Plymouth, and she was on her own with a brother she hardly recognised. Kenny had once been clever with his hands and fussy over his appearance. He had even let Mum give him dancing lessons. He had spoken properly and read books. A year ago he wouldn't have given his new pals Nudger and Spike the time of day. A year ago he wouldn't have spent half his life out drinking.

But, a letter came from Auntie. She was coming back home to Elson in time for Christmas. Daisy invited the two of them to spend the day with her.

'We ain't going – get that right out of yer mind. I'll drop in a note later to say that we're suited for the day. No good gawpin' or grizzlin', that's it, end of story.'

Auntie Daisy had called round once while Pearl had been at Mrs Padgham's, cleaning. Kenny had spun her some tale about his sister having gone away. She kept hoping to bump into Auntie when she was out shopping but she never did.

Now, on Christmas Eve morning, Kenny stamped down the stairs into the kitchen. Pearl flinched at his approach. She was sitting in her nightdress with one of Dad's old jumpers over the top warming her hands around a cup of tea.

'Right,' he said, 'you'll be getting money this morning from that old woman, I'll have what you've got in your purse, now.' Before she could stop him he had taken it out of her bag and stuffed the ten-shilling note into his trousers pocket. 'I'm gettin' the meat and you get the veggies and stuffin' and such like.'

Pearl wrote on the back of an envelope with a pencil stub. 'I'll get some crackers and Mrs P's given me a pudding and some custard powder. We could have a really nice time.' Even she could hear the whiney pleading note in her voice.

'Won't want crackers. Ain't kids no more. Me and my pals will be into the cider.'

53

'Thought it would be just us.' She hated his friends. They were loud and rough-mannered – slouching at the table, eating open-mouthed, and farting.

'You thought wrong,' he shouted, making her flinch and hurting her shoulder where his fingers pinched. 'Off out now. All you gotta do is cook the grub then make yerself scarce. Don't want yer miserable clock spoilin' the day.'

Pearl blew her nose and thought about the box of decorations she'd sneaked in from Dad's shed. The more Kenny scorned her Christmas the more she clung to it. Now she had borrowed a screwdriver and put a proper lock on her door she could have Christmas in her bedroom whatever went on downstairs.

After lugging home a bag of potatoes, carrots and sprouts she left them in the kitchen and set about her own festivities. By six o'clock she had put freshly ironed sheets and pillowcases on her bed, polished the furniture and set the Christmas angel on top of the dressing-table mirror. Standing on the bed and then on an upturned tea-chest she had hung the chains around the picture-rail. Pearl went downstairs and made a pot of tea. She lit the oven and opened the door to heat up the kitchen. In the bread-bin was a slice of dry bread, which she toasted under the grill.

When she had searched Dad's shed for the decorations there had been a box of photographs. He must have put them out there after Mum died at the sanatorium. Looking at them was such a joy to her. Hungrily she scanned the faces, and recalled the occasions when they had been taken. There was one of her and Kenny taken about five years ago, when Pearl was eleven and he was fourteen. They were walking over the mud with the wooden pattens Dad had made for them strapped to their feet. Kenny was holding up a flounder he'd caught with a hand-line. Her head was tilted back and she was really laughing. In another, Mum and Dad and Kenny were blackberry-picking at the bottom of Ham Lane. They had been a happy family once. How she had looked up to her big brother. From the shore at Hardway he could look across the harbour and name every ship. He would borrow Dad's binoculars and see those tied up across at Portsmouth, and the pensioned-off hulks in Portchester creek.

'Sharp as a needle is Kenny,' her mother had said proudly. She always brought out the best in him, made him bask in the warmth of her affection. Slow and timid Pearl had always been Daddy's girl.

The key turned in the lock. Her stomach lurched. She grabbed the box of photos and rushed upstairs with them.

'Get down here. Got sommink to show ya.'

She heard his footsteps on the stairs. 'Want me to come and fetch ya?'

Pearl just had time to slip the box under her bed and turn around before he reached the top stair.

'Watcha think of that?'

Laid out on the kitchen table was a dead turkey, complete with head, feet and feathers.

Kenny seemed well pleased with himself.

'Enough there to feed the five of us. Get the stuffing up his jacksy and we'll be quids in. You got the veggies?'

Pearl gulped. 'I've never plucked a bird and, what about the rest of him?'

Kenny spread his hands. 'There's a chopper under the sink – be able to take the head and feet off, easy-bloody-peasy. See ya tomorrer. Happy Christmas,' he called over his shoulder. 'And leave them lights on.'

The turkey's head trailed over the edge of the table. The thought of touching it made her shudder. Each Christmas, it had been Dad who transformed their bird into the golden-breasted resident of the roasting-tin – now it was her job. Got to do it, got to. Panic set her pacing around the kitchen. Passing the dresser for the third time she looked at the lone card on the middle shelf, sent by Mrs Padgham. The robin on the painted snow chirped soundlessly at her, its eyes bright and challenging. She dried her eyes on the sleeve of her jumper, then dragged on her coat and Wellingtons. Gritting her teeth, she slid the turkey into her shopping bag.

Shuddering, she folded the head and feet back over the sides, then pressed newspapers over the top to protect it from the snow. From one coat pocket she pulled out her gloves and from the other her beret. The winter air needled her face as she trudged down the path. She switched on her torch and shone it in front of her. Mrs Padgham would know how to turn the feathered corpse into a Christmas dinner. She was such a dear. Likely she would make some hot chocolate:

her spirits lifted at the thought. She rapped the knocker almost as loudly as Kenny would have done – and then she remembered.

'Shan't see you 'til Wednesday, Pearl dear. I'm off over to my sister's place in Fareham. I shall bring you back some of her cake. Happy Christmas. Here's a card for you, not worth putting it in the box you living so near.'

Inside had been a ten-shilling note and a handkerchief with a *P* embroidered on it.

All her hopes melted like the slush beneath her feet. 'Got to do it, got to.' The words drummed in her ears: cut off the head, sever the feet, clean out the innards. Fleetingly she thought of going over to Daisy's house and asking for help. It was quite a walk to the other end of Elson and the torch battery was on the blink. Kenny would soon know where she was and come and get her. He'd be polite but she'd have to go with him. When he stared at her she was helpless, like a rabbit caught in the headlights of a car. Besides, if Daisy really cared wouldn't she have come round a second time to see her? No, the invitation was just politeness, probably relieved they weren't coming.

Half-way home the torch died along with her hopes. She caught hold of the fence and felt her way up to the front door. Her pockets were empty, useless tears welled in her eyes. The key was on the dresser next to Mrs Padgham's Christmas card. As she stood in the porch rubbing her nose on her sleeve, she thought about the turkey. If it were alive now it would scurry across the ground to the hedge and seek shelter. She thought, fleetingly, of hiding there.

But, once, she'd seen a rat there darting between the roots. The thought of it gnawing at her frightened her more than Kenny. She unscrewed the torch, re-screwed it more firmly, and banged it on the step. It stuttered back into life. There was an old door leaning against the wall in the porch. Dad had been going to use it in the house before he went away. If she could just wedge herself behind it away from the wind and the rains, she'd be safe 'til the morning. Kenny would be back eventually. If Pearl didn't get herself hidden away soon he'd hit her for certain. The noise he'd make swaggering home would be bound to waken her, but she'd just have to stay quiet and find some way of getting in when it was light and she could see what she was doing.

Pearl took a newspaper from her bag, and spread it on the floor of the porch, and managed to creep into the little tunnel behind the slanting door. Folding the last one into a rough pillow she curled herself into a ball, dragging the turkey in beside her. Clamping her eyes shut, Pearl tried not to choke on the reek of cat's pee. She forced her mind on that blackberry-picking snap. Coiled in the dark, she tried to draw the heat of that September day into her bones.

Daisy Fletcher looked at the scrawled response to her Christmas invitation. *'Don't want to come. Pearl and me fine. From Kenneth Bunting.'*

She threw the paper into the fire. She was going round there tomorrow and he could bloody well lump it. That woman at the post office today had set the alarm bells ringing good and proper.

Hadn't mentioned Pearl by name but Daisy knew it was her she was on about.

'Poor little kid, thin as a lath she is. Looks frightened out of her wits half the time.'

'Ooh I know,' said the woman behind the counter. 'Comes in here every Thursday with that brother of hers. She draws the allowance her Dad sends her but I'm sure she doesn't see much of it. Looks a proper spiv he does.'

'Used to be such a pretty little thing, when her mother was alive. Comes to do my cleaning. Try and feed her up I do.'

'Never know what's going on behind people's front doors, do you. He wants getting away into the army. A bit of square-bashing, that'd bring him up with a round turn.'

Now she had made up her mind to it Daisy felt better. She concentrated on finishing her letter to her husband Frank away in Singapore. He was on the same ship as her brother Graham Bunting, Pearl's dad. When he got to hear about what was going on he'd be onto the welfare pronto. Better still if he could be drafted back home. Daisy sighed, even better if her Frank could come with him – she could do with a good seeing-to. If his old mother could look down from heaven and see her Franky being a really naughty boy she would be speechless. Giggling to herself, Daisy copied out the slogan that had won her three pounds in the Air Raid Precaution competition. *'A ready population is the foundation of security.'*

As she sipped her hot milk she studied the hyacinth bulbs in a pot on the windowsill. The buds were on the verge of opening. Perhaps they would make it for Christmas Day tomorrow. It was no good, her eyes were closing, she would have to give in and join that hot-water bottle waiting in her bed. Early next morning she would cycle round to those kids before they'd made a start on the cooking. Down in the larder, the turkey sat stuffed to the gunnels with sage and onion. If anyone knew how to cook a Christmas dinner it was Daisy Fletcher. As she drifted off to sleep under her blankets a rhyme jingled in her head. *'Bye baby Bunting Daddy's gone a hunting to get a little rabbit skin to put his baby Bunting in.'*

Kenny staggered up the path, stupid with drink. The scabby landlord had slung him and his mates out of the pub, before they'd ordered so much as lemonade. Gone to the off-licence they had, asked for cheap sherry and mixed it with nettle beer at Spike's place. Rotten-tasting it was but it hit him like a truck, making his head spin. Couldn't stop laughing. It was a wonder that Nudger could ride his bike he was that sozzled. Still chuckling, Kenny drew out his key and, after the third time of trying, fitted it into the lock.

Fear prowled in his belly. He'd have her, not leaving the light on. Knew how he hated the dark. Slow Pearl was, and the way she looked at him under her lashes made him so wild. Had to hit her, couldn't help it.

'Pearl, Pearl,' he yelled, rushing through the house, switching on the lights as he went. He crashed her door open and pulled off the bedclothes. Fear whispered in his ear – alone,

alone. The kitchen table was bare and the back door locked. What was she playing at? Would she have sloped off to Daisy's taking the turkey with her? If she had, by Christ she'd be sorry. He had things running sweet. The last thing he wanted was that great lump muscling in on things.

He hated being on his own. It was then that his mother called to him.

'Kenny you're my good boy. Help me sit up. Hold my hand, there's a love. I'm so tired. It's getting all dark Kenny. Please Kenny make the darkness go away.'

He whimpered to himself as he wandered through the silent rooms. All that stuff about Pearl being upset – what about him, mad with missing her, he was. She had loved him more than ever she loved his sister. Pearl had been a proper daddy's girl. Mum had taught him to dance. He had whirled around in her arms while his sister wound up the gramophone again and again. He closed his eyes and her scent came back to him and her voice whispering in his ear.

'One, two, three, one, two, three, that's it Kenny you're really dancing.'

In six months she was dead and within a year Dad had packed and gone. Who cared whether it was Singapore or bloody Timbuktu.

'Now your mother's gone and I'm going away, you'll have to be the man of the house. Take care of Pearl. She's so upset – different from you. I've made out the allotment in her name – she'll draw it each week.'

Why, why, why, hadn't Dad trusted him?

At work, all his enthusiasm for engineering had

been whittled away. Kenny couldn't concentrate. Only fighting and drinking, noise and danger drove it away. When he could hear himself yelling and see the fear on people's faces then he was alive.

Coming back into the empty house always tore away the sticking-plaster, leaving him raw and raging with loss. It was dark outside and Kenny was afraid. He crashed a plate on the floor just for the sound it made. Noise, booze and company, that's what saw off the voices. He rampaged through the house, crying and swearing. In the sideboard in the front room was Dad's bottle of navy rum. Hated the taste and wasn't even thirsty, but Kenny forced down the treacly liquid, desperate to drown out his mother's voice, staring all the while at the naked yellow light bulb.

Daisy carried her breakfast toast and tea upstairs to eat while she read George's letter marked, *'Not to be opened until December the twenty-fifth.'*

But Pearl was in the back of her mind, making her uneasy. She should have called around weeks ago. It was no good, the letter would have to wait. Peering at the clock beside her bed she saw that it was half-past eight. She'd just scoff her toast and give herself a quick lick and a promise before getting over there. Whatever she found it would all go into a letter to her brother, Graham. He'd have to get himself home to his family if the talk was only half-way true.

In spite of her anxiety the white silent world had her singing carols as she cycled along. Her breath smoked ahead of her and the wheels wobbled over the rutted snow and ice. 'Oh come all ye faithful, joyful and triumphant,' she warbled.

Daisy flung her bike in the hedge then stepped into the porch. The force of her hammering was enough to wake the dead. She peered in at the front window through the yellowing net curtains. The light was on. Kenny was slumped in the armchair, facing her, an empty bottle at his feet. His head was thrown back and face chalk-white. Rage boiled inside her. She fished through the letterbox for the key. Thwarted, she searched the front garden for a stone or something, anything to smash the glass. Oh hell and damnation! Failing to find anything, she wrenched the lamp from her bike and was about to crash it against the lead lights in the front door when she thought better of it. Shame to break them. No, she'd have a crack at the window, wake up that Kenny. Turning around, she smacked the door perched in the corner with her fist and sent it crashing into the garden. She stepped back in fright and put her foot through the handles of a shopping bag and fell onto the path. 'Oh buggering hell,' she yelled, rubbing her grazed knees. As she disentangled herself a dead turkey slithered onto the ground in front of her. Daisy shuddered. This was a nightmare. She turned and thrust the bird back in the bag. There was something wedged in the corner. With shaking hands she picked up her lamp and directed the beam onto a muddle of newspapers. She made out a body with Wellington boots at one end and, Oh my God! it was a beret. 'Pearl!' Daisy knelt and shook her, calling her name. Fumbling with the buttons, Daisy stripped off her coat and rolled Pearl up inside it. She took off the sopping beret and replaced it with her own.

Careless of the lead lights, she smashed them with her lamp. Picking some shards of glass aside, she slid her gloved hand through the hole and managed to open the door. Daisy wrenched off her gloves, knelt beside the girl and felt her wrist. Nothing! Pearl's skin was warm. But she must be quick in getting her out of the cold. Warm or not, she could still be dead.

'Kenny, wake up,' she raved, rushing into the room and giving him a shaking.

Kenny snored on.

'Bastard! Get up, get up,' she screamed.

'Wassup? No! Leave off, you mad cow.'

Crack! Her well-aimed blow set him howling. 'Get up them stairs and fetch some blankets.'

'Broke my nose you 'ave,' he whimpered.

'Blankets,' she screamed, 'or I'll kill ya. Your sister's bin out all night in the snow, if she dies I'll see you hang.' Grabbing him by the arm she dragged him out into the hall and pointed at Pearl lying lifeless on the tiles.

Blood trickled through Kenny's fingers as he held his throbbing nose. Looking down at Pearl's waxen face and blue mouth, fear drove out pain. Gasping and snuffling he lurched up the stairs.

'Hurry, hurry,' Daisy roared after him. Christ, the room was cold as a tomb. She clamped her hand over her mouth to stop herself from crying. Pearl's face was streaked with dirt but it was her stillness that frightened her. Heat, that was it.

Turning to the grate she set about getting a fire going. Paper, matches, where the hell was anything in this bloody house? Stamping and swearing, she roared into the kitchen and found the oven door open and the gas alight. Daisy dragged Pearl along the passage and laid her on the kitchen floor in front of the stove. Again she felt for a pulse. Was there a thread of movement beneath her fingers or was it wishful thinking?

Upstairs, Kenny wished he had a shovel to smash in Daisy's face. If only the ground would stop spinning. Running up the stairs was the last thing he needed. Blood from his nose bled over the blankets as he dragged them off the beds.

'We're in the kitchen. Fill the kettle and get some tea going,' Daisy barked at him. No sooner was that done than she was on at him again.

'Get my bike. Go down Avery Lane for Doctor Kean. Tell him it's urgent. Don't just stand there. Get the hell out of here.'

The whirl of activity distracted him from the terror lurking in his belly. She could die, his sister could die and it was his fault. Christ, they really could hang him. As he pedalled towards the doctor's surgery his brain teemed with possibilities. If she died he was a gonner. If the doctor saw all the bruises, Daisy would be sure to point the finger. What if he just laid low over at Nudger's? Now Daisy was fussing over her, Pearl was sure to pull through. Christ! If Dad found out he'd knock his head clean off his shoulders. Well, he'd have to find him first.

5

On Boxing Day Albert Pragnell stretched out his hand. In half sleep he could deceive himself with wishful thinking. Wakening to the empty space beside him was a daily grief. Each morning he had to wind himself up like a battered old clock. It was Beatrice's love that had kept him ticking. Without her, life had neither flavour nor purpose.

At his stirring, Towser, his newly acquired mongrel, leapt on the bed. The dog tilted its head enquiringly. The brown eyes beseeched him to get up. Albert fondled one of his silky ears. 'Just let me get into the rig of the day and grab a sandwich then we'll be off,' he said, pushing the dog onto the floor.

They had fallen into the habit of breakfasting in the woods together. Albert let the dog out into the back garden of his cottage then returned to splash his face in cold water before dragging on a jersey and trousers. He slid a thick slice of turkey between two slices of bread then wrapped it in newspaper. In his jacket was a flask of whisky. He rationed himself to one tot a day, fearful of becoming an old soak.

Taking his breakfast opposite Beatrice's empty chair had been a lowering experience. An hour in the woods in the frosty air enlivened him and Towser bounded ahead, tail up and ears pricked. Albert shut the gate behind them. At first he had thought the winter wood silent and lacking in interest. But now he was attuned to the stirrings of birds and small creatures, and the soughing of the wind through the trees. It was not a dead landscape but one in which new life lay waiting in the wings. All it needed was more warmth and light to stir the earth into activity. Soon there would be snowdrops. He ventured to hope that he too was lying dormant, and come spring he would emerge from his pall of grief to some useful purpose.

Albert reached the fallen oak that served as his breakfast bench and brushed off the snow before sitting down and reaching for his flask. After sharing his sandwich with Towser he spent half an hour or so following his usual path to the stream, noting the minute changes from the day before. There was a robin chirring from the skeletal branches of a willow tree. In the pale winter sun rooks could be seen swooping and falling in a mysterious dance. Frosty long grass crunched under his boots. 'Come, Towser,' he called, 'we have visitors today. What will they think of you, I wonder?'

Outside the Nile, Dad stood by Rosie's motor bike blowing on his hands and stamping his feet. 'What you want to take that old thing for beats me – mad as a March hare you are.'

She laughed. 'Dad, it'll be perfect. I know he'll love it.'

Rosie drew on her gauntlets and pulled her scarf around her mouth. She kicked her bike into life and swung onto the saddle. 'You get in the warm,' she shouted over the noise of the engine to her father waving from the door. She approached the Air Balloon pub in Mile End where she was due to pick up Blyth. He wasn't there. She pulled back her glove and saw that she was ten minutes early. Cursing her eagerness, she rode down the whole length of Commercial Road and back again. No Blyth. She was sick with disappointment. Blinking back tears she was about to drive off to Romsey when a figure jumped out in front of her. 'You daft bugger, you nearly had me off,' she shouted at him as she slammed on the brakes and swerved to a halt.

'Happy Christmas,' he said, pulling down her scarf and kissing her. His face was cold and his eyes sparkled. 'Shall I climb aboard?' He stood there grinning at her, wearing his cap and swathed in a scarf with a rucksack on his back. He winked at her.

Rosie was excited and furious. Not trusting herself to speak, she waited for him to climb up behind her. Feeling reckless, she increased her speed and swerved around the corners as far over as she could go. The air rushing past stung her face, making her eyes water. They zoomed past Portchester Castle with its helmet of snow and on through Fareham. Rosie had taken this route often and knew it in all its seasons. The fields were thick with snow. Now and then a lone figure could be seen coming out of a byre or going through a gate with a dog bounding behind.

Blyth tightened his grip and Rosie laughed out loud, feeling the bike throbbing beneath her. They skirted Southampton, passing through

Swaythling and then on to Romsey. As Solent Cottage came into view she slowed the engine and freewheeled down into the yard. She switched it off. Almost immediately Uncle Albert hurried out of the kitchen door towards them. A black-and-white dog yelping with excitement leapt around him. 'A thousand welcomes both of you,' he cried. 'Here, give me something to carry.'

Rosie hugged him fiercely. 'Happy Christmas, Uncle Albert, it's so good to see you.'

'Great Heavens,' he said, looking at the laden motor bike. 'Father Christmas has been busy. Beatrice would have been thrilled.'

Rosie gulped. He was an older, less certain Uncle Albert without the shine that Gran's company had given him.

Blyth pulled off his gauntlets and shook the old man's hand. 'Good morning, sir. Thank you for letting me come to see you.'

Albert smiled. 'Cut the formality, old chap. Uncle Albert was good enough when you were a young shaver, it's good enough now.' He turned to his dog. 'Towser, say hello to my visitors.'

'Towser, eh,' said Blyth, patting him on the head. 'We had a Towser when I was a nipper. I curled up to sleep with him lots of times, 'specially if I wasn't well.'

'It's the reason I named this little creature Towser, brings a bit more of Lemon Street out here.'

Laughing, Rosie scooped the dog up in her arms. He licked her face. Between them all they made their way into the kitchen laden with gifts. 'Smells good,' she said, 'bangers and mash like

69

you promised.'

'What's this?' laughed Blyth, setting down the long parcel that had been strapped to the carrier. 'It weighs a ton.'

Rosie pointed to her nose. 'All will be revealed after dinner,' she grinned. 'Dad reckoned I was mad to bring it but I knew it was perfect.'

'Take it all in by the fire and sit up to the table. I want to dish up immediately. Then we'll have a glass of Aunt Olive's blackcurrant wine.' He winked at them. 'One glass only, it's too early in the day to get squiffy.'

Rosie laid the white starched tablecloth and scrabbled in the drawer of the oak dresser for the cutlery and napkin rings. They were jumbled together and in need of a good polish. Blyth looked up from stacking the parcels around the fireplace and winked at her. They even managed a kiss before Uncle Albert came in carrying a tray laden with food.

'Rosie, will you fetch the plates out of the oven? Use the oven cloth darling, they're very hot.'

'Take your place Blyth, there facing the window. No, Towser,' he said to the dog. 'Your dish is in the kitchen. I'll go and get the wine.'

They helped themselves to slightly charred sausages and great spoonfuls of mashed potato and swede.

Albert laughed. 'It's my new invention, putting the two vegetables in the same pot. I think it improves their flavour and saves on the washing-up.' He uncorked a dusty bottle and filled three glasses to the brim. Turning to Blyth he said, 'Our toast, what shall it be?'

'To Granny Pragnell, she was my best friend, always. Nobody like her.' He winked at Rosie. 'Her jam tarts saved my life.'

They all laughed.

'To Gran,' they both said, clinking their glasses.

'To Beatrice,' said the old man. He smiled at them and she could see something of the old Albert. 'Eat hearty, as Beatrice would say. There's one of her puddings steaming on the stove. I even managed to make some custard without any lumps.'

While eating, Rosie looked around the room. On the mantelpiece and grouped on a side table were photographs of Gran. The furniture needed a good polish but the framed photos were dusted every day, she was certain of it. She could not imagine what it was like for Uncle Albert to be without his wife. He had been the only one to call her Beatrice. He had loved her all his life, even when she married someone else. Then when she was widowed, he had waited over twenty years for her to say yes. Would Blyth become the love of her life, she wondered. Helping herself to more onion gravy, she asked, 'How was Christmas Day up at the farm with Uncle Samuel and Auntie Olive?'

'Strenuous, we were all trying so hard. I had to keep eating more and more to show my appreciation, and opposite me was the empty fourth chair. Escaped as soon as I could.' He patted her hand. 'D'you know, I've taken to eating my breakfast in the woods. Towser and I have a good root about together. I think my healing will come from nature.'

There was a long silence and Rosie rushed to fill it.

'It was odd at home,' she said. 'Of course, we were busy with the pub open half the day but when we were closed and had our dinner it was strange. There were holes in the day that Gran would have filled up with all sorts of nonsense. We all tried to be extra jolly but it was strenuous.'

'And Blyth, how did you fare?' asked Albert, helping him to more sausages.

'Oh you know, naval Christmases. I was over at *Daedalus*. Nobody wanting to be there, food overcooked and too much booze.'

Albert smiled fondly at him. 'I remember them only too well. Where is your family based, now?'

'Big sister's at Wymering: she's married again. The twinnies away all the time in a concert party and big brother Harry and Dora running a pub in Plymouth.'

'All change then,' he said, setting down his glass. 'And how is my old chum Fred?'

Blyth paused. 'Poor old Dad died a couple of years ago. Went in his sleep. Nobody had much good to say about him. But in the end we rubbed along quite well. My inheritance was a coal shovel and his knot board.'

'Dear Fred! What a facility he had for rope work. Such a kind soul he was. Used to show me your letters, proud as punch he was when you passed out first in your dockyard apprenticeship. Said to me. "That won't be the end of it, my boy'll go for a sailor, it's in his blood."' He struggled to his feet. 'Now if you will just excuse me a moment I will go and check the pudding, mustn't let it boil dry.'

Blyth reached across the table for Rosie's hand and kissed it. Here with Uncle Albert he was different. She sensed that he was acting the suave young pilot a lot of the time, but here he was less armoured, more at ease with himself. Blyth smiled at her and her heart thumped.

Uncle Albert came back into the room with the pudding flaming on the dish. They cheered and Rosie hurried to get the dishes from the dresser. As she ate a dark, fragrant spoonful she felt that Gran was with them in their enjoyment.

When they had finished Blyth cleared the plates. 'You open your presents,' he insisted. 'I'll square away then I'll set you both up with a rum toddy. I brought all the makings with me.' He shooed Rosie out of the kitchen.

When he had gone Albert fetched a fat envelope from the drawer in the tea trolley.

'Your grandmother thought long and hard before making this decision,' he said. 'I am deeply grateful that she considered it her most valuable possession.'

Rosie was intrigued. At the sight of Gran's writing her eyes filled with tears. It summoned her up more clearly than any of her bits and pieces lying around. Opening the envelope she spread out the one sheet of paper and began to read.

My Dearest Granddaughter,
By the time you receive this I shall be long gone.
Don't grieve for me I had such a long and happy life.
Like me, live your own to the full and regret nothing.

We are here to learn how to be fully human and it takes a lifetime to get just an inkling of what that means.

I thought about leaving you my diaries but finally entrusted them to your sister Lily, her being the eldest. I have left for you the painting Albert did for my birthday one year. It hangs in the Marine Artists Gallery in London. You won't be able to redeem it until you have a home of your own and even then you'll need a blooming big van. When you go to the museum, you will be able to see it along with all the other paintings by members of the Marine Artists Association. Keep the ticket safe. Giving you my painting is an expression of my love for you. I hope it will give you as much joy as it has given me.

If you remember anything of all the many talks we had together let it be this: 'If you do not grow up to help other people, you are not worth the upbringing.'

Love you always,
Gran

Rosie looked at Albert; there were tears in her eyes. 'I remember Mum and Dad talking about seeing it before you took it up to London. Saying that it was your love letter to Gran. I remember asking them how a painting could be a letter. Mum promised to take me to see it one day but we never did go.' She settled herself on the carpet at his feet. 'Tell me about it,' she said.

'My darling, talking about it would be as unsatisfactory as describing the taste of a pudding. That can only be experienced in the tasting and a painting has to be seen. I tried to hold up a

74

mirror to your grandmother and all the other women of Portsmouth. But I don't want to say any more. I want you to find in it what you will.'

'It's a wonderful present, Uncle Albert. Not just because of what it is, but because of what it meant to Gran.' She turned and kissed his hand. 'But, I wish she was here with us.'

'I know my darling,' he said, patting her shoulder, 'but we were lucky to have her at all, weren't we? Now, look inside the envelope and you'll find something else.'

It was a white card with the address of the gallery on one side and on the other the words: *'Property of Mrs Beatrice Pragnell.'*

Rosie already had a picture of Gran, on her bedroom wall, but this painting was special. She remembered her saying that Albert had got a gold medal from some naval society for a painting. Could this be it? She handed him back the envelope. 'You look after it for me. We'll go together as soon as we can, shall we?'

'That would be wonderful,' he said, tucking it into his jacket pocket. 'Now, I think it's my turn for presents by the look of this heap here.'

Rosie pointed to the long lumpy parcel. 'You can open the others whenever you like but this one is especially from me.'

'Great heavens, what's this?' Albert stripped off the newspaper, and then the blanket that had been used to cover Gran's bed when she slept at the Nile. He gasped then settled the gift carefully on the mat beside him.

Rosie turned the battered metal over to reveal the words *'Lemon Street'*.

75

Albert wept. 'Oh, take no notice of a senti-mental old fool,' he gasped. 'You have brought the mountain to Mohamet. I thought Lemon Street was gone for good.'

'Almost. Dad and Joseph had a real tussle with the council workmen: had to promise them a good few free pints to part with it. Where will you put it?' Rosie asked

'It would be logical to set the sign outside but I wouldn't want to confuse the postman. I shall have it on the kitchen wall facing the door. It will be the first thing my eyes will look on every morning.'

Blyth knocked the kitchen door and she ran to answer it. He came in with a loaded tray. The room was filled with the scent of lemon and hot rum. As he set it on the table he saw the street sign lying on the floor. He laughed delightedly. 'Never expected to see that again. Where d'you get it?'

'Dad was down at Queen Street with Joseph and this dustman was loading it onto his cart. Had a real struggle with him.'

'Would you like me to put it up somewhere for you?' he asked.

'No, dear boy, Samuel and I will tackle it tomorrow. It will give me something to look forward to.' Albert smiled at him. 'This is what this place needs, laughter and young voices. I remember this young man not much more than seven beating me at chess. Scruffy little Herbert he was, but so thirsty for knowledge. Let's try your rum punch then, Blyth. You'll have to go a long way to beat your father's.'

76

'Cheers,' they said to one another, clinking their glasses.

Albert switched on the lamp beside him and the room came alive. The light shone down on his silver hair and the bronze scuttle near his feet. A log fell on the tiles and Blyth grabbed it, tossing it into the grate. Red spark-fairies glittered on the sooty fireback.

'Mm! It's delicious,' said Rosie licking her lips. She saw Blyth watching her and felt giddy with desire.

The clock on the mantelpiece chimed five.

'You must not leave it too late to set out. The roads are treacherous. Perhaps before you go we should have a cup of tea. That toddy has made me feel quite squiffy.'

Rosie wrenched her eyes from Blyth, and went into the kitchen shivering at the change in temperature. As the kettle boiled she set the table with cups and saucers. It had been a day full of sweetness, one that she would revisit often and often. Gran's gift to her had been a complete surprise. It would be ages before she could make it hers, but it was waiting for her in that London gallery like the crock of gold at the end of a rainbow.

'God bless you both,' Albert said, standing at the door swathed in Gran's blanket. 'Go safely. I shall go to Samuel's up at the farmhouse. Get your mother to phone me there the moment you arrive home. Good fortune, Blyth. Drop me a line sometime and let me know your exploits. And, if ever you need a bolthole this is your home.'

''Bye Uncle Albert, you take care of yourself.' Rosie hugged him.

''Bye Uncle,' said Blyth, shaking his hand. 'A great day, thank you.' He turned to her. 'Can I drive? I've got a pilot's licence.'

'You take care,' Rosie said, pushing the switch under the fuel tank. Blyth stood astride the bike and kicked it into life. She clambered quickly behind him. He swung the bike out of the farm gate and they were on the road. The sky was streaked with orange as the sun went down. She leant her face against his back and closed her eyes, swerving with him as they followed the curves of the road out of Romsey.

Rosie felt hungry for change. She wanted to feel alive – for her heart to pound and her skin to prickle. To be so frightened that she forgot to breathe, or so happy that she would shout out loud.

They had ridden for some miles with the engine throbbing beneath them when Blyth turned onto a path leading up to Portsdown Hill. At the top he swerved onto the grass and brought the bike to a halt. They both dismounted and looked down at the lights of Portsmouth winking far below them.

'Scruffy old gal is Pompey,' he said. 'Game, with her sparkling lights and tarry seaweed skirts, out to give a sailor a good time. Miss her when I'm at sea, yet no sooner home than I itch to get away. She'll be right in the front line if this war comes.'

Rosie shivered.

Blyth unwound her scarf and drew her to him. His face was cold but his lips warm and persuasive. His kisses were gentle, then deep open-mouthed exchanges that took her breath away. 'I shall miss you,' he said.

'What d'you mean?'

'I'm back up to Peterborough to complete my flying course, then off all over the place: Wales, Scotland and God knows where. Next time you see me I'll have my wings and a gold stripe on my arm. It will be goodbye to bell-bottoms.'

Rosie drew away from him. 'Why didn't you tell me before? Getting me all excited and then you're just going to flitter off here, there and everywhere. Ooh,' she yelled. 'I could kill you.'

'Calm down, calm down! Didn't we have a great day together? That's what matters. Got to go, you know that. Rosie,' his voice was pleading, 'we can't think long-term. You're the best thing that's happened to me in ages and ages. You're sparky and funny and I want you, all of you. But, we'll just have to make the most of being together when we can. No promises, no ties. Agreed?'

Rosie nodded, her face stiff with disappointment.

6

Pearl swung between sweats and chills, nightmares and daydreams. It seemed that whenever she opened her eyes Daisy was there, sponging her face, bringing her a fresh hot-water bottle or a cooling drink. As the fever receded, it was enough to lie there watching clouds drift by the window. Daisy had set a bowl of hyacinths on the dressing-table. Each morning Pearl watched the tight-fisted buds release more flowers. She never tired of gazing on their blueness or drawing in the richness of their scent.

Her ribs had stopped aching. Now she was well enough to go to the bathroom on her own and tip lavender bath salts into the steaming water. This last week she had managed the stairs on her own and sat with Daisy listening to the wireless.

'You're spoiling me,' she breathed. 'Shan't want to go home.'

'Here for the duration, love, you're bunked in with me 'til your Dad gets back.'

'What day is it?' she asked, watching her friend flick through a gardening catalogue.

'It's Tuesday the thirty-first of January, bin here a whole month you have.'

Pearl smiled. 'I knew I'd missed Christmas – but all this time! I didn't realise.'

'What d'you remember?'

'Being afraid. Always being afraid. Standing at

Mrs Padgham's with the turkey. Don't know nothin' else 'cept waking up here thinking I'd gone to heaven.'

'Well you're safe now, my pet. All you got ta do is build up your strength.'

Pearl swallowed. 'Where's Kenny gone?'

'To hell in a handcart if I had my way – I don't know, my duck. Sent him off on my bike to get the doctor. Ain't bin seen since. Bin over and locked up the house, and told the police all about him and the scum what he keeps company with. Bit of luck they'll all get scooped up in the army and good riddance.'

Fear clutched at Pearl's chest and her mouth dried. She fiddled with the ribbon on her nightdress. He knew where she was and was likely keeping a watch on Daisy's place. Kenny would wait until Daisy went out to work then sneak in and steal. He would terrorize her into silence. The prayer she'd said over and over came back to her. 'Let there be a war and let Kenny be taken.' It was a wicked, wicked thing to ask for.

'Talk to me, Pearl,' said Daisy, coming and sitting on the arm of her chair. 'What's frightening you, now? He'll be out of your life, I promise.'

Pearl began to cry, sinking down into herself, holding her hands over her face.

Daisy knelt on the floor beside her. She sat there saying nothing. From time to time she patted the girl's foot.

Pearl couldn't stop. Tears trickled through her fingers on to her nightdress. She gulped and shuddered and gasped. A great store of grief burst out of her. It went back to her being brave at her mother's funeral, handing out the sandwiches while Dad opened the whisky. Kenny had been mute, fidgeting with the starched collar of his shirt, easing it away from his chafed neck. She had waved bravely when Dad's ship left from Farewell Jetty over in Portsmouth. She had waved and waved and smiled and smiled. Afterwards she and Kenny had been locked together, the terrorizer and the terrified – alone in their pain. And then she had started praying. At first it had been for Dad to come home. But then he had written to her and said she must be brave and take no notice of Kenny – saying two-and-a-half years was not that long. When she saw Mr Chamberlain and Hitler on the news at the pictures she knew that the German would win. He was wild-eyed and strutting like Kenny. She prayed for Hitler to start the war and for Kenny to be taken. She meant more than being put in the army – she meant– No, she couldn't even think it.

Daisy sat there solid and still. When at length Pearl came to a juddering stop, she said, 'You reckon you're done, now?'

She nodded.

'We best start on the repairs then. Look at ya, puff-eyed and snotty-nosed, let's get a nice warm flannel and a towel. Fancy a cup of tea?'

Pearl blinked.

Later Daisy washed her face and dried her eyes as if she were a two-year-old. She folded her hands around a mug of tea and set a plate of biscuits on the arm of the chair. The big woman helped herself to three spoonfuls of sugar and stirred her cup.

'You bin in the wars, girl, and had a good buffeting, but now you're safe home with me. All that's bin cried out and in the past. You gotta stop being sorry and start being mad.' Daisy laughed, a rich rumbling sound. 'I'm gonna start up a sorry-box and every time you says it in will go a sixpence.'

Pearl gave the ghost of a smile.

'You'll have to rehearse that smile a bit more, wouldn't convince a fly.' She reached across and took a digestive and dunked it into her tea. 'If I had bin in your shoes, you know what? I'd have stoked up such a hate for my brother as I'd want to poison him or shoot him or pray for him to be took.'

Pearl was astonished. 'Would you really?' She darted out her hand and ventured a custard-cream.

'Punch his lights out soon as look at him. I know what you're thinking. Hefty great slab like me, easy-peasy. What you gotta get into that head of yours is that you deserve to be treated with respect.'

Pearl frowned. It wasn't a word she associated with herself. Respect was for the doctor or the teacher. 'How d'you mean?'

'Got a right to be safe and not to be hit. Every creature walking on this earth's entitled to that. Why, if I had a dog I'd care for it better than he cared for you.' She snorted. 'Cared for, what am I talking about? He didn't care one iota for ya. Neither did you. What d'you think your mother would say if she could see her precious Kenny, now? Not got an atom of pride, let himself get boozed up and slummocky. I know he was knocked over by her going but that don't justify.'

'I prayed for Hitler to come and kill him.' Pearl gasped it out, staring at Daisy. Waiting to be branded wicked. Waiting for the blow to come.

'Don't blame you, gal.' Daisy swept up another biscuit. 'War will have to be dealt with best we can, but I'm leavin' that on the back-burner. D'you fancy some liver and bacon? I got a powerful fancy for it.'

'You don't think I could make it happen? The war and things?'

'Blimey Pearl, you ain't bloomin' Jesus. What's up with ya?' She got to her feet. 'We better cut the cackle and get ourselves organised. Got plans for the afternoon. You get yourself back up to that bedroom and put on some warm clothes.'

In the kitchen, while slicing onions and putting the potatoes on to boil, Daisy's brain was working overtime. She could see that getting Pearl over the bronchitis had been a simple matter of care and Dr Kean's medicine. Now she had to get her up and about, then, turn her from an apologetic punch-bag into a self-respecting young woman. If her plans were to come to anything she must get cracking. In six days time they both had an interview up at the ordnance depot.

At first she had thought of just applying herself and leaving Pearl at home to do the cooking and cleaning. Then she had spotted Kenny. It had been one afternoon when she had gone back to the house to get the girl some clothes. Stood at the bedroom window she was, putting some photos into a carrier bag. Just happened to look up. He was getting out of the shed window. Could hardly recognise him from the lad she used to know. Wild hair and thin, God, she almost felt pity. Then there was her brother Graham. Surely to God he could have got a home draft in the circumstances. To go away so soon and leave his kids to fettle for themselves was bordering on criminal. But then he had thought, good old Daisy would keep an eye. And she had made a few visits, issued a few invitations and bin took in by Kenny like everyone else. When Frank had gone down to Plymouth, all her energies were put into going down there as often as she could to see him. And then when he went off East she had put off and put off going around to see those kids. Enough! Raking over the past was a waste of time.

Seeing Kenny still free to sneak about, in spite of her calls to the police and Dr Kean's report on Pearl's injuries, decided her. They would go off to Priddy's Hard together. Who was she kidding about keeping the house clean and tidy? Always bin a messy mare, she had. The two of them would muddle through and they certainly wouldn't starve. Now, where in God's name had she put the Bisto?

'That looks better – don't it feel better to have yer clothes on?'

Pearl smiled.

'Have to get you some new stuff once we bin working a while.'

'Working? What, up the laundry?'

Daisy laughed. 'Jacked that in ages ago. Got

fresh plans for the pair of us, up at Priddy's.'

'What, the gunpowder factory?'

'Yeh, you and me are gonna have an explosive time together.'

Pearl bit her lip and looked down at the floor. 'I don't know if I can, if I'm up to doing anything like that.'

'Well, we won't know 'til we tries, will we? You seen the Bisto? Had it here yesterday.'

'I'll get it. Left it in the sitting-room by the wireless.'

'Ta, Babes. Loads of different jobs up at Priddy's, ain't all big bangs you know. Hundreds of Gosport people up there working; when the war comes there'll be hundreds more. Be like the last time: they'll wheel all us women out of our homes and set us doin' all sorts.'

'What did you do, Auntie Daisy? Last time I mean.'

Daisy grinned. 'I got stuck in. Beginning of the war my Dad died and Mum, your Granny, moved down to Devon to run a little pub. Your Uncle Henry was posted off to France in the army. I got a job down in Gosport as a conductress on the trams. Worked with a great bunch of girls – then, this young woman come over from Pompey, needing a place to live. Expecting a baby she was, used to look after the place while I was down the depot. Miriam, she became my dearest friend. Great times, great times.' Daisy paused. 'Now where was I? Dig out the spud masher, will ya. In the back of the drawer somewhere.'

'Did you enjoy the war, then?' asked Pearl, fascinated by the picture her aunt was painting.

86

Daisy stopped smiling, and tears gathered in her eyes. 'It was bloody terrible. Reading every night them great lists of men killed over there. Seeing all the women and the nippers crying without their husbands and dads. There was all the muddles of men gone missing, and the waiting, and waiting and not knowing. You were too young to know my Henry. He was a lovely shy feller, taught me all I knows about growing things. Hale and hearty, never so much as a sniffle. Come back from France like a bloomin' ghost. Always sickly after that. Dead within five years.'

'I'm sorry, didn't mean to…'

'Where's that bloomin' sorry-box?' said Daisy, wiping her eyes with the sleeve of her blouse.

Pearl gave an uncertain laugh.

'You wants to do that more often, Babes. It suits ya. War is terrible, like I said, but you have to bear it the best way you can. And of course there's bits that lifts yer spirits, you even laughs, but by Christ we could well do without it. What comforts me about my Henry is that I cared for him right to the last and he died in clean sheets, not in that stinking French mud.' She took a hankie from her sleeve and gave her nose a resounding blow. 'Right now, Pearl, sling the knives and forks round and we'll get this grub down us.'

'I was thinking. What's happened to Mrs Padgham?'

'Gone off to her sister's in Fareham. Says we can go up and see her one Sunday, watcha think?'

'I'd like that. She was good to me. I suppose I could write to her.'

'Please her no end that would. Good soul is

Florrie Padgham. Puts me in mind of a robin, bright and cheery.'

'What sort of things would we do at Priddy's?'

Daisy felt a glimmer of satisfaction. The girl was picking up, showing interest. Soon she'd be back on her feet. 'From what I hear tell there's all sorts. There's making the special clothes what they wear, sewing munition bags, working in the canteen, office stuff, loading the barges what take the shells and stuff to the ships, there's even a little railway, and then of course there's the cordite and fuses and shell filling. What d'ya think? In for a penny, in for a pound?'

Pearl smiled. 'If you think I could do it, Daisy. I'll give it a try.'

Daisy slapped her on the back. 'Knew there was a tryer in there somewhere. Now this afternoon we gotta treat. You and me are going to the hairdresser, get you a proper hair-cut.'

It was the darkness that woke him. Crouched under a shelf in Dad's shed the fear clutched at him. He had gone to sleep like always with the torch clutched in his hand. Bleeding batteries must have run out. He crawled out of his bed made up of newspapers and a pair of his father's overalls, and rubbed a clear patch on the windowpane. He stared at the glimmer of daylight. What time was it? As he held his wrist up to the light it came to him that his watch was gone. He'd had to part with it to get money for food. Only got five bob from some tight-arsed sailor – worth tons more than that. The watch had been a present from Dad when he got the apprenticeship at Fleetlands. Kenny had lived in a different world, then. It had been a world of clean clothes and good dinners. He had had a fountain-pen in his top pocket and a slide-rule in his case.

It was that interfering Daisy's fault.

'If she dies I'll see you hang,' she had screamed at him.

Christ! he was hungry. Shouldn't have fallen out with Spike and Nudger. Gone mad he had. Laughed at him over not liking the dark. Led to a scrap between the three of them. Spike had blown out the candles. Been living in an old caravan on waste ground near an allotment. Nearly turned it over with their lunging at each other. Bloke banged on the door. Had a dog with him. Said he'd call the police. The two of them had chucked him down the steps. All night he'd lain under that van, terrified of the dog getting him in that dark hole between the wheels. Wet himself he had. Kenny looked across at his home, locked against him. If he could only get in and switch the lights on – get some sleep. Couldn't break in or they'd be on to him. Already, the other night, two of them had been snooping around with their torches. He'd had to lie there with his switched off while they rattled the shed door.

It was all falling apart. He was sick of it – the hunger, the dirt, and the fear. Couldn't bear his stink.

Perhaps he'd sneak off to that fat Daisy's place. Might be able to sneak in there and grab some grub. If Pearl were there she'd know what was good for her and keep quiet.

Kenny stared out of the window, watching the daylight spread across the sky, driving out the darkness. Dodging through alleys, over fields, he made his way to Daisy's house. He hid behind her dustbin, watching and waiting. Nearly had him she did. Came out of the back door with a parcel in newspaper. It was grub – he could smell it. Crouched double he was. Lifted the bin just a foot from where he was then clanged it down again. He heard the bolts being drawn across the kitchen door. Kenny waited. With exquisite care he lifted up one edge of the lid and slid his hand inside. His fingers closed over the parcel still warm from the plate.

God, it was good. Liver and a bit of bacon mixed up with jam tart and custard. He ate it off the paper, snuffling like a dog. In daylight with food inside him, Kenny began to feel better. The scheming part of his brain reasserted itself.

7

Blyth couldn't help admiring himself as he looked in the dormitory mirror at the figure in sub-lieutenant's uniform. He drew his left sleeve across his chest so that the gold stripe on his cuff was visible. It curled around the letter A, denoting the Fleet Air Arm officer. Better still were his pilot's wings above the stripe. 'Hello Gorgeous,' he said, kissing his reflection, 'your place or mine?'

'Oh darling,' breathed a voice behind him, 'sweep me off my feet. Transport me.'

Together they waltzed between the beds to the wolf-whistles of their classmates.

'Let me go, let me go, Daddy will be here at any moment, unhand me you cad,' said his dancing partner. Laughing, they collapsed in a heap on the floor.

Justin Croxley disentangled himself. 'Christ! You're a conceited bugger,' he said.

Blyth grinned. 'To love oneself is the beginning of a lifelong romance.'

'It is if you're a fucking worm,' snorted Inky Pen.

'Must go and phone the old man, he'll be like a dog with two tails,' Knocker White called, and his classmates rushed downstairs with him to the phone box.

Blyth had no plans to call anyone. Even if Dad

were still alive he couldn't have reached him at home. Lemon Street hadn't run to such luxuries as telephones. Probably he would have got him at the Captain Hardy and shouted his good news over the hubbub in the public bar. Dad would have been legless in half an hour on congratulatory drinks bought by his pals. The need to have his father's congratulations surprised Blyth, but then, only Dad knew what an achievement it was.

It had been a steep climb from that ragged kid in Brotherhood boots to Fleet Air Arm pilot. He remembered every rung along the way. It started with him taking back empty jam jars to the corner shop to earn his Saturday sixpence. At a halfpenny each, he'd had to scout around the neighbourhood dustbins. Following that had been his stint at the barber's as a lather boy, having to stand on the stool to reach the customers' faces.

What had really focused his ambition was the arrival in Portsmouth of Sir Alan Cobham's Flying Circus on his thirteenth birthday. There had been a 'Stop Me and Fly One' tent, and Uncle Albert had given him the five shillings entry money. Those ten minutes were burned into his memory as the plane bumped across the grass, then the surge as it accelerated into the wind. Passing over roads the cars looked like toys, and in the harbour ships were minute grey blurs. The thrill of rising through the clouds, the blue of the sky and the sun glinting on the wings was magical. After landing, he'd plagued the pilot with questions. To shut him up the pilot had asked him something.

'OK here's one for you. Say two planes are a mile apart, flying towards each other at the same altitude and a speed of 100mph: how long before the point of collision?'

'Eighteen seconds,' he snapped back.

The pilot gasped. 'Little Einstein, you are. What action should the pilots have taken?'

He had thought for a moment. 'They'd both have to turn right.'

'What does this tell you?' asked a bystander.

'There must be rules of the air which pilots follow to avoid collision.'

'Very good! Right pilot, take him up again for a free one, he's earned it.'

'Yes, Sir Alan,' said the pilot, 'you're the boss.'

'Jammy blighter, he's taken to you. Carry on like that, you'll make a pilot one day.'

'Right, Salisbury it is,' Justin said later, as they left the air station for a celebratory run ashore. 'What's the programme?'

'First stop the Lamb and Lark in Shadwell Street, then big eats at the Crowthers,' said Inky. 'There's a little nippy there with the trimmest arse. Gave me the glad-eye last time I was in – on to a certainty there. Blonde-haired, blue-eyed poppet she is.'

Blyth smiled at Inky Pen. He had seen the ring on the girl's finger and not thought the game worth the risk – besides she wasn't a patch on Rosie. They roared through the Wiltshire country-side in Justin and Inky's cars, mayhem in mind. The evening raced along in a fog of food and booze, and endless toasts ranging from the excellence of Tiger Moths to Betty Grable's legs. Blyth had no memory of returning to the base.

He awoke at seven in a state of fumbling excitement with Rosie on his mind. Her head was thrown back and she was laughing. Always, in his imaginings, she was wearing that jumper thing that clung to her breasts and showed a teasing glimpse of cleavage. With Rosie, there was none of the come-on then let-down he'd had from other girls holding out for an engagement ring. She was open and passionate and didn't play games. With her, he could be honest about his past. Yet, knowing her family complicated things. Uncle Albert was the nearest thing he had to a grandfather. If Blyth and Rosie fell out and the old man thought he had treated her shabbily, Blyth would lose his respect. Albert had taught him chess and bought him his first slide-rule. Albert's good opinion mattered to him. With a twinge of guilt Blyth realised that he'd been away for months and only sent her a couple of letters. He had some serious making-up to do.

In the Labour Exchange on the corner of Lake Road, Rosie picked up the green card: *'Join the WRNS and free a man to join the FLEET.'* She studied the conditions of entry. She must be aged between seventeen and forty-five and not be engaged in a *'Reserved Occupation.'* Requirement number three made her grin: *'You have good health and your teeth are in good condition.'*

She was tempted to add, *'Only good biters need apply.'* The work categories were: clerical, communications, domestic and transport. There it was: despatch rider. Her heart sank at the words, *'There is not much demand in this group.'* Well, tough! She'd just have to wait 'til they needed her. References were no problem, what with her employer, Claude Treagus, Uncle Albert and her old headmaster in the Isle of Wight more than willing to say what a great girl she was.

Blyth will be impressed, she thought, posting the envelope to the C-in-C Portsmouth Command at the end of March – if he cares at all. There had been two letters in three months. Lying on her bed, she reread his last one for the hundredth time.

Porthcawl
10th March 1939
   Dear Rosie,
   It's bloody freezing up here for all it's supposed to be spring. Hardly given time to breathe it's nearly all flying. We're up there from morning to night: aerial dogfights, high and low-level dive-bombing at targets in the sea. I love it. It's high risk and you have to concentrate every second not only on what you're doing but anticipating the other plane's next move. On the ground they hit you with all the theory, maths, aerodynamics and instrument flying.
   Soon we'll be off to Netheravon in Wiltshire to get our wings and be promoted to Sub-Lieutenants. Goodbye to bell-bottoms at last.
   Hugs and kisses,
   Blyth

Mentally she paraded her past boyfriends in front of her. Some had really been fun and others she'd thought herself in love with for at least a week. Tested by time they had all come to grief. With Blyth there was an immediate charge of excitement. They challenged one another. Just as she thought she knew him, he pulled the rug away and she was again uncertain. What would Gran have thought of them getting together? Grinning to herself, she invented the words Beattie might have said: 'He's got the face of an angel and a mind as sharp as a razor-blade. My stars, girl, you'll have to hang on to your drawers with that one. A real heart-breaker.'

'Stay with me at Hazlewood overnight then I'll drop you down to Pompey the next day. You can meet my sister Delia. It'll save you hanging about for trains.'

Blyth hesitated. He was impatient to see Rosie, yet Justin was his chum. They had joined up together at St Vincent in Gosport and stayed together ever since. Juss was his only real friend. Academically they were equals, yet Juss was having real difficulties with flying. Blyth couldn't understand it. With him it was instinctive. He wanted Juss to succeed, they were oppos. He stood looking at Delia Croxley's photo waiting to be packed in his friend's holdall – quite a looker, or would be when she had shed that eager puppy smile. He was curious. Another reason to stop off at Justin's was the spare overcoat he could lend him. With few relatives and none with any spare cash, Blyth suffered a clothes famine, and had been rescued more than once by his friend's generosity. 'You're on,' he said, 'as long as you drop me down early to Pompey. I've got some catching up to do.' Blyth slipped the card for Rosie in his pocket. He'd forgotten last night, intent on posting it before leaving the air station.

The journey passed in a blur of fields and farms as they rushed out of Wiltshire, through Hampshire and across to Surrey. And then they turned onto a shingle path surrounded by flowerbeds alive with daffodils. Munstead House came into view – a broad flat-faced building with a central porch. The walls glowed a pale honey colour in the morning sun. Blyth was enchanted by its simplicity. It reminded him of pictures in the storybooks he'd read as a child. He had never been interested in houses, but this one with its sloping buttress at one side and little gate leading out to the garden intrigued him. It reached out to him in welcome. One day, he thought...

The car crunched to a halt and they were caught up in a melée of barking dogs. At the sound of the horn a girl erupted through the front door in a blaze of red hair.

'Darling Juss,' she cried, wrapping her arms around her brother. Behind her was a woman in tweeds, with greying hair hanging down her back in a thick plait.

'Come in, come in, my dear sweet boy. Delia, unhand him.'

'Mummy,' said Justin, hugging her.

Blyth stood around like a spare part watching them. They were a different tribe entirely. He struggled to stop a liver-coloured spaniel from licking his face, and turned to find Delia tugging at his sleeve.

'Blyth, I'm so sorry, I do apologise. You must think us frightfully rude. Hello.' She grabbed his hand and pumped it vigorously.

He took off his cap and smiled at her. 'Hello, Delia,' he said. With that fantastic hair and those green eyes she could in time be quite stunning. First, she would have to stop all this horsy carry-on. Stepping forward to greet Mrs Croxley, he became aware of another figure behind her in the doorway.

'Pa,' said Justin, turning to embrace him.

The man came out onto the path. To Blyth, he resembled a whittled stick.

'Justin, good to see you, my boy,' he barked. 'Who's the chap behind you?'

'This is my chum, Blyth. This is my father, Commander Croxley.'

'Good morning, Sir.' Blyth held out his hand and with a jolt found his fingers closing over a metal hook. Embarrassed, he attempted to shake his other hand, annoyed at being placed at a disadvantage. 'Pleased to meet you, Sir,' he said.

'Blyth?' the Commander barked, 'What sort of name is that?'

'A short one,' he replied, refusing to be cowed.

'Hrrrmph! Come in, come in.'

Fairy castle complete with ogre, thought Blyth, following him into the house.

Mrs Croxley took him to her capacious bosom in a tweedy hug. 'Blyth, I'm delighted to see you. Justin has told me so much about you.' Her voice was like dark chocolate and her smile wrapped itself around him. 'This will be such a treat for Felix,' she nodded towards Justin's father, 'he loves to talk to flyers.'

'Play chess do you? Any good?' asked her husband abruptly.

'Yes, Sir,' said Blyth staring him out, 'I'm very good.'

'Hrrrmph,' the man barked before stumping away down the passage.

Blyth looked about him. The hall was large and thickly carpeted. Doors led off to the right and left. On a ledge above one of them was a pair of stag's antlers. In front of him was a broad staircase with a carved pineapple on the newel post. The place smelled of old dogs, old wood and beef stew. His mouth began to water.

'Delia, show Blyth up to the guest room, darling. See you boys for a sherry in ten minutes.' Her plait swinging, Mrs Croxley marched down the hall and out of sight.

Picking up his holdall, he followed Delia up the stairs and down a passage over uneven creaking boards. She held a door open for him. 'I hope you're not too good at chess,' she said. 'Pa will sulk for days if you beat him.'

He grinned at her. 'Good job I'm only staying one night,' he said.

'We must make the most of you,' she blustered, not looking at him.

He took her hand and kissed it. 'Thank you for making me feel so welcome.'

'Not at all,' she said, blushing and withdrawing her hand. Delia was about to leave when she turned and said, 'Blyth, may I write to you? I write to Juss but,' she looked at the carpet and scuffed her toe across a rose motif, 'but that's not quite the same.'

He hesitated. Flirting was one thing but writing? 'I'm a terrible correspondent,' he said. 'Let's just see where life takes us, shall we?'

'I shall write even if you don't answer,' she persisted.

She hasn't got any idea, he thought idly, but it might be fun to teach her. Smiling, he took hold of Delia's shoulders. 'You do what you like and now I'll do the same.' He kissed her lightly on the lips and then released her.

'I must go,' she gasped, 'Mummy will wonder.' Then she was gone, galumphing down the passage.

Blyth stood by the window, looking down at the garden with its flowerbeds, rustic benches and a giant oak complete with a tree-house. A radiator clanked as he turned to hang his jacket on a hook. Sitting on the edge of an armchair Blyth changed his boots for shoes. Beside him on a table was a china bowl heaped with dried flower petals, and on the shelf below a stack of magazines. Idly he flicked through them: the *Field*, *Tatler*, and *Horse and Hound*. He sifted the flower petals between his fingers – it was all so seductive. Reaching up for his coat again he remembered the card he'd meant to post to Rosie.

Assembling her crepe paper, glass shelves and ticket-box, Rosie began dressing the sweetshop window. The centrepiece was to be a golden basket heaped with foil-covered eggs. Set on the handle was a violet bow with a card attached. The message read: *Win this wonderful Easter gift. A raffle ticket with every purchase. The draw will take place on Saturday 8th of April.* It had been her idea, and Claude had for once been enthusiastic. She built up the shelves with dishes of sweets interspersed with fluffy chicks, aiming to enchant her young customers. It was half-way through the afternoon when she stepped outside to survey the effect.

'Very pretty, Miss Forrest.'

Before she could turn and see the speaker, she was swung round and round in his arms, drawing a cheer from people waiting at the bus stop.

'Blyth, Blyth, put me down you daft ha'p'orth,' she shrieked. 'When did you get here? Why didn't you let me know?'

He grinned at her. She took in the sub-lieutenant's gold stripe on his sleeve and knew he was waiting for her congratulations. Well, he was going to have to earn it.

'Fancy a meal tonight? I've booked a table at the Parisian for seven.'

'You're sure of yourself,' she said. 'How d'you know I haven't got plans already?'

'Have you? I could change it to another night.'

It was tempting to knock the gilt off his self-assurance, but equally tempting was the thought of dinner in a posh restaurant. 'A quarter to seven at the Nile, any later and I'll change my mind.' Smiling, she closed the door in his face.

In her bedroom that night she settled on a white blouse with a deep V-neck, and a black flouncy skirt. Sliding her feet down into a pair of Cuban-heeled shoes, Rosie could feel the *femme fatale* in her rising to the surface. To complete the effect she borrowed Mum's *L'aimant*, rubbing the glass stopper against her neck and between her breasts. 'Blyth,' she whispered.

'Hello Gorgeous,' he said later, when she met him in the lounge bar.

They walked across the Guildhall Square towards the Parisian Restaurant. Rosie concentrated on not tripping over her heels. It was the night she'd dreamed of, speaking might burst the bubble.

'Reservation for Vine,' Blyth said to the waiter, who helped Rosie out of her coat.

'Certainly, Sir, let me show you to your table.' He held her chair for her and Rosie seated herself, trying to appear as if she dined out every night of the week. He handed her a menu.

The food was listed in swirly copperplate and set out in sections: hors-d'oevres, entrées, poisson and desserts. Looking at the prices, Blyth would be lucky to have any change from a ten-pound note she thought. Well, she was worth it.

'Wine list, Sir?' A man with a napkin folded over his arm stood there holding out a card. He bowed towards them, features set in an unctuous smile.

Rosie looked around her at the mirrored walls, the candles at each table, the crisply starched napkins and gleaming glasses. She smiled at the woman opposite in a feathered hat, who raised a thin eyebrow before turning away. Rosie grinned to herself. 'Red hat and no drawers,' would have been Gran's estimation of her.

Blyth looked flushed. 'A bottle of Sauterne, please,' he said, brushing imaginary crumbs from the cloth. 'Have you chosen?' he whispered.

'What you whispering for?' she challenged. 'We're not in church.'

The waiter returned. 'May I take your order, Madam and Sir?'

'Let's not bother with horsydoofers or the soup. I'd like roast guinea-fowl, pommes frites, whatever they are, and cauliflower cheese. Do we do the puddings, now?'

The waiter shook his head. 'And, for you, Sir?'

'I'll have the same,' he mumbled.

The wine waiter reappeared and poured a dessertspoonful of Sauterne into Blyth's glass. He tasted it, giving a fake smile before nodding for Rosie's glass to be filled.

Its sourness made her gasp. 'Uggh! It's like vinegar. I'll have water, thank you.'

'What did you say that for?' hissed Blyth.

Rosie glared at him. 'What's up with you, tip-toeing about? Our money's as good as theirs. No good getting your gold braid if you can't act up to it.'

'I thought you hadn't noticed,' he sulked.

'Stop giving them permission to look down on you.' She had looked forward to the evening all day. Had dreamed of being alone with him, and now it was all falling apart. He was about to say something when the food arrived. Rosie took her napkin and spread it on her lap. What a palaver it was getting the food served. The waiter juggled it onto their plates between two dessertspoons. The guinea-fowl were tiny and tasteless and the chips cold. Forking a spoonful of cauliflower cheese to her mouth she thought wistfully of fish-and-chips in paper, liberally sprinkled with salt and vinegar. They should pay up now and cut their losses.

Blyth ate silently, staring fixedly at his plate. Rosie wanted to hit him for disappointing her. She had been looking forward to seeing him and now he was here, a pale imitation of the larky fellow she'd fallen in love with.

'What would you like for dessert?' he asked, after putting down his knife and fork.

'Spotted dick and custard,' she said, grinning at him. Why couldn't he thaw out and see that the only way out of the mess was to laugh?

'It's not on the menu, I'm having the peach melba.' His face was set like a stubborn schoolboy.

'Blyth, this is daft. The wine's cat's pee, the food's rubbish. Why don't we leave?'

'Sit down,' he ground out the words, as she got to her feet.

Rosie took out her purse and put two pound notes on the table. 'I'm going, Blyth. You're no fun to be with. Getting your stripe has turned you into a po-faced snob.' Not looking back she rushed through the restaurant and dragged her coat from the rack. As she hobbled back into Commercial Road there were tears in her eyes. Whether they were from anger or disappointment she wasn't sure.

8

From his vantage point behind the water-butt Kenny watched his aunt and sister lock the kitchen door and leave the house by the back gate. It was early, with the frost stiff on the grass. Where were they going? Must be work. It was the first time he had seen Pearl since Christmas. He felt relief. By now her bruises would have faded and it would be just their word against his.

The thought of having an entire empty house to himself spread a grin across his face. There'd be food and warmth, maybe a chance to sleep in a bed. Kenny laughed. Daft pair they were, locked the back door and left the key to the front one under a flowerpot by the mat.

With the aid of his torch and its stolen batteries he crept down the alley and round to the gate. As he was closing his fingers over the key someone came out of the adjoining house. Kenny thanked God for the height of the dividing fence. A man's voice spoke to a dog. 'Hang on, Bosun, let me fix your lead, boy.'

Making sure they had got to the end of the road he stood up and opened the front door. Warmth enfolded him. The house smelled of polish and toast. Kenny drew the bolt across the door. In the kitchen he switched on the light. Christ! How he had missed it all. On the table were a butter-dish and a jar of blackberry-and-apple jam. There was bread in the bin and in the cutlery drawer clean knives. Under its woolly cosy the teapot was still warm. He reached down a clean cup, saucer and plate from the dresser and located the milk jug. Taking up a saw-toothed knife he cut two doorsteps of bread and slathered them with butter and jam. He poured a cup of tea and helped himself generously to sugar from the basin with *Weymouth* painted on it.

Other possibilities presented themselves. Finding a tray he carried his breakfast up the stairs to the bathroom. He lit the geyser with the matches nearby and began to run the water into the bath. Kenny sat on the laundry-box eating his breakfast and watching the steam rise. On the window-ledge was a glass jar of bath salts. He set down his tray and flooded the water with a shower of yellow crystals. 'Lemon Verbena, why not, Kenny lad,' he crowed. Then he began seriously eating. God! It was good. Turning off the hot tap he dribbled in the cold water. While it was trickling in he went in search of clothing.

Daisy's room yielded plenty of Uncle Frank's stuff. Pity he was such a great slab of a bloke. He would lose himself in that big jumper and the trousers would look as if he'd come from a circus. Just have to tuck them in and turn over the waistband. Might be able to find some cash to buy some new togs. Now the chance had come to get some clean clothes, he could not stand his own fetid rags a minute longer. Rolling them up in his greasy raincoat he stowed them in the laundry-box. He peed in the lavatory then set his new wardrobe in readiness on the lid. With a sigh, he slid into the scented water.

As he lathered the soap over his body he thought of the films he'd seen of men on the run. The grainy, black-and-white world of barking dogs and police whistles didn't begin to capture it. It was a life on the snatch. Snatching sleep, snatching food and snatching chances. The flicks could never convey the exhaustion and gnawing fear, or the boredom. As the grey scum rose from his body he slid deeper under the water and closed his eyes.

Pearl hurried along Green Lane to Priddy's Hard arm-in-arm with Daisy. She couldn't remember ever being out so early in the morning. Her heart thumped with a mixture of fear and excitement. After their medicals the pair of them had had to sign the Official Secrets Act. They were now sworn not to mention a word of what went on behind the gates of the naval ordnance depot. Gunpowder fuses, TNT, who knew what they would be dealing with. They were not alone. Men swarmed past, dark blurs behind winking cycle-lamps.

At the gate a large policeman stared down at them. 'New ladies, are you?'

They nodded.

'Come in the gatehouse 'til the rush has died down.'

Pearl watched everyone taking numbered brass tokens out of a box. When the swarm had slowed to a trickle the policeman asked them their names.

'Mrs Daisy Fletcher and Pearl Bunting.'

He consulted a list. 'Ah yes. You'll be on cordite. I've got your tokens here, number 368 and 369.' He called to a woman emerging from the lane. 'Poppy Dundas, that you?'

'Whatcha want, Harry? Not late am I?'

'Got two new girls for your section. Here you are, Mrs Fletcher and Miss Bunting.'

Poppy rested her bike against a railing and followed the policeman inside the gatehouse. Her face was plump and rosy like an apple. Her dark eyes darted from one to the other. 'Hallo you two,' she said, thrusting out a gloved hand. 'I'm Poppy, pleased to know ya. Just pick up me token and we'll be off.'

They followed her through the gates, down a road and over a bridge. 'They tell ya up at the office what you'd be doin?' she called over her shoulder.

Daisy laughed. 'Told us heaps but it went in one ear and out the other, didn't it Pearl?'

'Same here when I started, learning by doin', that's favourite.' Poppy led the way to a large wooden building with a notice painted above the door. *Shifting-Room Number 28.*

They followed Poppy inside and found several other women all in different stages of dressing and undressing. There were wooden partitions and hooks all round, with outside coats and even skirts and jumpers hanging up. Down the centre of the hut was a wooden ledge set into the floor and painted red.

'This side, where we are is dirty. So we gets our clothes off down to vest and drawers and bare feet. Then we steps over the ledge into the clean side. See the girl over there, putting on them overalls and turban and tying up them shoes?'

Pearl nodded.

'She's all got up in her clean stuff ready to go off to the Igniter Labby. You two are coming along with me and Ruth here and Marj to the Cordite Labby.' Poppy smiled. 'Remember when I first started, talk about a babe in the wood. You'll pick it up, won't they girls?'

The others smiled encouragingly.

'Step over with me, when you're ready. Can only take a hankie, glasses and yer wedding-ring across with ya and your token. They're kept in the labby as a check of who's in or out.' Poppy scanned the hooks. 'Here you are, 368 and 369.'

Stepping over, Daisy laughed. 'Don't take a genius to work out which is which. Me and you is like Jack Sprat and his wife.'

The other women joined in.

'Don't never fit propply,' the woman called Marj said, smiling at her. 'In the summer they itches sommink cruel.' She was about the same age as Daisy, with ginger hair in a plait tied off with a strip of bandage.

Pearl smiled at her. The work clothes consisted of a man's suit in thick white serge and a round brimless hat of the same material. On the floor beneath her numbered hook was a pair of shoes with wooden nails and tape laces. Daisy's clothes barely fitted her while Pearl swam in hers. Marj came over and helped roll up the trouser legs while Pearl did the arms.

Back on the hook was a small bag of the same serge material.

'Hangs it round yer neck and puts in personal stuff, hankie, glasses and such like. Don't take snuff, do ya?'

Pearl shook her head.

'I has me snuff-box with me. Don't half clear your head of a morning.'

When all the women were fully dressed they left the shifting-room and made their way across a field strewn with huts divided from one another by high grassy mounds, each fronted by a large cement slab. They stopped at Lab number 16.

''Bye, girls,' called the igniter girl, going further on.

'It's another world,' said Daisy, as she watched Poppy take the bolts off the door and put them in a wooden box before pulling the door open with a rope handle.

'Gets used to it,' Ruth said. 'I'll nip around and switch the lights on.' She smiled at Pearl. 'All the switches are fixed to the outside, and heating. So's there's no chance of a spark. Not so important with us with cordite, but when you're dealing with gunpowder–' She clapped her hands. 'Poof!! It's another thing all together.'

'There's rail-track here,' whispered Pearl, looking down at tracks that seemed to loop in and out of the porch.

'For the train, it goes back and forth to all the labbys, bringing us stuff and fetching away what we've finished.'

'Where does it go then?' asked Pearl, her curiosity overcoming her fear. Ruth was not much older than herself and she had a friendly, freckled face.

'Taken to the magazine store or out on to the shell or powder pier, then on barges to the ships.' Like Daisy said, it was a whole different world.

Inside, the room was little more than a wooden box with a long table down the centre. Poppy hurried over to a corner, lifted up a loose board and put a newspaper package inside. She tapped her nose and smiled. 'Tell ya later,' she said. 'Right girls, Daisy, you come alonga me and Pearl you go with Ruth.'

There was the blast of a whistle and the train backed into the porch. It resembled a train for children, in size, without the bright paintwork. Poppy went out and talked to the man at the controls and brought in a wooden box packed with mysterious grey spaghetti.

In the meantime Marj had set a pair of scales on the table, and bundles of white tape. Poppy heaped the spaghetti up in front of each of them. Pearl looked questioningly up at Ruth.

'This is cordite and we bundle it up and tie it together in a reef knot with this tape. It gets weighed and then we put the fuses in and they're put in cloth bags and sewn up and we gotta put our number on a ticket with them.'

'Why have you got to weigh them?'

'It's all to do with arithmetic. Sailor using it knows it'll travel a certain distance in a certain time, according to how much it weighs. Got to be able to trust us that the weight is accurate. Too heavy, and it might fall short of the mark, and too light might go too far. Could mean putting those blokes in danger if their munitions fall short.'

Pearl swallowed.

Ruth smiled at her. 'Don't worry, Chick. It's easy-peasy.'

Once they had fallen into a routine, the women they worked with settled down to their usual chat.

Poppy was engaged to a sailor in a place in Scotland called Donnybristle, and lived at home with her parents and a confusing collection of brothers and sisters. Marj was a free spirit living at home but still not spoken for.

'Likes all my chaps for a few weeks or so then gets used to them and the magic's gone. 'Sides,' she said, looking down at the table. 'If a war comes, don't want to get fixed on someone then have them killed. Our sister's chap got killed in France last day of the last lot. Mum says she went mental. Never had another chap.'

'Chancey business is life,' Ruth said. 'My chap is in the Fleet Air Arm at Charlton Horethorne in Somerset. Getting married on his next leave. Expect it'll be Easter.'

'What's his name?' asked Pearl.

'Jeff, a big dark-haired lad, ever so jolly. What about you?'

'Live with Daisy. She's my auntie. Dad's out east in the navy and Mum's dead.'

Ruth put a hand on her shoulder. 'Oh Babes, ever so sorry.'

Pearl swallowed and looked at the floor.

'Time for a brew-up,' said Poppy, going over to a corner of the shed and lifting a loose floorboard.

She took out a teapot and shook in some tea. At one of the steam heating-pipes she twisted a valve and filled the pot with gurgling steamy water. 'Afraid there's no milk but plenty of sugar, we'll have to share the cups. Anyone fancy a sandwich?'

'Whatcha got this time?' asked Marj. 'Not more liver sausage.'

'Yer favourite,' laughed Poppy. 'Beetroot and mashed spud.'

Daisy looked at Pearl and raised her eyebrows. They grinned at one another. It was just one new experience after another.

After their tea-break they packed everything away and settled back to work. At twelve o'clock a whistle blew and the whole process was reversed. Back in the shifting-room, they changed into their outside clothes and handed their tokens to the gate policeman before hurrying home.

'Better not stay above a half-hour,' said Daisy, as they hurried down the road. 'Reckon tomorrow we'll leave something ready before we leave for work. It'll save a deal of time.' She turned to her niece. 'What did you think of it all? Reckon we'll stay the course?'

Pearl smiled. 'Liked the girls. They were nice.'

Daisy laughed, 'You've certainly come out of your shell and no mistake, Pearl Bunting.' Turning her key in the lock, Daisy frowned. 'What's happened here? Blooming key won't turn.'

She peered through the letterbox and sniffed. The house smelt different. What was it? Blimey! It was Lemon Verbena. Daisy frowned – it seemed unlikely that a burglar would take a bath. The main thing, she decided, was not to put the wind up Pearl. Poor kid was just getting her confidence back.

'Tell you what, love, I've a powerful fancy for something salty. Nip down to Bargent's will ya, and get us a couple of packets of crisps?'

'Right ho, Auntie.' The girl dashed down the road to the grocer's without a murmur.

Looking about her, Daisy walked down the side alley and round to the back of the house. The bathroom curtains were drawn and the window closed. She was equally unsuccessful at gaining entry at the back door. Peering through the kitchen window she saw half a loaf on the table and the lid off the butter-dish. Daisy fumed. It was that bloody Kenny. If it weren't for Pearl she'd go crashing in and punch his lights out. No, she'd try another tack. Keep it in the family – she had just the fellow in mind.

The phone-box was on the corner by Bargent's. She'd make a call. Smiling to herself Daisy came out of the box as Pearl left the shop. 'You best go back in and fetch us a Swiss roll or something and a bottle of Tizer. Have to have a bit of a picnic in the shifting-room. Well and truly locked out we are.'

'Don't understand. We had the key, didn't we?'

'All be sorted time we gets back tonight. Tell ya what, we'll have that little tin of salmon what I was saving for my birthday. Mash it up with the left-over spuds and have some fish-cakes.'

Arm-in-arm, they walked back to the Green Lane Gate and smiled at the big policeman. They were different women from the ones that passed through at seven that morning – part of the workforce now.

Kenny woke up in cold grey water. He shivered. Wrapping himself in the towel, he sat on the lavatory lid and examined his fresh clothing. It was laughable – like little Stanley Laurel trying to wear Oliver Hardy's jacket and pin-striped trousers. Still, all he had to do was stick it on just to make his getaway. Shoes would be a problem. He took eight and a half and Uncle Frank size ten. Then he thought of Pearl: she might have some plimsolls. He scratched his head: little weed that she was, they'd likely be too small. 'Friggin' hell,' he muttered. Thwarted at every turn, he was. Have to get a pair of her clean socks and wear his wrecked lace-ups.

Rolling up the sleeves of the shirt, and turning over the waistband of the trousers several times, Kenny padded out of the bathroom and into the small bedroom.

He hadn't expected to see the photo of his family looking out at him from that day out in Weymouth. It was on the dressing-table in a wooden frame. Kenny sank down on the bed. The pain at seeing his mother with her hand on his shoulder made him gasp. He knuckled the tears from his eyes. 'Mum,' he sighed, 'oh Mum.' Everything had become pointless. His life had gone down the plughole. As he had done when a small child, Kenny rocked himself back and forth snuffling and crying. When he had come to a shuddering halt he thought he heard something. Christ! What was it? Someone was in the house.

He got up and looked around him. Beside the picture was a china pig with a slot in its back. Kenny shook it. It was heavy, the coins packed

115

tightly together. Again he listened. They were downstairs. With the pig under his arm he went over to the window: below it was a short drop onto the roof of the kitchen. He'd have to go barefoot. As footsteps sounded on the stairs, he undid the latch and pushed up the bottom half of the window. Bloody thing was stuck with new paint. Sweating, he knelt on the floor.

The footsteps had reached the landing. Kenny sprang away from the window and drew the bolt across the door.

'Too late, old son.' It was a voice he knew.

'Got my constable down in the garden, and a ladder. Just be a race between me kicking the door in or me mate reachin' the winder.'

Kenny smashed the photo on the dressing-table and picked out a long shard of glass.

He sat on the bed and gritted his teeth as he drew the glass across his wrists.

9

Swathed in blue-and-white striped scarves and waving wooden rattles, the supporters from the Nile were worked up to a pitch of excitement. They were off to Wembley to support Pompey against Wolverhampton Wanderers in the finals of the FA Cup. Never had their team done so well. Connie Spooner was there with Arthur, her sailor husband, and twin sons Rodney and Clive. They were all in uniform sporting their *Royal Oak* cap ribbons. Bernice was there, too, smoking for England. Lionel, perched on Joe's shoulders, was beaming from ear to ear.

'The chara's here, everyone ready?' yelled Alec, taking a roll call. He kissed Miriam and Rosie. 'Shouldn't be any problems. I've changed the barrel. You're all stocked up and we'll be back before closing.'

'Never mind about us, you keep charge of everyone and don't lose Lionel.'

''Bye, Babes,' said Thelma, leaving a jammy lipstick kiss on Lionel's cheek.

'Yuk,' he growled, scrubbing it off with the back of his hand.

The charabanc departed with enough beer and sandwiches to withstand a siege. Rosie, Thelma and Mum stood waving until it was out of sight.

'Just time for a cup of tea and a bacon sarnie, you two girls fancy one?'

Rosie grinned. 'As long as there's some HP sauce you're in business.' She didn't feel a bit like smiling. Since the evening at the Parisian she had heard nothing from Blyth. That had been the first day of his fortnight's Easter leave, yet he had not contacted her. Was his pride so important to him that he would let her go rather than admit his own foolishness? Or had she been suffering from false pride in thinking she mattered to him? There was no news from the Admiralty about her application to join the Wrens either. And yet she had seen several women wearing WRNS armbands when she was down near the naval barracks in Edinburgh Road. Something had got to happen or she would die of boredom. She wanted to be up and away. In the Wrens there was the added bonus of being with girls of her own age. They could go out together and do things. She wanted to show Blyth that she had a life of her own, and was not just waiting for him to show up whenever the mood took him.

The morning passed with nothing like the speed of a normal Saturday, with half the customers on the road to Wembley. Old men sat about over their halves of bitter, and a gang of sailors lined up their pints on the bar while they played darts.

'Wonder how they're getting on up in London?' Thelma said. 'Bet our Li's enjoyin' hisself – loves your Joe, don't he?'

'Hope he doesn't get lost,' said Miriam.

'No danger, stick to your lad like glue he will.'

'Who's coming upstairs to listen to the match?'

'Much obliged, Mrs Forrest,' said Garth, the

old man who looked after the horses in the stable next door.

Rosie shook her head. 'Got a book on the go. I'll bring you in a cup of tea at half time.' In her bedroom she sat on her bed rolling a cigarette. If she was wasting her time on Blyth Vine and if life was boring she had only herself to blame. Tomorrow she would get on her bike and whiz off somewhere, shake the dust of Pompey from her feet and make something happen. Full of resolution Rosie went along to the kitchen and filled the kettle. While it boiled she blew smoke rings out of the window. Carrying the loaded tray along the passage, she could hear cheering coming from the spectators glued to the radio set in the living-room.

'Got two goals and first half ain't over yet,' said Garth, beaming at the radio.

'Oh, ta, love,' said Mum, 'my throat's that dry, what with all the cheering.'

'It's all down to that Worral and his lucky charms. Reckon he'd a horseshoe in his pocket, a bit of white heather down his socks, and a white elephant tied to his garter.'

'Bad as that manager Jack Tinn and his lucky spats,' snorted Garth. 'Pompey don't need all that mumbo-jumbo, they're the better side by miles.'

In spite of herself, Rosie got caught up in the excitement of the second half and cheered as wildly as Thelma and Garth when the final whistle blew and Pompey had beaten Wolverhampton four goals to one.

It was a good-natured laughing crowd in the

119

Nile that night. Pompey had won the cup. Who'd have thought it after all those years of trying?

'Cor, each of them players is getting forty-seven quid fer winning. Kicking a ball around fer ninety minutes. Money for old rope.'

'Not stopping in London, they're coming home tonight, probably be back by nine. You going down the Guildhall to meet them?'

''Course! A moment in history. Sort of thing you'll tell your grandkids.'

'You coming, Thelma?' asked a sailor, cap swept back on his head and cigarette dangling from the corner of his mouth.

'No she isn't,' snapped Miriam. 'Thelma, get out there and collect those glasses.'

Sulking from every pore, the barmaid tottered around to the front of the bar and did as she was told. By half-past nine the pub was shorn of men in the stampede to the Guildhall to welcome back 'Our Lads'. At ten, Mum brought down a plate of ham sandwiches and a bowl of pickled onions. 'Dig in, girls,' she said.

Rosie grinned. Was it the free food or being called 'girls' that had put such a spring in their elderly customers' steps?

'Four port and lemons and one for yourself, Rosie love,' said one of the matrons, clutching her purse.

Mum looked at the clock. 'You'd best bed down in the spare room, Thelma. God knows when the chara will be back.'

Sulks forgotten, Thelma grinned. 'Ta ever so Mrs Forrest, what a day it's bin. Don't reckon our Li will forget it fer rest of his life.'

Rosie smiled at her. Tonight even Thelma's scrounging and tartyness failed to get under her skin.

It was half-past eleven by the time the women heard cheers, whistles and the rat-tat-tat-tat of the wooden rattles, putting paid to further talk between them.

'They're back.' Thelma rushed out of the bar and into the street.

'Rosie, stick those sausage rolls in the oven for five minutes,' said Miriam. 'By the sound of them they're well oiled. Have to make do with coffee.'

'Play up Pompey, Pompey play up.'

'Bin down the Guildhall, seen the lads come back in their coach. Couldn't move across the square. Everyone's gone mad – be some thick heads in the morning.' Dad lifted up the bar-flap and pulled Mum into his arms and danced her around the room.

Rosie clumped about with Joseph, and when he set her down someone else took her in his arms.

'Hello, Rosie.'

'What you doing here?' she accused him, 'who said you'd be welcome?'

'Aren't you pleased to see me?' Blyth grinned at her. 'Hitched a ride down specially. Have to sleep in the park tonight, I've got to be back in Greenwich tomorrow for Church Parade. But it'll be worth it just to see you.'

'You can sleep in the spare room,' invited Joseph, who seemed to have become a bosom friend to Blyth in the coach journey down from Wembley.

'Thelma and Lionel are in there,' snapped Rosie. 'Let him sleep in the park for all I care.' She wanted to hit her brother, shoving his oar in where it wasn't wanted. 'I'll go and get the sausage rolls.'

'Night everyone,' said Thelma, carrying Lionel up the stairs. 'That your bloke?' she asked as Rosie helped open the bedroom door for her. 'Good looker, ain't he?'

'You can have him,' she whispered. 'Thinks too much of himself, needs taking down a peg or two.'

'You let me know when you're finished with him. Reckon I'd be killed in the rush. Throw my knickers at him any day of the week.' Thelma yawned. 'Trouble is he'd probably throw them back.'

Rosie laughed in spite of herself. Quickly she set the sausage rolls on a plate and made the coffee in a jug. Setting cups and sugar beside it, she carried the tray down the stairs.

Mum had pushed some tables together, and Connie, her husband and her twins Rodney and Clive were sat there laughing with Blyth.

'You're a lifesaver, my darling,' said Dad, taking the tray from her.

'I'm going to get that spare eiderdown and a couple of pillows,' said Miriam. 'Blyth can bed down here. What time's your train in the morning?'

'Ten past six.'

They were all ganging up on her. She sat down next to Connie and bit into a sausage roll. Blyth was watching her, she could feel it. Her skin tingled and she stared at the sugar basin, fiddling with the spoon. No, he had got to say sorry.

'Well, Mrs Forrest, we're gonna love you and

leave you,' said Connie, getting to her feet. 'I'm done for. Me throat is hoarse from so much shouting. What excitement! Reckon I won't forget it as long as I lives.'

The twins and Arthur followed her out.

'I'm off to my bed,' said Dad. 'You'd better get back to the section house, Joseph. Thought it was a rule you didn't sleep in licensed premises.'

'I'll sneak back early,' her brother said.

Still Blyth sat there. Rosie wanted to go and wanted to stay.

'Here you are.' Mum appeared with the bedding and dropped it down on the carpet. 'Won't see you in the morning, Blyth. Sunday's my lie-in morning.'

Blyth got up and shook her hand. 'Thank you very much, it's very kind of you, Mrs Forrest.'

Mum smiled at him. 'I remember you staying with us when you were not much more than five years old. You were a charmer even then.'

'I don't think your daughter agrees with you,' he said, doing his little-boy-lost routine. Rosie wanted to smack him.

'She's like her grandmother. You won't pull the wool over her eyes. See you in the morning, Rosie. Don't be long, love, it's gone twelve.'

What did she mean? On the one hand she was almost turning down the sheets for her and Blyth, and yet she was telling her to get up to bed as if she were a six-year-old.

Rosie looked up from the sugar basin to find that she and Blyth were alone together.

'What do you want from me?' he asked, taking the basin away from her.

'An apology would be a start.'

'For what, staying there like a lemon and footing the bill?' He took out his wallet and set down the two notes. 'What am I saying sorry for – letting you make a fool of me?'

'Why did you take me there? It was only to show off. Then when you got there you let them humiliate you. I was supposed to drink that pissy wine and half-cooked food just so you could look Mister Big in front of everyone. You picked the wrong girl.'

'How about if we both say sorry?' he said. 'I made a horlicks of it. Got myself into a bind I couldn't get out of. And you say sorry for leaving me to face the music. I just wanted to impress you. I was so pleased with myself, a proper Narcissus.'

Rosie began to thaw. 'All right, I'm sorry for making you look more of a prat than you were already. As to Narcissus, you know what happened to him. Fell in love with his own reflection. Being handsome, you've had it too easy, Blyth Vine.'

'Christ! Is that what you think? It was easy being brought up by a drunk and a loony?' Blyth got to his feet and began pacing the floor. 'Going to school with no breakfast, sharing a bed with my sister 'til I was nine. Dragged off to see my mother in the loony bin, sat on the bed of this woman with wild hair, gibbering away to herself and tearing up bits of paper all the time. Then Mary says "Kiss your Mummy." Had nightmares for ages afterwards. When she died, this Auntie came down from up North somewhere wanting to adopt me. 'Course I didn't know what was going on. All I remember was Dad raving at her and the two of them nearly pulling me apart. If it hadn't been for Mary and your Gran and Albert, God knows what would have happened.'

Rosie sat there not knowing what to do. There was no satisfaction in getting the apology, and they were still not reconciled. 'What can I say, Blyth? I just thought you were showing off. I'm sorry.'

'I felt I was entitled to but I got it wrong. We should have gone down to Norris's in Queen Street for fish-and-chips.'

Rosie smiled. 'I would have liked that.' She walked over to him and took his hands in hers. 'Can we start afresh?'

'You don't know how hard it's been climbing out of that pit. You sit there with a gran that loved you, a proper mum and dad, and judge me.'

'No, no I don't. I just hated seeing you letting that waiter make a fool of us. You're worth more than that, and so am I.'

'How much more, show me?' He smiled at her in the old teasing way he had.

Rosie stepped up onto his feet and slid her arms around him bringing her face level with his. She kissed him, tasting his lips, sliding her tongue between them, pressing her body against him. Blyth began walking slowly with her entangled about him, across the room to where the eiderdown and pillows lay heaped together. They stopped every few steps to kiss one another. 'Let me hold you, Rosie, just hold you,' he whispered, setting her down. 'You know you want to.'

'I don't know.' Desire, fear and curiosity surged

through her. What would it be like to lie together skin against skin? What if they went further than holding? What if someone came down and found them? Was it likely? Dad and Joseph were well oiled and likely to be snoring by now, and Mum was exhausted.

It was not the most romantic of places, the lounge bar, reeking of beer and cigarettes. But at least it had the edge on the public bar in having a carpet. She watched Blyth shake out the blanket and the eiderdown and plump up the pillows. He went over to the switch by the door and turned off the light.

'I'll get undressed and wait for you,' he whispered.

Rosie stood in the darkness hearing the sounds of Blyth taking off his clothes: the swish as he undid his tie, the rustle of his shirt and the clink of his belt buckle. She wanted to go and she wanted to stay. At any moment they could be discovered, at any moment she could make discoveries of her own. No, it was too risky. 'I'm only taking my shoes off,' she said.

'How about your cardigan? I reckon I'm worth that.'

'You're on shaky ground, yet. This is my territory and I'm making the rules.' She smiled to herself as she undid the cardigan and left it on a chair.

'Come here my love, here, take my hand.' Blyth reached out to her, his hand brushing against her leg. He drew her down to him and covered her with the eiderdown. 'That's it, lie still against me and let's hold you tight.'

Rosie lay on her side while he curled himself around her, wrapping her in his arms. Blyth kissed her neck and she felt the warmth of his body steal over her.

'I love you Rosie,' he whispered. 'Ever since I saw you at the funeral I've wanted to be with you like this. To be stroking and kissing you, and being close.'

'I want you,' she said, 'but I'm afraid. I can't let you run away with me.'

'I know but it's tempting isn't it?' His fingers stroked her neck and hovered over the buttons on her blouse. 'You know all that mix-up at the Parisian? It was because I wanted you to be proud of me. It would have been the icing on the cake.'

'I am proud of you, but I won't be sweet-talked into anything. You've got to be straight with me and stop being Flying Officer Kite.'

Blyth giggled. 'You can be very cruel, Rosie Forrest. Now turn around just for a little while and let me feel you against me.'

'Blyth, this is so dangerous,' she whispered.

He kissed her lips and pressed her hand over his chest. Rosie was confused and excited. She felt inhibited by her clothes, wanting to seal herself to him, skin to skin – and yet, and yet – Blyth pressed himself against her and she could feel his body hard and urgent. He took her hand and pressed it to his belly.

Rosie took her hand away as if it were burning. 'No, you're going too fast. I can't, Blyth, no, no,' she slid away from him.

'Oh Rosie, you're tying me up in knots. Phew! You don't know what you're doing to me, slamming on the brakes like that.' He reached out for her in the darkness and found her shoulder. 'It's all right, it's all right, I'm cooling down now.'

'I'd better go,' she said, still holding his hand.

'Just lie with me,' he pleaded. 'You can be on top of the clothes. Don't go yet. I don't know when I'll see you again.'

She sat down on top of their bed.

'Rosie, you are my posy,' he whispered against her ear. 'You don't know how exciting you are. Please, please, lie down and I'll wrap you up and keep you warm.' He took his side of the eiderdown and coiled her up in it like a Swiss roll. 'Isn't that cosy? Now kiss me.'

As she leaned towards him, the bar was flooded with light. Joseph stood there in his stripey pyjamas grinning down at them. 'I didn't know we were doing bed and breakfast,' he said. 'What's it to be, Sir, one egg or two?'

She slid down so that her head was hidden in the quilted folds of the eiderdown.

Joseph laughed. 'Too late, I've seen you. Cripes, Rosie, you took a risk.'

'You won't say anything, will you?' she pleaded.

Joseph went over to the table and picked up his tobacco tin. 'I reckon you should pack up now. Dad'll be down at the crack of sparrows to get everything shipshape. But please yourself, I'm saying nothing.'

'Thanks Joseph,' said Blyth, looking up at him. 'It was my fault. I shouldn't have let things get that far.'

'Fair enough. I'm off back to bed. See you sometime.'

'Don't look so worried.' Blyth leant on his elbow and smiled up at her. 'Could have been a lot worse. It could have been your dad.'

'Don't even say that,' Rosie said, unrolling herself. She felt as if she had fallen off the helter-skelter. Everything had been so intense between them and now she felt foolish, especially at being caught by Joseph. Hurriedly she buttoned up her cardigan and slid her feet down into her shoes.

Blyth sat up and ran his hand through his hair. 'I'm sorry, Rosie, not for what happened but for not waiting for the right time.' He smoothed out a place for her beside him. 'Are you all right? Not angry with me?'

'I think I just feel silly and embarrassed.'

'Don't be, my sweetheart. We'll get the right place and lots of time, I promise. But it won't be soon. I'm off to Scotland on Monday for two months and this time I'll write and tell you all the things I didn't say tonight.'

'Promise?' She demanded.

'Promise.'

They kissed one another and Rosie waved from the doorway, creeping up the stairs her shoes in her hand. Was she relieved that Mr Succulence had not had his wicked way with her, or disappointed? She wasn't sure.

10

Kenny awoke in a clean bare room with the light on. His wrists were bandaged. He could not think beyond the moment. Someone had washed him and dressed him in freshly laundered pyjamas. A tall man with a moustache came and went, and there was a woman who sat beside the bed with her sewing. They let him be. It was a floating world, with the two of them moving through it, occasionally stopping by his bed with food he couldn't eat and medicine he could hardly swallow. It was enough. His life had paused, and he had no desire for it to move on.

Daisy looked down at him. Kenny was a wraith. She had come to rage at him, but what was the point?

'He is severely malnourished and his mind is fragile. Rest is what he needs. Retribution can come later.'

'I'll give him fragile,' she'd raged at the doctor. 'Wasn't too bloody fragile when he beat up his sister. Led her a dog's life, he did. Wants putting away.'

Jacob Silverman and his wife Rachel were an exotic pair, darkly handsome and foreign-sounding. He was the police doctor and, against his colleagues' advice, had taken Kenny into his home. They had strange things in their house: a large candle-holder, and embroidered hangings with funny writing on them.

'We are Jewish, Mrs Fletcher,' his wife had said. 'These things are symbols of our faith, like your crucifixes and texts from the scriptures.'

Daisy had blushed at being caught out gawping. 'I see,' she said, 'very nice.' What a stupid thing to have said. Beliefs were things people died for. It must be those beliefs that made them take in that cheapskate in that bed upstairs. Nodding and smiling, she took her leave of them.

Daisy sighed. At least she knew where he was. It was all over, now, thank God. At first she had been exasperated with Pearl when the girl refused to bring charges against her brother. But then, she thought, if she wants to let it go it doesn't mean I have to. Daisy smiled grimly. Everyone thought she was a pushover – fat, slummocky and good-natured. Well, they were in for a shock.

'I've got a new life, now, Auntie Daisy. Even got some friends. Don't want Kenny put away, won't change anything. I just don't want to see him anymore.'

She was a funny little thing. You thought she was a dolly daydream but she had a will of her own. Her aunt smiled: they were both taken at face value. Quietly determined, that summed her up. The other women at work had taken to her, especially Ruth. They had chummed up together outside work, and went off to the pictures at the Ritz and over on the ferry to Portsmouth for shopping. She was a real help at home, too.

'Why don't you do the garden and the cooking and I'll see to the house?' she'd suggested.

131

Daisy smiled to herself. Poor Pearl can't stand living with a slut, she thought. All to the good, they'd both got the best of the bargain. Frank would think he'd come to the wrong blooming house, what with ironed sheets and polished chair-legs. And, the garden would be a picture in the summer. She'd got the seeds all planted and coming along nicely in the little greenhouse. This year, she was going to have a herbaceous border to knock spots off any of the neighbours': dahlias, hollyhocks, lupins, night-scented stocks, and a lovely blue blur of forget-me-nots as well as bachelors' buttons and Canterbury bells.

Due home round about March 1940, Frank had only a year to go. 'Please God don't let there be a war,' she breathed. Pressing her hands deep into her pockets, her fingers closed over his last letter.

I miss you my Daisy. I lie awake amongst all these naked sweating oppos of mine and long for Gosport in the rain. What I wouldn't give for the afternoon in bed on a Sunday, just the two of us, our bellies rumbling from one of your roast dinners topped off with treacle tart. Knowing at any minute my missus is going to have her wicked way with me. Then later both of us snuggled up close like a couple of birds in a nest billing and cooing. I tell you my babes I can't leave the navy soon enough. Whatever you feel for me double and treble it …

At the sight of the smashed picture and the blood, Pearl had felt as if she were going backwards into that pit of fear she had lived in for

132

so long. Kenny had been in her room – he had touched things. But Daisy washed the bedclothes and bought some more glass for the picture, and the door was mended. From what she told her, Kenny would take a long time to mend. He had tried to kill himself.

Pearl had once wanted to die. But to really want it bad enough to slash her wrists – she didn't know if she would have had the courage. She could see that it was the way that Kenny would choose, cutting and bloody and violent. All she had wanted was to be rescued and she had been, in the end. Daisy had been angry when she had wanted to drop any charges against him. 'It would mean going over it all again and having to see him. I'm happy with you and the work. Let's just forget it.'

She didn't really know what she felt. On some days, Kenny's terrorizing seemed like a bad film that she'd seen at the Ritz: and on others, when she awoke sweating at the memory, she hated him. Just because she'd dropped the charges didn't mean she'd forgiven him. It was just that her life had changed, and she didn't want dragging backwards into how it was before.

Things were better, tons better. She loved it up at Priddy's. At first the cordite had given both of them fierce headaches but now they were used to it. In the little wooden hut the five of them were pals. Things had settled into little routines. Pearl always got the hot water in the mornings for the tea, and between them Poppy and Daisy took care of the sandwiches. Friday lunchtime they bought fish-and-chips from a van that came to the gate. It was pay day. What with Dad's money still coming through, and her wages, she was able to save a pound a week. Friday was also cleaning afternoon. The floor was swept and washed and then coated with strange gluey stuff applied with a brush. Then the fun started. To give it a polish they put an old army greatcoat on the floor. Being the smallest, Pearl sat in the middle of it while the others grabbed hold of the sleeves and hem and pulled her back and forth like a human duster.

She and Ruth sometimes went to the pictures at the Ritz in Gosport High Street, and this Sunday she was going to her friend's house for tea. Even better than that, she and Dad were back letter-writing to each other. Pearl leant across to the dressing-table and opened the chocolate box in which she kept his letters.

My Princess,

I am so pleased to get good news at last and know that you are safe and well. I can't forgive myself for not foreseeing the danger of leaving you both with no support. Thank God for Daisy.

As for Kenny I hope the police find him and throw away the key. It will be a long time before I can even think of him without wanting to kill him. Enough said.

Just think a year today, March first. I will be out of the navy and a free man. We'll be back in our house starting a new life together.

Perhaps you and Daisy could go and see what needs doing to make it ship-shape again. I'm sure the outside needs a fresh coat of paint and there are all sorts of repairs I meant to do. Ted Greenaway in Ivy Lane is a good chap who would take on the job. I'm going to send you a cheque that you can cash at my bank for the work. The place needs living in. Perhaps when it's back on top line it could be rented out for a while and the money saved. What do you think?

I am sitting in the Botanical Gardens, a blessed cool spot. I shall send you a photograph but black and white just doesn't do justice to the wonderful colours of the flowers and butterflies here.

Take great care my Princess I loved you more than life itself.

Your devoted Dad.

Pearl saw herself in the mirror smiling. She had friends and work and a life again. There was plenty of time to take care of everything.

'What will you do, Kenny, when you're well?'

He looked at Mrs Silverman, or Rachel as she had asked him to call her. She sat opposite him in the living-room. Kenny liked looking at her, she was peaceful. Today she had on a cream lacy jumper and an amber necklace that brought out the gold-and-brown glints in her eyes. Rachel was able to be with him without words – to quieten him simply by being there. It was to her that he poured out the poison of the last couple of years. She had let him have the light on at night, and it was here that he had slept in darkness again.

'Don't know. An apprentice boat builder once, I was. Like to be out in the open.'

'Working on the land, do you think that would

appeal to you?'

'I don't know. Just want to be here with you and the doctor.'

'This is a temporary arrangement Kenny, I'm afraid. I have some of my family coming over from Austria – two boys, Saul and Rubin. We'll be going up to London to get them in a couple of weeks. We'll have to find somewhere else for you.'

'Couldn't I live in that shed in the garden and do things for you around the place?' He was near to tears.

'Kenny, you're free now. The charges have been dropped against you. Perhaps in time you can be reconciled with your family.'

'No,' he said, his disappointment giving way to anger. 'I don't want that. If I can't stay here I'll go away somewhere. Won't stay where I'm not wanted.'

'I won't argue with you, Kenny,' Rachel said, getting to her feet. 'We have time to find something better suited to you. Two weeks is a long time, and you're getting stronger every day.'

When she had gone he lay there fretting. He didn't want to share her with some other blokes. He didn't want life to start up again and have to make choices of where to live or what work to do. Kenny knew he couldn't live the hand-to-mouth existence of the last few months again. It would kill him. The weeks with the Silvermans had been clean, calm and ordered. They had restored him to himself, and he dreaded losing that sense of recovery. The thought of Rachel giving that level of attention to someone else stirred up his anger, making him tremble. No, it was all or nothing with him, always had been.

He was being cast out. The days and hours and minutes would drain away like sand through an hourglass. Only so many more nights of quiet sleep, so many more meals, so many more moments of being with her. Kenny knew himself to be greedy for things: a car, good clothes, drink and money in his pocket. Yet being with Rachel was beyond things. With her he was remade. He had shown her the emptiness of his life, even the badness of it, and she had still wanted to spend time with him. There was nothing he wanted more than to be with her. If she sent him away it would all begin again, he would be driven back into the darkness of himself. Kenny knew that he could not survive without her.

'I have told Kenny about the boys coming.' The relieved smile on Rachel's face wounded him. He looked at her husband and wanted to kill him – sitting there, old and boring and kind. What would he say if he told him he wanted to sleep with his wife?

'It is good of you, Kenny, to be so understanding. These two little boys have suffered much disturbance in their lives. It is most generous of you.'

He nodded, too angry to speak. What did he care about the foreign nippers? They were nothing to him.

Dr Silverman was called away and he was left in Rachel's company. Thirteen more suppers, thirteen more breakfasts: no, he must not think that way. Every moment must be stored against the famine to come. As she came back into the room, Kenny concentrated on stirring the sugar round and round his cup. If he looked into her face, into those eyes, he'd be done for.

'You are looking so well, Kenny. Your face has lost that pinched look. It's good to see you like this.'

'All down to you,' he said. 'If I go away I'll be done for.'

'Don't do that.' Her voice was sharp.

'What? What am I doing?'

'Two things.'

He looked away, and she took his face and turned it towards her. 'You are throwing my care of you back at me.'

'I'm not. Without you I'll be a goner.'

'Kenny, I have just given you the physical care anyone could have given. The rest and sleep have repaired the physical damage. Youth and resilience have completed what I started.'

'Said there was two things. What's the other one, then?'

'Blackmail.'

'What!'

'Kenny, you aren't stupid.' She had gone away from him. 'You think that if you make me feel guilty for removing my care, I will let you stay.'

'I'm not ready.' He despised the whining note that had crept into his voice. He took her wrist and gripped it. 'Please let me stay.'

'Let go of my hand.'

He tightened his grip.

'Kenny!' Her voice was sharp with dislike.

No, she couldn't look at him like that.

Rachel peeled his fingers away from her wrist.

'Go upstairs, now, and I won't tell my husband. If you strike me I shall strike you back.' There was a cold anger in her that frightened him. 'You'll have to go tomorrow. You know that.'

It was broken.

Kenny left in the morning before it was light. He had arrived in rags. Everything that he now stood up in, Rachel had given him. Yet, he left with nothing. The shame was physical, he burned with it. So consumed was he by his own misfortune that he failed to notice the man step into his path.

'Good morning Kenny, going somewhere?'

It was the policeman who had kicked the door in over at Daisy's house. 'Like to have a talk with you. Where's it to be? Back inside Dr Silverman's or down at the station? Weren't thinking of breaking your bail, was you?'

'No,' said Kenny. 'I wasn't thinking nothing.'

11

Crail
Scotland
August 1st

Darling Rosie,
I have time to miss you even though they're working us to death. I miss you in the gaps between taking off and touching down and just before I fall asleep and when I wake up in the morning. Specially then I try and remember exactly what you felt like beside me in the dark last time in the pub. Do you think of it and wish we'd had longer before your Joe burst in on us?

Rosie remembered the warmth of him and his breath on her neck – the secrecy and closeness. It was hard to keep that understanding going when there were such long stretches between their meetings. There was more memory than reality. Every time they saw one another they had to remake things. And, there was the charge of attraction that sparked every time and led them away from talking. Yes, she would have liked more time in the darkness where they sensed rather than saw one another. When he told her things he would not have risked in the light.

We are doing ADDLES a good name for it because addled is what you get trying to master it. It's called

140

Aerodrome Dummy Deck Landings. *It's mad. We take off and land on a stretch of grass as a rehearsal for the flight deck of an aircraft carrier. We'll see how it pans out later on HMS* Unrivalled *out in the Firth of Forth. But this is the real news. We are back at Daedalus, at Lee-on-Solent, for ten days arriving on Friday the fifth. Please, please say that you can come over on the Sunday. I could meet you at the Gosport ferry. Can you bring the bike? We could go to the beach at Lee and have the whole day together. Just think, you and me and a picnic, sarnies, cake and a bottle of Tizer. We could swim. Sun, sea and kisses!!! I'll see what I can rustle up over here in the way of treats. I want to hold you close and cover you in kisses. I want to hear your laugh and taste those juicy lips. I know so much about you and you know me but in some ways we're mysterious strangers. There is so much we don't know about each other. It's going to be so much fun finding out about you. I'll ring you when we get down on Thursday.*

Love and hugs,
Blyth.

A whole day together, Rosie was in a ferment. He would see her in her bathers. The pair she managed to drag out of the drawer were full of moth-holes. She went to the Landport Drapery Bazaar and found a Jaeger swimsuit for fifteen shillings. It was red, with white seagulls woven into the pattern, and fitted like a second skin.

When the phone rang on Thursday night she hurtled down the stairs, eager to hear his voice.

'Hello Rosie, it's me. We still on for Sunday?'

'Yes, we are.' She felt awkward and tongue-tied.

'Ten at the ferry, must go, Inky's outside wanting to phone his girl. See you Sunday, 'bye.'

On Saturday night she lay on top of the covers in the August heat, wishing the hours away. Questions teemed in her head. What would Blyth look like in his bathers, she wondered. How would they get undressed on the beach? If they began kissing would they be able to stop before they were swept away. Rosie wanted him to touch her. They had been on the verge of something when Joseph blundered in. What would it feel like lying naked together? Her thoughts raced ahead to what could be the consequences of an August afternoon alone with Blyth. Seeing Thelma with squinnying, pasty-faced Lionel was a sharp lesson in the outcome of an afternoon of passion. But then so was she, herself.

Rosie remembered asking Mum why she was in their wedding photo, aged three and laughing her head off. Her mother had blushed and looked as if she were about to cry. She had felt a sudden lurch of fear. They had sat together in the back garden of their pub in the Isle of Wight talking and talking. How brave she had been, hiding nothing. At thirteen, Rosie had been shocked at the thought of her parents' passion, then filled with anxiety.

'People are so judging,' Mum had said. 'Your Auntie Florrie went off to Devon and I had to go and live with a stranger. If it hadn't been for Daisy I'd have ended up in the workhouse. To some people a pregnant woman without a ring on her finger is only one step up from a prostitute.'

Rosie had not much experience of prostitutes.

142

They were not thick on the ground in Sandown. But, in Queen Street near where Gran had lived in Portsea, they swarmed around the pubs. She thought of the women she'd seen there, shivering in thin dresses, their faces larded with make-up, voices harsh and language ripe. How could anyone think of her mother like that? She had burst into tears. 'Did you wish you hadn't got me?' she had asked her.

Mum had hugged her tightly. 'Never, never, think that,' she said. 'Of course I was afraid and wished I wasn't pregnant, but the minute you were in my arms I loved you.'

'I don't think I want to grow up,' she had cried.

'Well, it's not going to happen in five minutes, my love. I know it's all been a bit of a shock but I don't want us ever to lie to one another. I trust you to keep this as something between us, something kept in the family.'

'Did Dad want me?' She burst out.

'It was complicated.'

'What d'you mean?'

'We were getting married, it was all arranged, and then it all went wrong. He had to go away in the war and I went to Gosport and we lost track of one another 'til the Armistice. He didn't see you until you were a toddler. But Rosie, you have always been his darling daughter. You know that?'

Looking back, she could still feel the turmoil of that day. There were things she wanted to ask her father even now, but the moment never came. She sometimes envied Joseph, born after Mum and Dad had married. The longed-for boy, to take the place of Andrew, her stepbrother lost at

Jutland. Had she replaced Lily, her stepsister, in Dad's heart, she wondered. It was a sore that she'd picked at over and over. He'd cried when she and Michael and little Beattie had gone to Canada – so had Gran. But Gran had left her painting to Rosie.

What would she say to her now, if she told her of her fears?

'If ever there was a girl that crossed her bridges before she came to them, it was you Rosie,' she had said, often and often. 'It's bad enough living through disasters when they happen, without running towards them. And worry-gutting robs you of little pleasures in the present that you're too wrought up to notice.'

The advice unsought by Thelma was another matter entirely.

'That sailor of yours is a real good-looker, you want to be careful. There are places where women can go to get fixed up, if they're planning to "go all the way" with their chap.' A visit involved going behind a screen and having a doctor fit a rubber thing called a Dutch Cap inside you. 'Every time you does it, gotta get that cap in or you're in the family way before you can blink. No good relying on the chap to use a French letter, it's not them that cops it. Wouldn't entertain it, wouldn't Fred. Like eatin' a toffee with the paper on, that's what he said. Then I was landed with Lionel. Thought you ought to know,' she said, one evening when they were working behind the bar. 'You can always get a ring from Woollies and say as you're married.'

Rosie shrunk from the idea. It was so

calculating and mechanical. Yet the thought of a baby was terrifying. Having your life snatched away before it was half lived must surely lead to resentment.

Through the open window she heard the Guildhall clock chime six as Dad's footsteps passed her door. He would be brewing himself a cup of tea before beginning the pub cleaning. Pulling on her dressing-gown she hurried along the passage.

'Hello, my love,' he said. 'You must have smelt the teapot. Fancy a cup?' He stood with his bucket in the sink watching it fill with water. They had never had a cleaner at the Nile, Dad saw to that. 'If I do it myself, the job's done to my standards. It's my routine to scrub out the bars and toilets then take your mother a cup of tea. When I can no longer do it, then's the time to take my name from over the door.'

'Reckon it'll be a fine day?' she asked, getting down the biscuit barrel.

'Be a scorcher. Off somewhere are you?'

'Meeting Blyth, going to the beach at Lee.'

Dad smiled and she caught a glimpse of what had attracted her Mother. 'You make the most of it, Rosie, and don't get sunburnt. Want a bottle of Tizer?'

And then the waiting was over. She could see him at the top of the pontoon as the ferry docked in Gosport. At the sight of him her fears evaporated.

'Hello, Gorgeous, you look a million dollars,' Blyth said, as she wheeled the bike towards him.

She grinned. 'Look good yourself.' Yes, the

145

excitement was still there between them.

He kissed her on the cheek. 'Shall I drive, as I know where we're going?'

Rosie nodded, sliding onto the saddle and holding him around the waist. They roared out of Gosport and on to Lee-on-Solent. Along the seafront were large villas, some with wooden shutters and others with striped awnings. Who lived in them, she wondered. The place was probably stiff with old admirals. On the other side were thick clumps of gorse, stretches of shingle and then the sea stippled with breeze. On they went, past Lee Tower with its pier and ballroom. There were beach huts nearby and steps leading down to the beach. He parked the bike and stood there taking off his knapsack. 'What shall we do first? Have an ice-cream at the tower or come back later for toasted tea-cakes?' Blyth patted his knapsack. 'I've got a flask of tea and ginger cake and a bottle of wine.'

He's already chosen for me, she thought as he stood there looking down at the beach.

'Let's go and paddle,' she said, slinging her bag over her shoulder and running ahead of him down the steps.

He caught up with her and held her hand. 'I feel like a millionaire with a whole day with you. I've only just unpacked, we've got hours and hours.'

Rosie looked about her. 'It's different over here. A proper holiday place.'

'It is until you go up the road to *Daedalus* and see all the planes spread out on the airfield. It's the flying navy over here and the sailing navy in

146

Pompey.' He stopped between two beach huts on a sandy path and took off his jacket. 'Let's go up into the gorse. It'll be warm and sheltered.' Kneeling down he spread a blanket over the sand. He looked up at her and smiled. 'What shall we do first? Have a picnic or paddle?'

Rosie stared out to sea, minutely aware of his inspection. 'Bit early for grub yet, I want to paddle,' she said, settling on the blanket.

Blyth knelt in front of her and began unlacing her boots. He peeled them off her, first over the ankle and then the instep – slowly, slowly until he had her bare feet resting on his thighs. Blyth kissed each toe before sliding his fingers under the hem of her trousers. Rosie could feel the heat of him through the soles of her feet.

'Mellifluous,' he whispered, leaning forward and kissing her on the mouth.

Her nerve-endings fizzed. Yet, as she melted under his tender invasion, part of her brain held out against him. It was too easy, too predictable. 'We paddling, then?' She ran down the path, slowing over the shingle to turn up her trouser legs. At the water's edge the breeze riffled the edge of her blouse and tugged at her hair.

'Whee!!' Blyth grabbed her around the waist and whirled her round and round. The intensity between them had evaporated. They giggled and splashed, running in and out of the water like children.

'Let's get into our bathers and have a swim before starting on the food. D'you want to go up and get changed first?'

Rosie was glad she'd thought to put on the

147

swimsuit under her clothes before setting off. She hurried out of her shirt and trousers, and ran back past him to the water. The sea hitting her belly made her gasp. Rosie tensed, then plunged under the water and up again, thrashing and kicking. It took some moments to recover from the icy immersion. Turning towards the shore she saw Blyth racing down the beach and diving straight in. He disappeared and she waited for him to resurface. Where was he? All the ripples subsided, and she was on the verge of alarm when he popped up in front of her like a cork from a bottle. He pulled her towards him and kissed her, his mouth cold and salty. It was Rosie who first broke free. Away from the shore he seemed a different creature. His hair was sculpted flat against his head and water beaded his lashes. Again he dived away from her, and she swam further out. Now they were both out of their depth. Behind them the beach was beginning to fill, there were the first deck-chairs being set out and children paddling at the water's edge.

He rose up behind her, thrusting between her legs and leaping up with her on his shoulders. Rosie laughed. No longer earthbound, they were weightless and carefree. He tossed her back into the water and she dived down and down, climbing up his body to the surface. Again they kissed. Blyth slid beneath her and held her around the waist. Kicking frog-like, he propelled them along. Rosie floated on top of him, her head on his chest, as they surged through the water. As she floated towards the shore the sea lost its chill.

Blyth swam from under her and took her face between his hands.

'You must be a mermaid, your lips are blue.'

'Perhaps I am,' she grinned.

'You're shivering, let's run up the beach and get warm.'

They grabbed their towels, and Blyth poured tea into the flask lid and passed it to her. They passed it back and forth.

'Stand up a minute and I'll smooth out the blanket,' he said. 'Let's have the picnic – I'm starved. What have we got?'

'Hand me my bag,' she said, rubbing her hair with the towel. 'Egg-and-cress sandwiches, crisps, ginger cake and Tizer.'

'Half a pork pie, tomatoes, a jar of salad cream, one chocolate éclair, a bottle of wine and two glasses.'

'Blimey, we'll be fat as fools by the time we've scoffed this lot.'

'We'll spread it out across the day,' he said, taking a corkscrew from his pocket.

They sat cross-legged, eating in no particular order but as the mood took them.

Blyth poured the wine and handed her a glass. 'To my gorgeous girl,' he said.

Rosie held it up and let the sun sparkle into its ruby depths. It was soft and fruity on her tongue. 'To Biggles,' she said, clinking her glass against his.

'Let's finish up with the éclair,' he said, handing it to her. 'You can have the first bite.'

'Quite the gent,' she teased. 'I can see you've been to Greenwich.'

'Oh yes, I've had all my rough corners ironed out, else you'd have to fight me for it.'

''Course, I haven't been to Greenwich,' she laughed, getting to her feet and running up the path away from the beach. She dodged down behind a bush and gobbled the cake in a couple of bites.

'Gotcha!' Blyth sprang on her and took her in his arms. He rubbed his fingers over her face then licked the cream from them. Dodging in and out of the bushes, they ran down to the water and splashed their hands in the sea. Arms swinging, fingers woven together, they walked back to the remains of their picnic.

'I'm going to shove all our stuff under the bushes out of the sun. We'll lie in the shade and cool off a bit.'

Rosie smiled to herself. Cooling off was the last thing she wanted.

They packed their bags and wedged them behind a tree-trunk. Blyth spread the blanket high off the path under the canopy of two gorse bushes. Rosie lay down on her back, slightly apart from him, and closed her eyes. The honey scent of gorse flowers and the heat of the sun made her feel drowsy. Running her tongue over her lips, she tasted the sweetness of the éclair and the acidity of the red wine. In the distance the sounds of children playing on the beach rose and fell. There were little buzzing and scurrying noises around her. Even behind closed eyes, she knew that Blyth was watching her. Rosie lay there minutely aware of herself. Every breath in caused her breasts to rise, and every exhalation made them fall. Her skin prickled and the blood pulsed through her veins. She was tinder-dry, waiting, waiting to catch fire. A shadow fell across her as Blyth bent to stroke her face. He caressed her eyelids and pressed his fingers against her lips. He kissed her mouth, deep drenching kisses that left her breathless. Touching, stroking, tasting, she wanted more and more. Blyth eased the straps of her swimsuit down her arms. The sun filtered through the branches, dappling her naked breasts. Every sense was alive to him, the taste of his skin briny under her tongue, the sound of his breath against her neck, the scent of his fresh male sweat, the sight of his tanned body with its wiry blond hair, and the touch of his hands as they stole over her. Yes, yes, yes.

'Wait, no, wait,' he whispered. Moving away from her. 'I've got to do something.'

'What, what?' She felt fuzzy and confused.

'I've to make us safe. Close your eyes.'

She heard him rummaging in his clothes, and then he was with her again. Stroking her belly, running his fingers between her legs, opening her secret place. Making her cry out with the pleasure of it.

'Shhh, shh,' he soothed, kneeling astride her and easing himself inside her.

It was a sudden sharp pain that made her gasp. Before she was conscious of what was happening to her body it was over. Blyth was lying across her, his hair drenched in sweat. She felt stranded. Tears pricked behind her lashes and fell down her face and onto her neck.

'Rosie? What is it? Just give me a minute and I'll

be back with you, sweetheart, don't cry.'

She lay there, not knowing what she should have felt, but surely not this.

'Tell me,' he said, taking her in his arms.

'I wanted more. I didn't know... Ooh, I feel I don't know.' She began to cry in earnest.

Blyth held her to him until she was still. 'My lovely Rosie,' he whispered. 'I'm sorry I got carried away. It'll be better next time. We'll find somewhere really private and we'll take our time.'

Slowly her sobs subsided.

'Better now?' he asked her, his face full of concern. He smiled at her. 'Let's go and have a swim and cool down then we can finish our picnic. Come on, my love, let me find your bathers. God knows where mine have gone.' He kissed her hand. 'Love you,' he said.

Hot and sticky, with leaves in her hair, she put on her bathers again.

'Well, we don't look as if we've been reading the paper. Tell you what. Let's run all the way down into the water without stopping.'

The stones were hot and sharp under their feet, and the sea an icy shock. Rosie swam under water and came up gasping and exhilarated.

Blyth swam across to her. 'Hello gorgeous, are you happy now?'

'I think I am,' she grinned.

Blyth turned away from her then leapt up and pointed to the sky. 'Look, Rosie, it's my Swordfish. I asked Inky to bring it down across the beach, specially for you. Isn't she beautiful?'

Blyth continued leaping and waving.

The plane swooped down over the sea. Rosie was stunned. She could see the pilot quite clearly in the open cockpit. He leaned out and waved to them, before rising up and turning away. She wanted to go with him. In those few seconds, she could understand Blyth's excitement.

'Take me up in her, promise me,' she shouted.

But he didn't hear her. He stood there still waving, his eyes tracking its course as the Swordfish flew out over the horizon.

12

Thelma shook Lionel awake. 'Come on Li, gotta get your clothes on quick. Off to Romsey with yer school, we got to be at the station by nine.'

'Wants to stay here with you and Nan.'

'Well, you gotta go and that's it.'

'Ain't going,' he whined, cocooning himself in his blanket.

Thelma wrestled the blanket from him. 'You're going and that's final.'

Lionel clung to the mattress. 'Bugger off. You're a cow you are,' he shouted at her, clutching the mattress.

Thelma resorted to hitting him round the head. 'Nasty little sod, be glad to be shot of you.' Still he clung on. Kneeling on the lino, she wrenched his fingers off the bed one by one. Lionel began to grizzle.

'For Chrissake, pack it in up there,' roared her mother, pounding up the stairs. 'Thelma, you get and see to the toast and Li, off downstairs, there's a good boy. Nan's put your clothes ready and there's a bit of crispy bacon waiting.'

With his hair sticking up and his nose dripping Lionel ran downstairs to the sink, where a slimy flannel floated in an inch of warm water. He dabbed it on his face, then dried himself on the scratchy towel. Shoving his feet into his lace-ups, he shuffled outside to the lavatory, laces trailing.

Thelma watched him through the bedroom window. Skinny little tyke he was, holding her back all the time and spoiling her chances. If that wasn't enough aggravation there was Mum nagging at her. If she didn't have her job at the Nile to go to, she'd be up the asylum. This war coming might be just what she needed to buck her life up. Give her a chance to spread her wings.

'You're a nasty bitch, you are,' Mum snarled. 'Couldn't send the boy off with a bit of a smile and a cuddle.'

'Christ, you've changed your tune. Who was it hit him with the copper stick just 'cos he trod on your glasses.'

Mum stood there squinting against the smoke coming from the cigarette stuck to her lower lip. 'That's as may be, today's different, poor little bugger's off to strangers. We gotta make a bit of an effort.'

Thelma glared. 'S'pose you're gonna stand at the door squeezing out the tears just so the neighbours thinks you cares.'

'Well, that's one thing they won't never accuse you of, my lady. You couldn't give a toss, never have. I'm off to get his breakfast. You get yourself together. I ain't taking him to the station. That's your job, madam.'

Thelma slouched back to her bedroom and gathered together the clothes she'd scattered the night before. She hated mornings, and didn't come to before the afternoon. Evenings she was ready to shine. Joe might have the night off and be in the public bar playing darts with his pals.

That always made for a bit of fun. If she could get Mum to iron her blue dress, she might be in with a chance.

As predicted, her mother stood at the door the picture of misery. She clutched her grandchild to her and insisted on a kiss. Lionel struggled out of her arms and scrubbed the kiss away with the back of his hand. He looked even weedier than ever, having just sicked up his breakfast.

There were other mothers hurrying towards the railway station, and grans and grandads waving. A man passed her on his bike, openly crying. 'Course, their kids was nicer than Lionel. He was not a child people were drawn to. Even she didn't like him much and, Thelma was certain, her son didn't think much of her. Mad for Li's dad she'd been. Fred Marsh, with his blue-black hair and dark eyes, had made her feel so special. He had only to look at her and she'd want him, so fierce. Even took her to his house, once, when his missus was away at her mother's. His smile got her every time. Wasn't smiling when she told him about having his kid. Mr and Mrs Marsh were off out of Landport, before she'd hardly begun to show – never left no forwarding address, neither. Thelma blinked. What she wouldn't give for another afternoon up in that back bedroom with Fred.

Li had been a big disappointment. She had hoped he would be a little reminder of Fred – a handsome nipper that she would take to. Instead he was scrawny and pale and always crying. Thelma looked down at him dawdling along as if they'd got all day – kicking a stone along the gutter. He had the little fire-engine that Joe from the pub had given him last Christmas – wouldn't be parted from it. 'Course, Joe was the one that he loved. Poor kid, she thought. 'I'll come out and see ya in a few weeks. It'll be good out there with all yer pals and the grub will be better than here. Be able to play in the woods and stuff.'

'Will Joe come?'

'Shouldn't think so,' snapped Thelma, aggravated that her offer of a visit meant so little.

'You ask him,' Lionel demanded. 'Gotta promise or I ain't going.'

'For God's sake pick up your feet, you'll have them new shoes scuffed before you even gets on the train.'

The station was packed with children, all labelled like parcels. Some were clinging to their mother's hand, others pent-up with excitement. Teachers and helpers were busy checking off names and herding them into lines. Thelma looked at the mothers' faces, raw with emotion. They were smiling down at the kids then looking away, biting their lips, their eyes brimming with unshed tears.

''Bye Li, you be good and do as you're told. Here's some sammidges and a bar of choclit.'

Lionel snatched it out of her hand.

''Bye my pet,' she said, planting a kiss on his cheek, as much for show in front of the other mothers as for any real affection.

Lionel walked away without a backward glance.

Thelma felt guilty at her relief in having got him off her hands. Always faking it she was – pretending she loved him, pretending her mother wasn't getting on her nerves, and pretending that she didn't fancy Joe Forrest something rotten.

As she stood about, bored and dying for the train to move, a woman screamed – a harsh animal cry. Thelma recognised her as the plumber's wife from down the street.

'Grace, my Grace,' she cried, flinging herself into the crowd of mothers, thrusting the porter aside in her panic. She wrenched one of the train doors open and yanked the sobbing Grace out onto the platform. The two of them, mother and daughter hand-in-hand, ran through the crowd and away out of the station. Before she could start a stampede of mothers, the guard blew the whistle and the train began to move. Women ran along the platform, fighting to keep their smiles still pinned to their faces. The train rushed away taking their smiles with it. Heads down they left the station, some biting their nails and others openly weeping.

Thelma felt a surge of relief so great she almost floated. Free, she was free. To celebrate she was going to the Labour Exchange to get a form about joining something, anything so she could get away from her mother. It would be a wrench to leave Joe Forrest, but she was kidding herself in thinking he would give her so much as a backward glance. Done everythink bar handing him her knickers on a plate. She would move on – it was time that Thelma Scoggins had a chance to kick up her heels.

Lionel was hot and tired and desperate to go to the lavatory. The train swayed alarmingly as he lifted the seat and tried to unbutton his trousers one-handed, so he didn't need to let go of the fire-engine. He had just got himself started when there was another lurch and the wee slopped all over his shoes. Re-buttoning was beyond him so he just pulled his jersey down over his trousers. He felt proud of himself that not once had he let go of Joe's engine.

Back in the carriage he took his seat next to Miss Fern.

'All right, Lionel?'

'Yes, Miss,' he mumbled.

Opposite was Gloria who sat next to him at school. She was clutching a rag doll and a bag of cakes that her mum had given her. Lionel's mouth began to water. Lived in a bakery, she did. He tried to guess what was in the bag. Could it be his favourite, lemon curd tarts, or mushroom cakes made of chocolate marked out in ridges, with a marzipan stalk? Perhaps it was one of those tower things covered in jam and rolled in coconut. He knew what was in his bag: horrible fish-paste sandwiches, a bag of crisps and a mingy little bar of chocolate. But, he couldn't eat nothing if he didn't have a drink. He licked his lips and looked out of the window. It was all sky and hedges and fields: blue and green and yellow. There were big spaces of nothing between the houses, spaces that frightened him. Ages and ages, it seemed to him, they were on the train.

It was all muddly when they got there. Gloria dropped her bag of cakes down on the line and started bawling her head off. Ginger Rolls from down his street tried to snatch his fire-engine.

Lionel kicked him in the shins. 'Bugger off,' he roared.

'Lionel, don't be so naughty.' Miss Fern gripped his arm, her fingers pinching hard. There were two angry pink spots on her cheeks and the flap under her chin that was like a turkey began to wobble dangerously. 'Say you're sorry, at once, now!'

Lionel stared at the scuffs on his shoes. He wanted Joe to come and hoist him up on his shoulder and run with him all the way back home.

They went to a church hall where they had a drink of orange squash and could go to the toilet. There were people looking at them and whispering to each other. Miss Fern had said they would be sleeping at Romsey and going to school here like they had in Portsmouth. She didn't say that they had to be picked out like things in a shop window. It seemed that the big boys got taken first, and the nice clean-looking ones. Perhaps if no one took him they might send him back.

'He'll do, the skinny one.' A woman with a thin slit of a mouth and lots of chins grabbed him. 'Not a bed-wetter are ya?' she shouted at him.

'I'll see you on Sunday, Lionel,' Miss Fern said. 'There'll be tea in the church hall and a treasure hunt in the woods.'

He wished he had thought to throw his sandwiches out the train window, like in the Babes in the Wood story where they kept finding their way home by following a trail of crumbs.

'My name's Mrs Neasom, and who are you?'

'Lionel Scoggins,' he whispered.

160

'Well, Lionel, you're gonna have to speak up. I got three lads at home. Have to sling you up in the attic. Pick up yer feet, got no time to hang around.'

He followed Mrs Neasom. Her big boots stomped down the hall and out to a van. She swung open the back doors. 'You get in there, over by them cabbages. Look lively now.'

It was cold and dark and smelly and Lionel was frightened. Suddenly he wanted to be back with his mum, even when she was being ratty. Even Gran moaning at him would be better than this. He sat with his knees up to his chin and his arms wrapped across his chest. In the middle of the tight little bundle was the red fire-engine.

13

Blyth crossed the flight deck to his Swordfish. This was it. His first take-off from the pitching deck of an aircraft carrier at sea. He walked down both sides of his aircraft from propeller to tail, doing the pre-flight check. Yes, the air-speed cover had been removed, yes, all was well with the ailerons and elevators on the back of the wings and yes to the condition of the wings and the tyres on the wheels. Satisfied, he climbed up the foot-holds on the fuselage and into the open cockpit. After strapping himself in, he connected the lead from his helmet to the flight radio and checked the controls. He warmed up the engine and held the Swordfish on her brakes, raring for the flight-deck petty officer to wave the green flag. Whoosh! With a roar of acceleration and a rush of cold air on his face he was up and into the wind – higher and higher until he had reached a thousand feet. He wanted to roll and soar and loop, to revel in the freedom of the air. Training overrode his excitement and Blyth turned left, waiting for the call on the radio to return. When it came he began the descent onto the down-wind leg and levelled off at the circuit height of 200ft. Below him the pitching deck of HMS *Unrivalled* was like a toy on a boating lake. Jaw clenched he released the arrester hook. Now he must trust the batsman.

'If your plane is properly maintained and you

obey me implicitly you cannot fail to make a perfect landing.' His arms were held parallel to the flight deck in the R for Roger signal.

As Blyth came over the stern of the aircraft carrier the batsman dropped his left arm and sliced his right bat across his throat, ordering: 'Cut your engine.'

He felt the very welcome deceleration as the hook caught the third arrester wire. Two flight-deck ratings ran out and released the hook. He was down. Blyth's jaw relaxed and he allowed himself a whoop of exhilaration – home and dry. Up he went again and again until he had completed his six qualifying deck landings. Switching off his engine, his excitement began to fade. His teeth chattered: he was bloody freezing. Clumsy with cold, he climbed out of the cockpit and crossed the flight deck, stamping life back into his feet.

He went into the island, the huge grey turret that was the operational structure of the ship, out onto the goofers' rail where he could watch Juss take off and land. Blyth realised he was more anxious about his friend making a success of it than he had been for himself. Juss was a brilliant mathematician and observer but a god-awful pilot. He was set on the thankless task of impressing Felix Croxley, his father. Blyth remembered his endless talk of his exploits in the Royal Flying Corps in the last war. Having beaten the old man soundly at chess, Commander Croxley had not warmed to him. In the Fleet Air Arm he and his oppo were both outsiders he thought – Juss because of his lack of talent and Blyth for his doubtful background.

163

Juss had got off safely. Blyth let out his breath in a rush of relief. All he had to do was get down again without making a horlicks of it. Where had he gone? Christ! He should be back by now. Where the hell? There he was. What was he doing? 'Too fast, too fast,' he wanted to scream. Furiously, the batsman waved him off to make another circuit. Blyth broke into a sweat. At the third circuit the Swordfish came down to a juddering halt having caught the last arrester wire more by luck than judgment. Why couldn't Juss pull it all together? It was baffling to Blyth, for whom it had become second nature. He went down to their cabin to avoid watching his friend get a shellacking from the furious batsman for not following his signals.

Tonight all of them would be off to the Cat and Corbie in Donibristle, and then carouse through as many other pubs as they could manage before drunkenness and pauperism set in. Blyth was looking forward to letting off steam, whereas poor old Juss would be drowning his sorrows. He had bumped and banged every landing while Blyth had touched the deck on all six landings in text-book fashion.

Later, he and his fellow pilots met up at the gang-plank for their run ashore. All of them were eager to get to the phone-box and get their congratulations from parents and girlfriends.

This time Blyth would make a call to Rosie at the Nile.

'Where's Juss?' asked Inky Pen. 'In hiding, I should think, after that last landing. Old Bats was foaming at the mouth.'

164

'He's seeing Commander Flying. Said he'll join us at the Cat.'

'Poor Juss, wouldn't want to be in his shoes.'

They all saluted the officer of the watch and rushed to the dockside phones.

Blyth felt a stab of disappointment when Mr Forrest answered the phone.

'Hello Blyth, how's things? Good, good, yes, she's here. Hang on, I'll give her a shout.'

He stood there with a heap of pennies on top of the coin box, impatient to hear her voice.

'Blyth, how are you?'

'Excited.'

'Why, what's happened?'

'I've passed all my deck landings.'

She laughed, and he wanted to hug her.

'Knew you would, clever old thing. We'll have to celebrate when you get back.'

'How?'

Rosie giggled. 'I think we'll find a way.'

'I can't wait but I'll bloody have to.'

Inky banged on the door of the phone-box.

Blyth glared. 'I love you, must go.'

'Love you too. 'Bye 'bye.'

Hearing her voice took the edge off his excitement. He wanted to be with her back on the beach at Lee but he also wanted to be flying. A greedy bugger that's what he was, wanting to have his cake and eat it.

He walked through the dockyard with Justin who ran to catch up with him. 'What did Wings have to say?' he asked.

'Bit of a stark choice, really, seems they won't let me loose on any more Swordfishes. It's either

165

changing to an observer or shipping out.'

'Christ, that's a facer. What did you say?'

Justin smiled. 'It was a relief. There's no joy in banging your head against a wall. I'm a bloody hopeless flyer but I am ace at finding my way around. So, let's get pissed. I'll navigate us to the Cat and Corbie and you can put your hand in your pocket for once.'

Deck landing in daylight was nothing to the challenge of returning to the carrier in the dark. Blyth, still fuzzy-headed from the night before, could hear the instructor's voice from earlier in his training ringing in his ears.

'Getting back to the carrier in the middle of the ocean is achieved by the accurate reading of the compass combined with good knowledge of the effects that the speed and direction of the wind will have on the course flown by the aircraft. Know your plane, read your instruments correctly, listen to your observer, and you should find your carrier every time.'

When they were fully operational, he hoped that Justin would be his observer, but for practice landing they flew solo. After all, if your observer bought it one night you'd have to manage on your own. He went through his usual aircraft check and clambered aboard his Swordfish. The procedure was much the same as daylight landing, with a few extra refinements. There were lights along the edge of the flight deck and the batsman had lighted directional wands. As he approached his landing he switched on the three lights on the Swordfish and tried to pick up the batsman's signals. By the time he had made his third landing he was exhausted. Aching from cold and tension, he staggered out of the cockpit and down to his cabin.

Their final night landings were cancelled and the *Unrivalled* returned to harbour on the first of September. Rumours were rife, as the countdown to the Sunday deadline between the British Government and the German Chancellery ticked away. In a couple of days they could be at war. All unnecessary personnel were landed, and the crew worked night and day to load fuel, ammunition and stores.

At midday, on the Sunday, the Captain broadcast to the ship's company.

'Today we have received the signal from the Admiralty that hostilities against Germany have commenced. I have every faith that in the best traditions of the service, together we shall meet and destroy the enemy wherever we shall find him. Good luck to you all.'

There were a few seconds' silence while each individual digested the news and then a loud collective cheer. This was it.

Blyth felt a surge of excitement.

Further talk was interrupted by the blaring of the tannoy. 'All pilots of 832 Squadron to report to the ops room, now.'

'I don't have to remind you,' said Commander Flying, pausing to look at each pilot in turn as they seated themselves, 'that the safety of this ship and the fleet will largely depend on you. The time of training and exercising is at an end, and the time to put into practice all that you have learnt is at hand. We do know that some heavy units of the German navy are at sea. We do not know where they are or in what numbers. The greater danger must come from U-boats. You will fly defensive patrols armed with depth charges. You will attack submarines on sighting them, report and shadow capital ships. You will not, I repeat not, attack them. I want no heroes. I want my planes back with their crews intact. Good luck and good hunting.'

At dawn the next day, three Swordfishes of 832 Squadron took off to carry out a defensive patrol.

Blyth had slept little and neither had Justin; they both wrote letters home. He sent a brief note to his sister Mary and a longer one to Rosie.

Dear Rosie,

So, we're at war. I'm sitting in my cabin with all sorts of feelings stirring about inside me; relief, excitement, fear. There's a big dollop of regret at not being able to say goodbye and to hold you close and love you. I tried to crystallize all my memories of you into one picture. You my lovely Rosie are lying on your back on the blue towel smiling up at me as I bend to kiss you. There is sand in your hair and it's all wet and salty. We have just made love and you lie there resting on your folded arms. You are glowing and there is so much I want to tell you. You are my safe harbour, my thrilling quest and my sheet-anchor holding me on my course. You cut through all my flannel bring me back to earth and yet together we fly.

Tomorrow we go to war. I can't promise you to come back safe and sound. We may not have any tomorrows but we have had some glorious yesterdays. I promise you that if I get back we won't waste a moment. We'll

168

live life to the hilt. And if this is goodbye remember the snot-nosed kid from Lemon Street who had the cheek to love you.

With all my love,
Blyth.

He sealed the letter and put it on the table ready for delivery for it to be censored before posting. Unable to sleep, he and Justin joined the others in the wardroom. The steward brought them cups of tea, and with the others they sat idly spinning yarns, some frayed from constant repetition.

'There was I at two thousand feet, flying upside down, coming out of a cloud without a clue where I was...'

'I said to her what d'you think this is, darling, a stick of rhubarb?'

'We know, she covered you in custard,' they all chorused at Inky's highly-coloured sexual fantasies.

Blyth's mind refused to rest. He was like an over-wound alarm clock ready to go off at any moment. Excitement and anxiety fought inside him. What if he funked it? What if fighters attacked them? Would he remember all that stuff they'd pumped into his head about evasion tactics? What about Juss, his observer, and Simmo, his Telegraphist Air Gunner or TAG? What if he let them down and they died as a result of his carelessness? While he was fretting, Lieutenant Jimmy Penrose, their flight leader, came in and sat down opposite him.

He looked at him for a moment before saying, 'By this time tomorrow, Blyth, we'll all be veterans. By the by, how's that girl of yours, Rosie isn't it? Comes from Pompey and rides a motor bike? Sounds like quite a girl.'

Blyth smiled. 'She's great thanks,' he said, encouraged by Penrose's friendly tone. 'Glad when we're off, getting cold feet.'

'You'll do fine. Being strung up is par for the course.' At first light, Blyth, Justin and their TAG Simpson, climbed into the Swordfish to do a wide sweep of the ocean investigating anything that floated. They attacked two submarines, forcing them to dive. Blyth felt exhilarated as he followed his leader down and released his bombs on the U-boat as it disappeared under the sea. One of the subs was an 'S' class of the Royal Navy. The tiny grey shapes were almost impossible to distinguish one from another. The bombs missed.

They had survived their first action of the war. As they turned back to the carrier Blyth felt neither veteran nor recruit. He was cold, hungry, and in need of sleep.

14

It was still dark outside. By rights Miriam should have been curled around Alec, fast asleep; instead she was in the kitchen making sandwiches. Not since she was a young woman with Rosie a child at the breast had she felt such dread. It dried her mouth and churned her stomach. It was today the deadline with Germany ran out. Later, Alec would bring the radio down to the public bar for everyone to listen to Chamberlain's broadcast. She had got to do something. What that was formed itself in the hours she lay awake, listening to Alec's breathing and the ticking of the clock.

'Mirry, my darling come back to bed,' Alec pleaded holding out his arms, as she carried in a tray of tea. 'What are you doing? It's only just gone seven.'

She sat on the bed and took his hand. 'Will you humour me just for the next hour?'

'I've done that for the last twenty years and more,' he laughed softly. 'What's so special about now?'

'I don't know what else to do.' She gripped his hand. 'I want all of us to have breakfast on the beach together. Before, before...' she turned away from him and wiped the tears away with the back of her hand. 'I need that,' she said.

Alec held her tightly against his chest. She could feel his heartbeat and the warm familiar smell of him. Miriam wanted to bury herself like a dormouse and wake up later to find the war melted away.

'You can have the top brick off the chimney, my darling,' he said.

'I'm so frightened for Rosie and Joe. We've done so well getting this far.' She took his hand and laid it against her cheek. 'When they were little and I was going to run across the road, I used to think, mustn't take risks, I've got to stay alive 'til they're grown-up. They need a mum and dad behind them. I can't do anything about what's to happen when they're grown up. All I can do is keep them safe now, and give them happy memories.'

'Is that what this picnic's about?'

She nodded. 'I want a picture of us all together on Gran's beach, being a family doing simple ordinary things. I want to hold it up and say this is the heart of a country: its people. These are the children we gave birth to because we thought they had a future.' She gripped his hand. 'I bet there's women in Germany feeling just the same.'

He took her in his arms. 'Christ, Mirry, d'you think there's anyone living around this pub that wants a war? Too many old sailors know what it was like. 'Course the young lads want it, a big adventure. Makes them look big to their girls. But we got no choice. Evil, terrible things are happening, Mirry. It's got beyond words.' He held her face between his hands. 'We've had happy times with our kids. Nothing can take that away from us. 'Course I'll come with you but,' he laughed, 'getting those two organised will be up to you. You'll have to phone the fire station. If Joseph's on duty you'll have to cancel.' He stood up and stretched himself. 'Must be back by nine. I've got the cellar to see to.'

Rosie was easier to convince. She yawned luxuriously. 'Mmm! That'll be lovely. What will we take to eat?'

Miriam smiled and bent to kiss her on the cheek. 'Doorsteps of bread and boiled ham. I'll go and make a flask of tea.'

As they all bundled into the car outside, Garth the stableman from down the street called to them.

'You ain't making a run for it, are ya?'

'Oh, yeah,' laughed Alec, 'we're scarpering with the Christmas Club money. 'Course not, you daft bugger, we're off for a swim.'

'Reckon you're the daft buggers. It's only half-seven. Reckon I'll get more sense out of old Fortune and Damson in there.' With a wave of his hand he shuffled back into the stable.

They stopped at the Fire Station in Park Road and a disgruntled Joseph came out to meet them.

'I thought there'd been an emergency,' he grumbled, getting into the car. 'What's so important about breakfast on the beach?'

'It may be a day of national importance but this is family importance,' Miriam insisted.

'Where we going?' Alec asked. 'Gran's beach?'

'We're going down by the pier, aren't we?' Joe said. 'Didn't you read in the paper? We're all wanted to fill sandbags. You'd think I'd had enough of that back at the fire station last week. Bags will be more shingle than sand.'

173

'You and Rosie can do that later. This is a family picnic, so it's Gran's beach, of course.' They went through the sally port and onto the stones. Alec and Joe spread out an old blanket and Miriam stood on the shingle looking about her.

Rosie pointed up at the blue sky. 'Fresh delivered from the laundry,' she said, slipping her arm through hers. 'That's what Gran would have said.'

'It's so beautiful I needed to be here.' Miriam gripped her daughter's hand. The beach was empty. The shingle, washed clean by the tide, stretched out to where the sea approached with nibbling white-capped waves. Above them to the east the sun rose in streaks of apricot cloud. It was going to be a warm day. 'I felt this morning she was talking to me. Wanting me to make a stand.'

'Stand? What d'you mean?'

'I don't know, really. I just followed my instincts, Rosie. This is a gathering-place for us. Beattie made it so, didn't she? I wish she was here to guide us, and then I think how sad she would have been to see everything falling apart again.'

Rosie smiled. 'Came here after she died. And threw stones in the water. I think her spirit's still here. Look at that seagull giving us a beady look. Do you reckon that's her ghost?'

'We having this breakfast?' called Joe. 'My belly's rumbling something cruel.'

They leant against the thick town wall sipping their tea and biting into the salty ham. A dog came over the shingle towards them. He cocked his leg and peed on a patch of seaweed. Joe laughed and tossed him the crust from his sandwich. Rosie sifted through the stones looking for one with a lucky hole in it. Miriam hurried over to the dog's owner.

'Could I trouble you to take a snap of us all together?' she asked, then sat herself between Joe and Alec. Rosie sat in front of them wiggling her bare toes. They raised their sandwiches in mock defiance.

When he had gone, Miriam turned to them. 'We must never forget this day.'

'Not likely to with old Hitler breathing down our necks,' Joe said.

'Shut up,' she said, fiercely. 'I want us to remember we were a family. If that snap comes out it's proof of it. Hitler or Stalin or bloody Mussolini can't take this moment from us.'

Alec leapt up and took her in his arms. 'After the war we'll come here again and have a victory picnic. I promise.'

Rosie raised her teacup. 'To Gran, our guiding star.'

'The best ham sandwiches in Pompey,' said Joe.

In Solent Cottage, watched by Towser, Albert was filling his flask. 'Won't be long old chap,' he said, 'you'll soon be out there getting a sniff of rabbit. It's corned beef this morning and the last of Beatrice's chutney.' He got his knapsack from the hook on the back door and packed it with all the necessities for their morning in the woods.

What would his darling have made of this day, he wondered. Probably filled Solent Cottage with children and kept him busy with instructions from morning 'til night.

As he walked with Towser towards the wood, Albert looked forward to some time for reflection. It had been a chaotic few days. He had been up at Olive and Samuel's helping their guests to settle in, a frazzled young woman in the later stages of pregnancy and her squinnying toddler. He had been in the town when the evacuees arrived, and witnessed the children's tired anxious faces. The young arrivals were viewed with suspicion. Albert's heart ached for the little Pompeyites. He smiled as he remembered one of his wife's salty sayings: 'A bugger-up in a pudding basin.' That just about covered it.

At the fallen oak he and Towser shared their sandwiches. Later, having judged that there was nothing else in the offing, the dog rootled off in search of his own amusements. Albert took out his book of poetry and turned to one by Wilfred Owen, a favourite of his, 'The Soldier's Dream'. It seemed appropriate.

I dreamed kind Jesus fouled the big-gun gears;
And caused a permanent stoppage in all bolts;
And buckled with a smile Mausers and colts;
And rusted every bayonet with his tears.

Albert sighed at the optimism of the first verse before turning to the second.

And then there were no more bombs, of ours or
    theirs;
Not even an old flint-lock or a pikel.

176

But God was vexed, and gave all power to
  Michael:
And when I woke he'd seen to our repairs.

Towser returned and looked questioningly at
him. Albert smiled. 'Your master is poor
company this morning old chap. Bear with me a
while and I'll try to cheer up.' He took a bulging
envelope from his knapsack and sifted through
the contents. He had promised to work out a
treasure trail for the afternoon, and write out a
list of clues for each child. Truth may be the first
casualty of war, he thought, but fun is not going
to be the second, if I can help it.

  Whistling to himself the old man took up his
stick and followed the dog further into the woods.

Alec carried down the radio from the upstairs
sitting-room, plugged it in and set it on the bar.
Miriam carried a glass of stout over to old
Connie Spooner and Rosie handed Wally his pint
of ale. Joe lit a cigarette.

  'Switch it on,' said Garth, pushing his greasy
cap further back on his head. 'Let's hear the
worst.'

  The voice of Neville Chamberlain sounding
brittle and exhausted filled the room:

  'This morning the British ambassador in Berlin
handed the German government a final note
stating that unless we heard from them by eleven
o'clock that they were prepared to withdraw their
troops from Poland a state of war would exist
between us. I have to tell you now that no such
undertaking has been received, and that

consequently, this country is at war with Germany.'

There was silence in the bar while everyone digested the news. Unnoticed by the rest of them, Bernice had sidled in. She went over to the piano and lifted up the lid and began to play. 'There'll always be an England,' she thumped out, and many took up the tune.

'Red, white and blue, what does it mean to you?' roared out Wally Organ.

Connie Spooner took a hankie from her apron pocket and dabbed her eyes. She thought of her husband and two sons on board the *Royal Oak* way up in Scapa Flow. 'Please God let them be safe,' she breathed.

Thelma felt a guilty thrill. She'd seen a poster down the Labour Exchange about war work. Good money there was in factories. Now Lionel was taken care of all sorts of possibilities beckoned. She might even be able to get away somewhere. Free of our Mum and Lionel, the prospects were dazzling. She suppressed a smile and went around collecting the glasses.

Garth went back to the horses.

Miriam stared at the Nile painting, peppered with holes from numerous inaccurate darts. Its dogged survival comforted her. Alec took her hand and she gave his a returning squeeze.

Over at Hardway Daisy leapt up, switched off the radio. She ran out to the shed and grabbed her fork. By the time Pearl followed her into the garden she was already digging. Dahlias, golden-rod, Michaelmas daisies – all were uprooted and tossed on the compost heap. She wrenched a marigold from its stem, tearing the petals.

Pearl chased after her. 'What you doing? No, stop, stop!'

She was flung aside. 'Out me way! Are you deaf or sommink? You heard old Chamberlain. It's war – you heard him. Won't be wanting these. Beauty and prettiness and manners'll all go to hell.' Daisy was panting and wild-eyed.

'Stop, stop it at once!' It was too much. Pearl wrested the fork out of Daisy's grasp and flung it aside. 'I've never heard anything so silly in my life. 'Course we'll want flowers and pretty things, stands to reason.'

'What bloody reason? Won't be any reason. It'll all be madness, madness everywhere.'

Pearl fetched Daisy a stinging slap across her face.

There was a moment of stunned silence then Daisy sank down on her knees, covering her face with her hands. Her body shook. She knelt there in the earth and howled.

Pearl felt an answering scream rise in her throat. Clenching her teeth, she swallowed it down. They had got to get a hold of themselves. 'We'll manage, we will, you'll see. Come on now, let me help you up, we'll go back in the house and have a cuppa.' She could hear the fear in her own voice, but kept on talking and tugging at her aunt's shoulder. 'Dinner'll be ready soon. That's it, up you get. Soon be back indoors. Have a nice sit down, I'll roll you a ciggie.'

Gasping and snuffling, Daisy allowed herself to be led back into the kitchen. Pearl got a flannel and a towel, and bathed and dried her aunt's face and hands.

Daisy slumped in the chair still gasping. 'Sorry, I'm sorry,' she whimpered, 'don't know what's come over me.'

Pearl smiled. 'Here, take this cup of tea, nice and hot and sweet. You're allowed one rampage a year and you've just used up your quota.'

Daisy smiled. 'This is a turn-up for the books, you taking charge of me. A real turn-around.'

'I surprised myself,' said Pearl. 'It was seeing all those flowers that you'd planted and watered and talked to, lying there. Won't they be what we'll be fighting for?'

'What, a bunch of friggin' dahlias?'

'No, being free to plant our flowers, going to the pub and the library, or staying in bed of a Sunday and reading the paper.'

Daisy chuckled. 'Be saying next as we gotta defend our treacle tart and custard.'

The two women hugged one another.

'We'll just have to muddle through.'

'No change then,' teased Pearl.

Daisy fetched her a swipe with the tea towel. 'Getting above yourself, you are, Pearl Bunting. Who'd have thought it, a little runt like you?'

15

Walking home through Victoria Park on a Saturday lunchtime Rosie fretted for something to happen, anything to get her out of the sweetshop. It was a pointless enough job in peacetime. With a war on it was ludicrous. What was she going to do to contribute to the defence of her country – fire humbugs at Hitler? Smack him one with her toffee hammer?

With Blyth away and possibly in the thick of the fighting, she was desperate for something to occupy her mind. That Sunday in August seemed like a dream, now, in the dreary days of October. Rosie tried to recover the simmering heat of those moments on the beach at Lee. If only she could feel again the pleasure of that afternoon alone with him. He had led her on a sensual journey, tempting her into unknown territory, taking her deeper, further and faster, making her senses sing. What she remembered above all were those moments afterwards when he had stopped her tears and brought her body to a pitch of melting content. And, he had kept her safe. Without his care she could have more than boredom to worry about. She could be expecting a child. Rosie treasured his last letter to her before the censor's blue pencil intruded on them. It had made her cry. She prayed the 'snot-nosed kid from Lemon Street' would come to no harm.

In contrast to Blyth's sorties at sea, war in Pompey was boring. There was the blackout, and a constant rain of leaflets telling everyone what to do from morning to night. She and Mum had taped up the windows, sewn blackout curtains while Dad reinforced the cellar. The birth, death and marriage certificates, along with insurance policies, had been locked in a tin box down there. Poor Dad, so used to the order and discipline of the navy, was driven mad by the attitude of his fellow air-raid wardens, especially her boss, Claude Treagus. He was proving to be a real Jeremiah.

'The bombers always get through. You saw the pictures of the cities in Spain. It'll be slaughter, you mark my words.'

Nobody wanted to be on duty with him. 'Tin-pot little general he is. Not been outside Portsmouth all his life, never so much as fired a pea-shooter. Now he's got a uniform, reckons he's God almighty.'

Caught between Claude, and the heated affair going on at the post between a young warden and her married boyfriend, Dad struggled to keep his patience. 'Mind you, there are some good ones among them,' he told her. 'Connie Spooner's brother Stan is a steady chap. We've got to all work together: us and the firemen and ambulance drivers, the gas company, the police and the bomb disposal and mortuary attendants.'

The mention of the mortuary had shocked her, making her realise how little she knew of war, or even of death. There had been Gran, of course, but she was an old lady and by her own admission had lived life to the full. If it had not been last year, it would have been soon.

As she pushed the door open and walked into the Nile she was hit by the smell of wet raincoats, tobacco-smoke and silence. It was Saturday dinner-time: what was up with everyone? No laughter, no thud of darts in the board, no one rolling a tickler, not even the crunch of a crisp packet – just silence and the early edition of the *Portsmouth Evening News* folded up on the bar. Rosie looked around her, trying to read the faces.

Mum came in from the street behind her. 'Have you seen Connie? Did she say anything last night about going anywhere?'

'She was off to the Landport Drapery Bazaar to have a perm.'

The clues all came together: the gloom in the bar, the newspaper, and Mum looking for Connie. Something must have happened to the *Royal Oak*. But she couldn't understand it. The ship was at the big naval anchorage at Scapa Flow. Rosie looked at Dad and he handed her the paper.

'Royal Oak *reported sunk loss of 100s of lives from a ship's complement of 1,200. The Admiralty announced the loss of the battleship HMS* Royal Oak *at 10.30 today. Survivors accounted for so far, 370.*'

Following the terse statement were a list of fifteen Portsmouth and Gosport survivors. There was no mention of Arthur Spooner or his twin sons. Rosie tugged at her hair. She could see them all bursting into the pub after Pompey's win at Wembley – the twins scooping up their

Mum and sitting her on the bar – Connie flushed and giggly on half a pint of stout. Rosie couldn't face her coming in with her hair all frizzy waiting for compliments. Couldn't face being the one who stole her family from her.

'I'll go down the barracks – they'll have the names of the survivors posted up on the gate.'

'What about your dinner and getting back to work?' asked Dad.

'I'll come too,' said Mum, going to get her coat. 'Thelma, you can manage, can't you?'

'Mirry, no, if Connie comes back here it's you she'll want, not Thelma.'

Always eager to skive off somewhere, Thelma went off to the lounge bar for a sulk.

'Can you ring old Claude, say I'm delayed,' said Rosie. 'I'll come back here first with the list. Got a pencil and paper in my bag.'

She hurried back through Commercial Road with its crowds of week-end shoppers. People were standing around the newspaper kiosks in anxious knots. Turning the corner into Edinburgh Road, she saw ahead of her a swarm of women gathering at the Royal Naval Barracks and at the officers' accommodation on the other side of the road. There were old couples arm-in-arm, young women with prams, children clutching at their mothers' coats. They pushed their way to the front of the queue, and scanned the list of survivors posted there. 'Oh! Thank God, Dad. Peter's there and Wally from down the street.'

'Name's gotta be there. Look again, Ruby,' urged a heavily pregnant woman, with a toddler beside her in a pushchair.

'Come here Ethel, don't take on so. This ain't the full picture. Bound to be chaos up there. Blokes lost their clothes, others bin hit on the head or sommink. Our Charlie will be back for definite. I owes him a quid.'

Rosie struggled to get to the front of the frantic women, and got out her pencil and paper. It was hopeless: she couldn't take down all the names, there were too many. Even so, there were only a few hundred when you weighed it up against the full ship's company. She bit her lip, feeling shame for her lack of interest when HMS *Courageous* was lost last month, just because she knew none of the men on board. God, she had got to concentrate. Finding the Spooner men was a matter of life and death. Even after the third reading she couldn't find them. As she turned to leave, two women were carrying a young chalk-faced girl into the barracks.

'Yes, Ma'am, we'll get her an ambulance,' the rating at the gates was saying.

Rosie ran up the road and on to the Nile. 'She here yet?' she gasped.

Dad shook his head. 'Mum's just come back from her house, no one in. Oh, and Claude says not to come back, he's shut the shop as a matter of respect.' He looked at her, his face grained with sadness. 'No joy?'

'No joy,' said Rosie.

'You go on upstairs, your Mum's got your dinner ready. Oh yes, I forgot this in all the excitement. It's a letter from a feller in Wales.'

'Thanks. I'll read it later,' she mumbled, sliding it into her coat pocket.

'Hello, my cockers, how's it going? I'm that thirsty from sitting in the hairdresser's. Me mouth's as dry as the bottom of a birdcage. Fetch us a stout will you, Alec.' Connie took off her headscarf and smiled at everyone expectantly. 'Reckon I look a right Shirley Temple. What say you, Rosie love?'

'Very nice, Connie.'

The little woman looked around her at the men. 'What's up with you all – looking very down in the mouth.'

This was out of their league. Breaking bad news and giving comfort was women's business. Even Thelma, normally not short of something to say, ducked down under the bar in pretence at finding something.

Rosie went and sat with Connie. 'Like to come upstairs and have some soup with me and Mum,' she said. 'You must be hungry. How long did the perm take?'

'Went at half-past eleven, what is it now?' She swivelled her head around to look at the clock. 'Blimey, just gone two, my Ginger will be sat at the back door with his legs crossed. Meant to let him out before I went but I was in such a rush. Nipped over to the post office to send a parcel off to the boys. Knitted them a balaclava apiece. They was telling me in their letters, ever so parky up there in Scotland.'

Out of the corner of her eye, Rosie saw a naval officer come through the door and walk up to her father. He asked him something and Dad pointed to Connie.

Rosie stared down at the table as the officer

approached. Any second now, she thought. He is going to break her heart.

'What about that soup?' she asked, getting up and pulling back her chair.

'Don't mind if I do, love. Just knock back the rest of me stout.'

'Mrs Spooner?'

'Who wants ter know?'

'Good afternoon, Ma'am, I'm Commander Fowler.'

'Well,' said Connie, 'pleased to meet you, I'm sure.'

'Why don't we all go upstairs,' said Mum, appearing from the side door. She slid her arm through Connie's, and Rosie and the naval officer followed after them.

'Rosie and I will serve up the soup. Can I offer you some, Commander, it'll warm you up.'

'No thank you, Mrs Forrest, I have many calls to make.'

'Of course, well, sit down please.'

Connie stared at the man, head on one side, and eyes watchful. Her earlier brightness quenched. 'It's about my man and my boys, isn't it?' she said.

Rosie stared at the lino, counting the green-and-cream squares, while the man in the navy raincoat began to speak.

'Mrs Spooner, there has been an attack on the *Royal Oak* in the early hours of this morning.'

Connie's hands flew to her face.

'There was an explosion on the ship and a number of fatal casualties. It is my sad duty to tell you that your husband and sons are amongst them.'

'Oh my stars!' She looked up at the man. 'There can't be no mistake? You sure as ever you can be?'

'They were identified, Mrs Spooner. I am so very sorry.'

'I only just posted off their balaclavas. Oh my poor, poor Arthur, my poor lads.' She began to rock backwards and forwards. 'Oh, oh my boys, my boys.'

Talking together, Mum and the Commander left the kitchen.

Rosie went to Connie and put her arms around her. 'I've got you,' she said, as if to a child. Still rocking, Connie gripped her hand. She smelt of stout and damp wool. Rosie blinked back her tears. The news had, in the instant of telling, sliced her family from her, leaving the little woman in ruins. In spite of the warmth of the kitchen fire and her thick coat, she began to shiver. 'I've got you.' Rosie held her tight. She heard the sound of Mum's quick footsteps on the stairs.

The kettle shrilled, invading the silence.

Connie stopped rocking. 'My Ginger will be wanting his dinner. Got his fish to give him on the back of the stove.'

'Rosie can see to that, love. Give her your key. I'll dish up the soup.'

'I need to be in my own home, with my things around me, specially my Ginger. Boys give him to me. Dockyard stray he was.'

'Why not let Rosie give him his fish and you have your soup? One of us will go back with you and stay the night.'

'It's on the chain behind the door, my duck,

like always. Didn't want my lads never to come home and not be able to get in,' Connie gasped and chewed her hand.

'Won't be long.' Rosie ran along the passage and down the stairs.

Number 20 Nelson Street was full of the lost men. Photographs, postcards and souvenirs from around the world covered the walls and the mantelpiece. There was even a snap of Connie outside the Nile last summer, between the twins. She was laughing. How will she bear it? Rosie wondered. Their faces are looking out at her from every corner. The place stank of catfish. Ginger, the large cat, slid off a stack of newspapers on a chair and wound himself around her legs. For all her care and affection, little Connie was merely his meal-ticket, anyone would do. Resentfully, Rosie spooned the grey fish onto a tin plate and set it on the mat by the door.

She reached in her pocket for her hankie and felt the crackle of the envelope. No, she couldn't read it here, it wouldn't be right. Ginger gulped down his fish and stared at her, his green eyes cold and calculating. She opened the back door and nudged him out with her foot.

Back in the kitchen, Connie and Mum were standing together arm-in-arm.

'Stay with her a minute, I'm just putting a few bits together. I'm staying the night with Connie. You and your Dad will manage. Don't let Thelma slope off early. Money in the tin, go down Queen Street and get yourselves some fish-and-chips, Joe will be off watch at six. Thank God we'll be closing in five minutes.'

'You told Ginger?' asked Connie, her eyes red from crying.

'I've left that for you,' said Rosie. 'He's had his fish.'

She put her arms around her neighbour, who leaned her head against Rosie's chest. Connie wore a string of glass beads, with a few bits of hair sprinkled among them, left unnoticed from the recent cutting. 'I don't know what to say,' Rosie whispered into the dry grey curls.

'Ain't nothing, love,' said Connie. 'Ain't nothing at all.'

Rosie stroked her back through the felted wool cardigan. Only touch can heal us, she thought. We need to be held in the warmth of another human being. What we're doing here in this kitchen will be repeated over and over again throughout the world, whatever the language spoken, whatever the beliefs held. She closed her eyes. Mum came in with her shopping bag and patted Connie on the shoulder.

'Let's take you home,' she said, picking up the little woman's coat and holding it open for her.

''Bye, Connie, see you later.'

Connie nodded and walked away hand-in-hand with Mum.

Rosie sat at the table resting her head on her folded arms. Tears leaked down her face, wetting the sleeves of her cardigan. In the distance she could hear the pub door slam and Thelma's high heels clacking down the road, followed by Dad's light tread on the stairs. He rested his hand on her shoulder.

'Thought you'd be reading your letter,' he said.

190

'Feel too sad,' she blubbered.

''Course you're sad, we all are, but you can't lie down under it. Seize all the joy and good things that come your way with both hands. The trick of it,' he said, taking out his tickler tin of tobacco and papers, 'is living each moment. Anything else is letting the enemy through the door. You go and read your letter.'

Sitting on her bed, Rosie peeled back the flap of the envelope and unfolded her letter.

Darling Rosie,

I'm cold and tired and missing you. I'd like to be tucked up with you in a warm bed with a fire crackling in the grate. That's something we have to look forward to, sleeping together. When I was small I used to wonder where I went to after I'd closed my eyes and how did I get back in time for school in the morning. Did you ever try to remember the exact moment when you fell asleep? I still wonder about it. Just a big kid really.

The ship is our whole world, now. It's a strange one without any women or pavements or chip shops. The worst bit is not being able to swap the company around. We all get on each other's nerves. Inky drives me mad, keeps pulling his fingers till they crack. Simmo our TAG whistles through his teeth. Juss tugs at his ear when he's reading and I, would you believe, play with bits of string. I'm looking forward to being with you long enough to find out your funny little ways.

You know that I don't trouble God very much but I thought you might like this special prayer used by us airy fairies.

191

'Almighty God, Who makest the clouds Thy chariot and Who walkest on the wings of the wind, we commend to Thy Fatherly protection all who ride the skies in the service of the Fleet, and those in whose work they trust.'

I wonder if you have joined the Wrens yet and what you are up to and when I'll see you. Where can we be together, my Rosie? Somewhere where I can have you to myself and hold you close.
See you on the Nile, my Cleopatra.
Simmering to see you,
Love Blyth

Rosie sighed. She wanted him here, and she wanted him now. Anything could happen. Look at poor Connie, her whole family gone in one night. Everything was grey and dull and uncertain. Living every minute, that was Gran's motto. Well, she had the minutes: all she needed was some living to fill them.

16

Thelma hugged herself with glee as the train bore her mother off to stay with Auntie Peggy in Plymouth. Now, she was free to make her own get-away. First stop the Labour Exchange in Lake Road. She had a fancy to join one of the Services. The Air Force uniform was the nicest – that blue would suit her and pick out the colour of her eyes. It was Friday the 10th of November; with a bit of luck she could be snug on an airfield by Christmas, with Mum and Lionel and Nelson Street just a bad dream.

'You have very little experience beyond bar work, Miss Scoggins. I think you should consider the Armament Depot at Gosport. The pay is very good, upwards of two pounds a week and the possibility of overtime, later.'

Thelma swallowed down her disappointment. Priddy's Hard was not at all what she'd had in mind, but it would be a start, especially at that money. Even Gosport would be a change from Landport. Over there were all those submariners at HMS *Dolphin* – supposed to be mad for a woman after being stuck under water for so long. She'd still have the chance of a boy in blue but it would just be a darker shade.

'What about your next of kin, Miss Scoggins? You haven't put that down, or your references.' The woman on the other side of the table gave her a sceptical glance.

Thelma thought quickly and went into her little-girl-lost routine. 'Ain't got no one close at hand. Me Mum's in Plymouth and that's it. I'm homeless, as of this morning. Got to get something quick or I'll be sleeping at the Sally Army. I forgot me references, they're in a case in the property locker at the railway station.'

'Very sorry, I'm sure.' The woman's voice softened at Thelma's straitened circumstances. 'I'll phone and fix you up an interview and a medical for you. You'll have to get yourself some accommodation. It's an early start, seven-thirty.'

Thelma had almost changed her mind. She sat biting her nails, waiting for the girl to come back to her.

'Right, Miss Scoggins, it's at half-past two this afternoon – over in Hardway. Leave yourself half an hour to walk from the Gosport ferry, someone over there will show you the way. They've probably got a list of billets, too.'

To cheer herself up, she'd gone down to Martha's in Commercial Road and stood herself a double gin-and-it. She sat chipping at her nail varnish with her thumb. How was she going to winkle her insurance card out of the desk in the Forrests' sitting-room? If she was going to disappear it was essential. The last thing she wanted was people going to the Nile and asking questions. Come Saturday night when she got her pay, that chapter of her life was going to be locked behind her, with no come-back. As she raised the gin to her lips someone tapped on her shoulder.

'I know you don't I? Thelma isn't it?'

194

She stared at the homely woman in the black beret and maroon coat. 'Dunnow, do ya?'

'I'm Daisy, Daisy Fletcher. Remember you from me sister's wedding. You got up and did the Charleston with that sailor. Wasn't you a pal of our Greta's? Over at the church hall in Gosport it was – couple of years ago. You was with your Mum and a little boy.'

Thelma's brain worked overtime. 'That was me young brother, he died of whooping cough and me Mum went down to Plymouth to stay with her sister.' She smiled at her cleverness in getting shot of her family all in one go. That silly cow Daisy had her face all creased up with concern. You could do a lot with people when they were sorry for you.

'Poor little mite, how old was he?'

'Eight. If you don't mind I'd rather not talk about him.' She even managed to squeeze out a few tears. 'I remember the wedding, beautiful cake and that satin ribbon round it was really classy. Better than them paper frills.'

Daisy glowed. 'I made the cake, my idea for the ribbon, too.' She went over to her table and brought her glass of beer and crisps back with her. After settling herself in her chair beside Thelma, she said, 'What you doing with yourself, now?'

'Going for an interview over at Priddy's Hard at the depot. Hope they takes me on, desperate for a job and a place to stay. Bin ill and lost me job and now the landlord's kicking me out 'cos I got behind with me rent.' Was she laying it on too thick?

No, Daisy was munching away and hanging on

every word.

'Snap!' she said, snatching the bait. 'I work at Priddy's with my niece Pearl. I'nt that a coincidence. What time's your interview?'

'Half two this afternoon.'

'We'll go over together. I can show you where it is. I bin off with this skin complaint – back on Monday though. If you gets the job you could bunk in with the two of us. Only lives down the road from Priddy's.'

Noticing the red skin above Daisy's cotton gloves, Thelma recoiled. She hated physical imperfections. Was it catching? She hoped not. Still, it would pay her to treat her right. 'You must be my guardian angel,' she said, treating Daisy to one of her smiles.

Daisy glowed. 'Tell ya what, let's get ourselves some fish-and-chips down Charlotte Street, then we'll catch the ferry and I can show you the way to Priddy's. After, you can stop by and let me know how you got on.' She patted her hand. 'Even if you don't get suited you can stay with Pearl and me while you look around. What d'you say?'

'I don't mind if I do,' grinned Thelma.

'Let's shake on it,' said Daisy, gripping her hand. 'You'll like Pearl, my niece,' she rattled on, as they made their way to the chip shop. 'She's a nice little thing. Be glad of someone nearer her age.'

Thelma doubted she'd like her. Wasn't one for palling up with women.

Back in the Nile that night, she congratulated herself on getting both a job and a home in one

196

day. There had been a few sticky moments over the references. She had copied one from a book in the library, of sample letters in a how-to-type manual, giving a Captain Marchant as referee. The name she'd got from the death column in the paper last week. By the time they checked it up she should have her feet under the canteen table. Then there was Wally Organ: she had persuaded him to get her some headed notepaper from the accountants he worked for – Glanville and Trenchard. Thelma had styled herself as a housekeeper for the captain, and a filing clerk for the businessmen. The medical had not been as straightforward as she'd hoped.

'Miss Scoggins, you are underweight. You must get yourself an iron tonic.'

'Once I'm earning again I'll be able to do that. I'll be staying with some friends. Daisy Fletcher, loves cooking, she does.' Good job she wasn't Pinocchio: with the lies she'd told her nose would be out the door and round the corner.

That last night behind the bar seemed to last forever, and she was almost caught with her hand in the desk drawer. She had to put her insurance card down the front of her dress, and pretended to Alec that Miriam had sent her upstairs for a postage stamp. Thelma smiled to herself as she said, ''Bye, everyone, see you on Monday.'

They all thought she was off to Romsey to visit Lionel. It would be a long time before she went there again. Last time he wouldn't even look at her and moaned all the time about wanting to be back in Nelson Street. No, this was her chance and she was going to take it.

'Give the little chap these marbles,' Connie Spooner had said, pressing the bag into her hand. 'Like to think of them being played with again.'

For a second or two she had felt a real cheapskate, but swallowed the guilt down with a smile. ''Course I will,' she said. Outside the door she laughed. They'd be one short, now. That Bernice would have to get her bum off that piano stool for a start. Her only splinter of regret was leaving Joe. But who was she kidding? He couldn't give a toss about her. Would have forgotten her name the minute she turned the corner.

Cripes! It was bloomin' freezing on the ferry, but that was a small price to pay for freedom. As she stepped onto the pontoon, on the Gosport side, Thelma threw her ticket into the water. Whatever happened next had got to be better than Nelson Street.

Lionel wedged himself into the corner of the porch and turned the crisp packet inside out and licked the salt off the paper. He was ever so thirsty but there was no chance of getting a drink for ages. The smell of the old dog beside him was making him feel sick. It was cold and cobwebby in the porch. Every so often waves of warm air, of shouting and laughter, seeped through the big wooden door of the pub. Lionel wanted to be back in his bedroom in the Neasoms' house, up in the loft with his feet on the stone hot-water bottle and Bob snoring in the other bed.

Tonight was Mrs Neasom's night out at the Red Cross hut. Lionel, who had been sitting by the fire drinking his cocoa and looking forward to a game of Ludo with Bob, heard shouting from the kitchen.

'Get that coat off, my son, where d'you think you're going? Gotta keep an eye on Lionel. My night off.'

'Can't he stay on his own? Ain't fair, me always having to look after him. Was meeting Eddie and Colin. Owhh!'

'If I find you've sneaked out there'll be hell to pay.' The back door slammed shut and Bob came in rubbing his ear. He glared at Lionel and slammed upstairs.

Lionel twisted and untwisted his pyjama cord. He liked Bob when he was on his own, away from Eddie and Colin. They played Ludo and Bob let him win every time. But when his two brothers were around he changed, and began punching and shouting at him like they did. But now that Bob had met this girl, and had got all soppy about her, he didn't hardly want to talk to Lionel at all. After his Mum had stormed out, Bob came down with his coat still on and wanted to give him a sixpence.

'You go on up to bed. I won't be long. You keep it a secret and you can have 'nother tanner tomorrow.'

'No, don't want to. Horrible in the dark, I hates it. No, no!' He had begun to cry. 'I'll tell ya Mum,' he shouted, as Bob grabbed the bicycle lamp from the shelf in the kitchen.

Bob stamped about then dragged Lionel's coat off the back of the door and flung it at him. 'You'll 'ave to come with us, now keep quiet and stay where I puts ya.'

'Have ter wait, I gotta get sommink.' Fighting

down his fear of the dark, he went upstairs, finding his way by the moonlight filtering in the window at the top of the stairs. Holding his breath, he felt his way over to his bed and grabbed the fire-engine.

With his coat over his pyjamas, he had sat on the cross-bar of Bob's bike, being jounced down the lane. The lamp on the front wheel flickered on and off and his ears stung with cold. Now, he had eaten all the crisps and drunk the glass of lemonade that Bob had sneaked out to him. His fingers curled around his fire-engine, and he wished he were back at the Nile.

It felt as if he had been living in Romsey for ever and ever, and he didn't like it one bit. Bob's brothers were big and loud, and hit him all the time. At tea-time they snatched the bread off the plate and left him with the mingiest sandwich and the driest bit of cake. On Sundays, they all got served out slices of meat and roast potatoes. Lionel ended up with the scraps and a shiny, white lump of suet floating in gravy. He would swallow it down with his eyes closed in the hopes of getting some pudding, and be rewarded with a burnt corner of jam tart.

Mrs Neasom was always tearing about from one thing to another. She tore him out of bed in the morning and flung him into it at night. Tore his hair with the nit comb, and hustled him into his coat each morning. The village kids stared at him. They frightened Lionel, jumping out at him from hedges. One day Miss Fern had taken his class for a nature ramble. They had walked over the lumpy fields and there were animals there. A cow came up to him, its pink bag with the titties wobbling and its brown eyes staring. It was ages and ages before he could drink milk again.

Mum had come once, all dressed up, and moaned about the mud on her shoes. She brought Mrs Neasom a box of biscuits and Lionel some new socks. Mrs Forrest came too.

'Can Joe come and see me?' he had whispered to her, when Mum was bent down wiping her shoes with her handkerchief.

She smiled at him. 'I'll see what I can do,' she had whispered back to him. 'But he sent you something.'

It was a smoking outfit with a liquorice pipe and sweet cigarettes. He hid it in the hedge behind the outside lavatory.

When the Neasoms were all sat round the radio listening to something called Itma, he got up his courage and ran down to the lav by the light from the kitchen window. He sat by the tiny oil lamp on the big wooden seat, chewing the pink-tipped cigarettes, thinking about the day Joe took him to the fire station. He'd tried on a big brass helmet and sat next to him on the engine. The best bit had been sliding down the pole on Joe's back. Then Joe had walked all the way back home with Lionel riding on his shoulders. Just as he was thinking of starting on the liquorice pipe, the door crashed open and Eddie Neasom, the oldest boy, stood there glaring at him. With one hand he tugged him off the seat, scattering his sweets on the floor, crushing the box under his feet.

'Geroff, kid,' he'd said, as he unbuttoned his trousers.

Lionel had waited shivering in the yard until Eddie finished, then he sneaked back and tried to find the scattered sweets on the floor. By the light of the flickering candle, he saw torn-up bits of the box floating in the lav. Once in bed, all his miseries came welling up, and he turned his face to the wall and cried himself to sleep.

Lionel was bursting to go to the lavatory, but he was frightened of the dark. He looked at the big smelly dog and wondered if he would come with him. Perhaps he could drag him along by his collar. The door into the pub opened, and a man stood there talking to his friend. Lionel slid between them and out onto the path. He stood near the windowsill, and by the chink of light leaking round the edge of the curtain he could see to unbutton himself. After he'd done his wee he felt even colder. Yellow beams swept the path as a car came to a halt at the kerb. After the driver had slammed the door, and gone into the pub, Lionel sneaked across and put his hand on the bonnet to warm himself. He walked around to the side and tried one of the back doors. It opened, and a warm leathery smell filled his nostrils. He only meant to sit inside until Bob came out to take him home. The seat was soft, and there was a rug in the corner. Lionel curled himself up in it and laid full length along the back seat. He closed his eyes, and after a few moments his fingers relaxed and the fire-engine dropped to the floor.

Albert stood by the back door waiting for Towser to cock his leg against the gate and finish rooting about the yard. Above him the stars looked down. What did they see he wondered – poor flawed humanity tearing itself to pieces? What would his Beatrice have made of it all? There were sailors she had spoken to at the Nile now lying at the bottom of the sea: children like Lionel dragged from their homes and all that was familiar to them. He had seen the young chap when he passed the school the other day. It was playtime and there were the usual games in progress: skipping, football and follow-my-leader. Lionel was kicking a stone across the ground, hands in pockets, scowling to himself. Albert had called to him, but he was so immersed in his misery he didn't hear him. He sighed. It was no good wringing his hands: he must do something. Tomorrow he'd go to the billeting officer and find out where the boy had been placed and who was looking after him. Perhaps he could come to Solent Cottage for his tea now and then. They could play Ludo or Snap, and Lionel might like to walk in the woods with Towser.

Across the darkened fields came the screech of an owl. Albert shivered. Out there, some small creature crouched in terror. 'Come on my lad,' he called to his dog, 'time to retire. I've a hot toddy waiting and I dare say we can find you a titbit or two.'

Later as he drew his bedroom curtains Albert thought about Blyth. Was he strapped into his Swordfish skimming across the heavens or tucked in his bunk, body tensed for the next sortie? Who would have thought that skinny urchin would have climbed so high. He and his Rosie were bright kindred spirits. Please God, let them have a pinch of time together and let it be a generous one.

'Good night my darling,' he whispered to the photo on his bedside table, later that night. He spread his hand across the space beside him wounded afresh by her absence. 'Beatrice, Beatrice,' he whispered into the silence. Was there a heaven, he wondered and was she waiting there for him? Dear God, he hoped so.

Alice Neasom stumped up the lane after waving goodbye to the others outside the church hall. She was starving. All the time that doctor had been wittering on about the dangers of tourniquets, she'd been tormented at the thought of that slice of Bakewell tart hidden behind the chutney in the larder. With three kids you had to be crafty to get a look-in these days. Then there was the little runt from Pompey to consider. Truth to tell, she hardly noticed him. Not like some of her friends, with big hulking evacuees eating them out of house and home.

Something wasn't right. She knew the moment the kitchen door was opened. Then checking the hooks on the back door she knew for certain. Bob's coat was gone and Lionel's. Alice climbed up to the attic, her heart thumping with rage. The bed was empty and the fire-engine gone. By God, she'd fetch that Bob such a clout when he got back. Simmering, she paced the kitchen, bamboo cane in one hand, Bakewell in the other. The clock on the mantelpiece showed the time as gone ten. After several laps of the kitchen table

Alice Neasom began to feel afraid.

What if something had happened to her son and that little runt of an evacuee? Only the other Saturday a woman had been knocked off her bike and killed in the blackout. Bob was the soft one, not like Colin and Eddie. He was always mooning about, not looking where he was going. While she was rampaging about Bob could be laying dead somewhere.

And, what about that little kid? That billeting officer had been really snarky when she came round last week. Telling her the kid looked pale and undersized. If anything happened to him she'd lose the six shillings feeding allowance. He had to be found. She'd mortgaged that money towards Christmas.

17

Ever since the OHMS envelope had arrived, with its travel warrant and instructions to be at New College, Hampstead, by 17.00 hours on Sunday 12th November, Rosie had not had time to breathe – certainly no time for second thoughts about joining the Wrens. When she phoned Uncle Albert to give him the good news, he had insisted on coming down to see her off.

'Your grandmother would have wanted to wave you away and wish you God speed, and so do I.'

'Must think a lot of you,' Mum said. 'It'll be his first trip back here since Gran died.'

London, she'd been there once with Gran and Uncle Albert. It had seemed huge. They'd walked along the river and then over London Bridge to the Houses of Parliament. Gran had cried when they went into Westminster Abbey and saw the tomb of the Unknown Soldier.

'Could be one of our lads from Portsmouth,' she'd whispered. Even Uncle Albert had tears in his eyes.

They had finished up at Lyons Corner House where she had scoffed three toasted teacakes and got butter on her chin. That had lifted the mood.

'What a day, what a place, Albert,' Beattie had said when they were back on the train. 'We've got ourselves a feast of memories that will light up many a dark day.'

'Rosie, you're stood there watching those veggies boil dry,' yelled Mum, rescuing the sprouts. 'How you think you'll be a Wren when you can't even watch a saucepan. Just go and lay up the table.'

Rosie didn't know what she felt as she said goodbye to everyone. Dad was being extra cheery and Mum was trying not to cry. The only one being himself was Joseph.

'Can I use your bike? I'll keep it in good trim. If it's not used it might seize up on you. Oh yeah, and if there are any good-lookers among your childbearing matelot pals, bring them down here.'

'You get so much as a speck of dust on it, I'll have you,' she threatened, swiping him round the head with the Sunday paper.

''Bye love, you take care now and give us a ring directly you get there. Shan't sleep unless I know you're safe and sound.' Mum hugged her fiercely then ran from the room.

Dad stood on the pavement waving until they were out of sight.

'Do you remember the little card that was with the letter your grandmother sent you?' Uncle Albert said, as he drove her to the station.

'Of course I do. Why are you asking?'

'I have it here for you. Perhaps you will have the time whilst in London to go and see your painting. I've put the card in an envelope with an introductory letter from me, explaining the situation.'

'Gosh, I hadn't thought of that. That would be good, I don't suppose they work us twenty-four hours a day. Be something to do on a Sunday.'

'If you do get the chance let me know what you think of it.' He smiled. 'I think it's my best work; it has to be, but I would value your opinion.'

'I'll write to you straight after I've seen it. Honest Injun.'

The old man had grasped her hand. 'It will be something to look forward to,' he said. 'Now, let's launch you on your new career.'

Arm-in-arm they walked into the station together. Having settled her luggage on the rack, Rosie leaned out of the carriage window talking with Albert. Something Gran once had said came to mind.

'I've hated stations ever since the war. So much grief there, soaked into the brickwork over the years. Young women trying to squeeze all their love into one embrace; to memorize every detail of their man's face in one last look; saying stupid things because the right words won't come.'

Behind Albert, a toddler was screaming and tugging at her mother's coat. The woman, trying to say goodbye to her husband, looked distraught. Rosie reached into her bag for the box of sweets Claude had given her. She gestured to Albert to take it over to the red-faced toddler. After a grateful glance in her direction, the couple were oblivious to their daughter who sat on the ground, her cheeks bulging with toffees.

Albert kissed her cheek. 'Goodbye, my dear, and God bless you.'

'Love you,' she mouthed to him as he stood waving to her, the wind tugging at his white hair. As the whistle blew and the train moved off, Rosie felt her excitement draining like sand through an egg-timer. What if she got lost? What if she didn't get on with the other girls? The letter told her to report at Waterloo to the Regulating Transport Officer. What if she couldn't find him?

The train snaked its way past the back-to-back houses in Fratton, past the hospital and then the graveyard where Gran lay. As it rattled on she fitted words to its rhythm. *I'm going away, to live a new way; not very sure but going to war. Fight the good fight, with all of my might.* They passed over the bridge at Hilsea, away from Portsea Island and onto the mainland. At the next stop a group of schoolgirls got on, swathed in scarves. They shoved one another, their voices breathy and confident.

Soldiers got in at the next stop and wedged themselves between the schoolgirls. Rosie was pinned against the rough khaki sleeve of her neighbour. Daylight was fading, and the soldiers pulled down the blinds. Overhead a blue bulb lent a ghostly tinge to everyone's faces. Across the carriage a squaddie chewed on a piece of gum, whilst a lad with acne coughed on a Woodbine. Just as the train was leaving Hazlewood, a girl flung herself at the door and almost fell into the carriage. Her beret landed at Rosie's feet.

The girl picked it up and plonked it on top of her long red hair. She grinned at everyone. 'Hello, I'm Delia, by the way, Delia Croxley.'

'Charmed, I'm sure,' said the gum-chewing squaddie, while the pimply lad blushed.

'Shove up, would you,' said Delia plumping down beside Rosie.

She couldn't resist her friendliness and held out

209

her hand, 'Rosie Forrest.'

'What a pretty name,' Delia said. 'I'm off to London. Where are you going?'

'Hampstead, New College.'

'How amazing, so am I. Are you joining the Wrens, too?' Rosie nodded.

'How super,' enthused Delia, 'it won't be half as scary if there are two of us.' Up until that moment the carriage had been thick with the pong of rain-soaked uniforms and male sweat. Now, as she struggled out of her coat, a new scent invaded the carriage, its floral essence lifting the staleness.

'I don't know how to get there from Waterloo,' confessed Rosie. 'We have to go and see the RTO at the station but beyond that I haven't a clue.'

Her new friend laughed. 'Getting to Hampstead is easy-peasy, but what an RTO might be I can't imagine.'

'According to my Dad it's a Regulating Transport Officer. He checks that everyone is moving in the right direction. Dad used to be in the navy, and my grandad.'

'My Pa was in the Royal Flying Corps and lost half his arm. Says it was the best time of his life, which is a bit mouldy seeing as it was over twenty years ago.'

The train slowed, then juddered to a halt. The soldiers helped the girls to get their cases onto the platform. Rosie spotted a group of sailors at a wooden kiosk showing their tickets to a bearded Petty Officer. 'He looks like the man we're looking for,' she said, dragging her case across the platform.

'Right, ladies, let's be having you,' he barked at them, as they held out their travel passes. 'Know where we're going, do we?'

'Yes, Chief,' said Rosie, 'we're off to Hampstead.'

'Right ho, you two,' said the RTO. 'Off you go on the double.'

Delia hurried Rosie over to a window and bought them two tickets for the Victoria line. Soon they were at the top of an escalator. Rosie looked down the long drop to the bottom of the shifting silver steps and froze. While she havered at the top, others ran down in front of her. Eventually Delia persuaded a stranger to take charge of the case. Clutching hold of the belt on Delia's raincoat, Rosie stepped on and closed her eyes, only opening when they reached the bottom.

'Quick! Step off, now.'

The roar of the tube, the cold and the grime of the underground platform, and the way everyone was packed together like ants, was a revelation. At their destination her terror began in reverse. Rosie got herself on the first step, trying not to scream.

'Sorry for being such a coward,' she said, as they reached the steps of New College.

Delia smiled. 'Wait 'til you see me on a motor bike. I'm an absolute ninny.'

'You'll get the hang of it,' teased Rosie. 'It's easy-peasy.'

Once through the door a large woman in a petty officer's uniform came towards them, hand outstretched. 'You must be the new pro-Wrens, Croxley and Forrest.'

'Yes, Ma'am,' they chorused.

'Petty Officer Challis. Welcome aboard.' She pumped their hands vigorously. 'Let's get the paperwork out of the way and then I'll show you where your cabin is.'

Rosie followed the solid bulk of the petty officer up the stairs, and down a dimly lit passage, to a long room fitted out with tiers of bunks three deep.

'Leave your things on those two bunks. The heads are next door, then hurry down to the dining hall downstairs and three doors to the right. That's it, chop, chop, now.'

'Heads?' Delia whispered.

'Toilets,' Rosie whispered back.

As they opened the door downstairs they were greeted by laughter, chat, and the clatter of plates. Heads turned to look at them and then back to their food. Delia smiled at everyone while Rosie hung back, feeling awkward. They followed the queue of girls, and held out their plates to receive a dollop each of what looked like macaroni cheese. There were large teapots and mugs set on the trestle tables, and heaped plates of bread-and-butter. Seeing two empty spaces at a table by the door they set down their suppers and took their seats.

'Hello I'm Delia, and this is my friend Rosie. Pleased to meet you.'

'Hello, that's Froggy and I'm Knocker.' The girl making the introductions smiled and held out her hand. She had a round freckled face and tight curly brown hair.

'Horrible being new, ain't it,' said Froggy, a

buxom blonde. 'First night, I wanted to turn round and go straight home.'

'Where's that?' asked Rosie, picking up her fork and looking doubtfully at the congealed macaroni on her plate.

'Derby, bloomin' miles away.'

'How about you, Knocker?' said Delia, smiling at her.

'Petersfield.'

'That's not far from us,' said Rosie. 'I'm from Pompey and Delia's from Hazlewood.'

'You two better stoke up on the bread and jam. There's nothing else now 'til morning. 'Nother cuppa each?'

For the first time since leaving home, Rosie began to relax. From their week's experience, Knocker and Froggy gave them a rundown on life in the Wrens.

'Got to strip and remake your bed every day. Got to mitre the corners of the sheets. That's it, you got it. No, Delia, for God's sake don't get the anchor on the counterpane on upside down. Leading hand will go spare if she sees it. It's called, "Going Astern." Devils for inspection they are.'

'What you like on motor bikes?' asked Froggy.

'I can drive a Rover,' said Delia, 'but I've never even sat on a bike.'

'Got smashing instructors, they're from the fire service. They'll see you right. Tall one with black hair's lovely. We call him Gorgeous George.'

'Not much good in a car,' said Rosie, 'but I've had my own bike for a couple of years.'

Soon it was time for lights out and the girls

went to the washroom. Delia stripped off without the least embarrassment but Rosie changed in the toilet. Lying on the top bunk in the dark, listening to the traffic going by and the sound of someone snoring, she reviewed the happenings of the day. Her confidence had swung back and forth like a pendulum. The lowest point had been the escalator, but she had swung back the other way when she'd told the others about her bike. It was strange sharing a room with so many other girls. Thank goodness for Delia. From her voice and clothes she was obviously from a posh family, but there was no swank about her and she seemed happy to muck in with everyone. Perhaps she would become the special friend Rosie had wanted for so long. From somewhere in the distance came the sound of a clock chiming twelve.

In the morning it was all rush and confusion. They all stood out in the yard, shivering in their coats while the Union Jack was raised, and sang 'Eternal Father strong to save' through chattering teeth. Then it was back indoors for a meagre breakfast of toast and strong tea.

Petty Officer Challis met them back in their cabin. 'Now girls, what clothes have you brought with you that can be worn for motorcycling? You will not get your uniforms until later.'

Rosie had some slacks and an old tweed jacket, whilst Delia had jodhpurs.

'There are two crash helmets and no boots, I'm afraid. But you'll have to make do at this stage. Here is one-and-six lunch money for each of you.'

They accompanied Knocker and Froggy across

214

London by bus to New Cross Racing Stadium. Rosie stared out of the window at the unfamiliar streets and listened to the varying accents of the passengers.

There were three auxiliary firemen waiting for them, with motor bikes parked in readiness at the side of a cinder track. As she could ride already Rosie set off around the track, stopping and starting to commands. It was not as easy as she had expected as the bike was far heavier than her old Norton, but she battled on, determined to make a good showing. Parking and starting quickly were also difficult with the added weight.

Then it was Delia's turn.

'Don't look so worried, girl,' said one of the firemen. 'I'll not let thee come to any harm. Up you get and I'll sit behind you.'

Not only was she a beginner, but being little more than five feet, holding the bike was quite a challenge.

Rosie looked at her face, pale and determined.

'Just get on and I'll sit behind you and explain the gears,' said Gorgeous George, smiling encouragingly.

After a few false starts, when Delia confused braking and acceleration, causing them to jerk along kangaroo fashion, they set off around the track.

'Stop,' he called and Delia jammed on the brakes. 'Start,' and she leapt up and down kicking madly.

'Get off now, Croxley and take a breather.'

'I feel such a great ninny,' she gasped, wrapping her arms across her chest and stamping up and down with the cold.

'You're trying too hard. Just relax and don't cling on so tight to the handlebars. Smoothly does it. We've got two weeks to get you roadworthy, not five minutes.'

At half-past twelve they broke for lunch and went into a café with oil-cloths on the tables and windows steamed up.

'Sausage sarnie and tea, and rice pudding with a dollop of jam, that's favourite,' said Froggy. 'Same all round?'

Rosie and Delia nodded, too cold to think.

Later Rosie stirred the jam into the rice, watching it turn pink before venturing a spoonful. She had enjoyed the morning and was eager for more. 'That wasn't too bad, was it? Least you didn't fall off,' she said to Delia, sitting beside her.

'Out in the traffic this afternoon,' said Knocker. 'You're lucky, you'll have Gorgeous George's arms around you all the way, 'til you gets your confidence.'

'No point in trying too hard then,' smiled Delia.

They all laughed.

'Think I'll forego the pudding,' said Delia, 'I feel queasy. Anyone else want it?' Knocker fell on it without a moment's hesitation.

Rosie made hungry gannet noises and they all laughed uproariously. Walking back with them arm-in-arm she felt part of a gang. Something she'd not experienced since schooldays in the Isle of Wight.

'All for one and one for all,' said Delia, as if she could read her mind.

18

He was rolling over and over and over – crashing, banging, shaking and then nothing. Even rolled in the blanket he shivered. It had been dark when it happened and now, as he pulled the blanket off his face, light streamed in through the glass. Everything was all mixed up. The window in the back of the car seemed to be up in the air and the front corner was squashed up like a concertina. Lionel reached up and touched his head. His fingers came back red and sticky. He tucked them up in his armpits out of sight.

Where was he and what time was it? Where had the man gone? Like a flicker book, pictures raced through behind his eyes. First he was bumping along on Bob's bike with the lamp going on and off, next he was wedged up beside the stinky dog in the porch of the pub, then he was lying along the seat of the car, his nose against the soft leather seat. The car had rocked, as the man got in and started up the motor. Lionel had fallen asleep in the dark with his fire-engine. If he could just find it and hold it he wouldn't feel so frightened. Sweeping his hands along the floor he felt something cold and wet. Screaming and thrashing about in panic, he banged his head under the seat. Reaching up, Lionel clung to the handle of the front passenger door and pulled it down with both hands. It swung open and pitched him onto the ground.

He landed on a tussock of frosty grass. Above him the sky was streaked with orange. Lionel lay there looking about him. He seemed to be half-way down a bank. At the top were railings all bent out of shape, and below him was a railway line. The car was wedged into a tree, its back wheels up in the air. Looking down at it, he began to shake. The cold slippery hand that he had touched earlier would not fade from his mind. His stomach rose up in his throat and he was sick all down his coat. Acid burned his mouth and furred his teeth.

Driven by thirst he began to climb the bank, clutching at bushes and clumps of grass until, gasping and crying, he reached the top. He slid between the railings and found himself on an empty road. On the other side were houses. As he watched, a door opened and a lady came out with a milk bottle. Lionel tried to call to her but his mouth wouldn't make any words. His legs got all wobbly and stopped working. Everything went round and round, and the road came up to meet him with a great smack.

Thelma hated early mornings. Half asleep, ratty and cold, she slouched behind Pearl and Daisy up to the main gate of Priddy's Hard. Worse still were the clothes she'd had to wear. What a sketch she looked in the lace-ups Pearl had lent her, and the raincoat. Navy didn't suit her, it drained her face of colour. The two of them nagged her to hurry, and she'd barely had time to put on a slick of lipstick or drag a comb through her hair. Back at the pub she used to take a good hour to make herself presentable – seeing to her make-up and getting the seams of her stockings straight, and all the little details that showed her off to the best advantage.

'Morning, ladies,' the policeman on the gate greeted them. 'Who's this then?'

'I'm Thelma Scoggins, just starting,' she said, glaring at him.

'See you at the canteen dinner-time, 'bye.' Pearl walked off arm-in-arm with her pals.

'Ah, yes, Scoggins. You're for the Rectifying Shop. Daisy, you're going with her 'til your hands are better. Harry Gibbons will be along in a minute. Come and stand in here.'

Cripes! What was rectifying when it was at home? This wasn't the job she'd hoped for. Thelma stood holding her brass token, scowling at the workers trooping through the gates, laughing and chatting as they went. For two pins she'd jack it in and go home. They wouldn't have missed her yet at the Nile, thinking she was still at Romsey with Lionel. She could nip back over the ferry and be back to Nelson Street in no time – except that she'd handed back the key.

'Harry, this is Thelma Scoggins, your new recruit, and Daisy Fletcher,' said the policeman.

Her heart sank. The man in the greasy cap looked a real old misery-guts, ugly too.

He took up his token and stumped off down the path. 'What bloody use are they gonna be, either of them,' he flung over his shoulder.

'You ain't no Prince Charming yerself,' she snapped.

Ignoring her, Daisy ran ahead and tapped him on the shoulder. 'You the Harry Gibbons what was in the Third Hampshires in the last lot?'

'What if I am?' he snapped.

'Served with my late husband Henry Spurgeon at Ypres, didn't you?'

Harry turned around and smiled at Daisy. 'You kin to Henry? Well! Don't that beat all? Fine chap he was 'til the gas took 'im.'

They walked on nattering together like she was invisible. Thelma could have flounced off if it wasn't for the two pounds in the offing at the end of the week. As they reached a tall corrugated-iron shed Harry stopped. 'Changing-room round the corner.'

Undaunted, Daisy went inside and took down two or three navy boiler-suits from the hooks along the wall. She took off her coat and skirt and began to climb into the legs of the boiler-suit, and then to button up the front. It had been made for a giant, from the length of the arms and legs. She sat on a bench and began rolling up the sleeves. 'Come on, Thelma,' she coaxed, 'give it a go. This pair looks more your size.'

'Wish I'd never come. It'll be bloody slavery and that old codger'll be a right barrel of laughs.' She snatched the overall from Daisy and wrestled herself inside. Between them they turned the scarves into reasonable-looking turbans, and after visiting the lavatory went through the large double doors of the rectifying shop.

Inside there were men standing at long work-benches, banging, screwing and drilling. There were sparks falling from welding tools.

'Daisy, you come alonga me, and you,' he glared at Thelma, 'over there with big Jim.'

'What's your name?' a slow-looking bloke with greasy hair and a moustache asked her.

'Thelma,' she muttered, staring down at her lace-ups.

'We're working together. You're me new mate.' He held out his hand and grasped hers in a vice-like grip. 'Over here we're rectifying the shells.' He handed her a wooden mallet and pointed to some large metal cylinders with pointed ends stacked in what looked like milk crates. 'See them dents? We gives them a bash with the mallet then it gets them all smooth-looking again.'

'What's the point of that?' she asked.

'Make them ready to use again. The flanges will be remilled, they'll be filled with gunpowder, sealed up, repainted and sent off to the fleet again.'

Thelma went at the shells with all her might. She belted the end with her mallet, taking out all her anger and disappointment.

'Jesus Christ, what you think you're doing? Putting more bloody dents in than you're taking out.'

'Do it yerself. Never wanted to come 'ere in the first place.'

Harry stalked across from his bench and gripped her by the shoulder. 'You listen to me, you silly bitch. This ain't a game! Men out there on ships whose bloody lives depend on what we does here – ain't no glamour to this lark but we gotta keep the fleet topped up with the right goods. Can't beat them Jerrys with duff ammo, so stop buggering about and do what Jim tells ya.'

Thelma was almost crying with humiliation. Showing her up like that, the miserable old sod. Coming over to Gosport, she'd jumped from the frying-pan into the fire. Well, she'd stick it out for a few weeks and then look around her. There must be something better than this.

'Just stand there and watch me,' said Jim. 'You'll soon get the hang of it. The tea urn'll be round in an hour. Treat you to a cheese roll.'

Thelma gave him one of her winning smiles. She wasn't operating on full power but just enough to get the big dope on her side. Casting her eye around the shed, she looked to see if there was anyone worth the wattage. No, they were all either old codgers or sub-standard one way or another. Perhaps there might be someone in the canteen at dinner-time. Having someone fanciable at hand was what made life worth getting up for. Otherwise it was like eating food with no salt – hard chewing and no flavour.

From across the shed she could see that Daisy and Harry were yarning away together. That was the difference between them. Old Daisy made friends with men, whereas she wanted their attention, wanted to be centre stage. Ooh! roll on tea break.

No, she didn't like her, not one bit. It wasn't just that Thelma was pretty, something that was guaranteed to knock Pearl's confidence, but she was hard and calculating. Funny, what few bits and pieces she'd brought with her for someone leaving home. And what she had got was of no use at Priddy's. High heels and earrings, who did she think she was?

'We'll give her chance to settle in and then we'll see how things go,' Daisy had said last night, as the two of them had sat over their cocoa in the kitchen.

Pearl smiled; she was a dear, always thinking the best of people and giving them a second chance. 'How d'you meet her?' Pearl had asked.

'Told you, down at the pub near Charlotte Street.' Daisy turned the page of her gardening book.

'No, I mean how did you know her, first off?'

'It was at our Greta's wedding, me youngest sister. Thelma was a pal of hers. They'd met over at some dance hall in Pompey. After the wedding we had a bit of a do in the hall next to the church. Someone brought a gramophone. Put on a Charleston record, and Thelma and this sailor what she was with got up and danced.' Daisy smiled. 'Ever so good they was. Everyone stopped yarning and watched her. Like magic she was. All the men's eyes was sticking out like organ stops.'

Being a Sunday night they had gone to bed by ten, ready for the early start at Priddy's the next day. Before putting out her light, Pearl picked up the envelope with the French postmark and read the letter inside, once more. It had arrived on the first of November and had taken all her courage to open it and see what her brother had to say.

Dear Pearl,
I have joined up and am now a driver in the army. Been over here now for some time. I know more about

the roads of France now than any back home. Everything the army needs we carry: food, barbed wire, engine spares, ammunition, medicine, motorbikes, weapons and men. There are thousands of us over here getting stuck in. Mostly it's boring, no shooting or bombing just digging and building and bloody bullshine. So far Bluey Hayes, my pal and me have got along fine. I have tried to remember a bit of my school French and I'm adding to it every day.

I am billeted with a French family. The father Guillaume works in the local coal mine and his wife Therese and daughter Lydie work up at the local chateau where we've got our headquarters.

I have done some thinking. Mum dying and all that drove me mental. Now I am getting myself back on an even keel, so to speak. In the army you're fed and clothed and told what to do. The routine of it suits me. Bluey and I look out for each other. Sergeant says I got to give the address of my next of kin and make you a weekly allowance, so I have allotted you five shillings. You will get the payment book soon. Leaving Gosport and that madness saved my life. Been remembering stuff from when we were kids. Perhaps you and me can start again – we were pals once.

Bye, Kenny.

Pearl had not thought about him for months. 'All that madness,' as Kenny called it, had been locked away. Since moving in with Daisy she had become settled and happy. Stopped saying sorry, she had, and was laughing all the time. After all this time, she didn't know what she felt about her brother. Once she had loved him, but now? Pearl didn't think so. *'Perhaps you and me can start afresh.*' Was that supposed to be an apology? No, Kenny could stew a while before he got a letter from her. And as for the money – didn't he owe it to her after all his thieving out of her purse last year? Pearl realised with a jolt that she wouldn't care if she never saw him again. All she felt was anger at herself for not fighting back.

What would really set the seal on everything would be for Dad to come home safe and sound. His last letter had not sounded hopeful.

Your Uncle Frank and me had been counting the days 'til we got sent home but that doesn't seem to be happening. Most likely we shall have to stay out here until old Hitler's been given the push. You can bet that the pair of us were really chocker when we got the news. All of us will just have to make the best of it my sweetheart and as the song says, Keep smilin' through. *It is such a load off my mind to know that you are enjoying life with Daisy. She is a real brick.*

Pearl wondered about telling her father news of Kenny. No, she would wait 'til she got the payment book. No point in raising his hopes too soon. What she'd got to do was nerve herself to go back home and get the place cleaned up and ready for letting. No point in letting it go to rack and ruin.

They were all in the canteen on Friday dinner-time tucking into fish-and-chips. Daisy was wedged between Pearl and Thelma. Opposite were the other girls from the cordite lab: Poppy, Ruth and Marj. It was the best time of the week:

225

they had been paid and all the talk was of going to the pictures, of dancing, news of their boyfriends away in the services.

'You bin over Pompey to see *Wuthering Heights* on at the Plaza? Me and Poppy wept buckets, that Lawrence Oliver, ever so handsome, sort of dark and brooding,' said Marj.

'Where d'you go dancing over here?' asked Thelma, blowing smoke rings.

'Fort Brockhurst, and sometimes there's a dance at *Dolphin*. Them submariners is ever so friendly.'

'Might give it a try.'

Pearl watched her. Thelma never gave anything away, yet she got people to tell her things. She had her eye on the canteen manager. He was not good-looking but had a certain swagger. He also had a car, a fact not lost on Thelma, hence that business the other night when they were going home. She'd held back, saying she had left her umbrella behind, and then sailed past in his car.

Pearl was seething. 'Scheming bitch, told you she was only out for number one.'

Daisy had laughed. 'We'll have to give her ten out of ten for initiative. She certainly doesn't let the grass grow under her feet.'

It riled Pearl that Thelma practised the same initiative at home. She was always tired when it came to washing up or cleaning the house, even got Daisy to make her sandwiches.

'You got a flair for making them,' she'd said, 'besides never could cut bread straight.'

Had a nasty habit of borrowing stuff and never giving it back, had Thelma. Since she came to stay, Pearl had taken to locking her best things in a suitcase under her bed. She watched her, sitting at the table flicking through the pages of last night's *Evening News*, probably looking at the times of the pictures and the dances.

'Get us another slice of that jam roll, there's a love,' said Daisy, as Pearl went up to the counter to get her pudding. 'I feel ravenous today.'

Back at the table with the two dishes, Pearl picked up a copy of the paper lying on the seat beside her and began to read in between eating her pudding. It was the usual mixture of news: submarines sunk by U-boats, Hitler swaggering about all over the place, and police fining people for showing a light in the blackout. There were adverts for Christmas stuff in the shops and what was on at the pictures and then she noticed something else. *'Police Concerned for Safety of Evacuee Missing now for a Week.'*

'Eight-year-old Lionel Scoggins went missing in Romsey where he had been evacuated in the care of Mrs Alice Neasom. He had been left outside a local pub by Robert Neasom on Friday night and has not been seen since.

Adding to this mystery is the disappearance of Lionel's mother, Miss Thelma Scoggins, from the family home in Nelson Street, Portsmouth. She was employed as a barmaid at the Nile by licensee Mr Alec Forrest who said she had not arrived for work on Sunday night and has not been seen since.'

At first she couldn't believe it. The lying scheming bitch! Telling Daisy Lionel was dead, when all the time he was alive. A little kid shoved off to Romsey out of her way. Well, she'd have a few words to say to her, and the sooner the better. Looking across the canteen she saw that Thelma had left. Pearl got to her feet. She shoved the paper under her arm and made for the door. 'See you tonight, Daisy. I gotta bit of business to see to.' She wasn't going to let her soft-hearted aunt divert her from giving that selfish cow a piece of her mind.

'Thought you wouldn't be long,' sneered Thelma, as Pearl rushed into the shed, waving the newspaper in her face.

'Always thought you were a cold-hearted bitch, and this proves it.'

'Must have made your day, Miss Goody-two-shoes. Thing is I wasn't never meant to be a mother. He's better off without me, probably having the time of his life.'

'Won't be the only one – you don't think Daisy'll want you after all the lies you told. Your little Lionel might really be dead by now, it would serve you right.'

'Wasn't planning to stay around anyway. So you can tell who you like, Princess Pearl.' Thelma laughed. 'Should see your face, it'd turn milk sour. By the time you've told them all I'll be long gone.'

'Don't forget to leave my shoes and my raincoat,' snapped Pearl, maddened by her indifference.

Thelma laughed in her face. 'You can stick your shoes where the sun don't shine,' she said, grabbing her bag and flouncing out of the shed.

Pearl stamped back across the grass. She had

expected Thelma to be ashamed at being found out, and frightened at the thought of losing her job and a place to stay. But somehow Thelma had made it appear that she was in the wrong. Made her feel like the school sneak.

'Good riddance,' she yelled to Thelma's retreating figure hurrying towards the main gate.

19

Rosie and her classmates sat astride their bikes grinning at the camera. It was three weeks since they had arrived as raw recruits, and every waking moment had to be accounted for. When they were not in the London traffic they were scrambling through Epping Forest, spattered in mud.

'You must get used to driving over every sort of road surface, through all weathers, keeping your bike in peak condition. The signals are vital: from a change in sailing orders to the transport of essential pieces of equipment.' Petty Officer Lucas looked at them. 'What must you never forget?'

'The message must get through,' they would chorus.

There were hours of map reading, ages testing spark-plugs or changing tyres. They had been issued with their pay books and a complete despatch rider's uniform. They looked admiringly at one another clad in their navy hacking jackets, riding-breeches, and tough black boots. Rosie couldn't help strutting. She linked arms with Delia as they walked back to their cabin. 'Have you invited Gorgeous George, the fascinating fireman, to the dance tonight?'

Her friend blushed. 'He invited himself. Have you got anyone coming?'

Rosie shook her head. Who knew where Blyth was? Besides, she didn't really want to share him with the others. Delia was her friend, they told one another things: yet she had never talked of Blyth, nor even shown her his photograph. The others spoke of their romances quite frankly, and from what they said Rosie knew that she was the only one of them to have gone beyond kissing. She guarded their last afternoon at Lee, not wanting comment or judgment. The heat of the sun and the secrecy had ignited the spark between them, speaking about it would spoil things.

Delia took off her blackout bloomers and stepped into lace-edged French knickers.

Froggy whistled. 'Is that for Gorgeous George's benefit?' she asked.

'Of course not,' she blushed, 'I just hate those dreary drawers. Anyway folks, tonight my brother Justin's coming up from home.'

'What outfit's he in?' asked Knocker, taking the towel from Rosie's neck and shaking the mass of shorn hair out of the window.

'Fleet Air Arm, he's an Observer,' answered Delia. 'How about you? Have you anyone in mind?'

'My bloke's in France, probbly canoodling with some Fifi right this minute.'

Rosie pricked up her ears. Justin, it sounded familiar. Was Delia's brother Blyth's friend, Juss? She'd never heard his surname, so it was possible. She put on her clean white uniform blouse with the starched collar. It was funny, all the time she had been out of uniform she had been dying to wear navy blue: now she was dying to wear something pretty and feminine. That would be one of the things to look forward to

231

when the war was over.

Delia gave her a hug. 'I've been looking forward to a knees-up for ages.'

The dance was at the gymnasium. Petty Officer Challis was in charge of the gramophone. There were glasses of squash and sandwiches curling at the corners. On one side of the hall were the Wrens and opposite them were a few sailors, the fireman instructors and two lads in civvies.

'This is deadly, like a boarding-school hop,' whispered Delia. 'Justin will cringe.'

'Maybe not,' said a voice behind them.

'Juss!!'

Delia was whirled round and round by her brother. Then he turned and spoke to her. 'Rosie, I've been looking at your photo for the last year on Blyth's locker.'

Justin had the same red hair and green eyes as his sister, but sharper features. He was not handsome yet had an interesting face.

'You know Blyth?' Delia's voice was accusing.

'We grew up together.' Rosie was startled.

Her friend gave a relieved smile. ''Bye,' she said, going over to Gorgeous George, who was waving her over to the seat beside him.

'Are you feeling brave?' said Justin, moving to the edge of the dance floor.

Rosie smiled up at him. 'I've heard Blyth talk about you loads of times, but when Delia said she had a brother Justin it didn't click.'

'Worlds within worlds,' he said. 'I don't think Delia quite grasps that you and Blyth are more than chums.'

Rosie tried to follow Justin's lead. When had

Blyth met his sister? Delia was a beautiful thoroughbred and made Rosie feel like a carthorse. Her heart lurched. The record changed tempo. Anne Shelton turned into a squeaky soprano singing at twice the normal speed. Laughing, they gave up in defeat and collapsed onto their chairs.

Red-faced, Challis announced that, 'There will now be a twenty-minute interval,' as she took the record off the turntable.

'Cigarette?' Justin asked, offering her one from his silver case.

'Thanks,' said Rosie. 'I think that would be better than the sandwiches. I thought you were going to be at sea for ages yet.'

'We came into Pompey Dockyard for boiler cleaning this morning. We're hoping to be alongside for Christmas. Nothing's certain, of course, we'll probably get a few jobs flying crates and personnel round the country. But,' he smiled at her, 'you'll be able to ask Blyth yourself. He'll be here soon.'

Rosie swallowed. She had barely begun to guess at how Delia was involved with Blyth, and now he would be here any minute. She could see her rival talking with George yet, at the same time, watching the door. Let's see what Mister Succulence does with the two of us, she thought, grinding her cigarette into the saucer.

'Venture a quick-step?' Justin held out his hand.

They were passing the double doors when Delia rushed forward. Rosie's footsteps faltered as her friend flung herself into Blyth's arms. Justin was talking, but Rosie's attention was on

Delia carrying off her boyfriend like a trophy.

Justin whisked her diagonally across the floor towards them. As they approached the music stopped, and Blyth stood up to kiss her. Still Delia held his arm.

'We'll get some drinks,' Justin said, steering his sister away.

'See you later, darling,' she said, over her shoulder.

Blyth held out a chair for Rosie then sat down beside her. He rumpled her hair. 'So you're a Jenny Wren,' he smiled. 'How d'you like it?'

'Good, it's good. Get our postings next week.' Pleased as she was to see him, there was a worm of doubt nagging her. Was she making a mountain out of a molehill? All the flirtation seemed to be coming from Delia, but Blyth wasn't fighting her off.

'Gin all round?' he asked, topping up the squash with a bottle from inside his jacket. 'Where are you two girls hoping to go?'

'We both put in for Plymouth,' said Delia, resuming her hold on Blyth's arm.

Rosie sipped her gin. Everything had shifted. She wanted to snatch his arm away from Delia, wanted to scream and shout and rage, but sat there like a pudding.

The gramophone was rewound and the interval was over. 'Take your partners for a ladies' request quick-step,' Challis announced.

Rosie felt someone tap her on the shin. Blyth was winking at her. As Delia got to her feet Rosie grabbed his hand. 'Want to dance?' she gabbled.

'Thought you'd never ask,' he teased.

He smiled down at her as they whirled around the floor. 'What's up? You don't seem very pleased to see me.'

'Haven't had a chance with Delia mooning all over you.' How whiney and kid-like that sounded. 'It's just been such a surprise.'

'We've got to make the most of surprises, Rosie. Why didn't you invite me?'

'I didn't know where you were and didn't think you'd come.'

'If anyone made a play for you, I'd make sure that they knew that I was in the picture. One thing I learnt with my family.'

'What?' she said, staring at the paper flowers tied around the refreshment table.

'If you don't say what you want, you've no chance of getting it.' He swung her round the corner. 'Dinner-time in our house you were either the quick or the hungry.'

All the tension of the evening evaporated. 'What makes you think it's you I want?'

'The way you froze her out. But you'd have let her take over if I hadn't kicked you. Why?'

'It was up to you.'

'No, it was down to you. You never even said my name to her in three weeks. As far as she knew I was a free agent.'

'And are you?'

'What do you think?' he said kissing her again.

The music stopped and they went back to their seats. Delia was sitting with Gorgeous George and Justin was talking to Petty Officer Challis.

'I hear you're down in Pompey,' she said.

'Good, isn't it,' he grinned. 'You've got leave, I

hear. Delia's invited me down to Hazlewood but I could be persuaded to go back to Pompey with you.'

Rosie was tired of being played with. 'You please yourself,' she snapped, striding down the hall and just clearing the doors before she burst into angry tears.

I'm worth more than that, she thought, swirling her foot in a puddle and watching the rainbow slick of oil disintegrate. Her nose was running and she couldn't find her hankie. Angrily she rubbed her nose against her sleeve.

'We used to do that at home,' said a voice behind her.

'What you doing out here,' she snapped at Blyth, 'come to gloat?'

'Rosie, stop letting Delia piss us around.'

'You said you were going down to stay with her,' she sniffed.

'That was to get you mad, Miss Bloody-hard-done-by.' He kissed her. 'Let's talk about me seeing you at the Nile and testing out the bar-room carpet again.'

She punched him in the ribs. 'You are so pleased with yourself.'

'I need firm handling,' he laughed, holding her close and bending to kiss her.

They stood in an archway out of the light. He pulled her to him, pressing her body against his. She kissed him back.

'I want more than this,' he whispered. 'I want us to be somewhere where we can be really loving, not five minutes here and there but hours and hours.'

'So do I,' she said.

'So you're nailing your colours to my mast?'

Even in the dark, she knew he was smiling. 'Listen, I'm staying with Inky at his place in Dulwich. Can you meet me tomorrow? Anything special you want to do?'

'Let me surprise you,' she said. 'Ten o'clock by the lions in Trafalgar Square.'

They heard a low whistle. 'That's Juss. Better go back or you'll be locked out.'

'Trafalgar Square,' she said, as they met up with Justin at the door.

He kissed her on the cheek. 'Bye, Rosie, it's been a pleasure.'

'You be careful, Croxley,' said Blyth. 'I've got my beady eye on you.'

'Permission to warm the car up sir?' Juss gave a mock salute.

The cabin was in darkness. Rosie undressed and got into bed. She looked towards Delia's bunk, wondering what they would say to each other next morning.

When she woke up, Rosie gathered her clothes together and crept to the bathroom. She and Delia had tentatively planned to go for a look at Oxford Street. Rosie dropped a note on her bed and went down to breakfast.

The morning was cold and crisp. She went to the tube station and, holding her breath, stepped onto the escalator. At the bottom she stepped off smartly and smiled. Another hurdle cleared. Proud of herself, she negotiated the ascending escalator at Trafalgar Square and went out into the wintry sunshine. She remembered it from the

237

visit with Albert and Gran. Everything had been on a grand scale. Water gushed from the triumphal fountain and the statues dwarfed the people milling around them. Now, with all the statues boarded up and sandbags everywhere, she felt sad. But they couldn't shroud Nelson's column. Rosie felt a stab of homesickness. Her street had been named after him. He had left for Trafalgar from Gran's beach to fight Napoleon. Now there would be another admiral squaring up to Hitler. She bought a bag of birdseed, flinging a handful up in the air. The pigeons clustered at her feet, grey heads bobbing. 'Breakfast over,' she said, emptying the bag. They rose in a cloud and crossed the square to their next meal-ticket. The lions reminded her of the ones at the Guildhall, in Portsmouth. Lily had told her once about the Peace Pageant, after the war in 1919, how she and her friend Dora had climbed onto their backs to watch the procession.

She caught sight of Blyth walking towards her, and watched the smile break out and spread across his face. She was swept up into his arms, and he kissed her.

'Hello, juicy lips, what we doing?'

'Got to find Cork Street,' she said, taking his arm, 'we're on a special mission.'

After getting the directions from a paper seller they arrived at the Neptune Maritime Gallery. 'It's in here,' she said.

Blyth held open the door for her, and she was approached by a man in a black jacket and striped trousers.

'How may I be of assistance?' he asked.

Rosie took a crumpled envelope out of her pocket and handed him the card inside. 'The painting was done by Albert Pragnell, the marine artist, and won a prize.'

'I shall have to consult the catalogue,' he said, 'if you would like to take a chair, and you, sir. I shall be with you in a moment.'

Blyth took off his cap. 'You mean Albert's got a painting hung in here? Really?'

Rosie grinned. 'It belongs to me,' she whispered. 'I can't wait to see it.'

They sat on the gold chairs looking about them at the pictures of admirals glaring out of their frames, and sailing ships entering foreign harbours.

'You will find it in the Anson Portrait Room at the top of the stairs.' The attendant returned the card to her. 'Show this to Mr Spence, he will find it for you.'

Hand-in-hand they climbed the stairs.

'Number seventy-five, Madam, down the end there, past the second column.'

Rosie gasped. She had not expected such a large painting. She stood and stared at it, unable at first to make sense of it, there was so much to see. Blyth stood behind her with his hands on her shoulders. It was of Gran's beach. Far out to sea was HMS *Victory*, then passing closer to the shore was a modern destroyer. The beach was crowded with women waving and children throwing stones. There was the Round Tower where her grandmother had been found as a baby. Now she stood with Lily, who was waving a green shawl, and Miriam. 'Look,' she whispered, 'I'm there with my mum waving. And, I can see you with a telescope, and the twins.'

'There's my Mum smiling, and Dad,' whispered Blyth.

At the sides of the painting were little houses with women sitting sewing, or nursing babies or writing letters. All of them gazed out of the windows towards the ships. In the middle of the frame at the bottom was the title: *'Beatrice, a Woman of the Fleet.'*

Rosie stood, hands up to her face, gazing and gazing at it. There was her grandmother's life set out before her. It was, as Beattie had said, a love letter from Albert, and now it belonged to her.

Blyth's arms tightened around her and Rosie leant her head back against his chest. She felt blessed. It didn't matter that she had no home to put it in. Its mere existence was a joy to her. She could come and see it whenever she was in London, and feel instantly connected to all that her grandmother's life had meant.

'Oh Blyth,' she whispered, 'isn't it wonderful?'

'That's where we came from, who we are,' he said.

'I'm glad you're with me. I don't have to explain.'

Blyth gripped her shoulders, his voice faltering. 'Any time I pictured my mum she was looking mad and frightened. Now I can see her happy, I can get that into my head and cross out the other picture. Thought I couldn't remember her, but I've got this blurry bit of being danced around in her arms, she's laughing.' He said no more.

'Remember I took the old street sign up to

Albert? I thought it would be a great souvenir, but it's not the sign, it's the spirit in the people. All of them are on the beach there, even if they didn't live in Lemon Street, they have that grit and humour. Nelson Street's got that same spark too.'

When she turned around he rubbed his hand across his eyes.

'Come on, old raggy-britches, let's go and have a cuppa.'

Arm-in-arm they stepped back into London.

Blyth bought their tea from a kiosk in the park. She warmed her hands on the thick cup and stamped her feet. 'What's up? Still feeling sad?'

'Thinking,' he said. 'Why don't we get married?'

Rosie looked at him, amazed. 'Cripes, Blyth, what brought that on?'

'Looking at the picture. We belong, we understand what makes us tick.'

'Do you love me?'

'More than gobstoppers, or sherbet dabs, more than my Fairey Swordfish. With you I don't prat around, with you I'm me.' He tapped his chest. 'I know it in here.'

'Marriage,' she said trying out the word. 'It's a big leap in the dark, 'specially now. Shouldn't we wait 'til later, 'til the war's over?'

'We haven't got a later, you know that. I need you now.'

'You haven't asked me what I need,' she said. His blue eyes searched her face. 'Do you love me?'

'I've loved you ever since the day in the grave-yard. But marriage, I don't know. You've never

241

given me any hint we were heading in that direction.'

'Rosie, every time I leave the deck and fly out with Juss and Simmo it could be the last time. It's all borrowed time. I can't think or plan ahead.'

'Can't we just be together as if we were married, making love and being faithful?'

'I don't know, it's just a feeling.'

She took his hand. 'I'm not going anywhere, well, not in my head. You're my one true love, Blyth. Can that be enough just 'til I've really thought about it?'

'Just for today,' he said. 'But it won't stop me asking.'

They walked and talked and held each other, even managed a teacake at Lyons Corner House. And then in a flash they were back at New College saying goodbye.

'See you in Pompey next week,' he said. 'I'll be simmering to see you.'

Rosie ran up the stairs to the cabin, her face scraped red by Blyth's stubble. On her bed lay a note in Delia's handwriting.

Dear Rosie,

I have gone on leave. According to the board we are both posted to Portsmouth, so we shall have to clear the air between us. Why didn't you tell me about Blyth? I thought we were friends. Why didn't he tell me when he was home with us last time? He certainly didn't give the impression that he had a girlfriend. I've gone home to lick my wounds.

Delia

Rosie stood by the window watching the light fade, determined not to let her friend's heartbreak spoil her day with Blyth. He certainly needed firm handling and Rosie was determined not to be a pushover.

20

Lionel watched the nurse peeling the poultice off his chest. It had become cold and clammy. Soon she would open the tin and spread the grey paste onto a white bit of stuff and make it into a sandwich. After that, she would test it against the back of her hand and then bandage it around his chest where it sat cosy and warm.

'How's that, my little man?' She put her head on one side and winked at him.

Lionel winked back. Her liked her because she didn't keep asking him things. Questions made his head ache. He didn't know who he was or where he was. Sometimes he felt as if he were floating up by the ceiling and looking down on the boy that was himself. Sometimes his chest hurt, and thick gluey stuff came into his mouth and made him sick. Pictures flashed in his brain. He was falling over and over and everything was banging about. Then he was walking and crying for ever and ever.

It must be night-time because the nurse sat at the desk near him and put a green cloth over the light, it shone on her yellow hair, making her look like a lady in a Christmas card. She drew the curtains and he went to sleep. Every time he woke up the nurse was there cutting up bits of cloth and putting them in a big silver drum.

Now it was afternoon visiting time. Nobody

244

came to see him except sometimes a nurse would come and sit by the bed and chat. Then a man came with a camera.

'Hello, Sonny, what's your name?'

He looked at him. He was a bit like a pixie: the tops of his ears were pointed and behind one was a cigarette, and behind the other a pencil. Drawing up a chair, he turned it the wrong way round and sat across it resting his hands on the back.

'Dunnow.'

He took off his coat, and he was wearing a blue-and-white scarf.

'Play up, Pompey,' Lionel said. It was the day on the coach with Joe and everyone. They'd all been singing and he'd swung the big wooden rattle, clackety-clack.

The man took off his scarf and gave it to him, winding it around his neck.

'Can I keep it?' he asked.

'If you let me take your picture.'

The light flashed and he smiled again and then he closed his eyes. He wanted to be back on the big bus with the singing. 'My name's Joseph,' he said.

Miriam queued up with her neighbours at the Portsea Island Co-operative Society's offices in Fratton Road, simmering with excitement. It was divvy day. For every pound spent in their stores, the Co-op credited ninepence to each customer's account, provided they quoted their membership number with each purchase. It had been a special treat for her and Beattie, twice a year; one that the old lady came down from Romsey to share with her, even though she no longer had a Portsmouth number. The June pay-out was not as exciting as the December one, which came a fortnight before Christmas.

Once having got their divvy, she and her mother-in-law would cross the road to the main Co-op store and treat themselves to coffee and cakes in the restaurant. Afterwards, armed with their lists, they would work their way through the various departments until they were spent up. Back at the Nile a beef casserole would be pottering along on regulo 3 to be accompanied later with mashed potato – provided Alec had remembered to set a match under the saucepan – and topped off with an accompanying glass of stout.

'It's bin a Godsend to women, has the divvy,' Beattie would say, 'given them a bit of money of their own, a bit of independence.'

Today Miriam had invited Connie to accompany her. Her neighbour had knocked on the pub door promptly at nine o'clock, neat as ever, and wearing her favourite Yardley cherry lipstick.

'Me badge of courage,' she had said to her, after her men were killed. 'My Arthur liked to see me properly turned out. I owes it to him to keep me standards up.'

How brave she was. Her home was still as spick and span as ever, with the net curtains washed each week and windows cleaned. Having no one now to knit for, she had started making jumpers for the young woman next-door with young growing children.

Once Miriam had met Connie at the post-box in Commercial Road. 'Just sending off a letter to

Arthur and the boys.'

Miriam had stood there not knowing what to say, anxious that Connie was not coping with her bereavement as well as she had thought.

'It's a habit, d'you see, done it nearly all my life. Begun when Arthur and me was courting. Sixteen when I sent him the first letter. What's that, nearly thirty years ago? Only way I can cope is to think of them as being away and me keeping them in touch with what's going on.' She had touched her arm. 'You won't tell no one will you, my duck? I don't put my address inside and they don't go nowhere, just gets tore up by the post office.'

'Our secret,' Miriam had said, squeezing her hand.

'What d'you fancy?' she said now, as they sat together in the Co-op restaurant.

'A nice Congress tart please, duck, and a cup of coffee.' She nodded to a neighbour at a table near the window. 'Been looking forward to this.'

'Used to come here with Mother, she loved it. Doesn't seem possible she's been gone two years, now.' She felt awkward, as soon as she said it. What was the death of a woman in her eighties, who had led a full life, compared to Connie's loss?

'She was a gem. We used to get on like a house on fire. Always pictures her by the piano, singing along with Bernice. Her and Mister Pragnell was real love-birds, wasn't they? Haven't seen the old fellow down here for ages.'

'He came over when Rosie went off up to London, and took her to the station. Promised me he's coming down for Christmas.'

'Proper gent is Mr Pragnell. Our boys used to like talking to him about the sailing navy. Christmas, I don't really know what I'll do about that as yet.'

Miriam smiled. 'Well, there I might be able to help you. I've got a favour to ask. I wondered if you could see your way clear to giving Alec and me a hand for a couple of hours a day.'

Connie seemed to be gazing into space.

'You don't have to make your mind up straight away. But now that Thelma's hopped it we're a bit stretched. I wondered if you could give us a hand with a bit of cleaning and suchlike. Only if you've got the time.'

'Time! Cripes, Miriam I'm the millionaire of time. Don't know what to do with myself. By ten o'clock each day I've cleaned, tidied round and shopped and there's the whole of the rest of the day stretched out before like a bloomin' desert.'

'So, will you?'

Connie beamed. ''Course I will and gladly. Arthur will be really pleased when I tell him. Thought a lot of you and Alec, so did the boys.'

'That's settled then. After dinner we'll sort out your hours. Let's see what they've got downstairs. I've seen a red jumper with beads on that would just suit Rosie.'

Miriam linked her arms with Connie. 'Wish Beattie could've seen how she's turned out. She would have been so thrilled.' Again a vague depression settled on her. Soon it would be Christmas club night again and there would be no Mother, no Rosie and no Thelma. The war cast a great grey fog over everything. It wasn't just the blackout, though that was bad enough leaving everyone banging about in the dark, nor was it the daily diet of bad news, or the pictures of Hitler swanking about with his generals. There were new young sailors propping up the bar, now. How long would they last, she wondered.

They had all got ration-books and been told to register with their local grocers. After Christmas rationing would start.

'Be fairer all round,' Alec had said. 'Why should the nobs be able to stockpile stuff? About time they were put in their place.'

'You sound like a proper Red,' Miriam had teased. 'When's the revolution?'

'Soon as the pub closes me and Joseph will set up the barricades.'

'What it means is, we've got to make the most of this Christmas before the shortages start. Reckon sugar'll be one of the first things to go.'

After a couple of hours trudging between departments at the Co-op Connie and Miriam called it a day. Bags laden with family presents, raffle prizes for the pub and a couple of jars of mincemeat, they sank down on the back seat of the bus. When they arrived back at the Nile Miriam steered her friend to the armchair in the living-room. 'You sit down there with the paper for five minutes, while I get unpacked. We'll sort out the dinner, then Alec can have his with you while I go down with Bernice.'

Connie studied the paper, looking at photos of Nativity plays in infants schools in different Hampshire villages, a picture of Father Christmas visiting an orphanage, sailors delivering firewood to a pensioner. And then she saw it. It was him she was sure of it, the poor little bugger. She raced downstairs and into the bar. 'It's him, it's him, I know it.'

'Blimey, Connie what's up with ya?' asked Bernice, setting down the tray of empty glasses with a thud. 'Who d'you mean? King Kong, Adolph Hitler or Charlie Chan?'

'Our Lionel, look at him, sat up in bed with that scarf round his neck, 'course it's him. He's in the cottage hospital at Castlerise. Bin there weeks he has.'

Alec took the paper and Miriam looked over his shoulder.

'It is him! Listen to this! *"Young boy found unconscious near Botley Station almost a month ago has spoken for the first time. It seemed that he recognised the scarf worn by the reporter who tried to question him. His first words were:* Play up Pompey. *He says his name is Joseph. There is speculation about there being a connection with the evacuee Lionel Scoggins who went missing at the same time."'*

'We'll have to go and fetch him, straight away, no question,' said Connie.

'Hold your horses, girl,' said Alec, studying the picture. 'They don't just give kids away at the door you know. Besides, Thelma might have shown up already and carted him off.'

Bernice snorted. 'In a pig's ear she will. Couldn't care less about her nipper, couldn't Thelma. You can bet your boots she's shacked up with some bloke and bloody good riddance.'

'Castlerise is a hell of a way from here. Best

thing we can do is ring them up and see how the land lies about visiting him.'

'No wonder he's not said nothing,' Connie snapped. 'Poor little scrap, he's marooned out there without a single solitary soul what knows him. I bet if he got a glimpse of your Joe he'd start talking nineteen to the dozen.'

'How do you think you'll get out there?' asked Miriam, amazed at her neighbour's sudden show of spirit.

'Here's the lad that will take me.' Connie turned towards the door where Joseph stood, his face muffled by a scarf.

'Where we off to then? What you all so het up about?'

'You just cast your eye over that paper and tell me what you think.'

All eyes were on him as Joseph scanned the page.

'Jesus! It's Lionel, poor little bugger. What we gonna do? Have to go and get him.'

'I knew it,' Connie was triumphant. 'Knew he'd back me.'

'How?' said Alec. 'Got a car have you?'

'Could go on Rosie's bike.'

'What she gonna say? It's miles, you don't know the way, and the roads are covered in snow and ice.'

'Cripes, Dad, you're making out it's in the back of beyond. There's a road atlas upstairs.'

'What about you, Connie? Be ever so cold on the bike. You got a nasty cough.'

'Never bin more certain: it's what Arthur would've expected. That little lad and Thelma

251

and her mother was our neighbours. I don't know much about a lot of things, but rearing lads, I'm expert in. Rattling about in my house like a pea in a colander I am. If he wants to there's a home for Lionel with me. I won't let him down, you can depend on it.'

His legs felt wobbly and his nose was all sore and crusty. It was better being out of bed though. Tomorrow he was going to help the nurses decorate the Christmas tree. For now he was making a long paper-chain. There was a stack of coloured paper strips on the table and a big pot of glue. It had been better yesterday when the big boy was with him, but then his mum and dad had come and taken him home. Now, there was only him, a screaming baby and a girl, but she didn't count.

He was frightened that Mrs Neasom would come and get him. Would Mum come? P'raps she didn't know where he was. He didn't know where he was either, not really, just that it wasn't Romsey and it wasn't Nelson Street. One of the nurses had asked him what he wanted for Christmas. Lionel was scared to put it into words in case it didn't come true. And, if it didn't happen he didn't know what he would do.

Connie had never felt so cold. They had in the end not set off when she wanted but had gone on the Sunday two days later. Joe was on duty in the evening, so they left at eight in the morning. She was swathed in a balaclava, a scarf, mittens and Rosie's motor-cycle boots. She had wanted to come but it would be Joe that Lionel would want to see, not Rosie.

'You never liked him and he didn't like you,' Joe had told her. 'Just lend us the bike. 'Course I'll take care of it. You get the decorations up and stop bossing.'

The countryside looked like a Christmas card but Connie wouldn't want to live out here, miles from the shops. No, she was a townie: you could keep all this frozen scenery. Joe stopped the bike at a cross-roads and they both got off and stamped about. He got the road atlas out of one of the panniers, and rubbed his goggles clean with his handkerchief.

'Mad buggers, aren't we?' he said, as he stared down at the map, 'coming out here, this weather.'

'Be worth it in the end.' Connie dug into her jacket pocket and fetched out a bag of rum-flavoured toffees. 'Best I can do,' she said, unwrapping one for him.

'Ta. I got it, we turn left and it's up that hill there.'

'It's cured me of wanting a bike. Tell you, Joe, it's got to be a Rolls Royce or nothink. Right, we back on board?'

'Lionel, we don't have a Lionel,' the sister said. 'He calls himself Joseph Forrest.'

'Just let us see him, Sister, if you please,' said Connie. Woman was as starchy as her apron. 'Course, she had to be careful about the kids but surely she didn't think they'd come kidnapping out here – plenty of stray nippers in Pompey.

'I live next door to Lionel's family in Nelson Street in Portsmouth. Joe here lives in the pub

253

few doors along. Name's Joseph Forrest. Little boy looks up to him.'

'You're not his father then?'

Joe laughed. 'Blimey, I'd have to have got started at twelve.'

The sister blushed. 'Very well, now I don't want you to tell him anything. Just sit and talk with him and let the remembering come from him.'

'Any chance of a cup of tea?' asked Connie, peeling off her balaclava.

'You sit there and I'll get one of the nurses to fetch you some.'

'That's very kind of you, Matron.' As the woman rustled out of the hall, Connie winked up at Joe. 'A bit of soft soap works wonders.'

Lionel was seated at a table, swamped in a dressing-gown, looking down at a jigsaw. Joe walked ahead of her. She watched him take the other chair and held her breath.

Lionel continued to stare at the table.

Joe picked up a piece of jigsaw. 'Where d'you think this goes then?' he said.

Lionel looked up at him. 'Joe,' he whispered. 'Joe, Joe.' Pushing back the chair, Joe held out his arms. Lionel rushed onto his lap. 'Joe, Joe,' he gasped. Burrowing his head into the thick wool jacket he began to cry.

Connie had to make do with rubbing her tears away with her coat sleeve.

'I lost the fire-engine,' Lionel sobbed. 'The one you give me, I lost it.'

'Don't matter, mate. Make you another one,' whispered Joe.

21

Kenny Bunting stood outside the jeweller's in Les Armandiers comparing the merits of the various rings. In his pocket was a French dictionary in case he got into difficulties. As he stared into the window, his reflection stared back at him. He barely recognised himself as the person he had been a year ago. His life had been transformed.

It began the day he walked through the gate of Buller Barracks in Aldershot. He was plunged immediately into a world run on shouting, drilling and bullshine. It was like being sandpapered – everything rubbed against his nature. Kenny was forced into working and sleeping in company with the other squaddies, with never a moment to himself. That first evening, as he sat in the mess eating his supper, the lad opposite reached across the table and forked a sausage from his plate.

'Don't mind if I help myself? I'm bloody starving, bin sat on a train since yesterday – belly thinks me throat's cut. Name's Bluey Hayes.'

'Kenny Bunting – here take the rest of it.' He slid the plate towards him.

From that first exchange, the ramshackle lad from Barnsley had become his chum. He smiled at the memory. They complemented one another. Bluey was stolid and good-natured, slow to anger, and dogged in his determination to make a go of the army. Kenny knew himself to be quick on the uptake, and miles better at sizing up a situation than the trusting Bluey.

Since they had arrived in Boulogne in their three-ton trucks, they had become more familiar with the roads in France than any back home. The British Army Expeditionary Force was building a defensive link from the old Maginot line to the Channel coast. As part of the Army Service Corps, Kenny and Bluey were carrying men and materials to the front. Mostly the men marched but their equipment and the officers' baggage went by truck. Kenny marvelled at the enormity in numbers and variety of regiments that made up the British Army: Grenadiers, Coldstream Guards, Gordon Highlanders, not forgetting the Hampshires and the Welsh Fusiliers. The RAF was also there in strength.

So far no shots had been fired, no bombs dropped, and few accidents. The 'Phoney War' was what the papers from England called it. For the soldiers in France it had become a boring war: digging holes, building bunkers, and endless exercises. They were browned off and missed having a pint down the local, weekends at home, or sizing up the girls at the dance hall and all it might lead to.

Kenny and Bluey were constantly on the move. Soon they had established watering-holes along the roads from the ports to the supply bases. They picked up a bit of French, mostly from the bar girls, and sometimes more than the lingo was exchanged.

Bluey threw himself into these encounters. 'They can't resist me,' he bragged.

'If you say so,' Kenny said, knowing it to be more bluster than hard fact.

'I do say so. Look at those two we picked up yesterday. Crackers they were, and it was me that did all the chatting up. If it weren't for your Bluey you'd be going back to Pompey untouched.'

'If you say so,' Kenny grinned. For all his bravado, Bluey was shy with women and was destined to be an incurable virgin, unless some woman had lots of time and patience. Since his failure with Rachel Silverman, the doctor's wife back in Gosport, Kenny was wary of women. He was no good with them. He wanted too much and misread the signals. But the roadside encounters were light-hearted and wine-laced. They meant nothing. Kenny smiled: that was before he met Lydie.

At first when he had been billeted in Les Armandiers with the Brechards he had felt awkward and tongue-tied. It wasn't just the language, it was living so close together with strangers. To begin with he kept out of their way as much as possible. The old miner was suspicious of his intentions towards his daughter Lydie, and Kenny had no wish to stir up trouble. Madame Brechard, a small neat woman, was civil to him from the beginning. She was a good cook and a keen gardener. Lydie said little to him. She was tall, with a mop of dark curly hair and the bluest eyes he'd ever seen. Everything she did was carried out with an unhurried grace that drew him to her.

Sometimes up at the chateau their paths crossed. Once he had strayed by the kitchen. *'Bonjour,*

Mademoiselle,' he had said.

She looked up and smiled. *'Café?'* she invited, holding out a jug.

He had blushed, something he had not done for years. *'Merci,'* he mumbled, lumbering into the kitchen and standing by the back door.

She handed him the cup, indicating the sugar and cream on the table. 'For you, Kennet,' she said.

He smiled at the way she said his name but could think of nothing to say.

Lydie moved about the kitchen with assurance, setting a tray with coffee and crescent-shaped rolls. There was one remaining on the table. She spread it with butter and jam and cut it in half, then passed the plate towards him. They stood opposite one another, eating the warm pastry and smiling. Lydie licked her fingers. *'Croissant,'* she said, 'very good.'

'Krrrwason,' he attempted.

Lydie laughed.

From that incident their friendship crept up on them, made up of many more such moments. He took in the washing from the line and left it folded on a chair; Lydie darned a hole in one of his socks. Noticing the dilapidated state of her bicycle, he spent an afternoon cleaning it and pumping up the tyres.

Madame Brechard began to talk to him, teaching him the French names of the vegetables in her garden. One evening she and Lydie sat at the kitchen table, slicing runner beans and packing them in jars between layers of salt. Kenny gestured his willingness to help. He was not trusted to slice the beans but was allowed to pack in the salt.

October blended into November, and found him straying on a Saturday morning into the local church. It was quite large for the village of Les Armandiers, but there had been a miraculous appearance of the Virgin Mary in the last century and so Notre Dame des Armandiers had some importance in the area. The church smelled of old stone and incense. Up a flight of stairs was the balcony. There, the choir sat on Sundays, Lydie being one of them. Kenny had walked past there often and listened to them. He had heard her singing from the kitchen when he was in his room. Her voice was sweet and true. In a corner to the left of the altar was a statue of Mary with Jesus in her arms. It was carved out of wood. Its simplicity attracted him. He went over to it and touched the folds of the Virgin's gown, and then the infant's feet – they were rounded and chubby. Beside the statue was an iron rack filled with candles and, beneath, a collecting box and matches. On an impulse he searched his pockets for a coin and dropped it through the slot. He took up a candle and placed it in the rack, and struck a match to light it.

He sat back in a pew and stared into the small yellow flame. The silence was at first unnerving. It had been some time since he had been totally alone and without any distractions. As Kenny sat there it came to him that he had lit the candle for his mother. He was flooded with all the grief and chaos of that time, all his rage and destructiveness. How ashamed of him she would be if she knew.

He leant forward and rested his head in his hands, tears welling up inside him.

Small sounds intruded into the silence. He was not alone. Kenny tried to pull himself together, what a wreck he must look. But, what did it matter, he was among strangers. Who would care about a red-eyed squaddie miles from home, or, to be brutally honest, a homeless squaddie. Rubbing his eyes, he looked up to see Lydie placing the number cards into the hymn board ready for the Sunday service. Kenny could do nothing. Ashamed, he bent his head. The sound of the cards being slotted into place continued and then stopped. There were footsteps coming towards him, and then they stopped as she sat down beside him. He could not stop crying. Lydie said nothing, yet her presence calmed him. When it was that she slid her hand along the seat and folded her fingers over his, he didn't know.

Explanations for his tears were beyond him, but with Lydie they proved unnecessary. When at last he came to a shuddering stop she gave him her handkerchief.

'*Merci*,' he managed to mumble.

'I go,' she said, looking at her watch. 'I help *Maman* with *déjeuner*. You will come in a moment, Kenny?'

'Lydie, I'm sorry, I've made a fool of myself.'

'No,' she shook her head. 'It is the war, *la guerre*.'

He smiled, 'Yes, in a moment.'

Walking back to the Brechard home he felt a lightness of spirit that he had not known since before his mother's illness. Guillaume was still sleeping after his night work at the mine, and so he sat at the table between Lydie and Madame Brechard. She set down a plate of rabbit stew in front of him, and began cutting up some bread she had baked earlier. She held the round loaf against her aproned bosom and began slicing towards herself.

Kenny smiled. It reminded him of the way his grandmother did it. He struggled to tell them why. *'Vous, Madame, rappelez moi de ma grandemère.'* He knew it was probably not grammatically correct but the sense of it was there.

Lydie's mother smiled at him. She spread her hands as if encompassing the world. *'Tout le monde c'est pareil,'* she said. They talked and laughed together, but there was a difference. Although he could not understand what was being said, he felt included.

After the meal Madame Brechard settled herself in her chair and took up her knitting.

Lydie began to clear the table and Kenny stood up and carried his dish into the kitchen. He took up a tea towel and Lydie began to wash up.

As he stood there drying the spoons, he wondered if it would be possible to take their friendship any further. 'Films,' Kenny said. 'Do you like films?'

'Films?' She shrugged and spread her hands.

'Cinema?'

'Ah! *Oui*, I like very much.'

'You like to see films with me?'

'It is not possible,' she answered.

'Pourquoi?' he asked, stretching his French to the limit.

'My father he say no, and my mother.'

'Can I ask your father?'

Lydie shook her head.

'Can I ask your mother?'

She smiled at him and shrugged her shoulders.

Kenny laughed as he remembered their first date, with Madame Brechard seated between them eating the chocolates he had bought for Lydie. He could understand their reluctance. Many of the local young men had been called up and sent away from the village, and here were the English Tommies in their homes and eyeing up their women. The situation was not helped by one of the married sergeants leaving a local girl pregnant. Their friendship crept along, made up of meetings at the chateau, whispered conversations when Madame Brechard nodded off in the evenings, and lots of washing up.

Last night when Lydie was at choir practice he had summoned up his courage and sounded out her mother on the subject of marriage. He must know what his chances were. There was no knowing how long the army would stay in Les Armandiers, anything could happen. If Lydie was his wife, perhaps she could go to England and be safely out of the way before the balloon went up and the Germans arrived.

Madame Brechard passed him a skein of wool. He held it out between his hands and she began to wind it into a ball.

He cleared his throat. 'Madame, I like Lydie very much and I want to marry her.' After living with the Brechards for some months he had noticed that she understood far more than she said.

Continuing to wind the wool, Lydie's mother looked at him. Had she understood?

'What is the right way to do this? I ask her father?'

She patted her bosom. 'You ask me.'

'Madame Brechard,' he held her gaze. 'I love Lydie and I want to marry her.'

'Lydie,' she said, 'she love you?'

'I don't know. I know she likes me but love, I don't know.'

'You have a wife in England?'

'No, no, I am not married.'

'Your family?'

Kenny felt like a piece of toast under the burning eyes of Madame Brechard.

'My father is a sailor, a mariner – in Singapore. My mother is dead. I have a sister, Pearl.'

She smiled and patted his hand. 'You are sad, Kenneth?'

'Yes,' was all he could manage.

Seeming to have come to a decision, she put down the wool. 'If Lydie want you, if she love you, I will talk with Guillaume.'

Kenny sneaked a look at the clock. It would be another hour before Lydie came back. He didn't think he could sit still that long. He had not understood what his next move should be. Things were different in France. Did Madame Brechard intend that she should ask Lydie first, or was it now up to him to propose?

Giving him no clue, she took another skein from the sack and pressed it into his hands. He had begun to think that the clock had stopped when it began to strike eight. It was followed by the click of the gate and Lydie's footsteps up the path.

Madame Brechard got to her feet. 'I make *café*, you speak with my daughter.'

He stood waiting for the door to open, his mouth dry and heart thumping.

Lydie stood in the doorway holding her music case, smiling uncertainly at him.

'Kenny? There is problem?'

'No, oh no, it's just I want to ask you something?'

She blushed. Did she have some inkling of what he wanted? Anxious that her Mother could return at any moment Kenny pressed on. 'Lydie, will you marry me?' She said nothing but looked at him as if something more was required. 'Um,' he struggled on, 'do you love me?'

She giggled nervously. 'You love me?' she asked.

'Yes, yes, of course I do.'

'You wish me to be your wife?'

'Yes, yes, I do. What do you think?'

Lydie smiled. 'I think you good man, Kenny. I think may be I love you. I say yes.'

He crept across the room towards her, aware that at any moment Madame Brechard would come in from the kitchen. Quickly he put his hands on her shoulders and kissed her lightly on the lips.

She giggled and put her hand over her mouth. Kenny had just regained his seat when the kitchen door opened, and Lydie's mother came back into the room carrying a tray of coffee and biscuits. There followed a rapid conversation between the two women, none of which he could follow. Lydie kissed her mother and went upstairs to her room. At the door she crossed her fingers and held them up to him, while Madame Brechard concentrated on her knitting. The clock struck the half-hour. He took another biscuit for the sake of something to do. His mouth was dry, and he almost choked trying to swallow down the biscuit. It was purgatory sitting there under the inspection of her mother, yet how to escape? It was too early to go to his room. It had begun to rain, putting a walk outside his range of choices. Madame Brechard continued to knit, holding the garment under her arm and pushing the other needle rapidly through the stitches. Was there anything he could do to influence old Guillaume into giving his approval? Anything that would make him look favourably on a British Tommy? Whichever way it went, he would have to wait until the morning when he returned from the mine. Then Guillaume's only concern was to bath and have his breakfast before going to bed. Kenny got to his feet and began to collect the cups and plates. 'I will wash them ready for the morning,' he said.

'Ah, *merci*, Kennet,' she said.

It was a relief to move out of the searchlight of her gaze and have something to do. When he had stretched the task out as long as he could, he went down to the privy and sat there trying to calm himself. Lydie had said yes, that was the main thing. Yet he could not begin to rejoice until he had secured her parents' blessing.

'Goodnight,' he said, directly he returned to the house.

Madame Brechard smiled at him. 'Patience, Monsieur, all will be well. Goodnight to you.'

Two against one he thought, as he sat on the edge of his bed. It wasn't until the next evening when he returned from work that he got his answer. Unusually, Guillaume was up and dressed and waiting for him.

'Good evening,' Kenny said, standing in the doorway, trying to gauge the old man's mood.

'You,' he said, 'ask me something?' He raised his eyebrows enquiringly in case there was any misunderstanding.

'Monsieur Brechard, I wish to marry your daughter Lydie. Can I have your permission?'

The reply was long in coming. Kenny swallowed and listened to the ticking of the clock.

Monsieur Brechard got to his feet and crossed the room towards him. 'You marry Lydie, she go to England. Do it quick!'

It was a command, and not at all what he had expected from him.

The kitchen door opened, and Lydie and Madame Brechard came into the room with a tray of glasses and a small dark bottle.

Kenny looked questioningly at the two women. 'Why does your father want you to marry me so fast, umhh,' he struggled. 'To England, *vite, vite?*'

'Away from the war, I be safe,' said Lydie.

He looked at her mother. She said nothing, but he could feel her anxiety. Going over to her, he took her hand. 'I will look after Lydie,' he said. 'I promise.'

'Impossible!' she said. 'She go to England.'

Monsieur Brechard poured them all a measure

of thick red liquid. *'Vive le mariage,'* he said, kissing Kenny on both cheeks. The words were hopeful and celebratory but Monsieur Brechard was not smiling.

Lydie raised her glass. 'England!' she said. There was belief in her eyes and confidence in him.

'England!' he said.

The shop doorbell rang, drawing Kenny back to the task in hand. Coming out of the jeweller's to meet him were Lydie and her mother. As Madame Brechard turned to re-enter the shop, Kenny took his fiancée's hand and smiled at her. Lydie's face was flushed and her eyes were bright with excitement.

Christ, he didn't deserve her! This was madness, getting married in the middle of the war. Anything could happen. But what was the point of playing safe? Sane or insane, your life could be snatched away in an instant. Still holding her hand, he turned and pushed the shop door firmly shut.

22

Miriam set the tray down on her daughter's bed. 'How does it feel to be home again, love?'

Rosie yawned. 'It's good to be back in my own room and not have five other women with me, hearing them snuffling and listening to the beds creaking.' She grinned. 'And the food's better here.'

'I brought my cup along too,' said Miriam, 'we haven't had much time for a chat, what with one thing and another. I need to catch up with you.' Perhaps it was just seeing her daughter in uniform that made her seem a stranger. Rosie had only been away for a month but she was back now on different terms. She would be living in a Wrennery and doing a dangerous job. It would have been a man's job in peacetime. But they were at war, and now her daughter would be in the thick of it.

'The pub feels different, lots of new faces and all of them in uniform. You've taken down all the cap ribbons.'

Miriam sighed. 'It got me down, seeing them about the place, reminding me of all the men that have gone. Those big ships at the bottom of the sea: *Courageous, Royal Oak* and three of the submarines gone, and we're not even counting the merchant ships and fishing boats. Don't even have proper cap ribbons any more, just HMS, no ship's name or nothing. All those lads gone, that used to stand around the bar laughing and chiacking.'

'Any news of Lionel?' asked Rosie, spooning sugar into her cup.

'Well, he's turned up in the cottage hospital at Castlerise. There was a picture of him in the paper. He was calling himself Joseph Forrest. Connie insisted on Joseph taking her out to see him. She is all set to make a home for the little lad.'

'Good old Connie,' laughed Rosie. 'What about Thelma?'

'Vanished,' sighed Miriam. 'I know she used to drive me mad, but we're run off our feet now. Thank God Connie's lending us a hand. Then there's your Dad and his Air Raid Warden meetings. He and old Claude always sniping at each other.' She could hear herself rattling away. What she really wanted to ask her was a hundred miles away from the ARP and gas masks and all the other paraphernalia of the lousy war. She wanted to say, 'I'm frightened that our closeness has gone. Please, don't shut me out of your life.'

The letterbox rattled.

'I'll get it,' Alec called from downstairs.

Rosie put down her cup.

'Letter for Wren Forrest,' he rapped on the door.

'Dad, come in.'

'Morning, love.' He kissed her and held the letter teasingly by the corner. 'Says on the back it's come from Burma.'

Rosie blushed.

269

'Things must have progressed.' He took Miriam's arm. 'We'll leave you to open it in private. Looking at you I should open the window, you're looking a bit flushed. You running a temperature?'

'Oh Dad, just go away.'

Miriam knew what BURMA meant: 'Be Undressed and Ready My Angel.' The letter was from Blyth. She slammed down the breakfast tray, and went downstairs.

Back in the kitchen, she began to fill the kettle. She felt, oh she didn't know what it was, an unnamed knot of unease.

'You making us a cup, love, throat's as a dry as the bottom of a birdcage. Bacon sarnie wouldn't go amiss.'

'In a minute,' she snapped. 'Blimey, Alec, what did your last servant die of?'

'Hey!! I've been up since six and brought you a cuppa. Who's rattled your cage?'

Miriam burst into tears. 'I'm sorry, it's just, oh I don't know everything.'

Alec took her in his arm. 'Our daughter's grown-up. I've been knocked off my pedestal and a handsome sailor's likely having his way with her. Make's me feel angry, afraid, and if I'm brutally honest with myself, jealous.'

'Why jealous?' she asked, resting her head on his chest.

'Because I remember being a young man with all those feelings, that fantastic rush of excitement when you saw a girl that you liked the look of and she fancied you. Be honest, Mirry, wouldn't you like just for a moment to feel that surge? To look in the mirror and see your young self again?' He rubbed his chin reflectively. 'As you get older you become invisible. Don't have women sizing you up anymore.'

Getting older was something else. Getting old was folded away in the ironing-basket, to be thought about later. She moved away from him. 'What if she gets herself into trouble? What if Blyth pushes off and leaves her, what if he's killed?'

'Jesus, Miriam, what d'you think I am, a bloody fortune-teller? Blyth knows if he treats her wrong he'll have me to deal with.'

'D'you think I should say something about – you know?'

'If you want your head bitten off you can. He'll have had enough lectures on board, and enough free French letters to shag for the fleet.'

'Alec!' She laughed in spite of herself. 'You're wicked, you are.'

'Later, there'll be all sorts of things she might want to confide in you. But if you start prying now the trap-door will come down and you'll have lost her.'

'How come you got to be so smart?' she teased.

'Keeping one jump ahead of a beautiful woman what fancies me something rotten.'

'Give me a kiss, you soppy date.'

'I'd give you more than a kiss if I didn't have a pub to run. Just get that frying-pan on. What a man has to do nowadays to get some respect around here!'

Rosie opened the envelope. Why did he have to

embarrass her in front of Mum and Dad. Burma! SWALK, 'Sealed With a Loving Kiss', would have been harmless yet still affectionate. Affectionate! Surely it was more than that, much more.

My Darling Rosie,

Thank you for today, it was special. Looking at Albert's picture was painful. There were so many things going through my mind. All the fear and muddle and anger of my life as a nipper was stirred up, a lot of guilt, too. I remember how my sister Mary kept me safe and stood up for me always. She gave up her childhood for us. No wonder she was always in a rage. But I knew a softer side to her when she used to sing me to sleep. I owe her a lot. You know me, Rosie, who I am and where I come from. Just writing that and thinking about you makes me feel blessed.

Becoming an officer and a pilot is more than the technical stuff. It's climbing a greasy pole. You get big-headed when they accept you as one of them but there's always a minefield of class stuff that threatens to let you slip back down. I feel I'm in a no-man's-land. Too toffee-nosed to be at home with my family and too much an erk to be at ease in the wardroom. When I'm making them laugh and seeming to fit in I feel like a con man passing off dud fivers. Only you know what I mean.

Rosie, you're the 22 carat genuine article. Asking you to marry me wasn't a spur of the moment thing I knew it was what I wanted. Tell me what you feel and think about it, I shall be in a ferment 'til you do.

Love you, love you, love you,
Blyth.

Did she want to marry him? She desired him. Even thinking about him excited her. Rosie drew in the muscles deep inside her, trying to mimic the feeling of making love. Her body did not seem able to remember that growing intensity that built and built within her. Touching herself was a pale imitation of being touched. Yes, she loved him, but marriage? It was being half of a couple, the two of you always thinking what was best for the other. Trying to understand them and put them first. She didn't know who she was yet, or what she wanted. At one level they were perfectly matched by common experience. But you could live in the same street and still have a totally different childhood. She had been well fed and decently clothed all her life, yet for Blyth just a door away it had been sink or swim.

Something Gran had said popped into her mind. 'He may have gone about in rags but he didn't go short of love, that I do know. Mary idolised him and Fred would give him the top brick off the chimney.'

Did she really love him or was it sex that drew her to him? At that last meeting in London, there had been more than attraction. Rosie had felt an understanding, a fragile growing-together between them. Was it the time for promises? So far the war had barely touched her. She had been shocked by the loss of Connie's family, but loss of neighbours was not like losing family. If Joseph or Dad were killed how would she feel? It was too terrible to think about. If Blyth were killed, would she mourn him less if they weren't married?

She searched for her slippers and padded along

to the bathroom. Tomorrow she would move to Wren quarters in Southsea. Delia would be down from Hazlewood and they had some serious sorting out to do. It was the day after that that Rosie was looking forward to. The two of them were due to report to the Commander-in-Chief in Portsmouth dockyard. Their training as despatch riders would really be put to the test. She had been disappointed at not going to Plymouth, wanting to stretch her wings: but here she had local knowledge, which would save time on her first journeys around the city.

After getting dressed, she carried her tray back to the kitchen. Mum was ironing. 'Make me a warm patch,' she said.

Mum smiled, but Rosie could see she had been crying. 'Haven't done that since you were small.' Taking up the iron Miriam smoothed it over the end of the board.

Rosie held her hand over it until the warmth faded. 'I don't know what to take and what to leave,' she said. 'Can I have that photo of all of us on Sandown beach?'

''Course you can, love. Anything else?'

'I'll take my picture of Gran, and *Treasure Island*, and the brush and comb bag with my ribbons.'

Mum laughed. 'Whatever for? Your hair's far too short for ribbons.'

'It just reminds me of you doing my plaits and the talks we had.'

Mum put down the iron and hugged her. 'I thought you were far too sophisticated for that.'

'Only on the outside, there's still a bit of me that's not grown-up.' She took her Mother's hand

and turned her ring round and round as she had as a small child. 'I'll be back, Mum, lots of times. Now, after I've packed I'll take you over to Pittassie's and treat you to a Knickerbocker Glory.'

The two houses commandeered by the navy on South Parade were large and imposing. Rosie lugged her trunk through the gate, past the frosty lawn and up the stone steps to the front door. She could have got Dad to bring her in his van but it had been hard enough saying goodbye to Mum. No, she must start as she meant to go on.

The six other Wrens had got there before her, as well as Delia.

'Hello,' she said, going into the large sitting-room. 'I'm Rosie Forrest, despatch rider. Pleased to meet you all.'

'Sandie. I'm a writer.'

'Joan, signals.'

'Hilda, writer.'

'Gwyneth. I'm a driver, we'll probably see a lot of each other. I'm at the yard, too.'

She shook their hands and moved across the room to two other girls.

'Fiona. I'm a telegraphist with Penny here.'

'Let's hope the food's good,' said Gwyneth, a small Welsh girl. 'It makes all the difference. You a native?'

'Yes,' said Rosie, 'I'll have to show you the sights.'

'My brother wants a stick of Southsea rock.'

'Hello, Rosie,' said Delia, giving her a wary smile.

The Sunday dinner fulfilled all their hopes. Mrs Cherrit, the cook, served up roast pork, crispy potatoes and a steaming treacle sponge and custard.

'Let's go for a walk,' said Gwyneth, 'I'm full up fit to burst. We can unpack later.'

Rosie marched them along the sea-front, pointing out the Isle of Wight and taking them as far as Southsea Castle. It was deserted. In December it was hard to believe that in August the promenade would be packed with holidaymakers, many with sunburnt faces. 'Wonder if there'll be people on holiday next year?' she said.

'Well, I reckon if you were sitting on those stones in your bathers, now, you'd get frostbite,' laughed Fiona, pulling her scarf up around her ears.

Delia began to run back and the others joined her. With red faces and fingers tingling, they raced back to the Wrennery.

'Let's go upstairs and get unpacked,' said Delia. 'We've got the attic.' Rosie went ahead, bumping her trunk up the two flights of stairs, followed by Delia. By the time they had got to their cabin they were both breathless.

It was a bare room with bunk beds, a chest of drawers and a curtained-off corner for hanging their clothes.

'Top or bottom, you choose,' said Delia.

'Top, and I'll have the top two drawers,' said Rosie, not wanting to yield an inch.

They made up their beds and hung up their clothes, still barely speaking. After banging in a nail with the heel of her boot, Rosie hung Gran's picture high on the wall facing her bunk.

Delia cleared her throat. 'Are we still friends?' she asked.

'Do you want to be?'

'Of course I do. Rosie, I was a beast to you. Can you forgive me?'

'It depends.' There was still a hard kernel of resentment, she was not yet ready to yield. Earlier she had watched Delia charming the other girls with her breathy little-girl voice. She felt angry and sad, they had been good friends. But if it was Blyth she wanted, Rosie was ready for a fight.

'Honestly, Rosie, I had no idea about you and Blyth. Juss brought him home once and he was so charming, kissed my hand and I was instantly in love. I asked him if I could write to him and he said he didn't mind.'

'Did he write to you?' Rosie tried to appear indifferent.

Delia shook her head. 'When I phoned Juss, and he said that Blyth was coming to the dance I was in seventh heaven. All day I was thinking about him and how I could get him to really kiss me.' She looked accusingly at Rosie. 'Why didn't you tell me about him?'

'I don't know,' Rosie floundered. 'I'd not worked out how important he was to me. Besides, I didn't expect to see him so soon.'

'And how important is that?' Delia looked at her assessingly.

'He's asked me to marry him.'

'And what did you say?'

'I'm thinking about it.'

'I'd have said yes right away. After all, once you're engaged that's when your beau is really, seriously, off-limits.'

'I think Blyth has put himself off-limits. He's made his choice and I'll make mine.' She stared at Delia until she dropped her gaze. 'We've got to work together and share a room. How are we going to do that if we're at each other's throats or just making the best of a bad job? It's up to you. We had a great time in London, didn't we?'

Delia said nothing. Rosie wanted to smack her. 'I'm off to the heads.' She sat on the chill seat of the lavatory, angry with herself. She hadn't wanted to tell anyone about Blyth's proposal – it was all too new.

'Sorry, sorry,' said Delia, as soon as she returned, jumping down from the top bunk and flinging her arms around her. 'It's just so hard to let go. I'd got us married at St Paul's. I'd even chosen the bridesmaids.'

They both laughed. Rosie was in two minds about hitting Blyth for being so insensitive or Delia for being naïve.

They went down to join the others for supper, and afterwards stayed talking until nine.

'You'd better turn the light out, now,' said Rosie. 'We've to be at the dockyard early in the morning.' She lay awake too excited to sleep. Pulling back the curtains, all was darkness. The only sound was the sea washing the beach below. Where was Blyth, she wondered. Was he too tucked up in his cabin or was he up there in his Swordfish among the shivering stars?

In a house just inside the main gate of the Royal Naval Dockyard they met Petty Officer Marion Johns.

'Morning you two.' The Wren shook their hands. 'Which is which?'

'Wren Forrest, good morning.'

'Wren Croxley, jolly nice to meet you.'

'Right, I'll show you around. Next door is the post room where you will collect your signals. You log yourself in and out, and get a signature when you deliver a signal.' She took them outside again and pointed to two ancient push-bikes. 'You take those and familiarise yourself with the dockyard. Here's a map for the two of you to share – hand it back before you leave tonight. It's a huge place but you must learn your way around, even in the dark. Don't want you driving into the drink or falling into a dry dock. We've lots of Wrens but motor bikes are precious. You've got a week.'

'Jeepers,' said Delia, 'my teeth are chattering. Where d'you think we should start.'

Rosie spread the map across the saddle. 'Most of the signals will be to and from the ships. Let's get all the jetties weighed off. The one nearest the gate is the South Railway one, then there's King's Stairs. Let's see – next up is Boat House, Sheer House, North Railway then we're nearly up to the far corner.'

'Let's go right up there, then turn round.'

It was overwhelming. Dockyard maties loaded with toolboxes or bits of piping, valves, blocks and wedges, sauntered past them. Sailors hurried from place to place. Their ears were assaulted by a disharmony of sound, from the thud of the steam hammers, the clatter of riveting guns, the shrilling of steam whistles and the hooting of harbour craft. Here and there, they would see the flash of a welding torch and the red glow of a brazier on the dockside. They stopped at number 4 dry-dock, and looked up at the black-and-yellow splendour of HMS *Victory*.

'She's prettier than all the modern ones isn't she?' said Delia. 'The others are just great grey wedges. *Unrivalled* is here somewhere. I know Blyth and Juss aren't here but we could take a decko at her, what d'you think?'

'I bet she was that huge one down at the South Railway Jetty. We'll give her the once-over then go back to the office and see if we can get a cuppa.'

HMS *Unrivalled* towered above them, a grey wall of steel. They stood underneath the great overhang of the flight-deck, looking upwards. The wind tore along the jetty, making their eyes water and teeth chatter.

'Let's get back to the office,' said Rosie, 'I'm perished.' On the way back, Delia got the wheel of her bike stuck in the railway track and crashed onto the ground. In front of them a gang of maties took off their caps and cheered wildly. Delia, lying on the ground beside her bicycle, got scant attention.

'What a mingy lot,' said Rosie, helping her to her feet. ''S'pose you've got to break your neck to get any attention round here.'

Delia stood up and brushed down her coat, and held a finger to her lips. 'Shush!' she whispered. 'Didn't you see who that was?'

Rosie shook her head.

'It's the King and Admiral James.'

'Blimey, royalty on our first day?'

Delia tugged her arm. 'Don't just stand there staring. We'd better make ourselves scarce.'

The King wearing a naval greatcoat, talking to dockies! It was amazing. What would Gran have made of it all? Rosie smiled to herself. Why shouldn't he talk to them? They were as vital to the war as anyone. Dad would be proud.

'How did you get on?' asked Petty Officer Johns, holding open the door as Delia hobbled in.

'I fell off on the railway line, I'm afraid, but the bike's OK.'

'Not a brilliant start, but you'll avoid the track next time. I'll get out the First Aid box. Forrest, you can go into the kitchen and make us all some tea.'

As Rosie returned with the teapot and mugs, Delia was buckling up her boots.

'You'll do. Just a few bruises. You got off lightly. After your tea you can deliver a signal at the central post office.'

The two of them watched in amusement as Johns got out a battered tin, and threaded a cigarette end on to an open safety-pin and began puffing away. She squinted at them through the smoke. 'Forrest, you're a native aren't you? You can take Croxley with you. Show her around. Take the two Ariels out in the yard.'

'Why the post office?' asked Rosie, putting the signal in her satchel along with the logbook.

'It's an admiralty signal, with a list of survivors and the names of the dead from one of the ships on the Atlantic convoy picked off by a U-boat. They'll be turned into telegrams. At least you won't have to knock the door and face the relatives.'

Rosie and Delia left the office in silence. The excitement of the morning had gone.

23

Daisy picked up the letter on the mat. It was from Kenny. She recognised his handwriting from the letter that had come earlier. She had found it in a crumpled envelope in the kitchen bin weeks ago. She had been about to sling out a pile of old seed catalogues, and spied it just in time. Turning it over, she saw it had been opened. She thrust it down inside her skirt pocket to read later. Funny that another one should come today, just as they were going down to the house. At last Pearl had agreed it was time to give it a good going-through, and get it ready for letting. The girl had not set foot in the house since leaving almost a year ago. It was time she faced her demons.

In that time Pearl had been transformed, from the chalk-faced girl afraid of her own shadow to a woman with very definite opinions. Her dad would be proud of her: holding down a job, building up a tidy sum in her post office savings book, and taking a real pride in her appearance. Daisy would be the first to agree with him. She had succeeded with Pearl beyond all her expectations. But her battering at the hands of her brother had left a residue of bitterness that Daisy had been unable to shift. It coloured her attitude to people, making her quick to judge, and unwilling to understand the possible motives behind their actions.

Having come from a large, loving and chaotic family, it was hard for Daisy to stomach Pearl's sudden rages and need for revenge. But hadn't she herself punched Kenny so hard she had broken his nose? Reading the first letter from him she could tell he was sorry. Reading between the lines, a lot had happened to the lad since she'd chased him from the house. Daisy sighed. Dulcie, their mother, would be so hurt by the rift between them.

She knew that her brother Graham had not helped his children by going off to Singapore so soon after the funeral. He had been bitter, like Pearl.

'I'll never set foot inside another church again,' he'd railed at her. 'Don't tell me there's a loving God after he's took my Dulcie. I won't never forgive him.'

Well, thought Daisy, that was then; now we've got to pick up the pieces and make a go of things. 'Pearl, get yourself up, washed and down here. There's porridge spoiling. If you're not out of that bed in one, one, two, I'll throw this film annual on the back of the fire.'

Pearl had thought that if she kept putting it off Daisy would go down to Hardway on her own. Just the thought of going back made her hands sweat and her heart bang against her ribs. She had left all that terror behind her, and become someone else – a girl that laughed with her workmates, permed her hair and wore lipstick. They went off on their bikes to the pictures at the

Criterion and dancing at Fort Brockhurst. Last summer they'd picnicked at Stokes Bay. Daisy had packed them up with blackberry jam scones, and great slabs of fruit cake. It was Daisy who had rescued her, left to herself she could have died. Peeling back the covers, she ran shivering across the lino to the bathroom.

If Daisy was prepared to give up her Sunday to help her, Pearl had somehow got to screw up her courage and go with her. At least she knew for certain that Kenny wouldn't turn up, and if it got too much she could stick her coat back on and leave. Knowing how cold it would be in the long-unheated house, she put a thin cardigan on between her vest and jumper and two pairs of long socks under her trousers.

'That's my girl. There's a sausage sandwich with loads of HP sauce, and I've put a nip of rum in your tea.'

Pearl dredged up a smile. 'I've put on two of everything, bound to be cold down there.'

'I've thought of that. What we'll do is take a couple of those little one-bar electric fires with us. We'll load up our bikes and wheel them down there with everything we can think of. No good taking it for granted what's in the place, now. I've bundled up some newspaper, got me kneeling-mat, two scrubbing brushes, buckets, soap, chamois leather and all sorts.' She chuckled. 'We'll be the Mrs Mops on wheels.'

Pearl concentrated on swallowing down her sandwich. Her aunt's cheerful get-up-and-go approach seeped through her terror, making the day seem just about bearable. 'I'll treat us to fish-

and-chips for dinner and a bottle of Tizer.'

'That's the spirit. And next week we'll go over to the market in Pompey and get ourselves some fresh Christmas decorations. That old tree fairy needs pensioning off. This year we'll have a real knees-up, and bugger the expense. Got rationing to look forward to in January so we'll tuck in while we can.'

'That'll be good.' Pearl managed a smile. 'I love Charlotte Street.'

'Just sling the crocks in the sink, ducks, and we'll be on our way. We wants to be back here by half four – don't want to be pushing them bikes back in the blackout.'

All Pearl's courage dribbled away at the sight of her home. Just stepping over the doorstep made her sweat. All her gains dropped away, and she was back to being that frightened girl again. Going up the stairs to her bedroom made her heart race, and if Daisy hadn't been with her she would have taken off screaming down the path. Seeing the paper chain she'd hung around the mirror in her pathetic attempt at celebration, made her weep.

'Want me to clear your room for ya?'

Pearl dried her eyes on the sleeve of her jumper then shook her head. 'Just fetch us up that big cardboard box what's down the shed. Nothing here I wants to keep.'

'Right ho. Reckon we'll have a blooming great bonfire when we're through. Bring this old place up with a round turn. Won't recognise it by the time we're through.'

Daisy pushed open the shed door. 'My stars!' she gasped. Her brother's immaculate workshop had degenerated into a slum. There was evidence of someone having slept on the floor. The cardboard box Pearl had asked for had been pulled apart and flattened out to make an emergency blanket. There were spent matches, a broken torch and photos lying everywhere, speckled with mouse droppings. Kenny! 'Poor little bugger,' she muttered to herself. Rummaging about, she found an old sack full of photographic magazines. She lugged it across the garden and tipped them into a rusted lidless dustbin. They would make good fuel for the bonfire.

'Here, let me give you a hand,' she said, watching Pearl dragging the mildewed sheets off her bed. 'We'll boil them up and use them for rags later. You put all the paper stuff in the sack, and I'll get up on your dressing-table and lug down the curtains. I'll dig out some bedding from our house to get us started. Once you've got the rent coming in, we can dish this place up to something half-way decent. Perhaps the garden can be turned over to veggies. Never know, we might get some blokes here that like gardening. Far from home, they'll need things to do when they're not working. Let's hope we'll be luckier with our lodgers down here than we were with poor Thelma.'

Pearl stood with a heap of outgrown moth-eaten jumpers in her arms. 'What d'you mean, poor Thelma?' she asked.

'Well, she was a lost soul, wasn't she? Don't reckon she had a scrap of loving as a kid. All strung up with nerves she was. Flitter, flitter like a moth: all right while she's young and got her looks, but she's going to be a lonely woman later on.'

Daisy's words ignited all Pearl's buried rage. 'What about her nipper? Fancy telling you he was dead, that's diabolical, and all that tarting herself up and making eyes at the men. Sitting there smoking her head off while we waited on her. Selfish cow deserves all that's coming to her. Directly I read about her little kid, I told her to pack her bags. I knew straightaway that you'd want her gone directly you heard.'

Daisy stepped down off the ladder and sat on the bare mattress taking the hooks out of the curtains. Pearl thought she hadn't heard her, but that wasn't possible. She'd been shouting at the top of her voice. And then she turned and looked at her.

'Punishing her won't change nothing. With time and patience, we might have turned her round. It wouldn't have happened overnight but I'd like to have given it a try. Next time ask me,' she'd said.

Looking down the harbour, Pearl remembered her irritation at her aunt's words. She hated Kenny and she hated Thelma. There were good and bad people in the world and that was it – no argument. She loved Daisy, but sometimes it seemed that she lived in cloud-cuckoo-land.

When they trudged back home, Pearl went up to her room to get out of her clothes. They smelled of her old life, and damp and misery. She put on her dressing-gown and slippers and took her clothes downstairs to the laundry basket.

Daisy had set a match to the top of the stove and the stew was bubbling. She poured them both a cup of tea. As Pearl stirred in a spoonful of sugar, Daisy got Kenny's letter out of her pocket and gave it to her.

'Got a pen pal?' she asked.

'You can tear it up, nothing worth bothering about.'

Daisy picked it up again and studied the postmark then looked at the name on the back, as if she didn't know who it was from.

'No, don't read it. From Kenny – it's rubbish. I don't want to know about him.'

'Well, if it's only going to be ditched, won't hurt me reading it,' she said, taking the letter out of the envelope.

Pearl was fuming. Why hadn't she just thrown it away? Then he would have stayed missing and she could have slid the door tight shut on him.

Daisy read the letter out loud in spite of Pearl holding her hands over her ears.

Dear Pearl,

I hope you got my first letter and have now got a payment book for the allowance I put in for you. Hope it will help you and Aunt Daisy a bit. If you don't want to write to me I understand but if you could see your way clear to sending me my birth certificate I would be grateful.

Things have taken such a turn for the better I can hardly believe my luck. You would say I don't deserve to be happy and you're right. Pearl I'm more sorry than I can put into words for what I did to you and don't expect forgiveness.

'Just as well,' she snapped.

I told you about the people I am billeted with at Les Armandiers Madame Brechard her husband Guillaume and their daughter Lydie. I have asked Lydie to marry me and she has said 'Yes'!! We can't get married in church as I'm not a Catholic but will have a civil service in the town hall. It all depends on getting the certificate.

Afterwards Lydie was hoping to come to England but her mother has become very ill and so she will have to stay here. I am worried about this as there is no knowing when the Germans will break into Belgium and come pouring through here.

Please Pearl, for Lydie's sake if not mine. She is a dear sweet girl and I know you and she could become great friends if ever you met her.

With love to you and Auntie Daisy,
Kenny

'Well I'm glad, a second chance. I'll send it off to him pronto – 'spect it's in that bureau of your Dad's. I'll go over tomorrow and fetch it, and drop them a line giving my blessing.'

Pearl's temper boiled over. 'He can rot before I so much as lift a finger,' she said. 'Made my life a living hell. If he thinks I'm going to forgive him he can think again. Never Daisy, I won't never let him forget it. Hope he gets shot, then that'll be the end of him and good riddance.'

'Calm down and stop pacing, you'll wear a hole in the lino. Hand us over one of them digestives.' Daisy dipped it into her tea. 'All that falling out is in the past. I can understand how you feel, and I was more than ready to give him a right kicking – but that was then, a year ago. You're different and 'spect he is too. Kenny's making something of himself, and so are you. Besides, you'd be hurting a young girl what's never done you an atom of harm. It wasn't just his fault. Your Dad had something to do with Kenny going off the rails.'

Pearl had been astonished. 'Dad?'

'He pushed off abroad just when Kenny needed him most.'

'But it was the navy: he had to.'

'I reckon if he had had a talk with his divisional officer and the padre, something could have been sorted out. It was easier to bury his own grief in busyness and the navy was a good let-out.'

'I think you're wrong. He loved us, it was just...'

'Pearl, we've all got our weaknesses. It's not all black-and-white. When you first wrote to me I should have come round straight away, and not been bamboozled by Kenny's saying you was all right. Should've made sure, but I was caught up with going down to Plymouth to see George. Things go wrong for lots of reasons.'

'I know,' said Pearl doubtfully, 'but it's not Dad's fault. He loved us.'

'How well did he love Kenny?'

'You didn't really know him, Daisy. He was ever so upset about Mum it was just that...' Her voice trailed away.

'All I'm saying,' said Daisy, taking the last biscuit, 'is that we're all human. It's dangerous to make heroes and villains of people. Your Dad is a

291

nice bloke and he thought the world of your Mum, but he's got his faults. I'm his sister, I should know. Kenny's not all bad. Must've took a lot of guts to write to you, and he's making you an allowance.'

'That's 'cos he's got to.'

'Oh Pearl. If you could see your face, all twisted up with hate. How you gonna feel if he dies out there and you haven't forgiven him?'

It was so easy for Daisy to say, she hadn't lain terrified in her bed waiting for the blows to fall. She hadn't had her money nicked from her purse or her arm twisted behind her back. 'And,' she said, moving the conversation away from her own family, 'I can't see how you can stand up for Thelma after what she done.'

'Well it isn't easy, but neither is anything worthwhile. What I'm harping on about, is being too quick to judge. We never got the full picture, any of us. It's as dangerous making heroes of people as villains. Look at Hitler.'

'What d'you mean?'

'He's got the gift of the gab and people just hung on every word what he said. Stirred them all up full of hate and turned one lot against another. My Frank and your father the other side of the world and God knows if we'll see them again. Your Kenny in France and every other mother's son and daughter caught up in the madness.'

Pearl had been frightened. 'What d'you mean, if we see Dad and Uncle Frank again. You don't mean...' her voice trailed away.

Daisy set down her mug before answering. 'War is terrible, Pearl. It makes you live on a knife-edge, it steals everything: all your hopes and plans. Look at last time. True, your Uncle Henry come back safe from France but then I had to watch him die by inches from gas poisoning. We just gotta hope and pray that they comes out of it in one piece. Meantime, get on with our lives best we can.'

'But I couldn't bear it if anything happened to Dad.'

Daisy had waved her spoon at her, 'What you can bear don't come into it. If you're still breathing, you just have to set one foot in front of the other and survive the best way you can. Always, there's folks worse off than you.'

Still, she couldn't bring herself to write to Kenny. There was a hard kernel of anger that would not be dislodged.

Looking down the harbour, the next Saturday, Pearl remembered her irritation at her aunt's words. She hated Kenny and she hated Thelma. There were good and bad people in the world and that was it – no argument. She loved Daisy but sometimes it seemed that she lived in cloud-cuckoo-land.

'Right,' her aunt said, as her foot touched the pontoon on the Portsmouth side of the harbour. 'Last one up to the bus stop buys the bacon sarnies.'

Laughing, breathless, they clambered on the bus. With Daisy having a head start, it was Pearl who bought the sandwiches. The Saturday crowds, faces flushed with cold and eyes peeled for a bargain, milled around them.

Pearl looked at the toy stall stacked with dolls,

tin soldiers and tree decorations. There were bunches of tinsel, coloured balls and Christmas tree fairies.

'What you up to, feeling me fruit? How d'you like me to pinch your lemons?'

At the fruit stall, a blowsy matron roared with laughter. 'Me melons don'tcha mean?' she joshed, thrusting her vast bosom towards the indignant stallholder.

'Oh!' He stretched his hands, in their fingerless gloves, as if to cup her breasts, winking at the bystanders. 'Reckon I got the best of the bargain,' he chortled.

'Chas, you get and trim them caulis, else it'll be sommink else what gets trimmed.' His companion glared at the woman. 'You get a tune out of him, darlin', you're welcome. Need to dip it in a bag of starch to get any joy from our Chas.'

After chortling at the impromptu entertainment, Daisy looked at her watch. 'We better wire in, time's galloping. Let's get our tree bits then we'll work our way through the rest of the list. We don't want to come back here and find the best one bin took.'

They stood pondering the merits of the Christmas fairies.

'Hello, stranger.'

Daisy swung around and whooped delightedly. 'Miriam!' She flung her arms around the blonde woman who stood smiling at her. 'I'm that glad to see you.'

'Daisy, I thought about you so often.' There were tears in the woman's eyes. 'This is the best Christmas present. Seeing you again.'

They stood laughing and crying, while Pearl waited to pay for the fairy in the green skirt. Beside them, holding a Christmas tree, a red-haired giant smiled down at her.

'Joe Forrest, pleased to meet you.' He nodded his head towards the woman called Miriam. 'That's my Mum blubbing there.'

Pearl smiled, and held out her hand. 'That's my Aunt Daisy, I'm Pearl Bunting. Pleased to meet you.' For a few moments she could feel the warmth of him seeping through his gloves, and then he took charge of the Christmas tree again.

'You must be from Gosport, bet it was nippy on the water. I haven't bin that side for ages. What d'you do of an evening over there?'

'Us natives have come along fast, we even got the pictures and dancing.'

Joe threw back his head and roared with laughter. 'I walked right into that. I'll have to brave the ferry and bring you some beads and feathers.'

'Cheek!' She stamped on his foot, making no impression on his thick boots. Flushed and giggly, Pearl was having fun. She could have stood there forever trading insults with Joe Forrest. But Miriam and Daisy were winding up their conversation.

''Course I know the Nile,' Daisy was saying. 'That'd be lovely. I can't wait to see Rosie again. We'll be over about two. Give us a hug, gal.' She tugged at Pearl's coat. 'Here, say hello to my best friend ever.'

Reluctantly Pearl wrenched her gaze away from Joe. 'Hello, Mrs Forrest.' She looked at his mother. She didn't look like her son except for the blue eyes, but instinctively she warmed to her.

'I look forward to seeing you Christmas Day, Pearl. Hope you can come.'

'So do I,' said Joe, winking at her.

Pearl nodded and smiled then he and his mother plunged back into the crowd, but they were not lost to her. She stood watching him shouldering his way forward, the branches of the Christmas tree waving and his red hair getting more and more distant.

Daisy clutched her arm. 'Ooh, that's cheered me up no end. Never thought to see her again. I can't wait 'til Christmas Day to get a hug off Rosie.'

Pearl let her aunt babble on. She held her gloves up to her face and sniffed them. They smelled of warm wool and pine needles. She smiled beneath her scarf as she linked arms with Daisy. There was nothing like having something to look forward to.

24

It was Christmas Eve. Blyth got off the bus in Wymering and trudged up Kellaway Avenue to his sister Mary's house. It was four o'clock, just time for a glimpse in the front windows he passed before the blackout curtains were drawn. There were Christmas cards on mantelpieces, paper chains looped across the ceilings, and every so often a tree. His ears stung with the cold, and his shoulders ached from hefting a bulging haversack of gifts.

Tonight there was going to be a family party. Faith and Mercy, his twin sisters, were coming. The only missing members were his brother Harry and sister-in-law Dora, busy in their Plymouth pub. Since Dad died he'd not spent Christmas at home. It had been easier to pretend he was on duty. What had changed, he asked himself. He didn't know. All sorts of thoughts and memories had been stirring in him lately. Was it going to war that shifted priorities, or falling in love?

For years he had bypassed the lumber-room in his head where he'd slung his childhood. Among his oppos in the navy, he said as little as possible. It was seeing the painting up in London that had burst open a door in him which he couldn't seem to close. Seeing himself in his mother's arms, with her smiling at him, had stirred him to tears.

It had given him back those first fuzzy images of her from his babyhood. He could almost feel the giddy joy of being bounced and jounced and danced with.

Rosie loved him. Not because he was good-looking or because he had a gold ring on his sleeve. She loved the man he really was, beneath all that Greenwich gloss and wardroom skylarking. There had been a spark of attraction from the first moment he saw her. In the beginning it was physical. He was drawn to her dark eyes and full breasts. He loved her quick-wittedness and earthy humour. But there were many women that he desired, and he found seduction all too easy. He and Rosie shared an intimacy he'd never expected to find with anyone. With her he felt blessed.

By contrast, his relationship with his eldest sister was thorny. He knocked on the door of number 85, squaring up for a fight.

He was on the point of giving up and going back on board, when the door was opened and Mary stood there, plump and wary.

'Merry Christmas,' he said, setting down his bags and kissing her.

'Quick, get in. It's brass monkeys, you're letting in the cold. Shove your gear up in the small bedroom. I'll get Hope to sleep on the sofa.'

'I'll do that, I'm used to sleeping anywhere.'

'Uncle Blyth!' His niece, Hope, charged down the stairs and into his arms.

'Ginger nut, how are you?' He grinned at the freckled youngster.

'Fine,' she said, 'see ya later. Mum, I'm off to me friend's, back later.'

'You be back by six. We got things to do, my lady.'

The door slammed and it was just the two of them either side of the kitchen table.

He supposed that she was pleased to see him. Pleased was something his sister had never got the habit of showing. No, there had been that time when she was married and they lived in the houseboat in Gosport. Then, she had been more than pleased with her life. She had been fiercely happy, even called their baby Hope, for God's sake. But it had all been snatched away in less than a year. He didn't know her any more. Didn't know why he had invited himself to stay. It was something to do with Rosie's painting. Standing there he'd had a sense of what he owed his sister.

He didn't know her new husband either. He had a greengrocery shop in Wymering, a step up from his stall in Charlotte Street market. Once Mary had run a toy stall there; Blyth had even helped her make stuff for it. With her husband gone, everything went to pot. Mary buried herself with Hope in the houseboat in Gosport, while he was left in Pompey muddling along with Dad.

'So how's things?' he said, helping himself to a mince pie.

Mary smiled. 'Wouldn't risk them pies, our Hope made them. Pastry's like iron.'

'Test-driving the rolling-pin is she?'

'Sommink like that.'

She looked rounder and less defensive. Taking out a cigarette machine from her pocket she handed it to him.

'Roll us a tickler while I makes the tea. We'll go

in the front room. I've laid a fire in there.'

Blyth sat in the armchair. He fed the paper into the machine, licked the sticky edge, tamped down the tobacco, then closed the lid and turned the rollers to produce a well-filled cigarette. Then he rolled one for himself. 'This was Dad's, wasn't it?' he said, as she came in with the cups. 'Remember how he used to cut up bits of newspaper when he didn't have any money for Rizlas?'

'I remember cutting it up in squares and threading it on a nail with string in the outside lav. Used to get newsprint on your bum.'

They laughed.

He lit Mary's cigarette with his lighter, and watched her drawing in the smoke. She sat relaxed with the cup between her hands.

He laughed. 'You got fingernails, how long you had them?'

'Dunnow, a little while, I ain't got so much to bite me nails over now, with just me and Sid and Hope.'

'You happy?'

She stared at the bobble on her slipper. 'Content, I s'pose, safer than I've ever bin all my life. Sid's good to us.' She patted his knee. 'How about you?'

'Me?' He grinned. 'My favourite subject.'

'Don't bugger about, remember I know you through and through.'

'Well, I might be getting married.'

'Might be, what sort of carry-on is that?'

'She's thinking about it. See her tomorrow and then we'll see.'

'Sounds bloody lukewarm to me, what she

300

need to think about?'

'Rosie Forrest, you know, Alec Forrest's daughter.'

'I thought going in for this officer malarky you'd aim a bit higher.'

Blyth could feel a row coming on. 'Higher doesn't mean better, Rosie and me – we're good together. She makes me laugh, she makes me happy.'

'If you're so blooming happy together why she keeping you fannying around?' Mary blew a perfect smoke ring. 'What's her problem with saying yes?'

'Jesus! Why d'you always turn everything into a fight? I took her by surprise, I took myself by surprise come to that. There's a war on, in case you hadn't noticed.'

'Well, there's a bit of fresh news,' she snarled. 'I wondered why my neighbour's boy got killed. Then there was those bits in the paper from grief-stricken mothers and broken-hearted wives. Your Rosie wants to play it safe, does she?'

He stubbed out his cigarette in his saucer. There were times when he hated his sister. As he got up to leave her to it, she tugged at his sleeve.

'Sorry,' she mumbled.

Blyth sat down in surprise. This was new. Never in all their run-ins had she ever apologised. Oh, she'd leave a sweet on his pillow or slip him a penny after a bad flare-up, but sorry? He said nothing and waited.

'Wants you to be happy, Blyth, like me and Matthew was before he was took.'

'How was that?'

'Just knowing that nothink I did or said stopped him loving me. I'd carry on top ropes sometimes, and he'd say: "You feel better, now you got that off your chest?" and sometimes – you'll laugh at this–' she looked at him, gauging his response, 'he would read me stories like I was a kid. With Matthew I could be me.'

He hugged her. 'You're a wise old boot, when you're not being a right cow.'

Mary laughed. 'Smashing, having you here. Quick,' she said, 'before Hope comes back, I got sommink to tell ya.'

'All ears,' he said.

'I'm in the club.'

'What club?' he teased.

'Pudding club, you daft ha'p'orth, up the spout, in the family way.'

'A baby!' He danced her round the room. 'Mary, I'm pleased to bits for you.'

'See, if I can risk having a nipper in the middle of the war, you can get yerself married. What's up with that Rosie? You're a catch. Good-lookin' bloke like you. She need glasses or sommink?'

He was struggling for an answer when there was an impatient rapping on the front door.

'You go, Blyth. If it's the vicar tell him to sling his hook.'

'Faith, Mercy.'

His twin sisters burst through the door, smothering him with lipstick and gin fumes. 'Surprise, surprise,' they chorused.

'Mary, how are ya? Long time no see.' Faith perched her foot on the edge of Blyth's seat and began un-strapping her shoes.

'Blimey Mary, you put on a bit of weight, looks like old two-ton Tessie,' Mercy said, staring down at her eldest sister through sooty lashes.

'Who asked you to put your oar in,' snapped Mary, 'mouthy cow.'

'Mercy, shut up and put the kettle on I'm parched.' Faith took off her hat and shook her apricot curls.

Blyth laughed. 'Blimey, what bottle did that colour come out of? What brings you two down this way?'

'Two officers off a minesweeper give us a lift. Come along from Brighton, we're in the panto down there.'

'What, as the ugly sisters?' Mary asked, making room for Faith.

Blyth sat on the floor with his back against the sofa. Once Mercy went out to the kitchen the atmosphere eased. She had always been the acid drop, spoiling for a fight. Faith was her gentle counterpart and family peacemaker.

'No, it's *Sleeping Beauty*. We're fairy fireflies, in the aerial ballet flying out over the auditorium. You and Hope and Sid, I got you some tickets.'

'How we gonna get down there?' asked Mary.

Blyth sighed. They were an ungracious lot, his sisters, never yielding an inch. 'I'll lash you up to the train tickets. Be a treat for Hope.'

'What time we eatin'?' asked Mercy, handing her sister a cup of tea. 'Bloody starving, belly thinks me throat's cut.'

'About half seven, Sid won't be in for another hour. He'll want to have a wash and shave, and get into the rig of the day before we sits down.'

'Jesus, who does he think he is, Lord bloody Fauntleroy?' Mercy sneered.

'Just 'cos we had an outside lav and washed at the kitchen sink, don't mean we don't know no better. We got a bathroom now, and a bloody good job too. Wouldn't go back to Lemon Street for all the tea in China.'

'What we havin'?' asked Faith, winking at Blyth.

'Cold bacon, jacket spuds, pickled onions. Sid's bringing some crusty rolls and cheese.'

'I won a Christmas cake in the NAAFI raffle,' said Blyth, going out to the hall and fetching in his case. 'Got a bottle of rum and a bag of sausage rolls. There was a cocktail party on board when I got in last night. Got these off the steward.'

'Ooh,' laughed Faith, 'hark at him. Be bloomin' admiral of the fleet soon.'

The front door shut and Hope came in, carrying a torch, her face red with cold.

'Come and sit here,' said Blyth, 'you must be perished.'

'Hello Auntie Faith and Auntie Mercy,' she said shyly, joining him on the mat.

'You're a skinny one. Looks like your Dad.'

Hope blushed and subsided into the corner.

Blyth glared at Mercy. 'You're a bit long in the tooth to be a fairy,' he said wanting to repay sting for sting.

Mercy scowled. 'What d'you know about the theatre? Reckon you're some sort of Busby Berkeley do ya?'

'You bin hoofers for some time. If you were any

good should've seen your names in lights by now.' He winked conspiratorially at Hope.

'How old are you, Hope?' asked Faith, smiling at her.

'Fourteen, Auntie Faith, I never seen you dance.'

'What d'you like best, ballet or tap?' said her aunt, getting out of her chair and gathering up the cups. 'We could do a bit in the kitchen, if you like.'

Eagerly, Hope followed her out of the room.

Mercy yawned. 'Seeing as there's no grub around I'll go upstairs and have a kip. Where we kippin'?'

'Back bedroom,' said Mary. 'You can wash up later seeing as you ain't offered to help beforehand.'

'Oh welcome, Mercy, ever so glad to see ya!' her sister snapped, before dragging her case upstairs.

Blyth grinned at Mary. 'Nothing changes,' he said.

'Always were chalk and cheese, for all they're identical. Used to lead me a dog's life.' She laughed. 'I remember raving at her till me throat was sore. Never made an atom of difference. Could always get round Faith. Mercy would have the fillin's out yer teeth, a real wheeler-dealer. I used to be really jealous of them gadding about, having money to spend. Now,' she blew a smoke ring, 'what are they, twenty-nine? No home either of them, and not spoken for as far as I can see.'

Faith came back into the room. 'Can I make a start on anythink, Mary?'

'Tell yer what, if you and Hope wash the spuds and stick 'em in the oven on a regulo two, they'll be fine. Don't forget to prick 'em well with a fork.'

Blyth was getting to his feet, when Mary gestured for him to sit down. 'You stay put. This is a treat for me, putting me feet up and having you to myself.' She smiled at him. 'Make us another tickler, will ya?'

They sat together in silence, Mary smoking and Blyth watching a flame flickering in the grate.

'Glad you come up,' she said. 'We gotta make the most of things this Christmas. Rationing in January. We'll all be tightening our belts. This war got me scared. Thank God Sid's out of it. Hurt his back in the last lot, why he walks with a limp and Hope's too young to be sent off anywhere.'

'You've had your share, Sis. About time things were good for you.'

She gripped his shoulder. 'Few years back, me and Sid went to the pictures. Don't even remember what was on but there was this newsreel. It was about Spain when they was having their war. Christ! I'll never forget it. Showed this town what'd bin bombed to buggery. There was dead women and kids lying in the street, and a little nipper wandering about crying. They reckons we'll be copping some of that soon.'

From the kitchen came the sound of feet tapping over the stone floor, and Hope laughing.

'Should think you'd be safe enough up here,' Blyth said, trying to sound unworried. 'You've got a shelter, haven't you?'

'Sid put the Anderson in the garden few

months back, his brothers come over and helped him.'

'You just look after yourself and take care of the baby. What you fancy?'

'I'd like a boy. I was good with boys. Reckon I'll call it Matthew.' Again she gripped his arm. 'And I want you to be his godfather. So don't get yerself shot up or nothing.'

'Do my best. There are things I want to do. I'm not going to play the hero. I've got a girl to come back to.'

'D'you know, I been really missing old Beattie Pragnell, lately. She was a gem, wasn't she? When Matthew got took I reckon I would have gone under without her.'

'Better than any real grandma,' said Blyth. 'Reckon she grandma'd the whole street.'

There was another silence, and Blyth could hear the clock ticking and the coal shifting in the grate.

'It wasn't all bad when we was kids,' Mary said.

Blyth reached up his arm and took her hand in his. 'Remember when we used to sing in bed together. *If all the world was paper, And all the sea was ink,*' he began to sing. '*And all the sea was bread and cheese—*'

'*—What would we have to drink.*' Mary finished for him.

'Write to me, Blyth won't you,' she said. 'I'll worry about you.'

'And, you write to me,' he said, leaning over and kissing her on the cheek.

'Jesus!' Mary stubbed out her cigarette in her saucer. 'It's six o'clock. We better get our skates on. You better pull out the table and set the leaves out. Lay up for six, cloth's in the sideboard. I'll go and roust up those girls. There's bin lots of tapping out there. I just hope they remembered the spuds.'

The front door opened and a thick-set man in an overcoat and balaclava came in. 'Hello, Ducks,' he said to Mary, giving her a hug. 'Glad to get home, any chance of a cuppa?'

'Hello Sid,' Blyth shook his large work-roughened hand.

'Hello Squire, how ya keeping?'

'Good,' said Blyth. 'I'll go and chase up your tea.'

The next hour or so flashed by, and then they were all six of them sitting around the table, passing plates back and forth, laughing and chatting.

Sid, sporting a red paper crown, carved the bacon, and Mary sliced the potatoes and sprinkled the halves with grated cheese. Between them they polished off a trifle. After more iron-roofed mince pies they sat around the table, too full to move.

'Sid,' said Mary, setting down her empty glass. 'Bring down the gramophone. We'll get the twinnies to give us a turn.'

Blyth rolled up the mat and pushed back the table. Hope cleared a place for the gramophone.

'What'll we have?' asked Sid, setting down a box of records.

'How about Dad's old favourite, "Red, red robin?"' Blyth slipped it onto the turntable before winding up the handle.

Once the music started it was as if a switch had been thrown. The twins threw themselves into their performance, tapping across the floor, swinging their arms and grinning fit to burst. Faith beckoned Blyth to join them and he in turn coaxed Hope out to dance. Mary laughed out loud. Blyth blew her a kiss. For once all the sniping, jealousies and discontents were forgotten. For once, the Vines were almost a family.

25

It was Christmas Day. Uncle Albert was coming to take him back to Nelson Street and Auntie Connie. They would have their dinner at the pub and Joe would be there.

Lionel sat at the end of his bed, waiting and waiting and waiting. He had been kept awake by the icicle on the tree banging on his window. On the chair beside him were the balaclava and gloves that Auntie Connie had knitted him. She said that her twins Rodney and Clive wore them on their ship up in Scotland. Joe had sent him a copy of the *War Weekly*. Auntie sat with him turning the pages. When they got to the picture of a U-boat she ran out to the toilet. Lionel knew she had been crying because her eyes looked extra bright and she'd put powder over her tears. She asked him if he wanted to be in the navy but he told her he was going to be a fireman like Joe. Auntie told him his grandad Reggie Scoggins had been a submariner and a bit of a hero. Lionel was astonished. Gran always said that he was, 'a mean old bastard that drunk like a fish.' Perhaps in submarines you had to drink like a fish to keep the water out.

After breakfast the nurses came and stood in the middle of the room with their cloaks turned to the red side, and sang carols. Father Christmas arrived and put a present at the bottom of the other children's beds. He gave him a game of Ludo. Lionel began to feel frightened. Had Uncle Albert crashed the car?

And then he was there, tapping up the ward towards him with his gold-topped walking-stick. 'Merry Christmas, Lionel, how are you? Ready for the off?'

He smiled. 'Yes,' he said. After lots of shaking hands and thank yous they were outside in the freezing cold.

'Where would you like to sit, old man?'

The car scared him. Lionel gritted his teeth. If he didn't get in he wouldn't get to see Joe or have a proper Christmas. Tears were coming up into his eyes when he saw a dog looking at him through the window.

'Towser's not good in cars. I think he will want to sit with you. Is that all right?' Lionel nodded. 'I'll sit in the front,' he said.

The old man tucked a blanket round him and Towser leapt on his lap.

'Keep a look-out for dogs. It will distract him and stop him from being frightened.'

Soon he began to feel warm, and they laughed when Uncle had to stop at some traffic lights and an Alsatian was crossing with his master. Towser barked his head off. 'Your trick worked,' Lionel said. The dog smelt like wet wool and old biscuits. The little towns passed by, all white like Christmas cards. Now and then he glimpsed a tree in a window, and then there were boring bits with fields. What with the heat from Towser's fur and the steady purr of the engine, he drifted into sleep. And then the car had stopped and

311

someone was tapping on the window.

'Joe. Joe.' He couldn't believe it.

'Come on, my little mate,' he said, opening the door. 'Let's get you out of there and upstairs to see your Auntie Connie.'

Joe swung him up on his shoulders, and carried him into the pub and up the stairs. Everyone cheered, Towser danced on his hind legs, and Joe plonked him down on the sofa beside a load of presents.

'Merry Christmas, my little cocker,' said Auntie Connie. 'Let's get you out of your coat. What you needs is to get them hands round a mug of cocoa. Fancy some crisps?'

Lionel nodded. He sat and looked at the fire, wondering where his Mum was. When Joe carried him in, he'd looked down the street to his old house. Nobody had said anything. Was she dead? He knew that Clive and Rodney had drowned because one of the nurses' dads had been on the *Royal Oak*. Perhaps Connie was keeping it a secret, like not telling him about her boys. Perhaps if he didn't say nothing she might not be dead. Any minute, she could come up the stairs shouting at him, like always. Auntie came back with the cocoa, and he sat up and sipped it, feeling the warmth stealing back into his hands. Lionel couldn't seem to fix his mind on the presents. He felt half-way between laughing and crying, and ever so tired. Auntie read to him from the *Hotspur* about Biggles. Joe sat on the floor next to them and everything inside him settled down. He felt all smoothed out and perhaps even happy.

Pearl and Daisy waddled down the pontoon swathed in scarves. The deck was grey and mushy with melted snow. They stood together heads down, stamping the cold out of their feet. The wind was like a smack in the face, leaving their cheeks stinging. Pearl hoped there would be time to thaw out a bit when they reached the Nile. She wanted to change into her best frock and comb her hair. The last thing she wanted was Joe to see her before she was ready. He had been ever so friendly, and his smile had made her feel giddy looking up into those blue eyes. She hadn't washed her gloves since he'd held her hand. Beside her, Daisy wittered on and on, with hardly a gap to draw breath.

'I'm that excited, don't know what to do with meself. Ahh! Miriam was such a love when she stayed with me. She was so pretty, with hair like corn and those eyes, men was drawn to her like bees to honey – never anyone else for her but Alec. We kept each other going. And Rosie, she was a little angel.'

'Shall we get a taxi? My treat,' said Pearl, as they made their way up the pontoon at Portsmouth.

'Blimey, you're pushing the boat out,' laughed Daisy. 'Probbly be a bus down at the Hard we can get. Or we could walk, not that far. If we step out smart wouldn't take us above half an hour.'

Pearl could imagine them arriving all red-faced and sweaty. No, the taxi would be an investment. When she saw Joe again she wanted to look her absolute best. She didn't fool herself that he'd made as much of their meeting as she had. Probably had a girlfriend, even more than one.

This was her one chance to make an impression. She stepped to the head of the rank and tapped on the taxi door. 'The Nile in Nelson Street, please,' she said.

'Happy Christmas, mate,' said Daisy, getting in to the seat beside the driver. 'You workin' all day, bet you're chocker.'

'Off at three,' the man said, turning to smile at her. 'They'll wait for me 'til they haves their dinner. Missus is good like that. "Jim," she says, "it ain't what you got on yer plate but who yer eating it with."'

'Ain't that the truth,' laughed Daisy.

Garth filled the crib, one end with oats and the other with straw. He stood talking to the two horses, Fortune and Damson, as he fed and watered them before stepping along to the Nile for his Christmas dinner. 'It's big eats today, Fortune,' he said, holding the bucket of water up to the animal's head. 'I shall be sat there in me best bib like a lord.'

Fortune slurped noisily until the last drop. Then he ambled over to the oats and nibbled them, seeming to relish their taste.

'Good, ain't they, my old lad? I shall be tucking into turkey, down the road. I'm going next-door now to see to your sister.'

He filled the crib for Damson and went through the same routine. 'Merry Christmas, my lady,' he crooned, as she lapped up the water. 'You know it's cruel out, that wind must be coming from the Arctic. You two are in clover tucked up here in yer stalls.'

Damson, her brown muzzle speckled now with grey hairs, dipped her head into the oats. Her lips seemed to quiver in delight. Funny that was, how they loved them so much.

Whistling to himself he filled the bucket again and topped up the troughs in their stalls. 'Right my old pals, here's your treats then I must be off.' He reached into his waistcoat pocket and pulled out two sugar cubes and held them up to Damson on the flat of his hand. She drew them towards her with her soft velvety lips. 'Tell you all about it old girl, when I gets back.'

'Fortune, here's yours, me old bucko. That's it, see you later. Your master is off to fill his boots.'

Sitting in the saloon bar, Albert sipped his gin and looked about him. He'd thought himself well content in Solent Cottage pottering about to his own rhythm, but he'd been fooling himself. This was his world. He watched a sailor with a cigarette tucked behind his ear squinting before aiming his dart at the board. A skinny fellow, with a stick of chalk between his tobacco-stained fingers, was keeping score. He could tell, watching a man in a shiny suit, that he was working up to the climax of his story by the rapt attention of his companions, beer froth clinging to their lips.

'Right sweetheart,' said the soldier, 'you're getting six yards of that tomorrow.' The raconteur reached for his pint, and basked in the laughter erupting around him.

'Blimey, mate, where d'you get them from?'

'Trade secret, mate,' laughed the joker.

Albert itched to draw them all. In the last year

315

he had barely touched his sketchbook. Here, there was a raffish optimism in their faces, a particular Pompey style of smoking with the cigarette pinched between the thumb and index finger. Bernice, with her hectic rouge and bottle-blonde curls, was punishing the piano for all she was worth. If he closed his eyes he could picture Beatrice sitting there, sipping her stout, chatting with one of the locals. And, in Rosie's dark gypsy looks and boundless vitality, he could see the young Beatrice he had fallen in love with all those years ago.

'Let me take your glass, Albert,' said Miriam. 'It's good to see you here. I tell you, it's made my Christmas.'

He watched her serving drinks, washing glasses and keeping up several conversations at the same time. Christmas dinner for ten was a challenge to the family, especially with a pub to run. But Miriam had been adamant.

'War or no war, I'm keeping up the tradition we started when we moved in. Joseph is on night duty so he'll be able to eat with us. Rosie's off 'til Wednesday and we've got Connie and Bernice to lend a hand.' She smiled at Albert. 'It's what Beanie would have expected of us.'

Rosie felt like a clockwork mouse as she scurried back and forth from the kitchen to the lounge. She dodged between Mum and Bernice, filling saltcellars, polishing glasses, setting out the knives and forks. Her eyes kept straying to the clock above the bar. Blyth had promised to be there by two o'clock sharp. She ached to see him.

They'd not seen each other since that day at the gallery in London. There was so much to say, so many people, how would they get even five minutes alone together?

'Thanks, Love, you've worked like a Trojan. Go and get yourself ready. Connie's coming down in a minute. Lionel's sound asleep, poor little chap. It's just a case of bringing the dishes out onto the table.' Mum shooed her up the stairs.

In her bedroom, Rosie adjusted the neckline on her scarlet blouse so that it revealed just enough cleavage to be tempting but not vulgar. She put on the crystal earrings, and shook her head to watch them sparkle in her reflection in the mirror. Taking Mum's silk scarf she rubbed it over her hair to make it shine. The final stroke was a slick of Yardley cherry lipstick. She sat at the top of the stairs listening to the hubbub of voices. Rising with the laughter and chat was the aroma of roast turkey, and the orange and nutmeg in Dad's rum punch.

'What we've got, my girl, is riches without money.' She could hear Gran saying it almost as if she were beside her.

'Daisy, welcome love, come in, come in, and you Pearl. Tell you what, run your coats upstairs, you can sling them on my bed. Rosie, are you up there? Show Daisy and Pearl to our bedroom. Chop! Chop!'

Mum sounded so excited. This was her dearest friend, the one that had been there when her daughter was born. Rosie leaned down and called to her. 'Auntie Daisy, is it really you? I've heard so much about you.'

Directly she reached the upstairs landing,

Daisy swept her up in a great bear hug.

'Rosie my little Rosie, let's have a look at ya. Ooh, you're a beauty just like your mum. I bin looking forward to this party, couldn't hardly sleep for excitement.'

Immediately she liked this fresh-faced roly-poly of a woman. 'Lovely to meet you, we'll have a good natter later, let me take your coats.' She looked past Daisy to Pearl.

'Hello Pearl,' she said, giving her a kiss. 'I'm pleased to meet you.'

She looked like a child, wearing make-up and adult clothes for the first time. Her hair formed a frizzy blonde halo around her tiny face. But, as she smiled into Pearl's blue eyes, Rosie felt she was being assessed. There was an adult directness in her gaze. Whatever else, Pearl was not a child. 'I'd better go down and give Mum a hand. Her bedroom's in there. See you later.'

Downstairs she looked at the clock. Where was he? If he didn't hurry they would be sat down to dinner with no chance of a word alone together.

'Rosie, love,' said Mum, giving her a quick hug in passing. 'You look a star. Vivien Leigh had better watch out.' Seeing her daughter look at the clock again, she said. 'It's a long way down from Wymering and not many buses today. He's probably had to walk along to Cosham. What you need to do is keep busy. Here, fill this dish with nuts and find the crackers.'

After setting the dish on one of the side tables, along with apples and a packet of dates, she risked another peek at the clock; ten past two. On every trip to and from the kitchen, she was sidetracked into talking to someone. She smiled and laughed and chatted, forcing herself not to check the time.

At half-past two Dad blew an old boatswain's whistle.

'Ladies and gentleman, kindly take your seats and dinner will be served.'

Everyone rushed to the table and read their name on the cards that Mum had written. Rosie wanted to cry. Fixing a grin on her face, she took her seat and tried to avoid looking at the empty plate opposite.

'Hello, Gorgeous.'

She turned, and he was there behind her in his greatcoat, swathed in a scarf. He rested his gloved hands on her shoulders.

'Merry Christmas,' he said, kissing her cheek.

Her spirits climbed from the basement to the roof. 'Hello yourself,' she whispered, smiling up at him.

'Blyth, lad, nip into the public and sling your coat on the stand there,' Dad called from the head of the table. 'What'll you have, beer or punch?'

'Beer please, Mr Forrest. You carry on, I won't be two shakes.'

Rosie wanted to follow him, for a moment alone with him before he was swallowed up in the crowd.

Blyth came back, his uniform jacket slung over his shoulder, and he set it on the back of his chair. After seating himself, he leant across the table mouthing the words, 'I love you.'

'I love you,' she whispered back.

On her side of the table she was seated between

319

Uncle Albert and Joseph, while Blyth was wedged between Daisy and Bernice.

They smiled regretfully at one another.

She blew him a kiss and he winked at her. They both got caught up in passing plates back and forth and talking to their immediate partners. Joseph was grinning at Pearl, and she was blushing and giggling.

Every so often their eyes met. Rosie could hardly swallow. Talk swirled about them yet they heard nothing. Glances were thrown in their direction but they were not returned. They were enthralled by one another.

Somehow, roast potatoes passed up and down the table, followed by turkey, stuffing, sprouts, and carrots. They mysteriously found their way onto her plate. She ate without knowing what she was eating. Looking up, she saw Blyth put a slice of turkey in his mouth, she watched him chewing then licking his lips. She wanted him to kiss her, to uncurl his fingers from the fork and curl them around her waist. She wanted, oh she wanted...

'Rosie, are you deaf, or something? Pass us the sprouts,' demanded Joseph.

She turned back to her plate and knew Blyth was watching her. Slowly she drew a long sliver of potato into her mouth, closing her eyes as if it were the most succulent experience.

Blyth winked at her.

They were in a secret world, tempting one another, playing a wonderful game.

'Rosie, my dear let me fill your glass,' said Uncle Albert. She turned to him flushed and disorientated.

Bernice and Connie darted about, clearing away the vegetable dishes and the meat platter. Mum came in from the kitchen with the rum-soaked Christmas pudding set alight. Everyone cheered. Blyth passed her the jug of custard. She grinned at him.

'Fill yer boots,' yelled Bernice. 'Won't see the like of these in the New Year.'

And then Dad was on his feet. 'Friends and family, welcome all of you. Miriam and I want to thank you all for your kindnesses to us over the year – they have been much appreciated. Whatever happens, we at the Nile will go on into next year with the same spirit of goodwill to all that has always been a Forrest family trademark. This is the first Christmas of the war and the last before rationing falls on us. Eat hearty. I should like us to raise our glasses in memory of all the faces that are missing from Nelson Street this year, starting with my dear mother Beattie Pragnell. Then there are Arthur, Rodney and Clive Spooner and all the other men who have lost their lives fighting for their country. Especial mention must be made of Mrs Waller, who was run over in the blackout and died of her injuries. Bless them all.'

Everyone stood up and raised their glasses. 'Bless them all,' they cried.

'Our second toast is to all our friends who are away from home, serving in the forces, whoever and wherever they are.'

'Absent friends,' chorused everyone.

'Lastly I should like to toast this one little street in Pompey which represents the spirit of the whole country. It's full of hardworking, honest and lively people. Folk who have open doors and open hearts. I give you Nelson Street.'

Rosie wanted to fix the moment forever in her mind. She winked at Blyth then smiled at Mum and Dad. These were her people sitting here, tricked out in their best, eyes blinking in the cigarette smoke, just the right side of tipsy.

'Volunteers for washing up and tea-making,' called Mum, 'then we can settle down to the afternoon's entertainments.' She looked at Rosie. 'Fetch us some tea towels from upstairs, love. I reckon we'll need the lot with all these plates to dry. And Blyth, shift yourself, lad, you can bring down the prizes for the housey-housey we'll be playing later. They're in the sideboard.'

She ran up the stairs. It had been so hard being with him yet at a distance. She wanted to get closer to him. To peel off the face he showed to the world, and find the Blyth he became only with her. She knew the spark of attraction was still there, but Rosie needed to feel that open lack of pretence he had shown at the gallery that day. She needed to tell him all that she was feeling and to know what was in his heart. Then and only then could she give him her answer.

'Ooh come here,' he said, as soon as she shut the door behind them. 'God, that was torture. Kiss me, kiss me.'

Rosie stood on tiptoe, winding her arms about his neck. He moulded his body against hers and began to kiss her. At first they were gentle sipping exchanges, then drowsy, deep and drenching kisses that stole their breath. He held her face between his hands. 'Have you thought about what I asked you last time? Please, please say yes?'

Blyth was irresistible.

'I want you to say it again,' she insisted.

He went down on one knee and looked up into her face. 'Rosie Forrest, will you marry me? I love you.'

'Why do you love me?'

He smiled at her. 'Because I know you for what you are, warm and loving but more than that. We're like two bits of a jigsaw: the only bits that fit together.' He grinned at her. 'I'm a conceited pushy bugger most of the time. With you I find the best part of myself, the part that got left behind in all the ducking and diving. You rescued me and I want to stay rescued.'

'And?' she teased.

'I want to be with you always. I want to love you and make you happy. Marry me, Rosie Forrest. You can't say no.'

She burst out laughing. Only Blyth could make such a proposal. 'Yes, yes, yes, yes,' she said, punctuating her words with kisses.

He kissed her forehead, then her eyelids. 'Thank you,' he whispered. 'Thank you.'

26

Pearl sat in the shifting-shed on the first day back after Christmas, feeling as cheerless as the weather. The trip to the Nile had been a big disappointment. She had worn her best blue twinset and the pearls Mum had left her, even a dab of 'Evening in Paris' behind each ear, but it hadn't done an atom of good. Joe had been as nice as pie but she could tell he was just being friendly. Pearl had been desperate for him to like her, well more than like if she was honest with herself. Yet, all her smiling at him, all the accidental standing under the mistletoe, had achieved nothing – not a flicker of interest. What had really rubbed salt into her wounded pride was the announcement of Rosie's engagement to that naval officer. It was straight out of the *Woman's Weekly* stories that she read each week. The only way she had managed to get through the day was the thought of pouring out all her disappointment to Daisy on the way home. Some hopes! Aunt Daisy never drew breath, rattling on and on about how wonderful Miriam was and how pretty Rosie was. Pearl burned with the unfairness of it all. After the terror of last year with Kenny, she had been counting on this Christmas to make up for it. She deserved to be happy.

She slumped in the corner eating her marmite

sandwich and drinking the tea from her flask, while the others laughed and shared their news.

'Blimey, Pearl, what's up with you? Got a face like a kite,' said Marj, nudging her.

'Just things,' she said, near to tears.

'Give us a for instance.'

'What?' she mumbled.

'For instance, I can't hardly lift me face from the floor because I put a fiver on a horse and it come in last. Or, for instance I lost me diamond bracelet down the drain. Or this bloke what I fancies like mad won't give me the time of day.'

Pearl burst into tears.

'That's it, you have a good boo hoo, and you'll feel tons better.' Marj handed her a hankie and poured her another cup of tea. 'Was it that Joseph you was on about?'

Pearl nodded and sniffled.

'What I say is, if a chap don't fancy you, you just gotta look for someone new. Plenty more fish in the sea but who wants to marry a kipper?'

The others laughed, and even Pearl had to give a watery smile in the face of Marj's unstoppable good spirits.

'That's it, you go and give your face a splash under the tap and put on a bit of lipstick. Tell you what, there's a dance up at Fort Brockhurst on Wednesday – great band, the Golden Arrows. Fancy coming up with us?'

'I don't know,' said Pearl, blowing her nose.

'Come on, it'll be fun. Me sister Ruby's going too. Got a bike, have ya?'

'Won't it be dangerous in the dark and the ice on the roads?'

'Just have to go careful,' said Ruth. 'Right that's settled, we best get back to the labby or we'll be having our money docked.'

While the men stood round the tea-urn, Daisy took the letter out of her overall pocket. She had picked it up from the mat that morning while Pearl was upstairs getting ready. There was a French stamp on it. It would be news of Kenny's wedding, she was sure of it. Not a subject to bring up with Pearl, even at the best of times. And now with her disappointment over Joe Forrest, she was a nightmare to live with. Daisy sighed. The poor kid had built up her hopes sky-high. Being young was not all it was cracked up to be, not by a long shot. Thank God she had got her Frank, even if he was thousands of miles away. Who'd be seventeen again – certainly not her. After taking a swig of tea she opened the letter.

Dear Auntie Daisy and Pearl,
Lydie and I were married on the 23rd of December. It was bitterly cold but the sun was shining on the snow-filled hedges and fields. We walked together from her home to the civic office. Lydie's mother and father followed behind with a few friends and neighbours. One old man kept calling out, 'Vive le mariage,' or 'Long live the marriage.' The service was very short, hardly a service at all. I felt sad for Lydie that she was cheated of a church wedding and the chance to wear a bride's dress because I'm not a Catholic. But in spite of that she looked so happy and I couldn't stop smiling. My best man, Bluey Hayes has taken

some pictures. I will send one to you when they are developed.

We walked back to the house together, now man and wife. Her mother had roasted a goose and there was wonderful wine. Her father made a speech but I didn't understand a word of it. But, I could feel that everyone was happy for us in spite of the unsettled state of things.

Thank you for making it all possible by sending out my birth certificate. I wish you could have been with us both of you. There was a moment standing there when I thought of Mum. I would give anything for her to be with us to meet Lydie and know how happy I am. If only I could change the past. Then Pearl and I would be close like in the old days. But, then I would probably have joined the navy and not come to France and met my Lydie.

I know we're living in a fool's paradise in Les Armandiers, any moment our happiness will be stolen. I wish that I could have sent Lydie back to England but her Mother needs her here. A few weeks ago the doctor told her that she has cancer in her breast and Lydie can't think of leaving. Madame Brechard is a fighter and will keep going as long as she can. I'm trying to value every second with Lydie knowing each day could be our last.

Please Daisy, keep writing to me I need some home contact. Could you let me know if the worst happens and Lydie comes to England you will make her welcome, I don't deserve your kindness but she does.

Love to you both,
Kenny.

Daisy reached in her pocket for her handkerchief. Who would have thought a year ago that Kenny would have been capable of writing such a letter? Reading it had been a tonic. It justified her faith in people. Now, all she had to do was get Pearl to write to him. Even if all she did was to pour out her anger it would be a start. She smiled almost hearing her Frank's voice in her head.

'Daisy, you're a sucker for a happy ending.'

Putting the letter back in her pocket she went back to her bench. She had settled to the work in the rectifying shop. She and old Harry Gibbons were getting on a treat. She created none of the animosity and frustrations that Thelma had caused. Being married and homely-looking could be an advantage. Daisy found she had an aptitude for using machine tools: it was all to do with the feel of it. Harry showed her how to operate the lathe, the milling machine and the hand tools: reamers, scrapers, files, toffee hammers, mallets and gauges. She had been a willing pupil, and found satisfaction in acquiring new skills. There was a purpose and satisfaction in bringing the battered shell-cases back into operational use. It made her feel as if she was part of the war effort, just one little nail in Hitler's coffin. What she had realised was that she quite liked working with men. They were a lot less touchy, and the jokes were better. They treated her as if she was one of them, and perhaps she was. Certainly she had never mastered the primping and preening aspect of womanliness, but on the other hand she did enjoy sex. Her mind skated over that frustrating subject and addressed itself to why Harry was being so quiet. Subtlety was useless.

'What's up with you?'

'Bit of bad news, a real sickener, the missus got a letter from her sister up in Liverpool. Kath's boy is in the Merchant, their ship hit a mine. Blown out the water, no survivors. Only seventeen, poor little sod.'

'Oh Harry, I am sorry, that's terrible.'

'Missus was all for packing her bags and going up there, but Kath got her bloke at home and a couple of daughters so she don't want for comfort. Thank Christ we never had kids. They breaks your heart one way and another.'

Daisy said nothing, and concentrated on reaming the rough edges off the inside of a shell-case before testing it again on the shaft.

'Worst bit is feeling that we ain't making any headway in this war. Here we are knocking out ordnance at the rate of bloody knots, and Jerry is beating us hands down.'

'Are we downhearted?'

'Too bloody right,' Harry answered. He got out his snuffbox and laid a little heap of powder on his wrist before snorting it up his nose. It was followed by an explosive sneeze.

'Least your tubes is clear,' grinned Daisy. 'That's one thing you don't have to worry about.'

The workers went back to their benches. The rectifying shop was never silent. In the background to shouted conversations was the clang of metal as the brass casings were shifted from one bench to another, the clatter of hammers and the whine of machine tools.

'How about your Frank?'

Daisy paused. By rights he should have been

home by now, and out of the navy looking out for some cushy little number to see him right until retirement. Now, it was unlikely she'd see him 'til the end of the war. In spite of her surface cheeriness, she felt as gloomy as Harry about the outcome. 'Don't say much except it's hot and he's browned off being stuck out there. 'Course, what with the censoring he's muzzled so to speak. We just plans what we're gonna do in the future and goes over things in the past.'

'Might go to a dance on Wednesday,' Pearl said, as they sat in the canteen over a plate of corned beef hash.

'Good idea, what d'you reckon to wear?'

'That skirt I got that was too small for Marj. It's got loads of pleats and swirls about when you walk. Have to put my hair up in rags. The perm is growing out a bit now.'

Daisy debated showing Pearl the letter from Kenny, but decided against it. She'd wait until they were home sometime and her niece was in a really good mood. This dance night could go either way.

'What d'you think about me going on the bike? Is it a bit risky?'

'Everything's risky these days, Pearl. You could catch a bus but that means hanging about in the cold and the dark. Reckon if you're careful and you all stays together, you should be all right.'

'Could I stay the night at Marj's house and come to work from there?'

Daisy doused her plate with a liberal helping of HP sauce. 'It'll do you good to be with young girls for a change 'stead of being stuck with your old auntie.'

Pearl gave a rare smile. 'I'll tell Marj when I get back. What will you do with yourself?'

Daisy smiled. 'I think I'll settle down with a glass of the old raspberry wine and write to Frank. You written to your Dad lately?'

'Nothing to tell him.'

'I expect he'd like to know you were thinking about him and that you sent your love.'

'Fancy some plums and custard?'

Daisy winced. 'Too sour, sets your teeth on edge.'

'That's because of the rationing. They're cutting down on the sugar.'

Walking back to the shed, Daisy decided to nip over to the Nile on Wednesday night. Now she had got back in contact with Miriam she didn't want to lose touch again. They had hardly had time to say much over Christmas, but seeing her had really lifted her spirits. Yes, a couple of hours in the Nile going back down Memory Lane was just what the doctor ordered.

On Wednesday morning Pearl woke with a headache. She had slept with her hair tied up in rags, and they had dug into her head like lumps of rock. Carefully she folded her skirt and blouse and packed them in her case, along with a nightie and sponge bag. She would have to tie it onto the carrier on the back of her bike.

Daisy was busy packing up their sandwiches. Eating them at the morning tea-break instead of making breakfast gave them an extra half-hour in bed.

'What d'you reckon to chickens?' she asked, as Pearl handed her two paper bags.

'How d'you mean, chickens? Eating them or what?'

'No. I've a fancy to keep them. It'd be one way of getting some eggs and we could swap them for other things. Like we did in the last war.'

'Won't they keep us awake with their squawking? What will the neighbours say?'

'Should think they'll be only too pleased to have the chance of eating scrambled egg again. This rationing don't seem much now, but once it's really taken hold we'll be in for a lean, boring time on the eating front.'

Pearl handed over her coat and hat in the cloakroom at Fort Brockhurst and waited for her ticket. She was frozen after cycling from Elson. Ruby and Marj stood by the mirror combing their hair.

'Hope that Gordon's here. You remember him Ruby? The Scotch bloke with the wavy black hair. Ever so good at the tango, he was. Said I was a natural.'

'Natural what I'd like to know,' teased Ruby. 'Give us over that comb, you ain't the only one wanting to look her best.'

The hall was cold and smelled of chalk and dusty curtains. In front of her was a sea of khaki uniforms. As the band struck up a quickstep Pearl was reminded of her mother dancing around the kitchen with Kenny. They had cleared the chairs out of the way and she had sat on the table in the corner to watch them.

'The new Fred Astaire, that's what you are,' Dulcie Bunting had said.

Pearl knew that Daisy had had a letter from him yesterday. He had probably got married by now. She felt a spurt of anger. Why should he be happy and have things turn out well for him after what he did to her? Mum would be pleased for him, another voice whispered in her head.

'Like a dance?'

Startled, Pearl looked up to see a young soldier standing in front of her. He was blushing, and across the floor she could see his mates laughing and egging him on. If she said no, he'd have to slink back across the floor to further teasing. She smiled. He wasn't much to write home about but what had she to lose? At least a dance would warm her up a bit.

'All right then,' she said.

'What's your name?' he asked her.

'I'm Pearl, Pearl Bunting, what's yours?'

'Maurice Reeves.' Again he smiled. 'I'm afraid I've got two left feet. I'll apologise now before we start. I'm sure I'll tread all over you.'

'Let's see, shall we?'

After a couple of false starts they began to circle the floor. 'Quick, slow, quick quick, slow,' she repeated, and then he got it and they were away. When the music stopped they stood talking on the edge of the floor.

'Are you a local girl?' he asked.

'Yes, I've lived here always. Where d'you come from?'

'Dorchester, miles away from the sea, thatched cottages, that sort of thing.'

He was nice, she thought, polite and well-spoken. 'Have you been in the army long?'

'Three months, it's all been a bit of a shock.'

Looking at him, Pearl could see that Maurice was not the typical loud-mouthed squaddie. The band started up again and they quickstepped away with much greater confidence. Over his shoulder, she could see Marj throwing back her head and laughing. The soldier with her must be the Gordon she had been drooling about. He was flashily good-looking. Ruby was talking with another girl she'd seen at Priddy's. 'What did you do before the army?' Pearl asked.

'I worked in a bookshop. Rather dull I suppose,' he smiled apologetically, 'and a lot quieter than the army.' They did another circuit of the floor and then he said, 'What do you do, Pearl?'

'I'm at Priddy's Hard. Not allowed to talk about it, really, sort of top secret.'

'You mean you're a spy?'

They both laughed. The music stopped and everyone went back to their seats.

'I don't want to let go of you,' said Maurice blushing. 'I can't get you a drink until the interval.'

'Come and meet my friends,' she said, catching hold of his hand.

'Hello Marj, hello Ruby,' he said, when she introduced him.

'Charmed I'm sure,' said Marj, carelessly turning back to Gordon. Ruby giggled.

'Sit here,' Pearl made room for him. She felt angry with them. Just because Maurice wasn't full of himself didn't mean he wasn't worth knowing. In fact, she was beginning to quite like him.

'Did you want to join up?' she asked him, later, as they sat sipping orange juice on the other side of the room away from her friends.

'Not really,' he said. 'I want to be a forester, like Giles Winterbourn in *The Woodlanders*. Have you read it?'

Pearl laughed. 'I thought it was a pub.'

'No, I'd like to look after a woodland. I'm a countryman, I want to learn how to coppice and know more about trees. What's your special interest?'

She blushed. 'Don't know, haven't really thought about it.'

Maurice stopped dancing. 'You must have something that you really care about,' he said. 'It's what makes life worth living. What we're fighting for I suppose.'

Pearl was startled. Maurice was the most interesting man she'd ever met. Outside the hall, they arranged to go to the pictures the next Saturday.

Marj said that she would see them back at the house and disappeared with Gordon.

Cycling back in the dark with Ruby, Pearl felt she had had a good time. Maurice was not a heartthrob but he had nice eyes and he had set her thinking.

At the Nile, Daisy was enjoying herself: it was just like old times. 'How's things over here?' she asked, diving her hand into a bag of crisps.

Miriam paused to serve an old woman a glass of stout, then came back to the corner of the bar. 'You know, Daisy, we've been here before. War knocks the heart out of you. Oh I'm a hundred percent better than last time. I've got Alec with me, we've got our home and two good kids, most of the time. But it's what might happen to them that frightens me. And I didn't realise until she'd gone, how much I leant on Beattie.'

'Funny, when the war started we was all expecting to be blasted to kingdom come the first day. Now it's a waiting game. Gets you down sometimes. My Frank is out in Singapore 'sposed to have bin let go last year, now God knows when I'll see him.'

Miriam's eyes were full of concern. 'Oh Daisy, here's me wittering on and you're over there on your own.'

'I got Pearl and I got letters.'

'Paper kisses, I remember them.'

'Your Beattie was a jewel, wasn't she?'

Miriam nodded.

Daisy could see that her friend wasn't far off crying.

'Perhaps it was old Beattie, up in heaven pulling strings, that made us bump into each other again. She knew we both needed an old pal to shore us up a bit.'

'You think so, really?'

''Course I do.'

'Oh Daisy, it's so good to see you. You're better than a tonic any day of the week.'

'Miss Parish's Food, nineteen forty,' Daisy chortled.

'Let's make this a regular thing, every Wednesday. Never very busy, you could come early and have a bit of supper with us.'

Daisy smiled. 'That would be champion. It's a

date, I'll come straight from work.'

Sitting on the bus going back to the Hard, Daisy smiled to herself. That was the secret in life, having something to look forward to.

27

'Hello Gorgeous, it's me. Listen, I've not got much time.'

Standing in the hall at the Wrennery, Rosie felt her spirits plummet. They were supposed to be meeting tomorrow night. She had been counting the hours to have some time alone with him, after the squash of people at Christmas. 'Blyth, you're going to say it's off, aren't you?'

'I'm as sick as you are. But, listen, listen. There's a good chance of a forty-eight-hour pass this coming weekend.'

'You sure?'

'Sure as anything. I want you to find us somewhere where we can be by ourselves.'

'That's a – well, I don't know, it's a big step.' Her voice floundered.

'Rosie, love. This may be our last chance for a long time.'

Fear dried her mouth. If she didn't see him then it could be too late.

'Listen, I'll phone you Thursday night. I can borrow some transport. Just tell me where we're going and I'll be there Saturday lunchtime at the latest. Got to go, love you?'

'Love you,' she said, putting down the receiver. Hurrying up the stairs to the attic, her mind seesawed between fear and excitement.

'Morning, you're up with the lark,' said Delia,

emerging from her blankets on the bottom bunk. 'What's up – couldn't you sleep?'

Rosie sat on the floor. 'It was Blyth on the phone.'

'Crikey! At seven o'clock in the morning, he must be keen.' Delia pushed her hair away from her face. 'Not something serious is it?'

Rosie would like to have kept it a secret, but she would need her friend's cooperation if the weekend with Blyth were to become a possibility. 'We can't meet on Thursday but he wants me to arrange something for the weekend.'

'Well, I'm sure your mother could arrange things.'

Rosie blushed.

'Crikey! Rosie, what are you saying? Are you sure about this? Where would you go? Not some seedy hotel?'

'I don't know. It's all so sudden and I haven't even got a weekend. I don't know.'

Delia climbed out of bed and knelt beside her. 'That's easy-peasy. We can swap. I'll go home the week after.'

'But it's your birthday, you've been looking forward to it.'

'Stuff and nonsense! It's not as if I'll be having a party, all my chums are scattered to the winds.'

Rosie burst into tears. 'Delia, thank you,' she blubbered, 'you're a gem. Oh! My brain's in a whirl. I don't know, I don't know.'

'For Pete's sake, stop saying you don't know. Look, you've got the weekend free. I've seen to that – all you've to do is find somewhere.'

'Delia, it's a secret.'

Her friend smiled at her. 'Cross my heart and hope to die.'

'Oh God,' gasped Rosie, 'look at the time. We'd better get ourselves together.' Blyth was forgotten in the scrabble to be washed, dressed and breakfasted by a quarter to eight.

'It's freezing out there,' said Gwyneth, looking out of the dining-room window. 'We'll all have to wrap up. Glad I'm not you two out on the road all day.'

'What's for dinner, Mrs Cherrit?' asked Delia. 'It'll give us something to look forward to.'

'It's make do and mend,' said their cook, setting down a fresh plate of toast. 'Cottage pie and bread-and-butter pudding.'

'Will there be custard?'

Mrs Cherrit smiled at Delia. 'We'll see what we can do.'

Back in their cabin, the two of them dressed for bad weather. Delia had brought back two pairs of long-johns from Hazlewood, a present from her father, and Rosie had been given two balaclavas by Connie.

'I'd got them done for my boys but I'll be glad to see them put to good use, my cocker,' she'd said. 'You go careful, now.'

Petty Officer Johns had advised them to stuff newspaper into the front of their jackets to keep out the cold. And as a final precaution they had a pair of silk gloves each, sent to them from Blyth and Justin.

'We wear them under wool gloves and topped off with our gauntlets. Thinking of you wearing them will make me feel part of your trips and feel that I'm looking after you,' Blyth had written.

'You'd think we were going to the Arctic,' laughed Delia, as she climbed onto the back of Rosie's bike.

Since their first day on the C-in-C's staff, they had clocked up the miles around the Portsmouth area. They had familiarised themselves with most of the surrounding police stations, barracks and shore bases, and were beginning to be sent further afield. Now, in the first week of January, they waited expectantly in the office at the dockyard to see what signals had come in overnight.

'Forrest, there's a signal to HMS *Tigris* in Newhaven,' said Petty Officer Johns. 'It's a straightforward run but, with these weather conditions, go carefully. If you start out now you'll be back before blackout. There's a café on the road out of Arundel, the Black Cat, evidently they do great Chelsea buns. Good luck.'

Rosie spread out her map on the table in the office and studied her route. It was a straightforward run, as far as she could see, passing through Chichester, Arundel and Worthing, and from there along a good coastal stretch through Brighton and on to Newhaven. She was confident that she could make the journey with few problems. The only challenge was the weather.

'Where are you going?' she asked Delia.

'Aldershot. Might try and drop into Hazlewood on the way back and see Mummy. See what time I make. How about you?'

'Newhaven.'

'Crikey, that's miles. Take care, see you tonight.'

'Tell Mrs Cherrit to save me some pudding

will you?'

She put her despatch rider's satchel over her shoulder, wrapped her scarf around her neck. 'See you tonight,' she said, patting the saddle of her own bike before going over to the navy-issue Ariel. It took a lot of kicking before it sparked into life. The snow was falling in fat flakes as she drove out of Portsmouth and onto the road for Chichester. She was glad of the goggles keeping the snow out of her eyes. There was little traffic on the road, and she made slow but steady progress. When she was on the open road, Rosie loved to open the throttle and speed along, feeling the wind whistle past her face, but not today. The wind sliced at her cheeks making her eyes water. Twice she almost skidded on a stretch of ice. Traffic moved slowly, churning the snow and turning it from sugar crystals to grey slush. Past Emsworth, she waited for the sight of Chichester cathedral spire to appear pointing her in the right direction. But the visibility was poor, and it took all her concentration to hold a steady course. By the time she reached the Black Cat on the road down to Worthing, her hands felt as if they were welded to the handlebars. Blinking, she tugged off her goggles and clambered from the bike and dragged it back onto its stand.

The Black Cat was by no means a starched table-cloth and copper-kettle establishment, but a no-nonsense transport cafe. A bacon-scented fug enveloped her as she opened the door. 'Tea and a Chelsea bun, please,' she said to the woman behind the counter.

'That'll be a sixpence, Miss. Won't find better

buns anywhere.'

'So I've heard.'

Rosie stood battling her way out of her gloves, and then tackled her helmet and balaclava. By the time she had undone her jacket, her food and drink were slapped down on the counter. It was good to stand after being crouched in one position for the last hour or so. Looking around her, she saw she was the only woman driver and the subject of some curiosity.

'What sort of uniform is that?' asked an old man in a greasy cap and overalls, with a plate of fried bread.

'I'm a Wren,' she said, stirring sugar with a teaspoon that was chained to the counter. 'Despatch Rider.'

'You women's getting everywhere. I seed one the other day chopping up logs. Great big woman she was.' He shook his head.

Whether it was amazement or disapproval, Rosie wasn't sure. The tea was sweet and strong. She unrolled the bun and chewed piece by piece, slowly relishing the spicy cinnamon taste and the plump raisins.

'Got far to go?' asked the old codger, stirring his tea.

'Far enough,' said Rosie, conscious of the crowded café.

It was a performance getting herself garbed up to leave. 'Thank you,' she called, as the bell jingled behind her. In her haste, she had wound the outside of the scarf next to her and it lay wet and clammy against her face. There was a layer of snow on her saddle, which she rubbed off with her gloves. She switched on the petrol below the tank, and stood astride, kicking it into life. The weather had not improved, and there were drifts of snow building up on the bends of the road. Rosie drove on cautiously. From Worthing she took the coastal road all the way to Newhaven. The sea was a sullen grey and still it snowed.

All the while, ticking away in her head was the question of where they could go for the weekend. It was a huge step for her to take. She wanted Blyth, wanted to show him how much she loved him and to have him love her. The thought of two whole days together after the scraps of time they'd had to make do with so far, was overwhelming. At one moment she felt a rush of excitement, and then doubt seized her. The thought of signing a register as Mr and Mrs Smith was too sordid to consider seriously. If only Gran were there for her to talk with.

At the docks she asked the policeman for directions for HMS *Tigris*.

'Down there, she's the outside one of those three. The minelayer.'

Rosie approached the gang-plank of the nearest ship.

'Signal for *Tigris*,' she said to the duty quartermaster, holding up her pass.

'Right, Miss, come aboard. Careful as you go, the deck's slippery.'

The procedure was repeated twice more and then she was taken below to the wardroom.

'Signal, Sir, for the captain,' she said to the duty officer. 'Can you sign here, please?'

'Thank you, Wren...' He set down his coffee

cup and added his signature to her log.

'Wren Forrest, Sir.'

'Travelled far, have you?'

'Portsmouth, Sir, on the road since nine.'

'Must have had a hell of a journey. I'll get the steward to put you up a spot of lunch before you leave. Come along to the pantry.'

'Steward, this is Wren Forrest, Despatch Rider from Pompey. Put her up something, will you?'

'Certainly, Sir.'

'Come in, Miss, take your coat off and sit yourself down, there.'

''Bye, Wren Forrest, safe journey to you,' said the lieutenant.

'The name's Sharky,' said the steward. 'Sharky Ward. I comes from Pompey. Let's see what we can rustle up for ya.'

Rosie sat on a stool in the little cubbyhole, feeling quite at home.

'Cheese on toast, a bit of Worcester sauce, and there's a cold snorker what I can slice up for ya. Mug of mulligatawny should chase it down.'

'Champion,' grinned Rosie. 'Thanks, Sharky.'

'Here, let's stick your scarf on them pipes. It'll warm up a treat. Be just the job by the time you're ready to be on your way.' He kept up a constant stream of chat while moving around the pantry, slicing the sausage, cutting the bread, and heating the soup.

'Where you from?'

'I'm a Pompey girl, live in Landport in Nelson Street.'

Sharky's face lit up. 'Not far from my place. Missus and me and two kids got a flat in Arundel

Street. Her dad's got a fruit and veg shop up near Fratton Bridge.' After putting her toast under the grill he turned to her. 'You wouldn't drop off a letter to Betty, would you? It's thirty-two A, above the shop it is.'

''Course I will,' smiled Rosie, 'be glad to.'

'Be back in two ticks,' he said, setting the plate down in front of her. 'Dig in.'

Rosie looked at her watch. It was almost twelve. She had a feeling of satisfaction at having found her way and delivered the signal. She felt part of the Navy.

'Very good,' she said to Sharky, handing him back the plate, and tucking his letter in the pocket of her breeches.

Rosie sat holding the mug of soup. Her fingers stung as the feeling crept back into them. She was not relishing the return journey. 'I'd better be getting back, Sharky. Want to be home before blackout.'

'Rather you than me, mate,' said Sharky, handing over her scarf.

'If ever you're near Nelson Street, you must drop into my Dad's pub, the Nile.'

The steward chuckled. 'Bin thrown out of there, still, was a good few years ago. Don't 'spect your old man will remember me. You go careful, now.'

Stepping off the gang-plank, on the ship nearest the dock, Rosie shuddered in spite of the warm scarf wrapped across her mouth. Although it had stopped snowing, her saddle resembled an iced cake. Sixty miles, she thought with a sinking heart.

On the way out of Arundel she realised she was bursting to use the toilet, and stopped at a pub. She was directed through the public bar and down a passage over a threadbare mat. It was a performance getting dressed and undressed, but on the other hand she was glad of her many layers. On her way back along the passage, someone shook her roughly by the shoulder.

'Here, what's your game? Going in the Ladies, you a peeping Tom or something?'

Standing on her dignity, she said. 'I'm Wren Forrest in the service of the King.'

'Oh my good God,' the man gasped. 'Oh Miss, I'm that sorry. Let me make it up to you, can I get you a drink?'

'You can put a new toilet roll in there and a fresh bar of soap.'

She laughed to herself as she pressed on towards Chichester. It was the sort of incident that would have made Gran chuckle. How proud she would have been of her and Blyth, wanting to know every last detail of their new lives, relishing their excitement. How she would have loved to fly.

'Wonderful what the human brain can do, finding a way to leave this earth and soar up into the sky. Just as we set limits on what's possible, the boundaries are pushed back yet again. I've lived in a time of wonders, and you will too. When I was a child it was sailing-ships and hiring-fairs. Now!' She had spread her hands in amazement. 'There's motorcars, the wireless and aeroplanes. If ever you get a chance, Rosie, you get up there and do it for your old Gran.'

I will, she promised, battling on. Leaving Chichester, she was waved on by an army truck and given the thumbs-up as she passed; grinning, Rosie did the same. The engine thrummed on and the snow started up again: nearly there. And then, it came to her. Solent Cottage. Directly she got home she would phone Uncle Albert. He'd told her that on a Monday evening he would be up at the farm, visiting his brother Samuel.

Full of her plans, Rosie became distracted. Coming into a bend she failed to slow the engine. Suddenly she was slithering out of control down a snow-packed incline. It was a shock how quickly it happened. Once she knew she was in one piece, Rosie scrabbled over to her bike. The engine was still going and the back wheel racing. Rosie switched if off and struggled to get the bike upright. She was now faced with the problem of getting back onto the road. After several failed attempts to push it up the bank, she restarted the machine and rode it out. *Let that be a lesson to you*, she chided herself, while waiting for a gap in the afternoon traffic. A few miles on and she was back on Portsea Island and following the traffic down to the dockyard.

'Hello, Forrest, you've made good time, considering the weather,' said PO Johns, looking at the office clock. 'Make yourself a cup of tea, then there's just one last signal. The Royal Marine Barracks at Eastney.'

'Can I go on my own bike and go back to the Wrennery afterwards?' Rosie asked. The spill on the road had shaken her, and she wanted to get back to her cabin and get out of her clothes. And, there was the phone call to Uncle Albert yet to be made.

'Providing they've no messages for us,' said Johns, returning to her paperwork.

'Just in time,' said the Royal Marine Wren at the barracks. 'There's a signal for HMS *Vernon*. Our despatch rider is on her way back from Deal and it's urgent.'

'Yes, Petty Officer,' said Rosie, swallowing down her irritation. Back she went along the sea-front and down to the shore base for underwater weapons known as HMS *Vernon*. There was some delay in getting a signature, and she stood in the signals office champing to be off. At last the Lieutenant arrived, and after saluting him she was on her way back to the Wrennery.

Coming in through the back door, she could hear Mrs Cherrit talking to someone in the kitchen. Hastily Rosie went through to the phone, and dialled the number for Samuel Pragnell's farm.

'Rosie, my dear well, well, this is a surprise. I haven't seen you for years. How's that brother of yours, still growing? A giant he was last time I set eyes on him. Albert, yes he's here. Hold on my dear. Yes, I'll give your love to Auntie Olive.'

She stood in the hall with a heap of coppers ready, in case her money ran out.

'Hello, Uncle Albert, I've not much time and a great favour to ask you.'

'Rosie, my dear girl, how wonderful to hear from you.'

She could feel the warmth in his voice giving her courage.

'Ask away my darling. If it's in my power to grant it to you, you shall have it and gladly.'

'Blyth's got a forty-eight-hour pass for the weekend. I'd like to bring him to stay at the cottage. Is that all right with you?'

'It will be my pleasure, Rosie. I shall clear off up to Sammy's farm. When do you want to come?'

'Probably Saturday 'til early Monday morning?'

'Think no more about it. Everything will be spick and span, and I'll leave a stew bubbling on the stove. The key will be under the stone lion.'

'You won't say anything to–' She felt disloyal even asking, but Albert was ahead of her.

'Rosemary, you are an adult. What you choose to tell your parents is your affair entirely.'

'Uncle Albert, thank you, thank you. You're a jewel.'

He chuckled. 'A rather battered carbuncle I should think, by now. You know my dear, Beatrice would have been so thrilled at the two of you getting together.'

Rose smiled to herself. 'D'you think she would have given us her blessing?'

'Twice and thrice over, my darling.'

28

Connie Spooner laid the table for breakfast. It would be Lionel's first day back at Nelson Street School. His clothes were warming by the fire, and she had his mug of cocoa cooling on the table. She went into the kitchen to see how he was getting on with washing himself.

'Here, give us the flannel, my cocker, you could grow taters in them ears.'

'Owhh,' shrieked Lionel. 'You're hurting.'

'Such a fuss,' she laughed. 'That's better. You go and get yourself dressed and I'll make your toast.'

'Don't want to go,' he whined. 'I'm not well.'

'You was well enough to go to build a snowman with Martin down the road yesterday.'

'All me friends are in Romsey. I'll be like a new boy.'

'You don't want to go back there, do ya?'

'I just want to stay home.'

Connie sighed. It was taking her all her time to put a bit of spirit into the boy. The last thing she wanted was to have a whining invalid on her hands. 'Lionel, I want you to be a big boy and go to school. We all got to be brave. I don't 'spect Joe wants to go into places that's full of flames. Bet he gets the willies lots of times. Being brave is about doing things what scares us and getting over it. That's what heroes is all about.'

Lionel looked doubtful.

'You'll miss out on playtime. Thought you was wanting to take your marbles. Do you reckon those soldiers in them tanks we was looking at in the *War Weekly* wanted to be out there getting shot at?'

'Dunnow.'

'They wants to be back home with their pals, kicking a ball up and down the street, eating a bag of chips or sitting in the pub over a pint. That's it,' she said, handing him his jersey. 'Let me do your parting and we'll put a bit of Brylcreem on. You got a bit sticking up there at the back. That's my lad. You looks a proper boy. Not too cissy-smart and not too slap-dab. Sit up and have your breakfast. Ready for some toast?'

'Suppose so,' he said grudgingly.

'If you go to school you'll make new pals, and then there's no knowing what games you'll have.'

Lionel looked doubtful. 'When's Joe coming round again?'

'Well, he lives down the station house with all the other fire-boys. They don't get much time off at all. But, you know what he promised?'

'Every time he comes round to see his Mum he'll come and knock the door.'

'Well,' said Connie. 'He can't say fairer than that.'

While Lionel toiled at his toast she sat and wrote her shopping list on the back of an old envelope. She thought of her dead sons Rodney and Clive, lively harum-scarum lads. What was it that made them so eager to rush out into the world? And why was Lionel such a timid child? The answer was love. The little boy's courage and confidence had withered in the indifferent climate of the Scoggins household. Well, he'd been transplanted into Spooner soil, a richer substance entirely.

'Right, my cocker. Let's get down that school and see what's going on there. You ready?'

Lionel scuffed his toe across the mat. 'Yes, Auntie Connie,' he said.

He would do it, she had chivvied him into going, but wanting to go or even looking forward to going was a long way off.

Alec Forrest set the clean ashtrays along the bar and rubbed last night's score from the dartboard. Well, that was another Christmas done and dusted – the first of the war. He had no illusions that the present conflict would be over quickly. There was a tendency among the top brass always to underestimate the enemy. The German nation was highly skilled and disciplined. It had taken four years to knock them into submission, in the last war, and then they'd had the Yanks to help them. The losses at sea grieved him.

Thank God Joseph was not involved. Mind you, he was fooling himself there. If the German bombers came over and gave Pompey a pounding he'd be in the thick of it with his fire-fighting. As for Rosie, his precious daughter, losing her didn't bear thinking about. She was a beauty and the dead spit of Beattie – all that energy and fire. He had seen the looks exchanged between her and young Blyth, and felt a sudden fierce jealousy. He had been her hero and now he was what? Just Dad. Watching Blyth watching her, he could see the desire in his eyes. Jesus! If he ever hurt Rosie, he would – what? What could he do? His ARP work seemed futile. Traipsing round the streets, spying on his neighbours' blackout infringements, made him feel like a school sneak. Every week there was another leaflet to deliver – from: how to store your gas mask, to: masking your window against bomb blast and how to use a stirrup pump. The sandbags stacked around the public shelters were rotting away, swamped by rain, and more often than not soaked in dog's pee. Even the shelters had to be kept locked, to stop courting couples sneaking in there for a bit of a fumble. Mind you, he thought, it'll be a different story when the Jerry sends his planes in earnest.

There was a knock on the back door. Glad of the diversion, he opened it to Connie Spooner.

'Hello, Connie, come in, come in, you're as welcome as the flowers in May.'

The little woman smiled at him. 'Cripes, I wish it was May, my cocker. This cold weather gives me the pip.'

'Where's the lad?'

'I've got him off to school, not without a struggle.'

'Fancy a half of stout?'

Connie smiled. 'I reckon I got my work cut out with him. But we'll get there by and by.'

'Poor nipper, he hasn't had the best start. God knows where that Thelma's got to.'

'Funny you should say that.' Miriam came in with a laden shopping bag, on the end of Connie's words. 'Daisy was saying that she fetched up at their place. Got a job at Priddy's Hard. Seemingly she and Pearl had a fall-out over a piece in the paper about Lionel. November it was. Then she left and there's bin no word since.'

'Can't say I miss her,' said Alec, drawing himself a half of bitter. 'Moody and work-shy. We get on just as well without her.'

'Wrote to her mother down in Devon at Christmas, but not a word.'

Connie set down her empty glass. 'Right, where d'you want me today, Miriam? I got a couple of hours to spare before Lionel gets back. They're only in mornings for the moment.'

'There's a stack of ironing upstairs. I need to give the lounge bar a good sort out. I'll be up later for a cup of tea.'

'Right, my cocker,' said Connie. 'I'll have the teapot warming about eleven.'

'What's up, Alec?'

He smiled at Miriam and shook his head. 'Nothing, love, well nothing I can do anything about. Just the war and the winter, and feeling old and helpless.'

'Oh, that's nothing at all then.'

She came and put her arm around him. 'You're not used to being a civvy, where you can't do much and just have to make the best of it. It's all waiting and dreading.'

He squeezed her hand: she could read him like a book. 'When you're in the thick of it, at least you feel you can make a difference. Least you get to face the enemy and do something about him.'

'You get to kill some German mother's son, and your opposite number gets to kill one of our boys.'

'That's what war's about,' he said wearily. 'You can't believe that we should just stand by and let Hitler and his thugs get away with it?'

'I think they should have a boxing-match. Get some tough bloke like Churchill to get into the ring with Hitler. Have them knock seven bells out of each other, and that would be the end of it.'

'But Hitler's younger than Churchill. He'd be no match for him.'

'Well, I reckon Churchill would be crafty and bite his leg or talk him to death.'

They looked at one another and burst out laughing.

'What grieves me,' she said, 'is that those who take us into war are not the ones that get hurt. They talk and talk and get all the men fired full of hate, then go back to their posh houses while the young lads the world over get slaughtered.'

'Wish I could be out there doing something.'

'You think running a pub is nothing?'

'No, but I was a sailor. I know what those lads are feeling. I've got a skill.'

'That's just bunkum. Beattie'd have you for that. Everyone counts, not just the fighting men. We all got to hold each other up. What d'you think the Nile stands for?'

'What d'you mean?' he asked, surprised at the anger in her voice.

'It's where people meet to have a bit of a yarn, tell a joke or have a game of darts. But, it's more than that, Alec. Who supported Connie when her men were taken?'

'We did.'

'Not just us, it was our locals gathering round

her. How about all those little letters, and bunches of flowers out of their gardens, that people brought in when your mother died? Where does a sailor go when he's in a strange port? To a pub. Who gets out the ladder when someone gets locked out, who has a whip-round when they've fallen on hard times? Who's the first to put out the bunting, in good times? We are, and all the other little pubs up and down this country. How about when you're away? What's the first thing you promise yourself when you get back home – a drink with your pals at the local. It's like Beattie used to say; we're a first-aid post without bandages. And we should be proud of that.'

Alec drew her into his arms, too moved to speak. He felt ashamed of his grousing. Christ! What would he be without her? 'Love, I'm sorry.' He managed to choke out the words.

Miriam smiled at him, her eyes bright with tears. 'Least I got a hug out of it. Now give us a kiss to make my knees tremble, and we'll have a nip of rum apiece. That should set us up for the day.'

Alec laughed. 'If you'll stop talking I'll do just that. It's not your knees that should be trembling, it's mine.'

Connie stood at the doorstep, looking up the street towards the school. How had he got on, she wondered. One glimpse of him would tell her. There was beano pie waiting in the oven. It wasn't nothing much, just mashed spud, baked beans and a scattering of cheese over the top – comforting and flavoursome. Down at Woolworth's she'd got a magic painting book for him, and a bag of sherbet dabs. He'd have to earn them, stand on the stool by the draining-board and dry up for her. She'd got a book from an old teacher, with all the letters set out and tracing-paper in front of each page, so you could practise each one. She meant to bring him along like she had her own boys.

Lionel slouched towards her, head down and hands in pockets. Connie sighed. 'Well, my cocker, how'd you get on?'

He shrugged.

'Let's get in the warm and you can tell me all about it. Hang your coat up, that's it.'

She spooned out the pie and set it in front of the silent Lionel.

'Want some sauce?'

'What's a tart?' he asked her.

'It's a sort of cake made with pastry, and jam or apples and things,' she said, wondering where the question was leading.

'Grace Burgess said my Mum was a tart and didn't want me.'

So it had come, the question she was dreading. 'Well, I don't know how Grace knows anything about your Mum, Lionel. Anything you want to know about her you should ask me. I knew her, and your Gran.'

'She didn't like me, no one does.'

'I like you Lionel, you know I do and Joe does. You're his pal. Your Mum was unhappy and I don't think anyone loved her.' Cripes, she thought, I'm making a right mess of this.

'Was it Gran?'

'What d'you mean, love?'

'She was nasty to her, all moany. Sometimes she hit her with a stair-rod.'

'Did she hit you, Lionel?'

'No, me Mum wouldn't let her.'

'Well, there you are then. She must have liked you.'

'Don't think so. Never smiled at me, always telling me off.' He took the sauce and shook it on his pie. After eating a mouthful he looked at Connie. 'She said I was a big mistake.'

'We all say lots of things we don't mean. You know that. When we get angry and fed up with things. I reckon if we was to see your Mum now, she would give you a cuddle and say she was sorry.'

Lionel shrugged.

Connie wanted to weep.

'Well, I reckon you have come to me just at the right time. You and me can help each other. I've lost my husband and my boys, and your Mum has got herself lost.'

'Where d'you think she's gone?'

'There's lots of places she might be. Perhaps she's working in a pub somewhere, or perhaps she got hurt, like you, and she's in a hospital.'

He stared at his plate. 'Could be dead.'

'Perhaps she is, Lionel. I don't know.' Connie wanted to gather him up in her arms but she waited. Whatever happened, lying would solve nothing.

'Why didn't she like me?' He stared at the table.

'Because she was unhappy and didn't like

359

herself very much.' She went around to his side of the table and sat beside him in the other chair. 'I want my boys to come back and my husband Arthur, and you want your Mum. What can we do about it?'

'Dunnow,' he mumbled.

'We could be friends.'

Lionel pushed his plate away and leant over the table, his head in his hands. Connie took him up onto her lap. They sat together with her arms around him. His body was stiff with hurt. Connie waited.

Lionel gasped, and then the tears came. He slumped against her. 'I've got you, my love. Connie's got you,' she said, rocking him in her arms. In the end, she thought, it wasn't words that mattered, it was touch that healed every time.

29

Rosie parked the bike in the yard and looked about her. What a gift, Solent Cottage for the whole weekend. They had never had more than a few hours together, and now there would be a great sweep of time and privacy. She crunched over the snow to the stone lion and tilted it to retrieve the key. As she pushed open the back door a wave of heat engulfed her. Dear Uncle Albert, making sure they had a warm welcome before he went up to the farm. Everything was neat and tidy. The cottage smelt of lavender polish, and there was a stew bubbling gently on the back of the stove. She got a knife and lifted the lid on the iron pot. Saliva flooded her mouth – venison stew.

In the sitting-room the fireguard was wedged in place by the poker, and the scuttle was heaped with logs. She crept upstairs to the back bedroom and shivered at the change in temperature. On the dressing-table was a chipped willow-patterned jug with a spray of yellow winter jasmine, and beside it a sketchbook with a sheet of notepaper on top.

My Dear Rosie and Blyth,
Enjoy your time here. It comes with my blessing and that of Beatrice your Grandmother. Don't waste a second. I found this pad the other day and thought you might smile at these sketches from our time in

Lemon Street. The memory of those times may sustain us in a world gone mad. Take them with you as a promise of better times to come.

Your affectionate old Uncle Albert

She stood there in her helmet and jacket, turning the pages. They recorded the summer of 1920, when she was three and living in Lemon Street, next-door to Blyth and his family. There they were, the two of them in the back yard, with a bowl of bubbles between them. Blyth, his head a mass of curls, was holding a pipe towards her and smiling. He was dressed in a pair of ragged shorts. She feasted on the dimpled backs of his hands, and that smile. The child that was herself smiled back at him, in her gingham bonnet and sun-dress. Oh, she remembered those little canvas shoes, how they had rubbed her heels. Rosie turned the page, and her eyes filled with tears. There was Gran with the two of them, one on each knee, listening to one of her stories. 'Gran, you were lovely,' she whispered. 'I was so lucky.'

She began to unpack the few possessions she'd brought with her: sponge bag, underwear and a satin nightdress that Delia had lent her.

'I can't let you show up in those pyjamas,' she'd said. 'If I'm to play Cupid there are rules to follow.' She had waved away her thanks. 'You would do the same for me,' she grinned.

Rosie smoothed down the satin folds. Two whole nights alone with Blyth. It was a dangerous gift. They had never had much more than a few hours together, and now there would be this great sweep of time and privacy. In the normal state of things this weekend would not happen until her honeymoon, when she would have a ring on her finger and a marriage certificate in her suitcase. But she might never see Blyth again – never have another chance to show how much she loved him. She went downstairs and filled the kettle. On the table was a copy of The Times folded and unread. The war would have to wait, whatever the news, she would cry tomorrow.

Crack! A pebble hit the window. Blyth! She rushed downstairs and hurled herself into his arms. His gloved fingers on her face made her shiver. 'Ooh, you're icy.' She kissed his mouth until they were breathless. 'Come in and let me warm you up, there's tea in the pot.'

'Let me get unwrapped,' he said. 'I've been thinking about you all the way here, nearly drove into a hedge I was so excited.' He threw back his head and sniffed like a dog. 'What is that smell? It's making me dribble.' He licked his lips. 'Lead me to it.'

'Venison,' she grinned at him.

'Bit early for dinner,' he said, looking at his watch, 'only quarter to ten.'

While he took off his jacket and boots Rosie poured the tea.

Blyth took her in his arms and danced her around the floor, singing to her as they went:

'*Rambling Rose, Rambling Rose, I want to get inside your clothes,*
Want to tell you how I love you, Want to hold you in my arms.'

'Those aren't the words,' she giggled.

'Those are my words,' he whispered against her neck. 'This is our little world cut off from everyone else. There are no rules. Being together, that's all that matters.'

Rosie closed her eyes and leant her head against his chest. It was going to be all right. After another circle around the kitchen, Blyth led her to a chair.

'A cup of tea, wonderful.' He held it in both hands. 'Well, Rosie, are you pleased to see me?'

'Yes, yes, of course I am.'

'Hours and hours alone together. It's a gift.' He put down his cup and stood behind her chair, massaging her neck. 'Undo your blouse, that's it.' Again he sang to her: *Rambling Rose, Rambling Rose.* The steady pressure of his fingers unloosed the knots of tension. Still singing, he held open his arms and danced her towards the stove where the stew still simmered. He leant over and turned off the gas beneath it. They danced into the other room, over to the window, where he closed the curtains. Blyth took the guard away from the fire, and pulled her down onto the sofa beside him. He held her in his arms, and kissed her forehead and then her eyelids – little sipping kisses. He kissed her mouth until she was breathless.

They began to undress. Rosie's blouse was tossed on top of Blyth's shirt. When the heap of clothes was complete, they slid together onto the floor. He stroked her breasts and her body came alive under his touch. She pressed her fingers into the hollows above his collar-bones, and stroked the hair curling across his chest. Stroking, sipping, kissing, they aroused one another. She turned onto her back and he leant above her, smiling into her eyes, his body dappled by firelight. Slowly, tenderly, with his fingers and his lips he brought her to a shuddering release.

'Close your eyes,' he whispered, 'I've got to make things safe for us.'

She heard him rummaging among their clothes, and then he was with her again re-awakening her with his kisses. Rosie shuddered as he entered her. They were carried deeper and faster, moving as one, breath to breath, until they fell back into a state of melting content. Then he left her for a moment. Returning, he lay on his side, smiling into her eyes. Rosie wanted to hold the moment. I want this now not to pass into the future, she thought. I want it to go on and on, like the ripples spreading outwards from a pebble dropped in the sea. I want it rooted in me. She took his hand and kissed his open palm, then folded his fingers over the kiss.

'I love you, Rosie,' he said. 'Don't forget that and don't ever forget me.'

'How could I forget you?' she asked, his words bringing a sliver of dread into her mind.

'I might fly too near to the sun.' He stroked her hair away from her face.

'I will always love you,' she said. 'But, we can't think about always. None of us can. You said so.'

'I know,' he whispered. 'Just sometimes I want more. I don't just want to fizzle out unmarked, unremembered, with no flowers, as if I'd never been.'

She took his face between her hands. 'You will be in me like the letters in seaside rock. If they chop me up you'll be there in the pieces. Wherever I go, you'll be there in what I think or do, because I love you.'

They made love again, more assuredly, asking for and giving pleasure.

'Oh yes, touch me there, slower, slower, yes, yes.'

'Oh God, God, God!'

Rosie collapsed in laughter. 'I never knew you were religious.'

Blyth lay on his back grinning at her. 'Rosie Forrest, you could do more for religion in one day than a lifetime's preaching by the Church of England.' He shivered. 'I'd better see to the fire or we'll freeze.'

Rosie's stomach rumbled. 'I'll get washed and dressed upstairs and then we'll have the stew.' She carried a jug of hot water upstairs and quickly soaped herself all over with a flannel. Dragging on her slacks and jumper, she ran back to the kitchen and relit the gas. In the larder was a brown loaf and a wedge of cheese wrapped in waxed paper. There was a jar of pickled onions, and butter, and some strawberry jam. It was warm still in the kitchen, and she laid the table and sliced the bread while the stew came to the boil.

Blyth came into the kitchen with a bottle of red wine. 'This is a present from Juss. If you find the glasses and corkscrew, I'll make myself presentable. Any hot water?'

She grinned, wine from Juss and nightie from

Delia. The clock chimed twelve. There was ages and ages yet.

'To us,' said Blyth, raising his glass. 'You and me, for ever and ever.'

The wine was soft and fruity on her tongue. They finished the stew and mopped their plates. After washing up together they searched the sideboard and found a game of Snakes and Ladders and set it out on the mat by the fire. They finished up the wine and dozed on the sofa together with Gran's crocheted blanket draped over them.

The day slipped away. At eight o'clock they took a cup of tea up to bed. They talked by candlelight, shivering between the sheets. Blyth lay curled around her while she read to him from Uncle Albert's copy of *Treasure Island*. Finishing the chapter, she closed the book; Blyth had fallen asleep. She lay awake not wanting to lose a moment of their time together, listening to his breathing and watching the stars through a gap in the curtains.

Blyth uncurled himself and slid out of bed. He shuddered as his feet came in contact with the bare boards. They had come to bed naked. Not wanting to wake her, he tiptoed into the other room and took a blanket and wrapped it around him. He padded downstairs and dressed by the embers of last night's fire. While the kettle boiled he rolled himself a cigarette. In two more days he would be back on the *Unrivalled* and out to sea. Anything could happen. It was what he was good at, what he had trained for, and yet... No, he must compartmentalise in order to survive. Shove it back in the locker marked 'Navy', and go back to Rosie.

He stood at the end of the bed looking down at her, flushed in sleep. No one excited him as she did, challenging him at every turn, drawing him on. Twisting, turning, she never yielded an inch of who she was to accommodate him. Yet she could be so tender, reaching out to him and soothing his fears. What was she thinking, he wondered. Was she whirring along on her motor bike, was she dreaming of him?

He looked around the room and wished he had a camera to record the scene. Looking away from Rosie, his attention was drawn to the sketchpad lying on the dressing table. Idly he began to turn the pages. Albert was a wonderful observer of people. Blyth had forgotten just how good he was. He looked at the picture of himself as a boy, at the frayed trousers and bare feet, then turned the page. There was his sister Mary at about twelve years old, standing at the clothes-line with a peg in her mouth. He could feel her anger. On he went. There was Fred, his Dad, with some rope, showing him how to do a running bowline. His younger self stood there, fingers itching to try it for himself. There was Granny Pragnell with him and Rosie, showing them a picture-book. On the last page was him with the shoe-shine box. His brother Harry in his naval uniform was sitting on a chair laughing, while Blyth polished his shoes.

He sat on the bed and covered his face with his hands. The fear and boredom of much of his childhood washed over him. Never enough to eat, going to school with no underwear, the headmaster having to buy him a pair of rope sandals because his shoes had fallen apart. All the indignities were laid bare. There had been so few carefree times, and most of them had been with Uncle Albert and Granny Pragnell.

When he remembered his childhood, it felt like a lead weight dragging him backwards. He thought of his classmates at Greenwich last year, of their sports jackets, silver-framed photographs on their lockers of parents in evening dress. It wasn't the clothing or possessions he envied, but their easy confidence and settled family life. All his cleverness could not achieve an ounce of that privilege.

'Aren't they wonderful?' Rosie knelt up behind him, twining her arms around his neck.

'I'll get you some tea,' he said, throwing down the sketchpad, not able instantly to dispel the sudden fit of gloom.

'Blyth? What is it? Tell me.' She pulled off the quilt and wrapped it around herself before following him downstairs.

'You get washed and I'll see to the fire,' he said, pushing her aside.

'I want to know.'

'You're poaching.' He gave a fake smile. Then, 'I just need to be on my own for a bit.' Blyth slammed out.

'Is it me?' she persisted.

'Rosie, leave me alone.'

'Fine, bloody fine!' she snapped, filling a jug with water from the kettle and taking it back upstairs.

Angry with himself, Blyth slammed out into the yard. Christ! If he didn't pull himself together the whole weekend could be ruined. He took out his tobacco tin and rolled another cigarette. The air was cold and pure. There were icicles hanging from the hedge, and his were the only footprints to disturb the fresh covering of snow. Action, that was it: they'd go walking in the woods after he'd lit the fire and made her some gypsy toast.

Rosie felt frightened. How could everything change so fast? They had been blissfully happy last night, sleeping in one another's arms. And now? She scrubbed at herself with the flannel, trying to work some heat into her body. There were other ways to get warm, but looking at Blyth's face they didn't seem to be on offer. She dressed slowly, delaying the moment of going downstairs. As she combed her hair the smell of cooking wafted up the stairs.

Cautiously she ventured into the kitchen. Blyth's back was turned away from her. He was dipping bread into beaten egg and frying it. On her plate was the word 'sorry', cut out in toast. 'Oh, Blyth,' she rushed over to him and kissed the side of his face.

'I hope you're hungry,' he said, 'I've made mountains.'

Her heart lurched. 'I'm ravenous.'

'We'll go for a walk afterwards in the woods.'

'Afterwards?' Her eyes flirted with him.

He grinned and shook his head. 'Treats have to be earned. A walk first and then I might see myself clear to giving you a cuddle. Besides, we'll need to get warm, afterwards.'

At Blyth's insistence, they washed and cleared away before putting on their jackets and setting off for their walk.

The woods were full of small sounds: the stirring of the breeze, the drip, drip, dripping of melted snow, rustling of small animals and the chirring of a robin. Stripped of their summer leaves many of the trees stood like skeletons wearing borrowed garlands of mistletoe and ivy. Hand-in-hand they followed a path uphill and down dale, following the course of a stream. The water ran over a pebbly bed. Blyth knelt and dipped his hand down to the bottom and fished out a handful of stones.

'One for me and one for you,' he said. 'You choose, but we need two flat ones about the size of a halfpenny.'

She slipped a speckled grey one into her pocket.

Blyth chose a pebble that looked like a piece of toffee. 'I'll take it up with me,' he said. 'I need a good-luck charm. Inky's got a rabbit's foot and Juss has a crooked sixpence. Besides, it'll remind me of you.'

She stood on tiptoe resting her hands on his shoulders. 'Let's seal it with a kiss,' she said, reaching up to him.

He leaned down and cupped her face in his hands. 'I do love you,' he said, 'more than my Swordfish, and I need you more than breathing.'

They stood in silence, resting in the moment. And then the seriousness evaporated and they chased one another around the trees, laughing and calling. Back at the cottage, their lovemaking was urgent. Rosie clung to him, not wanting to let him go. She was filled with sadness. Tomorrow, early in the morning, he would be off to *Daedalus* and she must be at the Wrennery by half-past seven. This time tomorrow she could be anywhere.

'We'll scratch our initials one on either side, get a hole drilled through them. I've a chain on board. It'll have to do 'til I can get you a ring.'

'I expect there's someone in the dockyard can drill it for me,' Rosie said.

They sat in the kitchen scratching their initials on their stones. Then Blyth took her hand.

'We were reckless, just now,' he said. 'I've put you at risk when there's little chance I'll be around to help you. You could be pregnant and I'll be miles away. I'm sorry, I'd meant to stop in time. What will you do if you are?' he asked her.

'I will be very frightened at first, and feel that I've let Mum down. But, I won't regret it for one moment.'

'Where would you go?'

'I'd come here and stay with Uncle Albert until you came for me.'

'I'd come back to you somehow, wherever I was. I've changed my will from Mary to you. She's got a bloke now. It's you I must care for.'

'Hold me,' she begged him.

'Listen,' he whispered, 'we've had a weekend in heaven and it's not over yet. What we've had is stored in here and here.'

He kissed her forehead and her breasts. 'It's soldered into our hearts.'

'Blyth, I'll always love you. We're promised to each other as firmly as if we'd stood in church together.'

The day rushed on. Rosie foraged in the larder and made them a huge fry-up of bacon and eggs, liberally doused in HP sauce. They lay in bed that night talking by candlelight, reluctant to let go of their time together. And then it was morning. They made love for the last time, tenderly, regretfully.

'Rosie,' he sighed, 'I don't want to let go of you. Please don't cry. Come on, we've got to help each other.' He smiled at her. Just one last waltz:

'Lovely Rose, Lovely Rose, I've put you back inside your clothes.
I loved you truly, oh so newly, and I'll be back just Heaven knows.'

'Let me go first. Just kiss me now,' he said, holding out his arms. 'I won't look back or I shan't be able to leave.'

'Oh Blyth,' she gasped, hugging him fiercely. 'Take care of yourself.'

The thrum of his borrowed motor bike became fainter and fainter as Rosie wrote 'I love you,' on the frosty windowpane.

30

Pearl laid her faithful blue twinset and plaid skirt on the bed, ready to wear later. Maurice was coming to tea. She had spent the morning cleaning the house and baking jam tarts. That would be the limit to the cakes, since sugar was rationed, and Daisy still insisted on two spoonfuls in each cup of tea. They couldn't even get boiled ham for the sandwiches, but had to content themselves with sardine and tomato paste.

Daisy came in from the greenhouse covered in grime and cobwebs. 'I'm really pleased with myself. Clean as a new pin it is, and not a mucky flowerpot in sight. I shall have a bath then have a good look at the seed catalogues.' She stood in the kitchen helping herself to a tart. 'Ooh, blimey, nearly burnt me mouth.'

'Serves you right,' said Pearl, taking the plate out of temptation's way. 'They're for tea.'

'Oh yes, the Prince of Wales is coming, I quite forgot. I'd better put on my best bib and tucker. What time's he coming?'

'Half-past three, so dinner will be at twelve to give me time to clear round.'

'You done well, Pearl, it looks like a little palace. If Frank was to come home now he'd think he'd come to the wrong house.'

Pearl smiled, 'It's a nice house. It deserves looking after.'

'We'll have two houses by the end of this month, your Dad's and mine. You'll be a landlady. Four young blokes on the railways, so the billeting officer said.'

'It'll all go into the victory fund. I want to have the place like a new pin when Dad gets back. Redecorated inside and out, new carpets and curtains. I've written and told him so he's got something to look forward to.' Ever since she'd had the idea, Pearl had been looking in the furniture shop in Gosport High Street. She had a picture in her mind of her and Dad sat on their new armchairs, listening to Henry Hall's Music Night on the radio. There wouldn't be a trace of Kenny. She had scrubbed him out of their lives.

Daisy smiled at her. 'You're a proper little home-maker,' she said. 'Your Mum would be ever so proud of you. That reminds me, Mrs Robins next-door give me a letter for you. Must've gone to the wrong number. Looks like it's from your Dad.'

'Thanks Aunt Daisy, I'll take it to my room.'

Pearl ran up the stairs, it was turning into the best Sunday she'd had in ages.

My Dearest Pearl,

A new month, it always cheers me up to see the back of January. One month nearer coming home and seeing your own dear face at the window. I expect your Auntie Daisy is busy planning her garden. I miss England and all the flowers. Your Mum used to love catching sight of the first snowdrops. She said they were the sentinels of spring. Is our old rowing boat still in one piece? What fun we used to have in her, you, me, and Kenny.

I bet you thought never to hear me mention his name again. Well I got a letter from him last week, out of the blue.

Pearl felt rage bubbling up inside her. What was he doing in their business? Dad was nothing to do with him any more. She was the one Dad loved, not Kenny. Well, she'd just have to write and put him straight.

Why didn't you tell me he had got himself married? I can tell you when I recognised his writing I was all for chucking it over the side after what he put you through but it seems he's made amends. Joining up has been the making of him. I got a photograph of the wedding. He said he'd sent one to you and Daisy. What d'you think of this Lydie, pretty little thing from what I can see. Perhaps when this war is over we'll see something of the pair of them. I've no right I know to ask you to write to him after what he put you through but he is very sorry. It would mean so much to me to have our family re-united. Without your dear mother it will never be complete but I know she would want you to find it in your heart to forgive him.

Now tell me all your news. The last I heard you were going to a dance at Fort Brockhurst. How did that pan out? I have bought you a length of Chinese embroidered silk to make something pretty for yourself. But you will have to wait for it, I'm afraid.

Rushing to close to catch the post.

With love and kisses,

Ever your loving, Dad.

Pearl leapt off the bed and tore the letter into pieces. She was crying with temper. How dare Kenny muscle in on her territory. No, no, no! She wouldn't lift a finger to help him. She had nothing against his wife, but she wouldn't have him over the doorstep.

'Brought you up a cuppa, said Daisy, standing in the doorway. 'What's your Dad got to say for himself?'

'That Kenny's written to him worming his way back into the family. Makes me so wild.'

'I can see that.'

'Gone and sent a wedding photo out there. Dad's even talking about me making them welcome when they come over here.' Pearl paced about her bedroom, shouting at Daisy. 'If Kenny comes here he can knock the door 'til he's blue in the face. I sha'n't open it.'

'Aren't you forgetting something?'

'You won't get round me, whatever you say,' she snapped. 'He's not coming here.' Rage surged through her. How could Daisy not see how insulted she felt at Dad's letter? How quickly they'd all forgotten her powerlessness and terror!

'Pearl! Pearl!' Daisy's voice was sharp with anger. She held Pearl by the shoulders and forced her down into a chair. 'Be quiet at once. Calm down, now take a few slow deep breaths and listen to me.'

Something in her aunt's face made her bite back the next sentence. She stared down at her hands, twisting her fingers until they hurt.

'This is my house. I say who comes here and don't you ever forget it. No one, least of all me, has forgotten what Kenny did to you. It was cruel and wicked. Now you may never forgive him, that's up to you. But you will not dictate to me.'

'Where's the photo? You better not put it up or I'll smash it. I will, I will.' She couldn't stop screaming. 'You're stupid, letting him get round you. Stupid, stupid, stupid!' She banged her heels on the floor, and her heart was beating fit to burst.

Daisy left the room and came back with the jug from her bedroom; she flung the contents in Pearl's face. 'Right, my lady,' she said. 'I'm going to have my bath. When I get out I expect you to have calmed down.'

Pearl gasped as the water trickled down her face and seeped under the collar of her blouse. Her throat was raw from shouting. She flung herself on her bed and burst into loud sobs. What was she going to do? How could she face Daisy? She'd gone too far! Pearl felt like a runaway horse, exhausted and terrified. The room was cold, as her sobs subsided she began to shiver. Kicking off her slippers she crawled fully dressed under the covers.

Daisy tipped some bath salts into the running water. She hated losing her temper, it took her days to get over it. It felt as if she and Pearl had come to the end of the road. There was nothing she could say to her that made any difference. Such a pity – they had got on so well to start with. It had been a joy, watching her niece growing in confidence, settling down to a job and making friends. That first letter from France had peeled back the scab on Pearl's wounds, and left her smarting for revenge. What was the answer?

Daisy settled down in the water, shifting her bottom away from the gritty crystals that had failed to dissolve. Best leave her to calm down. A pity the letter had gone astray. If it had arrived earlier, the eruption and the consequent debris could have been swept up and the dust settled. Now, somehow, she and Pearl had to put the lid on their differences and make her boyfriend welcome. If it had been a better day, Daisy would have wrapped up and taken herself off down the garden, and left them to it. As it was, her only escape would be holing up in her bedroom, and writing to Frank.

It was hardly the behaviour of a responsible adult to leave a sixteen-year-old girl alone downstairs with a soldier. What ever would Dulcie say? As always in a crisis, Daisy's thoughts turned to food. Pearl was supposed to be cooking dinner. They had settled on rissoles, mashed potato and tinned peas. She would be pleased when her allotment was up and running, then they'd have a bit more choice. The price of carrots and parsnips had so infuriated her that they'd settled on the marrowfats from the store cupboard. It made her wild, the way some people made a profit out of a crisis. Daisy supposed the butchers would be throwing their weight about next. For some reason, Thelma came into her mind. She thought of her giving some poor bloke her come-hither look, then walking out with extra sausages. Well, her own homely features would hardly net her so much as a few ounces of suet. Should she start cooking or settle for a few slices of toast and that last scraping of apricot jam? No, she would have an unhurried soak, paint her toenails and get herself dressed. By that time Pearl should have simmered down.

She was cold, tired, and miserable. It wasn't fair. There was Kenny over in France with a new wife and everything, like a reward, while she was the one being punished. Even when she tried not to think about him something always led her thoughts back to that time. It seemed, now, that every fresh reminder fuelled her sense of injury. What was she going to do?

Never had she seen Daisy so angry. What would happen to her if she asked her to leave: where would she go? Next week the men were moving in to her home in Hardway so that option was no longer available. Besides, her imagined return had involved Dad being there. But now he wanted her to invite Kenny and his bride to stay with them everything was poisoned. Pearl knew she had to apologise to Daisy, and she had to get herself together.

There was the dinner to cook, and then Maurice was coming. He would be looking forward to a nice tea and a chat. There was even the chance he might kiss her. They had been going out together now for three weeks, and on their last meeting at the pictures he had held her hand. Maurice was nice. He wasn't at all the sort of boyfriend that Marj or Ruby would have chosen, but their only reason for being friends was being workmates. She hadn't even liked their family. They were always shouting at each other and the house was in chaos. She had even found a pair of knickers under the cushion on the sofa. And last time she had called round there, their dad was sat in the kitchen eating a sandwich while soaking his feet in a basin of water.

Maurice had told her about his mother. He had shown her a photo of Mrs Reeves outside their house. She looked gentle with a shy smile, just like her son's. The house looked so pretty with a garden full of flowers. There was even a dog, called Rags.

The sound of bath water running away and then the door opening in Daisy's bedroom, had Pearl on her feet. She would make her a cup of tea and take it up to her. If things were going to be right between them before Maurice came there was no time to waste. As she climbed the stairs, trying not to slop the tea in the saucer, Pearl tried to calm her breathing.

'Hang on a mo,' called Daisy, from the other side of the door. 'Right ho, ready now.'

'I've brought you a cup of tea.'

'That was kind of you,' said Daisy. She was swathed in a bath towel, with another one folded turban-like on her head. Sat on her bed she was, painting her nails. 'Was that all you wanted?'

Pearl swallowed. 'I'm sorry.'

'What are you sorry about?' Daisy wasn't her usual cheery self. She looked at her as if she was disappointed in some way. 'You see, I don't think sorry is going to be enough, Pearl. If we're going to live here together we got some serious sorting out to do.'

'It was just a shock, the letter from Dad saying as Kenny had written and that he wanted us to be all pally – like nothing was wrong. Even wanting me to make him welcome in our home.'

'That's a long way off. By the time this lot's over there may be no Kenny to invite, your Dad's homecoming isn't guaranteed, and if we get one of these air-raids they've promised us there may not be a house left standing.'

Pearl covered her face with her hands. She slumped onto the dressing-table stool, feeling sick. 'You're just saying that to frighten me.'

'No, I'm just trying to get you to face up to what's going on around you. All you can think about is getting back at Kenny. It's ruling your life. Whatever you want to do to him, the war will likely do it for you. And your Dad stuck out there in the Far East, worried sick about his family – how is it going to help him, if he gets a letter from you full of hate and revenge?'

'I can't forgive him, I can't.'

'What I want you to do is lock all this away. We haven't time to wallow in self-pity. You've got a job to do and a life to live here and now.' Daisy put down her bottle of nail varnish and smiled at her. 'I'm not the strong jolly soul you think I am, well not all the time. I need you to support me sometimes. Jesus, Pearl, don't you think I get downhearted with Frank away all this time, don't you think I get frightened?'

'Oh Daisy!' Pearl got up from the chair and flung herself into Daisy's arms. 'I'm sorry, I am, I really am.'

'Watch out for me toenails they're not dry yet.'

She hugged her then let her go. 'Go and get us a digestive then let me get meself dressed. Better get the spuds on the go if we're to be all shipshape for this Maurice.'

'Right, Daisy,' Pearl dabbed at her eyes with her sleeve, 'I won't be two shakes.'

By twelve o'clock they were sitting in the kitchen together tackling the rissoles. The air had been cleared between them, but Pearl still felt shaky. Daisy's words had been a shock to her. Somehow she had managed to slide the war to the back of her mind. Because no one she knew personally had been killed, or no bombs had been dropped, it hadn't been real to her. Even the newsreels at the pictures had failed to pull her head out of the sand. 'There's no pudding,' she said. 'I've saved that tin of peaches for tea, and the last tin of evaporated milk.'

'Well, he better be worth it.' Daisy got to her feet. 'You go up and pretty yourself. I'll square away here. Then I'm taking the paper upstairs with a cuppa. You can let me know when Maurice arrives.'

'Thanks, Auntie, you're a jewel.'

Daisy chuckled. 'Aren't I just.'

With the kitchen tidied and the tea poured, Daisy made herself scarce. She plumped up the pillows and opened the *News of the World* avoiding all the bits about war. What she wanted was a bit of scandal, something titillating to round off her dinner. *'Respectable Choir Member's Second Career'*: that sounded promising. But wait, what was this at the bottom of the page? *'Freemason's*

Apron and What it Concealed.' Daisy burst out laughing. Human beings were a funny bunch, especially where sex was concerned. The more po-faced and respectable they were, the more hilarious was their fall from grace. She and Frank used to marvel at the secret life of the high-ups.

'Never makes the news the other way round,' he said once.

'What d'you mean?' she'd asked him.

'Well, say a tart become a nun, we wouldn't hear nothing about it. Or a villain goes off and becomes a missionary.'

'Read us that bit about the headmaster what wanted to throw rice pudding at the girl in her undies. Ooh, that tickled me no end.'

'She can't have made puddings good as you, gal,' Frank had chuckled.

'Oh Frank,' she sighed, 'don't half miss you, love.'

At the sound of the door-knocker, Pearl hurried down the stairs. Maurice was early. She smiled, she knew she looked pretty, and the house looked really nice. Opening the door, the smile vanished.

'Pearl Bunting?'

'Yes?' she said. A soldier stood there shuffling his feet but it wasn't Maurice. He handed her a parcel.

'What's happened? Has Maurice sent you? Is he, oh, is he all right?' She couldn't bear anything happening to him. He was just beginning to be important to her.

'Nothing like that, Miss, just got posted. Says he'll write to ya, only he can't make it.'

'Oh, thank you.' Pearl took the package, and

the man got back on to his bike.

As she closed the door, Daisy called to her from the top of the stairs. 'What's happened?'

Pearl sat on the bottom step. 'Been posted. Man just brought me this.' She began untying the string. It was a book, *The Woodlanders* by Thomas Hardy. It was Maurice's favourite book. Inside the front cover was a prize-giving label:

Awarded to Maurice Reeves. First Prize in English. July 1935. Dorchester Grammar School.

Also inside the cover was a letter.

Sunday February 25th

Dear Pearl,

I'm so sorry to have missed having tea with you but we're on the move and I can't tell you anything. I would like to have met your Aunt Daisy. She sounds nice. I've given you my book to keep because I like you very much. Will you write to me? Let me know what you think of Giles Winterbourn. I so want you to like it.

Take care of yourself.

With love from,

Maurice.

Pearl turned and smiled at Daisy, coming down the stairs towards her. 'He's given me his school prize to keep and says he'll write to me. Oh, I do hope he'll be all right.'

'Well,' said her aunt, 'we'll have to try and cheer ourselves up. I reckon a couple of jam tarts might do the trick.'

31

Rosie and Delia crept down the stairs of the Wrennery at seven o'clock on Easter Saturday morning. They were off to Delia's home in Hazlewood, on a forty-eight-hour visit.

'You'll love it,' she had enthused, 'it's so pretty at this time of year, the garden will be a picture and Mummy will spoil you.'

Perhaps a change of scene and a bit of cosseting was what she needed. Since Blyth had gone everything had been dull, tasteless, and hard to bear. Her first objective on returning from Romsey, had been to get a hole drilled in the stone Blyth had found for her and threading it onto a chain. One of the dockyard maties in a machine-shop had done it with a high-speed drill. She had promised him a free pint at the Nile and the bargain was struck.

'I've got the best of it,' he said. 'What you want that old thing, God alone knows.'

Wearing her new necklace made her feel connected to Blyth. Her belief in his safe return teetered between confidence and despair, with a hundred tiny gradations in between.

As Rosie spent more and more time out on the road, there was little time to think of Blyth. Winter gave way to spring and the driving became less hazardous. On new journeys, she noted where the petrol stations were and any decent cafés. Being out and about so much she missed a lot of the disciplines of a Wren's life, such as divisions and kit inspections. Her time in the sweetshop belonged to another world.

As they approached Hazlewood, Rosie remembered Blyth's description of the Croxley family at home, and did not look forward to her introduction to Delia's father.

'If ever you meet him, just look the old codger in the eye and shake the hook if he offers it to you. Don't be bulldozed by him. He just likes to throw his weight around, and everyone has let him. But Juss's mum makes up for him, she's a gem.'

As they turned into the drive, Munstead House stood before her: sturdy, mellow and honey-coloured, just as Blyth had said. The air was scented with hyacinths, and when she switched off the engine, filled with birdsong. From inside the house came the sound of excited barking. The door was flung open, and two liver-coloured spaniels burst out making for Rosie, jumping all around her.

Delia flung off her helmet and ran to meet the woman rushing towards her.

'My darling, oh, let me look at you. Too thin – I shall have to feed you up.'

Rosie busied herself untying her case and heaping their luggage on the ground. Delia's mother came over and swept her into a warm embrace.

'Rosie, dearest girl, at last, how good to see you.'

'Mrs Croxley, thank you for inviting me. It's very kind.'

'Please, call me Hermione. Come in and welcome.' She drew Rosie's hand through her arm. 'Come into the kitchen, I'll make us some hot chocolate.'

The three of them sat around a large scrubbed table, exchanging news.

'Daddy will be home for lunch, off seeing his flying chums. It jollies him up no end.'

Looking at her, Rosie thought her a handsome rather than a beautiful woman. Her eyes were the same startling green as her daughter's, and her auburn hair hung down her back in a fat plait. Hermione Croxley was warm and genuine and perhaps, thought Rosie, a little batty.

'Your husband must be proud of Justin becoming a flyer, like him,' Rosie said.

'I would like to think so,' she said. 'Merlin is a very private man. Justin understands that.'

There was a silence, as Hermione went over to the stove to begin heating some milk.

Rosie struggled to think what to say. 'I met him in London,' she said. 'I thought Justin was a really good person.'

'Bless you, Rosie.' Hermione Croxley recovered herself. 'Off you go and settle in. I'll bring up the chocolate when it's ready. I've put you together in Delia's room.'

Laden like a Christmas tree, Rosie and Delia hefted their luggage up the front staircase, on up a smaller one then down a draughty passage.

'Welcome to my lair,' said her friend, flinging down her case. 'What d'you think?'

It was still a child's room, with dolls and a teddy heaped on a chair. Photos of Delia covered the thick white walls. She sat on a pony, receiving a rosette from a man in a tweed suit, then on tiptoe in a ballet dress, and one with Justin on a beach somewhere.

'With the pink curtains and frilly bedspread it makes me think of a birthday cake.'

Delia smiled. 'It is a bit girly, still. Mummy doesn't want me to change anything.'

And there it was again, thought Rosie, that sadness.

'Hello darlings.' Mrs Croxley set down the cups of hot chocolate on the dressing-table. 'Drink it while it's hot. Lunch at one, I'll leave you to gossip,' and then she was gone.

'She's adorable, isn't she?' said Delia, sitting at her dressing-table, combing her hair. 'All my friends love her.'

'What did she mean about Justin and your father?'

Delia stared out of the window. 'Daddy is damaged. I don't mean his arm, it's inside somewhere. He's furiously disappointed in life and takes it out on Juss.'

'That must be difficult,' said Rosie, not looking forward to meeting Mr Croxley.

'Sometimes yes, sometimes no. Oh, he'll be fine today. Seeing his old gang always peps him up.' She smiled apologetically. 'You mustn't worry. We'll have fun, whatever.'

'Merlin will be back later,' said Mrs Croxley, when they joined her for lunch.

They ate in the kitchen, thick vegetable soup and crusty bread.

'Prunes and custard for dessert,' she pulled a

face, 'not exciting I'm afraid, but tonight I can promise you a feast.'

Rosie offered to clear away but Mrs Croxley shushed her. 'Off you go, darling. Mrs Parrish will see to that later. Now, girls, it's a beautiful day – just right for a visit to the Easter Garden.'

Rosie looked enquiringly at Delia.

'It's a surprise over the fields. I'd better lend you some wellies.'

After trying on and hobbling in her friend's boots, she eventually wore Justin's with an extra pair of socks. They walked through the garden and out of the side gate, across the fields. Delia named all the flowers they passed. Rosie began to unravel from her pent-up anxiety.

'How d'you know them all?'

'Mummy loves the countryside. She's the one that does the Easter garden. It's over in St Anselm's down in the crypt.'

They went through the lych-gate into the flintstone church. The wooden pews gleamed, and above the altar was a tapestry of the Last Supper, with Jesus washing the disciples' feet. Delia led the way down a twisted staircase into the crypt. There on the stone floor was the Easter Garden. A mossy hillock had been created, and a cave with a stone rolled away. Inside were bandages heaped on the floor and, at the entrance, was a carved wooden figure of Jesus. Hyacinth florets were tucked between the rocks, along with wood anemones and violets. Above the cave were three little wooden crosses. Coming up the hill towards Jesus was Mary Madgdalene, her arms held out in wonder.

'They're beautiful,' said Rosie, 'where did they come from?'

'Daddy made them, the first year they were married in nineteen fifteen, before the accident.'

Rosie said nothing. Her earlier impression of Delia's magical childhood had been wrong. They raced one another back to the house and went laughing into the kitchen. A man stood there, flicking through the pages of the paper. He was hawk-like, with a needle-sharp nose and small bright eyes.

'Good to see you.' He leaned towards his daughter, and Delia flung her arms around his waist, resting her head against his chest.

'Had a good day?' she whispered. He stroked her hair.

Standing in the doorway, Rosie felt an intruder.

'Yes, my cherub,' he said. 'Guy and Willie were in good spirits, sank a couple of bottles of claret between us. Decent cook, Willie's lady, kedgeree would you believe? Now, what's the drill? Hermione says you've got a chum staying. Is this her?'

As he came across the kitchen towards her, Rosie reached out and grabbed Merlin Croxley's left hand. She looked straight at him. 'I'm Rosie Forrest. Good afternoon, Mr Croxley. Pleased to meet you.'

'Why?' he demanded.

'Curiosity,' she snapped back.

'What have you heard?'

'You like to frighten people.'

He gave a great barking laugh. 'Well, I shall have to try harder. Obviously I haven't rattled

391

your cage. Who told you that?'

'My fiancé, Blyth Vine.'

'Remember him. Beat me at chess by God, arrogant sod.'

'Got a lot to be arrogant about,' Rosie snapped. She might well have to ride home for her cheek, but she was determined not to be cowed. Merlin Croxley smiled at her, and she got a glimpse of the handsome man he must once have been.

'Where did you find her, Cherub? Sparky lass, I'll give you that.' He strode away from them, his walking-stick tapping on the tiled floor. 'Off for my siesta, see you at seven,' and he was gone.

Delia whistled. 'Rosie, you were splendid.' She hugged her.

'I was terrified,' said Rosie. 'Thought I'd be sent packing.'

'I'll make us some tea. Mrs Parrish makes a scrummy ginger cake.' Delia looked questioningly at her. 'I'd like us to get out all the old photos. Would you mind?'

''Course not.'

While her friend rummaged in a cupboard in the sitting-room Rosie sipped her tea. Grinning to herself, she thought about the letter she would write to Blyth, detailing her run-in with Croxley senior. He had been a surprise. Like his carved figures, he had been whittled down to the bare essentials and possessed a wintry charm.

Delia sat next to her on the leather sofa and spread the albums out on a low table. There were, it seemed, hundreds of snaps of Justin and Delia. In almost every one her friend was laughing, while Justin held back, looking posed and unnatural.

It was when they looked at the earlier albums of Hermione and Merlin that Rosie's interest sharpened. She looked at the picture of the young airman, cocky and self-assured. In their wedding picture they grinned fearlessly at the camera. And then, there was the young father with Justin. The small boy looked fearful, and Merlin with his empty sleeve – defiant. The rawness of the emotions made her look away.

'Let's tackle the gingerbread,' said Delia, sliding the albums off the table.

Relieved, Rosie took a bite. The cake was rich and sticky with slivers of stem ginger stirred through it. 'This is well, scrummy.'

The rest of the afternoon and early evening was taken up in frivolity. Rosie tried on Delia's clothes before sharing a bath scented with bluebell essence. She settled on a long black skirt and a fuschia jacket with tiny pearl buttons.

'Stunning!' gasped Delia, 'It does nothing for me, you can keep it.'

'It's far too expensive,' Rosie protested, hoping Delia would not take her seriously.

'It's mine to give, and Mummy will be only too pleased to see it put to good use. It was one of my mistakes. This is like being sisters,' she said, smoothing down the skirt of her simple black dress. 'I've always missed having one.'

'I've got an older sister called Lily but she lives in Canada. Haven't seen her for years. I just remember her playing with me a few times when I was little. Pretty she was, like Vivien Leigh but with dark eyes. Dad was married before but something happened to Lily's mother – it's never talked about.'

'Gosh, how mysterious. But your mother is lovely. I can tell your Pa is besotted.'

Rosie grinned. She couldn't imagine Dad ever using such words as besotted or adorable, he was much too matter-of-fact.

'What are you thinking?' asked her friend, busy fastening her brassiere.

'How we never see our parents in a romantic way, as if they'd always been Mums and Dads.'

'Mummy was a doctor before they were married. She was in France in the last war. That's why she's so good with him, putting up with his rages, and coaxing him round again. He was sent to Haslar hospital in Gosport, and she left the army and followed him there. Helped him write with his left hand, taught him astronomy, even bought him a telescope.'

'How about his family?'

'He was an orphan and because he was very clever he was sent to college. There was an aunt called Aurora who had been an actress. She drank like a fish and ponged of peppermints. Daddy's not good with families, that's why he gave Justin such a hard time.'

'I like Juss,' said Rosie. 'He makes you feel at ease and he's kind.'

'I just hope he meets someone who will love him as he deserves to be loved. Justin is very special. What about Joseph?'

Rosie grinned. 'What do you think of my brother?' she said, teasingly.

'I'm just mildly interested,' said Delia, blushing.

'He's always the same, larky and sporty and a terrific flirt.'

'I think he's beautiful,' said Delia. As she swept her hair up into a twisted knot at the back of her neck she said, 'He's almost edible.'

Rosie giggled. 'Croxley, you're shameless.'

The atmosphere was different when they joined Delia's parents in the dining-room. Merlin was in a maroon quilted jacket over a shirt and bow tie. His right sleeve was folded back and pinned in place. Hermione was in a voluminous satin blouse.

'Hello, darlings, what will you have? Rosie?'

'Gin and tonic, please,' she said. It wasn't a favourite of hers but she didn't think a shandy would be available.

'A gal after my own heart,' said Mr Croxley approvingly.

'Sweet martini and a cherry, Pa, please.'

The table intimidated her with its arsenal of cutlery. And then the meal started, served by an elderly woman in thick spectacles. The food was delicious: mushroom soup followed by roast lamb and new potatoes. Rosie found the meal fraught with difficulties. Merlin always seemed to ask her a question when she had her mouth full, and when she replied he didn't always hear what she said. Rosie had just taken a mouthful of boiling hot lemon pudding when Merlin smiled at her.

'Delia has been fortunate in finding you, Rosie. You'll likely be lifelong chums. Do you pass by Hazlewood often on your journeys?'

Rosie swallowed a piece of suet crust, searing her

throat and making her eyes water. 'Sometimes,' she gasped, pouring herself a glass of water.

'You must drop in and see us, isn't that so, Hermione?'

'Of course you must, darling. Stay overnight. Treat it as your second home.'

'That's very kind of you,' she smiled, shyly, at both of them.

'Utter rot,' he said dismissively. 'I don't go in for empty gestures.'

'Or kindness?' she dared to ask.

Merlin laughed and she could not help joining in.

'Not one of my faults,' he said.

By the time they went up to bed Rosie was exhausted. After talking 'til way past midnight, she fell asleep only to waken in the early hours full of anxiety. The photos of Delia's father kept floating behind her eyes. Blyth had that same confidence, verging almost on arrogance, that the young Merlin possessed. How would he react to having his charmed life snatched away, she wondered. Would he hit out at people, wounding them as Merlin did? How would she cope if he became bitter and distant? Did she have Hermione's capacity to forgive and forget? There were huge differences in the life that she and Blyth would lead than that of Merlin and Hermione. Rosie could see that living in his wife's family home on her money must have eroded his pride. That would not be a problem they would have to tackle.

Tears filled her eyes and trickled down her face. The thought of Blyth struck down and dependent frightened her. She remembered how in the first few days after their time in Romsey she had hoped their lovemaking would result in her carrying his child. When her period came she had felt desolate. But it had been a foolish whim. Later, she had been relieved to have her freedom still. Tears welled in her eyes and Rosie lay in the darkness, listening to the dawn chorus, before dropping down into sleep.

32

In Les Armandiers, Kenny was jolted awake by someone hammering on the front door. When he opened it Bluey stood there, fully kitted out, his face flushed. 'The balloon's gone up. Jerry's broken into Belgium, we gotta be at the compound by eight, load up the trucks, and move out.'

Kenny's heart dived. All his promises to Lydie were now like chaff in the wind. Last night she had told him about their baby, due to arrive in October. It was a gift beyond anything he'd dreamed of or deserved. Christ! October, he would be lucky to last uninjured until tomorrow – six months ahead was never-never-land. Kenny turned around and she was there behind him, smoothing her hair behind her ears in that so familiar way of hers. He wanted to cry.

Lydie smiled at Bluey. 'Good morning, can I make you some *café?*'

Kenny glared at him. 'You going,' he said, 'or do I have to spell it out?'

His friend blushed and shuffled towards the door.

'Goodbye Bluey,' Lydie said, touching his arm. *'Bonne chance.'*

''Bye, girl, I'll look after him, bring him back to you.'

Kenny sluiced his face at the kitchen sink and

went back into the bedroom. Birds twittered in the almond tree. Looking around, he tried to record every moment spent in the room; every caress, every word of whispered conversation.

He took the coffee from Lydie and looked into her eyes – words were useless. Setting the cup on the bedside table, he took her in his arms. They made love with none of their usual tenderness. His only concession was to kiss her belly.

'Tell my baby Daddy kissed him goodbye,' he whispered. As he dressed he tried to think of everything he needed to say to her. 'I will come back,' he insisted. 'Don't leave the house, you're all safer here than on the road. Promise me.'

'I promise,' she whispered.

'If you get no word, you must go to England after the war to Pearl and Daisy.' Again he kissed her. 'I love you and I'll never, never forget you,' he said.

'*Au revoir.*' She touched her belly. 'We love you Kenny, we will wait for you.'

Walking away from her he kept turning and waving, his body marching on in spite of himself.

That night in their room, Lydie tried to rewind the spool of time and have Kenny walking up to her home, again, that first time in October. She smiled, remembering them sharing a croissant and Kenny laughing. When she had found him weeping in the church she sensed his grief was as much about his sister as the death of his mother.

His aunt Daisy wrote from England, wishing them well, but there was no word from his sister. There were no photos of his family for Lydie to look at, and read their characters. If only she could speak to Pearl so much would be explained.

If it had not been for the war they would not have met. Because of the war their time together was tenuous. That uncertainty was behind every word and glance. If Maman had not become ill, Lydie could have gone to England. Would she have been welcomed? Lydie held Kenny's pillow to her face, drawing in the scent of him before losing herself in sleep.

The next day weary Belgians walked through Les Armandiers leading their cattle. There were loaded wagons, with old people and children wedged between bedding and cooking pots.

Neighbours gathered in Monsieur Brechard's house. The old miner sat at the table jointing a rabbit he'd trapped the night before. Lydie, pale and nauseous, sat beside him.

'We must go,' said Marcel, the butcher. 'We'll try to get to St-Paul and then to England. We must go soon or the bridge will be blown and there'll be no choice then.'

Her father threw the rabbit pieces into the pot with herbs and onions. 'Tonight I shall have my stew. Tomorrow we will put it to the vote. I must stay behind for my job and try and keep the home together. Thérèse is not fit to travel.'

'She can travel in my cart,' Marcel offered, 'beside my mother.'

Madame Brechard was adamant, 'I stay with my husband. The rest of you must decide for yourselves. Lydie, you are a married woman, now. It is up to you.'

That night the German planes came and bombed the trains waiting in the sidings, loaded with ammunition. They bombed the tar factory. When Lydie and her mother stood in the doorway the next morning, the air was acrid and choking with tar fumes. She ran down the garden and vomited into the hedge.

'My situation is the same as it was yesterday,' her father said to his neighbours as they gathered in the kitchen. 'As for the rest of you, things have changed. Who is for going and trying to reach St-Paul?'

'I will stay with my husband, as I said yesterday.' Her mother took hold of his hand. 'Whatever happens we will face it together.'

'Lydie?' asked her father.

She looked at her parents and then at Marcel and his family. There was the baby to consider. How could she stay if she was barely able to breathe?

'I'll go with them,' she said.

On that first day they had walked until they were exhausted. Soon after they set out her father had caught up with them on his bicycle, leading Lydie's bike beside it.

'What were you thinking, leaving it behind? Here, tie the case on the carrier, sling this bag over the handlebars. There's a bottle of blackberry wine and a loaf of bread.' She hugged her father not wanting to let him go.

He kissed her, his beard scraping her face. 'God bless you and keep you safe,' he said turning quickly away.

The road was crowded with people, mostly on

foot. Some had babies on their backs, while others pulled carts. Anxiously they scanned the skies. Soon German planes swept low strafing the terrified line of people. The lucky ones flung themselves into the ditches. Lydie cowered there beneath her bike. Rejoining the road, she found one of her schoolteachers lying dead beside Marcel's cart. It hurt her to leave the body uncared for on the road. A man helped her set her bike upright again and on they trudged. A young girl was limping, her feet a mess of blisters. Lydie untied the bag from the saddle and gave it to Marcel's mother up in the cart. The girl, Colette, sat on the bike and Lydie pushed it until they sighted another plane. Once more they scattered in terror.

They had set out by nine in the morning, and ten hours later they were still some miles from St-Paul. Marcel spotted a barn and left the road to investigate.

'It's dry and full of straw, we can hide in there until the morning.'

Lydie pushed the bike across the field, and Colette got down from the saddle and walked barefoot to the barn. They were exhausted. Mothers slumped down against the straw and suckled their babies. A man scouted outside for some wood and they built a fire. Marcel and his son dragged the cart through the field gate up to the barn and, unhooking an old black cooking pot, he disappeared in search of a well. When he returned his mother heated the water, drank black coffee and shared what food they had. Lydie gave the wine to Marcel and shared the bread with her new friend. Someone brought back another bucket and Lydie drank a cup of cool, clean well water. She took off her shoes, untied her coat and laid it on the straw. Her skin was itchy with dirt but she was too tired to care. Marcel's mother gave the two girls an old curtain for a bed cover. 'Tomorrow everything will seem better.' Lydie pulled the curtain over her. 'Good night, God bless you,' she whispered. Having someone else to care for eased her loneliness and distracted her thoughts.

At dawn they were greeted by the call of a cockerel. The occupants of the barn roused themselves, yawning, stretching and pulling straw from their hair. Lydie and Colette went down to the well and pumped up another bucket of water. They splashed their faces and dried them on their skirts. Colette stood in the bucket to soak her blistered feet. Lydie gave her a piggy-back across to the barn.

The morning meal was much the same as the night before, with smaller rations of bread. Marcel and his son set out to see what they could scavenge for the journey. They returned with eggs in their caps and pockets full of onions.

Some of the party wanted to rest up in the barn while others wanted to go on. An old man said, 'We must stay together to keep each other going. St-Paul is only thirty kilometres away. We can do it.'

Lydie refilled the wine bottle with water, and Colette climbed back onto the bike.

The road was crowded with a convoy of British soldiers riding down the centre of the road, flanked by weary French civilians. The sight of the Tommies lifted Lydie's spirits. Perhaps Kenny would come for her like he promised.

By ten o'clock, when they had not seen any German planes, the party from Les Armandiers' spirits rose. At the next village, soldiers wearing the red caps of the military police stopped them. They were ordered to clear a path for a convoy to hurry up the line. They met a crowd of their villagers returning the way they came.

'The bridge is blown. We'll be safer at home than on the road,' they cried.

'Maman,' Colette called, recognising her father's cart. She kissed Lydie before being reunited with her family.

The journey back was sombre. Now Lydie had the blisters on her hands from gripping the handlebars of her bike. Marcel's mother helped her climb up beside her and her son rode the bicycle.

Many in the party muttered against the British for blowing the bridge.

Lydie slept beside the old lady.

'When you get home, you must hide your wedding photos and your marriage certificate from the Germans. Pray he will come back for you in happier times,' the old woman said.

Lydie lay awake in a fever of anxiety. Were her parents safe? Was Kenny still alive? Would they meet again? Tomorrow was her eighteenth birthday, the fifteenth of May. It did not seem possible that a year ago she had been so concerned about embroidering the church banner. In one day, their safety had vanished like dew in sunlight.

Yesterday she had seen things that sealed her past life away forever. Her teacher lying dead, her hair matted with blood, and the baby shot in her mother's arms. Loving Kenny had put herself and her family at risk. She stroked her belly, thinking of their child. As if in response to her touch there was a flicker of movement – no more than a feather-stroke. Could it be her baby responding to her touch? Lydie wanted her mother. She was carrying a child and knew nothing about how to care for it. But ignorant or knowing, minute by minute this hidden life beneath her fingers was moving towards birth. It would be their child – hers and Kenny's. Dulcie, Melisande, Guillaume, the names threaded through her thoughts like the beads of a rosary.

She was awoken the next morning in the barn by the smell of eggs cooking. Two women were carrying roasting-dishes filled with slices of omelette. Lydie took a piece of paper out of her bag to hold it with.

At nine o'clock they were back on the road walking home to Les Armandiers.

Daisy sat in the kitchen, drinking her tea and reading the paper. The early morning sun crept through the net curtains and shone on the knife blade as she cut her toast. The birds sang in the oak tree but Daisy was oblivious. Her heart was wrenched by the words in front of her detailing the army's retreat from Dunkirk:

'There was a touch of glory about these returning men

as I saw them tramping along the pier, still in formation, still with their rifles... They were exhausted. They had not slept or eaten for days. Many tramped in their stockinged feet. Many had wounds. Many had torn uniforms, and their tin hats blasted open like metal cabbages... The men came ashore in heaps, scarcely able to stand. Yet they pulled themselves into straight lines and walked to the harbour gates.'

Poor buggers, she thought. There had been no word from Kenny for weeks, or that Maurice that Pearl was so fond of. She doubted that her niece had given a thought to her brother and his plight. All the other soldiers would be only too glad to see the cliffs of Dover. What would Kenny feel, leaving his wife behind with the German army pouring in? Say he did get back to Hardway, what reception would he get from Pearl?

Thank God their mother, Dulcie, wasn't here to see the mess the world was in and her children scattered. She rummaged in her pocket for her last cigarette. Finding her matches, Daisy went out into her garden. She smiled at the wallflowers and sniffed their scent. As always, the sight of things growing gladdened her heart. Some of those soldiers would have been gardeners, she thought. Bet they were missing all the little routines of planting out, pushing in the canes to support the dahlias, stringing up a trellis for the runner beans, sharpening the shears for trimming the lawn. Bet there were German gardeners, and Italian. One thing she felt certain of, Hitler couldn't be a maker and grower of things. How could he be and then want to uproot everything?

No, he was a destroyer and he must be overcome.

Pearl poured herself a cup of tea and stood flicking through the pages of the paper. Her stomach clenched as she read: *'I saw one man with a handkerchief tied over his head wound. Another with a torn trouser leg soaked with blood. Another with his arm tied in a scarf. There had been no bandages.'*

Was Maurice one of them, she wondered? There were anxious girls at Priddy's Hard, waiting to hear from husbands and sweethearts. Here at Daisy's, one of the neighbour's sons was in France somewhere. Even out shopping in Gosport you saw little knots of people looking worried. It was ages since she'd heard from him, and as she wasn't his next of kin she was unlikely to be told if he didn't make it. Pearl bit her lip. There had been so little time, just a handful of meetings. So much she had wanted to tell him, so much she wanted to know.

For the first time she thought about Kenny's wife. Whatever Pearl thought of him, Lydie must love him. It must be even worse for her. Even now the Germans could be in her village. There was no chance at all that Kenny was with her. Even now she could be a widow.

'Pearl, you got the sandwiches on the go?' called Daisy from the garden, 'time's ticking on. I got a fancy for some of that pilchard and tomato paste. What d'you reckon?'

'Right ho,' she said, glad to be distracted from her thoughts. 'Shall I slice up some of those gherkins?'

Lately she had a passion for anything salty. All the alternatives to meat and cheese seemed so flavourless. Daisy was at the other end of the scale and desperate for sweet things. She was even talking of bee-keeping. Before she came in from the garden, Pearl hid the newspaper under the bread-bin. If only there could be a day off from war, like a bank holiday. It was the constant hearing about it and reading things that wore away at your nerves.

As she walked down the path with Daisy to pick up their bikes, the scent of wallflowers wafted by her. Pearl felt her spirits lift. It was going to be a lovely day.

33

'What is our aim? I can answer in one word: victory – victory at all costs, victory in spite of all terror, victory however long and hard the road may be, for without victory there is no survival.'

When he had read Churchill's words early in May, Alec had not been swayed by them. Only when he listened to him on the wireless a week later was he fully convinced. *'We shall fight on the beaches, we shall fight on the landing grounds, we shall fight in the fields and in the streets, we shall fight in the hills, we shall never surrender.'*

It was a strange voice, upper-crust with a hissing lisp, and yet it stirred him with its passion. But, how was he going to wrest victory out of the defeat in Dunkirk? Whatever the courage of the little ships, and the doggedness of the soldiers standing waist-high in water, it had been a bitter humiliation. Could this baby-faced toff with his big cigar really stir the blood and stiffen the sinew of the man in the street?

His customers at the Nile were not optimistic.

'Christ, he ain't offering us much to look forward to,' Garth muttered. 'Blood, sweat and tears, we got that already.'

'Least he ain't giving us a load of flannel. He's laying it on the line, letting us know what we're in for.'

'He was behind Gallipoli.' Claude wagged his finger. 'If you ask me...'

'Oh yeh,' sniffed Bernice. 'The Claude Treagus plan, drawn up in a frigging sweetshop. Don't make me laugh.'

'There's something in his voice,' Alec said, 'that puts new heart into you. It's about time we got our chins off the floor and talked about victory.'

Garth shrugged. 'Be a bloody long time coming.'

'"*Arm yourselves and be ye men of valour – and be in readiness for the conflict...*"' Albert stood in the doorway smiling. 'Those aren't Churchill's words, but he knew their value. Men of valour – what a stirring phrase, don't you think?'

'Albert, what a surprise! Seeing you is a real tonic. Miriam will be chuffed to bits.' Alec shook his hand. 'What can I get you?'

The old man took a seat near the bar and smiled. 'Good morning everyone. A gin and a splash of tonic, if you please.'

Garth nodded to Albert before leaving. 'Things don't look good to me.'

Alec carried the drink over to the table. After setting it down he went back behind the bar and picked up a hand-written card. He took it to the old man and said, 'Thought I'd put this up here by the cigars. What d'you think? *This house believes in Victory*".'

'Admirable sentiments,' said Albert, 'just the thing to rouse our spirits.'

'What brings you down here, Albert? Lovely to see you of course, but what with the petrol rationing thought it would be a while before we saw you again.'

'It's a joy to be here, Alec. I had the chance of borrowing my brother's car having used up my coupons and took the opportunity for a visit. I want to catch up on all your news and possibly get a sniff of the sea. Romsey is a tad quiet for an old sailor, as you can imagine. It was fine when Beatrice was with me, but now,' he shrugged his shoulders, 'far too quiet.' He looked around him. 'Where is the lady of the house?'

'She's up in the kitchen. Why don't you go up and see her? Stay the night, why don't you?'

Albert finished his drink and patted Alec on the shoulder. 'It's a very tempting offer. I'll let Miriam persuade me.'

'Morning, my cockers, morning Albert, what you looking at?' Connie peered up at the card and then grinned, 'That's the spirit. You don't get nowhere being downhearted. I'm upstairs to see what needs doing. 'Bye chums.'

Alec smiled to himself. There was hope yet.

Thelma looked at the poster of the girl in RAF uniform and wanted to tear it off the wall. Serving your country was all a load of hooey. What had her country done for her? Since that row with Pearl, the last six months had been a nightmare. If the silly cow hadn't read that bit in the paper, about Lionel being missing and her being the wicked mother, things could have been sweet. What was that Pearl carrying on about? Lionel was probably right this minute tucked up snug somewhere. Bet he wasn't thinking about her. She walked past the shops to her lodgings in North End. She wasn't never meant to be a

411

mother, it wasn't in her. Look at her Mum, nagging from morning 'til night – not an atom of love. If she ever spoke back, it was a whack round the legs with the stair-rod. Dad had never been around. The fact was, everyone had let her down, except perhaps Daisy.

Since leaving the Nile, she had gone round in a big circle and ended up a mile away from where she started, and back in the pub trade. Being so near Nelson Street, she was fearful someone would see her and rat to the police about her neglecting her kid. As a precaution she'd stopped bleaching her hair, and started calling herself Vivienne Marsh. She had been at the Sailor's Farewell for a month now and hated it. The landlady spied on her and her husband. Who was she kidding? Lardy old bugger! Beryl Kendrick stuck wave-clips in her hair, making it look like a railway track. Got a corset like a suit of armour. If Lenny wanted his oats he'd have to get a tin-opener.

Lately a new bloke, Alan Dale, had come to the Sailor's Farewell – a real good-looker, just like Clark Gable. Thelma knew he was interested. Had a silver cigarette case with his initials on it. She liked the slick way he opened it with one hand, and sparked his lighter with the other. Last week he had lit two cigarettes and passed one on from his lips to hers. Well Alan, she thought, it's time you showed a girl a good time.

Her lodgings were in one of the many long avenues running between North End and its neighbour Copnor, at the other side of the city. The houses had square bay-windows and lead-lights set into the front doors. Thelma had a room next to the shared toilet. The kitchen was shared, too, with the other six lodgers. It was aggravating living like that. Whenever she wanted to wash her hair or have a bath there was always someone in there. Bath! That was a laugh, two inches of water and that was your lot. Her room was damp, and if she wasn't careful and wrapped it up, her bread got green mould growing on it. The lino was cracked and the mattress lumpy. She was going backwards. Even if Alan showed a real interest she couldn't bring him back here. For a kick-off, she doubted the bed was up to it. He'd likely take one look at her crummy place and scarper.

Thelma took a piece of meat pie out of her handbag, along with a bag of crisps. She fished out the screw of blue paper and sprinkled the salt over them. She'd sneaked them out of the pub. Getting a ration-book was tricky when you'd changed your name.

She looked at the sun streaming through the window. Flipping July, it didn't feel a bit like summer. There was barbed-wire strung out across the beach now, and they'd taken the slot-machines off the pier. War was boring. The only bits she liked were the Spitfire pilots on the newsreels at the pictures.

Thelma sighed. If she was going to knock that Alan dead tonight she'd better get her gear together. On her chest of drawers was a tube of leg make-up called 'liquid stockings'. 'Course, what she really needed was someone else to draw a line up the back of each leg to look like seams, with eyebrow pencil. They were her best feature. Fred had always liked her legs. She'd press that navy-and-white dress with the deep V-neck. It clung to her hips and showed off her cleavage.

First, she'd have a nap. At night she couldn't sleep. The thought that she might have to, one night, go down into that air-raid shelter in the garden terrified her. Covered in earth, it reminded her of a tomb – like being buried alive. Perhaps the bombers wouldn't come, or would be seen off by the RAF before they got here.

Thelma stripped to her petticoat and slid into bed. She hated the room. What if she never got anything better? In the pub she could fool herself, buoyed up by the customers flirting with her. The married blokes winked at her behind the wife's back. She was the one they wanted, but it was the missus they went home with. Sometimes, escaping to the pictures in the afternoon, she watched the film stars living life without the boring bits, and felt panic churning in her stomach. Was this to be her life? Hours bored stupid, and just now and then a few heart-stopping moments of excitement. She lay on her side, arms folded across her chest. She just wanted to fall asleep in someone's arms, and have them still with her in the morning. That was the only thing she had liked with Lionel. If he were frightened he'd come into her bed and snuggle up. Thelma lay sucking her thumb, tears leaking out of the corners of her eyes.

Lionel lined his shoes and slippers up under his bed. Thursday was inspection day. Mr Forrest would come along and make sure he'd got his room shipshape. If he thought Lionel had done a good job he would get a threepence and a bag of crisps.

'I got to do the same, Lionel, over in the section house,' Joe had told him. 'If you get used to doing it now, when you get to be a fire-boy it'll be a piece of cake.'

There was a sixpence from Auntie Connie every Saturday. At first he had tried to get out of all the jobs she wanted him to do, but it wasn't easy. Everyone thought she was kind but there was no getting round her. If he didn't 'come up to scratch', there was no pocket money and no *War Weekly*. When he'd cleaned all the shoes, dried up every day and made his bed, she would say the same thing every week.

'Lionel, my cocker, you are a credit to yourself,' and they would shake hands and she would give him the sixpence. Best of all was when she took him to the pictures. She would be waiting outside school with the flask of cocoa and a bag of sandwiches.

Lionel had always hated school. He couldn't seem to work out how to put the words together for reading, and writing was even worse. The pen slid out of his hand and the letters were shaky and miles too big.

'It's because I'm stupid,' he told Connie.

'Never say that again!' She had been frightening in her fierceness. 'You and me will tackle this together. There ain't nothing we can't do once we puts our minds to it.'

He had tried to get out of it saying he had a

pain in his belly.

'That's a shame,' Auntie Connie had said. 'There's them books upstairs belonging to my boys: sea stories, cowboys and Indians. Be a shame if they went to waste.'

Every night they did ten minutes reading and writing, then he went out to play. There was no argument. She just gave you a look that meant you'd let her down.

'Neat as a new pin Lionel. Now, I think it's someone's birthday on Saturday.'

'I'm nine, Mr Forrest,' said Lionel, jumping up and down. 'James is coming to tea.'

'I shan't see you on Saturday then, you'll be too busy. Here's your early present,' Joe said, handing him a parcel.

Lionel gave a whoop of joy. It was a cricket bat made 'specially for him, with proper string wound round the handle, and the bat shaped in at the sides just like a real one. 'Thanks Mr Forrest, it's smashing. Look, Auntie Connie, look.'

She smiled at him. 'I reckon Jack Hobbs probably started out with one like that. Off you go, my cocker, and see if your pal fancies a game.'

Thelma woke up at half-past four feeling muzzy. Cripes, she'd better get a move on if she was to be up at the Sailor's Farewell by half-five, looking a million dollars. No time for a bath. She'd just have to wash the important bits and trust to a splash of perfume to carry her through. Oh bugger! She hadn't ironed the dress – too late now. Thelma splashed her face in cold water and passed the flannel under her arms. She sprinkled talcum powder on her cami-knickers and did up the two pearl buttons between her legs. It wasn't the effect she was hoping for but it would have to do.

As she got off the bus at Kingston Cross, she saw him walking towards her just like in the films. It was the last thing she saw, that Clark Gable smile.

No sooner had the sirens whined than the planes zoomed overhead. With a sickening whistle the bombs fell. In front of their eyes the Sailor's Farewell was reduced to rubble. Shoppers were caught in the street amid the falling bricks and shattering glass. Bleeding and panic-stricken, they milled about in confusion. The local ARP and rescue squad swung into action, ambulance bells clanged and fire-engines sped to the scene. Beryl Kendrick was helped out of the debris to a chair across the road. She couldn't stop trembling. Tears channelled through the brick-dust down her cheeks.

'Anyone else in the building, Mrs Kendrick?' asked the warden. 'Staff, customers?'

Beryl couldn't seem to make out what he was saying.

'Mrs Kendrick, listen to me. Was anyone in there?'

She put her hand to her mouth. God, that silly bitch had been just going in. 'The barmaid, Vivienne Marsh.'

Bernice was coming out of the shoe shop with a new pair of extra-wide slippers. She stood in the crowd, looking at the ruins of the pub, her hand to her mouth. There was the sound of another bomb up the road somewhere. Everyone screamed and ran into the shops. Across the road, the warden was helping an ambulance man lift someone onto a stretcher. It was impossible to recognise the still figure coated in brick-dust.

'Is this Miss Marsh?' asked the warden.

'I don't know, could be. Yes, oh yes, that's her shoe. Poor kid.'

'She got any relations?'

'Bit of a loner, sorry.'

Another warden put a battered handbag on the end of the stretcher.

Bernice knew that bag. Seen it often enough, behind the bar. She could almost say from memory what was in it. She took a shuddering breath and went over to the warden. 'I think I know her. It's not Vivienne, it's Thelma.'

'You'd better make sure, Miss.'

Bernice was trembling so much she could hardly open the bag. Inside was the blue compact with the flowers on the front, and that grimy powder-puff. There was a photograph of Thelma and Joseph, with Lionel on his shoulders. Bernice's face crumpled. 'It's Thelma's, Thelma Scoggins. Used to work with her over at the Nile.' She went over to the stretcher. At first she thought she'd made a mistake, looking at the brown hair sticky with blood. But it was her hand with the bitten fingernails, and the burn scar on her arm from upsetting a teapot when she was a kid. 'It's her, I'd swear to it. I gotta go to work. Be at the Nile, name's Bernice Fowler.'

Half-way down Kingston Crescent she sat on a low wall and eased her shoes off her swollen feet. Then, in her new slippers, she made her way back to Nelson Street.

Because the raids had not come on the first day, or even the first week, and because of so many false alarms, Miriam had somehow believed that the war would stay over there. She would be able to turn off the wireless and ignore the newspapers, and push it to the back of her mind. It was a foolishness that evaporated at the sight of Bernice. She sat blubbering and incoherent with shock. There were cuts on her face and her make-up was awash with tears and blood.

'Terrible, it was terrible. Just come out of Bata's with me slippers and the siren went. No time for nothink, planes over, then wallop. We was all in the street. The pub just crumpled in front of me eyes. And then,' she broke into noisy sobs, 'they brought her out on a stretcher. Terrible, all in a flash it was.'

'Who was it? Did you know her?'

Miriam turned and shook her head at one of the locals.

'Drink this brandy, love,' she said. 'I'll hold it for you, then we'll clean you up.'

'On this stretcher, landlady said she was her barmaid, Vivienne Marsh.' Bernice broke down again into loud sobbing. 'It was her, it was her, Thelma.'

All the locals gasped.

'Was she? Oh Bernice!' Miriam set down the

419

bowl and the brandy glass, and took her in her arms.

'She was gone. I knew it was her from the handbag. There was that compact, and a photo of her with Joe and Lionel outside here.'

'Here have another drop.'

'Miriam, no, give us a cup of tea. Dry as a bone.'

'Warden asks if I knows her and I had to say, yes.'

'D'you want to come upstairs, love, and have a bit of a lay down?'

'I never liked Thelma,' she burst out suddenly, 'she was a selfish bitch but she don't deserve to be killed.' Poor Bernice, always so sharp and funny, was babbling on, looking every day of her forty years. 'Pub just fell to bits in front of me. Just as we're picking ourselves up, there's another bloody plane come over and another bloody crash down the road somewhere.'

Nobody said anything, but as they looked at one another Miriam knew they were thinking, 'Who's next?'

Miriam ran down to Connie's house, anxious that Lionel should know about his mother's death before he read about it in the paper.

'Poor silly Thelma, at least she's at peace now,' said Connie. 'As for Lionel, I'll tell him in the morning. Bad news can always keep a while.' She took Miriam's hand. 'You all right, my cocker?' Her bright eyes were full of concern. 'Give old Bernice my love. Bet she's been knocked sideways.'

When Alec came home from his warden's

duties, the full extent of the air-raid became clear. 'Twenty bombs,' he said. 'The school in Drayton Road was hit. First-aid post it was, eleven killed. Loads of houses up there wrecked. Gas holder up at Rudmore caught on fire.' He took her in his arms. 'God knows what the total of dead and wounded will be,' he said. 'We're in the front line now. Poor bloody Pompey.'

Connie didn't know quite what was going on in Lionel's head. She had sat him down before breakfast the next day. 'Listen, my cocker,' she'd said. 'I got something important to tell you. You're a big boy, so the best way is for me to tell you straight.'

'Is it about the planes, last night?' He looked at her, his hands fiddling with the elastic band on his match-stick gun.

'Yes. It killed a lot of people in North End. One of them was your Mum.' She wanted to cuddle him up, in her arms, but instinct told her to wait.

'What was she doing there?' He stared at the table.

'She had a job there. The pub was bombed and she died straight away. I'm sorry, Lionel, I know you wanted her to come and see you. I'm very sorry.'

She thought he hadn't heard her. Then his head came up and he stared at her.

'She didn't care about me. I don't care about her.'

Well, she thought, we'll just have to bide our time.

Evening News Spitfire Fund

'In launching our fund to buy a fighter for the RAF, Portsmouth gives a proper answer to the enemy who seeks to lay waste our homes. I await the success of your efforts with confidence that you will provide us with a powerful reinforcement of the squadron patrolling our shores and smiting our foes. The sum required is £6,000.'

'You read that very well, Lionel,' said Connie, on the following Monday tea-time.

'What d' you think about it?' he asked her.

'A good idea my cocker, we'll see what we can scrape together.'

'It'll take ages and ages.'

'I don't know, there's millions of people living in Portsmouth, if they all give something it won't take long at all.'

Lionel turned another page and suddenly saw his mother's name: *'In memory of Thelma Scoggins of 21 Nelson Street aged 26, mother of 9-year-old Lionel. Killed in air-raid 11th July 1940. Sadly missed by all at the Nile Tavern.'*

Was his mother sadly missed? He didn't know what he thought. He didn't think about her very much at all. But when he did, she made a muddle in his head and a knot in his stomach, with anger all mixed up with sadness.

34

The siren went and everyone rushed to the nearest shelter at Priddy's Hard. It was dinner-time, and Pearl had been sitting with the others on the grass between the labbys, about to eat her sandwiches.

'Quick, take the grub and the flasks,' said Marj.

Fumbling in panic, Pearl dropped her paper bag, then turned around and trod on the tomato sandwiches she'd made earlier.

'Come on, bugger the food, you want to be killed?' Poppy grabbed her arm.

The six women rushed through the door along the path and down into the brick shelter. They sat on the benches looking at one another, as they heard the sound of aircraft thrumming overhead.

'Could have waited 'til we'd had our dinner.' Ruth's voice was shaky with fear.

No sooner had they shut the door and settled themselves on the wooden benches than the battle began overhead. Then came the thuds and crashes that terrorized them. Marj poured some tea from her flask and handed it to Pearl. Her hand was shaking too much to get the cup to her mouth, so she passed it on to Poppy. If only Daisy were with her. Just the sight of her round freckled face would be enough to calm her. Please God, let her be safe in her shelter.

Overhead a battle raged. Planes whined and bombs whistled as they fell towards the ground.

Machine-guns stuttered as the RAF fighter planes wheeled into attack the bombers. The noise of explosions was interspersed with the rumble of heavy anti-aircraft batteries, while from the ships came the staccato rattle of the pom-poms.

Instinctively the women held hands.

Ruth stamped her feet and began with: 'Pack up your troubles'.

One by one the others joined in singing and stamping. Fear stalked them. Crash after crash! They seemed to be coming closer. It took them all their concentration to get their mouths to move and brains to remember the words.

'Run, rabbit, run rabbit, run, run, run,' they shouted, then cowered as aircraft thundered overhead. It seemed that they could only remember the first line of each song. 'I've got sixpence, a jolly, jolly sixpence,' was followed by, 'When the saints go marching in,' and then, 'Roll out the barrel.' What happened if they ran out? 'Red white and blue, what does it mean to you,' they gabbled. They sang them over again, their voices hoarse and throats sore. When they thought they could bear it no longer, the all-clear sounded and they rushed out up into the air, weepy with relief.

Above them the sky was criss-crossed with vapour trails. Everyone wanted to use the toilet. They sat in the shifting-shed, eating their sandwiches and drinking their tea.

'Ooh, tastes like nectar,' gasped Marj. 'God, I nearly wet my knickers, I don't know about you.'

Pearl felt exhausted. Please, let it be home-time soon, she prayed. She wanted to see Daisy and know she was all right. There were notices saying,

'We can take it' outside bombed shops on both sides of the harbour. There were times when Pearl felt she couldn't take another solitary second. She wasn't brave like Daisy, or Marj.

When they thought they could string out their late lunch no longer they went back to the labby. Soon the train slid into the back of the shed and big Jean stepped out to collect the boxed fuses.

'All hell let loose over in Pompey, reckons the harbour station's copped it,' she told them. 'I was down at the shell pier. Thought me ears would burst.'

'Bet there's damage over this side,' Ruth said. 'Those planes were right on top of our heads.'

When they left, at five o'clock, Daisy was waiting for her, scanning the faces as they left the gates. She ran towards her, flinging out her arms and hugging her fiercely.

'You all right love? Let's get off home, quick as we can.'

'Dunnow if I can pedal the bike, my legs are that shaky.'

'Don't matter, we'll walk. God, I was bloody scared I can tell ya. Wished I'd bin with you. In the shelter with the men, they was all swearing at Hitler and getting all worked up. Scarin' me as much as the bombs.'

'Oh Daisy, it's just good to be alive,' gasped Pearl.

'Too right, what we need is to sit in the back garden, have a cuppa, and look at the flowers. Gather ourselves together.'

'What's on the wireless?' asked Pearl, craving normality.

Daisy began to sing: 'It's Monday night at eight, oh! can't you hear the chimes?'

Pearl joined in. 'They're telling you to take your easy chair, to settle by the fireside and take up your Radio Times, for Monday night at eight is on the air.' Walking down the road pushing her bicycle with Daisy was bliss.

A soldier was sitting on the front wall, a big shy-looking blond lad. He stood up as Daisy opened the gate and pushed her bike up the path. 'Are you Daisy and Pearl?'

'I know you from the wedding picture, you're Bluey, Kenny's pal.'

'Pleased to meet you,' he said, shaking their hands. 'You're Pearl,' he said, 'I can tell.'

She had hoped it was someone from the Sherwood Foresters with news of Maurice. There had been no news since the middle of May. Of course, she wasn't his next of kin, so whatever happened she would not be the first to know. Perhaps there was no need to worry. He might be staying with his mother, picking up his strength.

Pearl managed a smile and held open the door.

'Bet you're gasping for a drink,' said Daisy, 'Go out into the garden with Pearl. What'll you have, Bluey, tea or beer?'

'Beer be favourite,' he said.

They sat together awkwardly. She didn't know what to say. In the end she managed. 'We had an air-raid at work, I just come out of the shelter.'

He smiled. 'Bit of a relief?'

She nodded, liking him in spite of herself.

'Dreamed of gardens, flowers and stuff over there. When we reached Dover, wanted to get out and kiss the ground. Times when I thought we wouldn't make it.'

Pearl nodded. 'Was Kenny with you?' There, she'd said it without shouting.

'No, he stayed behind.'

'What, with Lydie?'

Daisy brought out the tea and Bluey's beer. She dragged a chair across to where they were sitting on the bench. 'We want to know about Kenny, don't we Pearl?' There was a warning note in her voice.

Pearl nodded, not knowing what she felt anymore.

'Ta, Daisy,' said Bluey, taking the beer and gulping thirstily. He set it down on the little rickety table.

Just being out in the open air was enough for Pearl, after the fear and frenzy of the afternoon. It was like seeing things for the first time. She noticed the scarlet flowers on the runner beans, the peeling paint on the greenhouse door, the floor-cloth draped over the upturned bucket. She was alive; whatever Bluey had to say didn't matter – she had been given a second chance. While Daisy prattled on, Pearl could feel Bluey watching her. He was waiting for her to ask again.

'You said Kenny stayed behind, what did you mean?'

'It's a long story.'

'We ain't going nowhere,' said Daisy. 'You tell Pearl, I'll knock up a few sandwiches. I'll leave the door open save you having to tell it twice.'

'We chummed up in Aldershot last year. Both

misfits. Kenny was wound up and wanting to be on his own. I found all the shouting and the bullshine and doing things by numbers...' he shrugged to show his bewilderment. 'He was quick at picking up things and I was slow,' Bluey gave a shy smile, 'like Laurel and Hardy. Once we'd learned how to drive lorries and keep them running, we were off to France. All over the place we was.'

'How did Kenny meet Lydie?' asked Daisy, coming back into the garden with a heaped plate of tomato sandwiches and a bowl of radishes.

'We got to Les Armandiers in October, and the top brass commandeered the chateau. Lydie worked there in the kitchen, and we got billeted in the village. I was with an old widow and he was with the Brechards, Lydie and her Mum and Dad.'

'What was she like?' For the first time Pearl wanted to know.

'First thing you notice is her eyes, very blue, startling, then her long black hair. Funny when you can't talk the lingo,' he said, giving a shy smile, 'you still manage to get a sort of idea of people – whether they're wrong 'uns or genuine. I didn't think she'd ever had a boyfriend, and her Mum and Dad were strict with her.'

Pearl thought back to the wedding picture on the wall in Daisy's bedroom. For some reason the other day when she'd taken up some ironing, she had stood in front of it looking at Lydie. Perhaps they might have been friends.

Bluey laughed. 'When Kenny took her to the pictures her Mum went too, sat in between them and ate up all the chocolates.'

'What did they think about Kenny wanting to marry her?' asked Daisy, dipping a radish in a bowl of salt and crunching in her teeth. 'He was an English soldier. Can't have been what they wanted.'

'Wasn't. Bin a sergeant there, a married bloke, got one of the girls pregnant. Their blokes was away fighting so they were suspicious, couldn't blame them.'

'Did they like Kenny?'

Daisy studied the toe of her sandal, afraid to look at Pearl. She felt as if they were pushing open a door. At any moment it could be pushed too far and then slammed shut.

'Bit by bit. He worked at learning French and helping in the garden. He mended things. Think he missed having a home and a family. Funny. It was the first time I heard him really laugh, you know throw back his head, and roaring.'

Pearl looked away down the garden. When was it they had all been laughing? It was out in the summer before Mum died. A seagull had wheeled overhead, and left a message on the top of Dad's head. His indignation had made her and Kenny hysterical.

'Poor bloke, the night before we had to leave she told him she was having their baby. Ever so brave she was but you could see she was frightened. It was bloody bad luck. Just as they was so happy it's all snatched away.'

A baby, over in France there would be a baby belonging to her family, hers and Kenny's. She would be Auntie Pearl.

'Poor bugger, he was so worried about her. Every day we passed women on the road carrying kids on their backs. The Jerry planes would sweep along and strafe them, there was bodies in the fields and dead animals.'

Pearl felt her stomach churn.

'We was being shot to hell, sleeping under our trucks, running out of food, no clean clothes. Fighting Jerry day and night. Once we managed to get back to Les Armandiers but Lydie was in hospital with measles. He had to go on. Her mother said she was coming home the next day, and to tell him the baby would be called Dulcie.'

'Poor lad,' said Daisy. 'He must have been in a terrible state.'

'We all was. By the time we got on that beach, nearly done for. Our officer had been shot up and we were carrying him between us. Hours we were stood in the water. In the dark we told each other things.' He looked at Pearl. 'Kenny said that he'd made your life a misery, knocked you about. Didn't expect you to forgive him but he wanted you to know he was sorry.'

Pearl began to cry.

When Bluey went to touch her arm, Daisy shook her head. It had been a long time coming but now Pearl had got to let go.

She was overwhelmed. All her sorrows welled up, layer on layer: the loss of Mum and then Dad going away before he had had time to comfort her. She had lost Kenny, the brother she had known, to a violent stranger. And now it was all beyond repair, all too late. She couldn't just stay there blubbering in front of Bluey. 'Got to go,' she gasped, pushing back her chair, rushing into the house and up the stairs.

Bluey stared at his boots, looking as if he too might cry.

'You said he was on the beach with you and this officer,' Daisy said. 'How come he didn't get in the boat?'

'At the last minute, there was a bloke behind him in a real bad way. His mate couldn't hold him no longer, so he asked Kenny if he'd let him go first.' Bluey looked at Daisy. 'I think he changed his mind, and thought if there was just the chance of him finding his way back to Lydie he was going to take it.'

She looked at the lad. It must have been an effort for him to relive those days in France, especially the last moments on the dunes. 'Bluey,' she said, reaching out and touching his arm, 'it was good of you to come. Pearl and me, we appreciate it.'

'T'ain't no trouble, least I could do. I best get back.' He stood up and made as if to leave.

'What's your rush, Bluey? Only just got here, at least let me cook you something. Where are you staying?'

'I'm in barracks over in Portsmouth, there for a few weeks, 'til they decides where to send us.'

'What time you due back? Can stay the night if you like. We're up at the crack of sparrows for work. The ferry will get you across before seven. What d'you reckon?'

'Champion,' he said, smiling shyly at her.

'You sit out here and I'll scare up some grub. If you want it there's the lav down the end. Oh and here,' she handed him a packet of cigarettes and a box of matches.

Bluey looked awkward. 'Sorry about Pearl, I didn't meant to, I mean...'

'Don't you worry about her,' Daisy smiled up at him. 'It's bin coming a long time. I'll nip up and see her in a tick. You relax, lad.'

What a day, she thought rummaging in the cupboards. We've been scared out of our wits and now we're having our hearts broken. This calls for a good fry-up: potatoes, onions, a couple of rashers and a tin of beans. She would throw it all in the oven and let it get on with it. Poor Pearl, poor Kenny – well the cork was well and truly out of the bottle now. It would all be cried out, given time.

Pearl felt as if she had lived through a month instead of one day. She had been angry, scared, and grief-stricken. Now she felt empty. The blaming was over. She didn't know if she could forgive, but she certainly wanted to step away from that part of her past. There was nothing she could do about Kenny, now. Perhaps she would write to Lydie if that were possible. The first thing to do was thank Bluey for coming. Getting up off the bed, she knelt down and slid out a box of photographs. Pearl splashed her face with cold water and combed her hair. As she carried the box downstairs the smell of fried onions made her mouth water.

Bluey was sat in the garden smoking.

'I've got some pictures to show you,' she said, 'of me and Kenny when we were little.'

432

Looking out at them talking together, Daisy shook her head. All her talking and chivvying had achieved nothing. It had taken an air-raid to bring Pearl to her senses. Why did human beings have to be pushed to the edge, she wondered, before they saw what really mattered? What was that saying? An eye for an eye makes the world go blind. Cripes, they had a long way to go before they got a glimmering of what life was really about. Outside in the garden she heard Pearl laughing.

35

The Wrennery October 1940

Darling Blyth,
I am writing to you from my cabin up in the attic.
It's half past six in the morning and in the bottom
bunk Delia is snoring merrily away. I have just
peered out of the window and the sun is getting up, the
Isle of Wight is all smudgy, a sign of good weather.
Now that I am on night duty I shall be able to enjoy
it. There is just a tiny patch of beach that we can
sneak onto and I shall do just that.
I rode through a forest the other night on very
dipped headlights. It was scary but magical. The
moon appeared and disappeared behind the clouds. I
was so tired I took off my goggles and got a face full of
dew. There's a velvety blackness in the woods at night.
Now and then you see the eyes of ponies lumbering by.
And, if you get there at just the right time you hear the
birds' dawn chorus.

Blyth felt a wave of homesickness wash over him.
He wanted Rosie here and now in his cabin.
Most of the time his head was full of flying,
briefing and de-briefing. There were moments of
panic, excitement, and troughs of boredom or
exhaustion. It was almost a year now since their
weekend at Albert's, and there seemed little
likelihood of seeing her in the near future. He

picked up the letter again.

Our friend Froggy French is now a Royal Marine Wren and lives down the road in a beautiful Wrennery with a green-tiled roof It's called Pantiles *but since the party the other night it's become,* Panties. *A young marine was having an L of a time and stole the letter.*

Blyth chuckled. It was the sort of thing he would have done.

Delia had an adventure the other day. Her little Ariel developed a puncture in the back tyre. She pushed it to a nearby barracks and they said they could loan her something else to complete the journey and would have her bike ready for when she got back. They loaned her a Harley Davidson!!! *She was thrilled and terrified. Having helped her on, her biggest fear was how to get off.*
Looking out of my window at the sea reminds me of our time sizzling on Lee beach among the gorse. It feels like it belongs to another lifetime. Then better still is the magic time in Solent Cottage. God, I don't want our life to be just a bunch of memories. I keep looking at your photo. I'm afraid I shall forget what you look like. Won't it be strange to make plans and even have time to be bored with each other? What luxury to sleep in your arms and wake to find you still with me in the morning.

Blyth kissed her photo on the shelf over his bunk. Christ! He hated the separation and all the time wasted apart from one another.

Please take care and know that I love you full strength and forever. Give Justin a hug from me. Hope I don't have grey hair and wrinkles before we see each other again.

All my love,
Your Rosie

He folded the letter back into its envelope, then added it to the others in his locker drawer. Before switching out the light he touched the stone hung around his neck, for luck and fell instantly asleep.

The next morning he woke to the news that they were going into battle. This was it, the long-planned attack on the Italian fleet at anchor in Taranto. It would be a date engraved on his memory, November the 11th 1940. His enthusiasm was tempered by regret that his crew would not be with him. That morning, Justin had tripped on a patch of oil and badly sprained his ankle, ruling himself out of the operation. Space was critical, and the need for an extra fuel tank meant Simmo had also to step down. Working with an unknown observer was an added complication.

He sat on the edge of Justin's bed in the sick bay and punched his arm. 'Amazing! Some blokes'll go to any lengths to avoid action. Bad enough losing Simmo without you playing hookey.'

Justin smiled ruefully. 'Look on the bright side. With Dicky Bird you've got the best observer in the fleet, barring me of course.'

'So I've heard. If he's that good I might not want you back.'

''Bye Blyth, see you tomorrow – mine's strong tea, two sugars and one digestive. Make sure you set a course for home before the fireworks start. You know the drill. Dicky does too, but just the same–' Justin's smile was forced.

Blyth cursed the oil slick. He and Juss were right together. However good this Dicky Bird was, there would be an edge of uncertainty about the whole thing. Back in his cabin he sent for his gunner. 'Sorry Simmo, you won't be with me this trip. It's the extra fuel. Can't be helped.'

Simmo shrugged. 'That's OK Skipper, could do with a night in my pit 'stead of freezing me balls off in the string-bag.'

Blyth went down to the hangar deck and saw the Swordfish all crouched together, wings folded like conspiring moths. The fitters were swarming over them, doing their meticulous last-minute checks. Soon each plane would be moved one at a time onto the elevator, and taken up to the flight deck where its wings would be unfolded and locked into place.

After a briefing from Commander (flying), Blyth and the other pilots and observers in their bulky suits and flotation vests began to climb into their planes, assisted by the deck crew. Blyth patted a pocket in his flying jacket for luck. Inside was the little brown pebble he'd picked up from the Romsey stream the last time he was with Rosie. And then all thoughts of her were extinguished. He and Dicky Bird flew north-west and were forced up to 7000ft by cloud. Cramped in the small space behind the auxiliary fuel tank, and having to contend with the roar of the engine and the wind plus exhaust fumes, Bird did not have it easy. It was an observer's night, and he was constantly checking the compass, wind gauge and star sightings. Blyth kept the plane in formation with the other aircraft and wondered if Bird was as cold as he was.

'Skipper, should be on target in fifteen minutes.'

'Thanks, Dicky, we'll be in for a hot reception, place reported to be ringed by anti-aircraft-guns. There's at least six battleships, four heavy cruisers and up to thirty destroyers, and God knows how many auxiliary aircraft. They'll fight like hell to protect the big fellows.'

'What's the plan, Skipper?'

'Go in and hit the biggest target we can see, and get out as fast as the Pegasus engine will take us.'

'I'll give you the course for home, before the action starts. It's south-east, and we should be able to pick up the ship's beacon, and the destroyer screen will be keeping a look-out for stragglers.'

'Christ!! Have you ever seen anything like that, Dicky?' The sky was illuminated by thousands of lights, and the thunder of exploding ammunition fired by all the land-based guns was terrifying.

'Passing over the Cape, now, Skipper. There's the town, a real bomber's moon, can see everything as clear as daylight. God help anyone under that hail of shrapnel. Watch out for the barrage balloons.'

'Be under it ourselves soon, Leader's on his way down.' Blyth clenched his teeth and willed himself not to panic. 'Hang on Dicky, here we go.' He put the nose down into a solid wall of lights coming up to meet the Swordfish. The whole fleet had opened up in a monstrous barrage of sound.

'There's the eastern shore, Skipper, go right, go right.'

'Must get lower, get under this fire.' The plane dived down into the storm of flashing lights and thundering ordnance.

'Have to shout, Skipper, can't hear you.'

Christ he must pull up, he'd nearly put them in the drink. What was that great flash to starboard? There's a solid object dead ahead spewing out a great shower of lights like bonfire sparklers. 'The bastard has opened up on us, Dicky.' I must go to port, he told himself. Now, swing out wide to starboard, got her at midships, level off. Blyth pressed his thumb on the button to release his torpedoes. Relieved of her weighty burden his plane rose into the maelstrom of flying metal. Up and over the ship she went with every gun on board following his tail. The Swordfish shuddered out of control and dipped down towards the sea. Haul back! Haul back on the stick, Blyth shouted to himself. Thank Christ, I've got her and we're level. Oh Christ, we're hit, we're hit. Bullets peppered the fuselage. Caught in a searchlight, the plane juddered as rounds of ammunition slammed into the cockpit, destroying the instrument panel, but she flew on. As quickly as they had joined the battle they left it. The steady strum of the engine took over from the clamour of the guns. Moonlight replaced the hectic sweep of searchlights. 'Dick, you still with me?' he called, aware that he had not heard from him in the intensity of the last few minutes.

'Sorry Skipper, your course is 136.'

'You'll have to guide me, Dicky, my instruments are shot away and the old girl's not responding like she should.'

'I think I've bought it this time, Skipper.'

Blyth had to strain to catch what he was saying.

'You're heading due south, come round to port. That's it Skipper, 136, keep her there.'

'Christ, Dicky, how bad are you hit?' Blyth's stomach lurched. 'Can you get a dressing on? We need you to get us back.'

'I'm leaking like a sieve, Blyth, you're falling off to starboard again. Come back to port that's it, 136, now stay there. Use the moon and the stars as your compass. There's a little group at about five to twelve, get them dead ahead, and about one hour and a half you should pick up the ship's beacon.'

'You're the best, Dicky.' Relief flooded his tired brain. 'Stay with me, keep talking.'

The cockpit remained silent save for the steady strumming of the engine. Pain flared in his back. His legs were leaden and stiff. Concentrating on the group of shivering stars was so hard when all he craved was sleep. Without Dicky, his only company was the noise of the engine.

'Rambling Rose, rambling Rose,' the words of the song sauntered through his brain. They were waltzing slowly round the room and he was singing to her. And then they were climbing up the stairs lingering on each step to kiss. Blyth thought of her that last time, her face flushed and hair tumbled on the pillow. He longed for Rosie, longed to be held in her arms and lost in her warmth and sweetness. Afterwards he would drift down into sleep, and later, much later, wake with her beside him. She was his harbour and his place of safety. You must get me back my Rosie, he breathed.

Christ! He'd lost the stars. Oh! Thank God, there they were. He must bring her round to port and fly on. 'Bobby Shafto went to sea.' He was a little boy singing it at a party in Granny Pragnell's house. Everyone loved him, he could feel it in their smiles. Mary held out her arms and swept him up in them. The Swordfish dropped down. He jerked back into wakefulness and hauled her back on course. Poor, poor, Dicky Bird. Still, thank God it wasn't his pal Juss. Good bloke Juss, the best. Down and down she drifted.

Blyth woke with a start. He was skimming the sea. Haul back, he told himself, putting every last ounce of strength into pulling the stick towards him but he had not the strength to do it. As he drifted again Blyth thought of his brother Harry. He was standing in Lemon Street watching for him to come home. When he was sick with waiting, Harry would come whistling round the corner. Blyth felt again that excitement as he tore down the road and threw himself at Harry's legs.

'Hallo, tiddler, pleased to see me?'

Perhaps that was my first experience of flying, thought Blyth. That rush of joy, as I was swept up by Harry, and set on his shoulders before he ran down the street with me, my knees gripping his neck, and arms held like wings.

God! Where am I? He awoke with a start. There

441

were white-crested breakers ahead and his trusty Pegasus coughed and juddered. 'Rosie,' he gasped. 'Rosie, Rosie.'

Exhausted from keeping their vigil on the flight deck, Justin and Simmo went below; one trudged to his mess and the other hobbled to the sick bay.

He must get her head up. The plane shuddered as her wheels hit the turf. Blyth used his last reserves of strength to keep her level. The engine died and she dropped like a stone onto the wet sand that held her fast. As he began to lose consciousness he said her name.

36

After a cold journey to Southampton and back, Rosie went into the office hoping for a local journey to round off the day. She unbuckled her helmet and began peeling off her gloves. It was half-past two and with luck she could be back at the Wrennery by five. There might be even greater luck – a letter from Blyth.

As she stood in the office stamping warmth back into her feet, Petty Officer Johns looked up at her. 'How was the trip?' she asked.

'Freezing, I'm gasping for a cup of tea. I hope there's nothing else come in yet. I need to thaw out.'

'The tea will have to wait. Commander Barnaby wants to see you, pronto.'

'D'you know what it's about?' asked Rosie, a range of possibilities passing through her mind, from special escort duty, to a reprimand for speeding.

Johns looked uncomfortable. 'I'll see you later.'

'No chance of a cuppa first then,' she said.

'Best get it over with. I'll have a cuppa waiting for you.'

Crossing to the Commander's office Rosie felt a faint stirring of doubt. Johns had seemed odd somehow and, offering to make her tea? She tapped on the door.

It opened immediately and Commander

Barnaby stood there, holding out his hand. 'Wren Forrest. Good-day to you,' he said.

Rosie was taken aback. Normally his Wren secretary or a lieutenant would be there for such trivialities as door opening. And to have shaken her hand – she was startled and uneasy.

'Come in, come in. Take a seat.'

In the midst of her anxiety she remembered Delia saying how handsome Barnaby was, how like the film star Tyrone Power. How stupid for that to come into her mind at this moment.

'I believe your fiancé, Lieutenant Vine, is serving on the *Unrivalled*, flying Swordfishes? Jolly brave chaps.'

Rosie nodded. It seemed a preliminary, like the spoonful of sugar before a dose of cascara. In the distance something was waiting, she knew it.

Barnaby studied a piece of paper in front of him. 'Last night, the Fleet Air Arm was involved in a successful attack on the Italian fleet in Taranto harbour. It's believed that their action has changed the whole naval balance of power in the Mediterranean.'

Rosie sat there saying nothing. What was the balance of power to her?

'I have to inform you, Wren Forrest, that Lieutenant Vine and his observer are posted as missing.'

She sat forward, gripping her hands between her knees. She stared at the gold ring on the Commander's little finger. Missing, that wasn't dead, but what? What did it mean?

'I must hasten to add that his plane was seen to leave the battle area intact. There's every chance that he has survived. There are many islands in the area where they could have come down. The Italians are very quick to report planes downed, and captured air crew.' He spread his hands. 'There has been nothing. And rest assured the navy will be conducting its own search of the area.'

Rosie blinked and the ring became a gold blur. She put her hand up to her throat and patted the stone hanging beneath her shirt. Not Blyth, please God, not him. He'd promised to come back – he had to. She thought of Justin and Simmo. What would Delia do if her brother were lost?

'Can you tell me the name of the observer sir? Wren Croxley shares my cabin and her brother Justin is Lieutenant Vine's regular observer, and Petty Officer Simpson is his TAG.'

'On this mission there were no TAGs carried, and the observer I have here is not Lieutenant Croxley.'

This man has the power to break my heart, she thought, but I won't let him. I won't let him. Missing is just not found yet, missing is not dead.

'You are listed as Vine's next of kin, Wren Forrest. Is there no family then?' He asked.

'There's a brother, Harry, in Plymouth and three sisters. Mary lives in Wymering, I should go and tell her today.'

'Under the circumstances I want you to have two days' leave. This must have come as a shock. You'll need some time with your own family.'

No, she couldn't just hang around, she must keep busy. Of course she wanted to see Mum and Dad, but not now. 'Sir, can I just carry on? I'd feel better being at the Wrennery with my friends, and

I'll get any news quicker than at home.'

'As you wish, Forrest. Be assured, whenever I have any new information you shall have it immediately.'

Rosie got to her feet and Commander Barnaby escorted her to the door. Again he shook her hand. 'Good day to you, Wren Forrest, and good fortune.'

'No tea, thanks,' she said to Johns. 'I'd better get up to Wymering and tell Blyth's sister.'

'Are you sure you don't want to sit down for a minute? It must have been a shock,' said Johns. 'Well, you don't need to come back 'til Thursday.'

'I'll be in tomorrow,' Rosie insisted. 'Can't mooch about. 'Bye.'

Outside, she started up her bike and rode north out of Portsmouth onto the mainland, up the hill to Wymering and Mary. Rosie had a feeling of unreality. An hour ago her only wish was for a cup of tea and a warm by the fire. Now, she wanted to rewrite last night's battle and for Blyth to be back on board laughing with Justin. Telling Mary was not going to be easy. Blyth had said she could be prickly and bad-tempered. Standing shivering at the front door, she didn't think she could cope with either.

The door swung open, and Mary stood there with a baby curled into her shoulder. For a second they looked at one another and then she smiled. 'Standing there in that motor-bike clobber, you must be Rosie. Come in quick, it's brass monkeys out there.'

Rosie followed her down the passage into the kitchen. The baby was a surprise. Blyth hadn't said anything about a baby.

Rosie followed her into the kitchen. It was heaped with piles of washing, newspapers, and on the table the makings of a stew.

'Sit down then if you can find somewhere, shove those papers on the floor. I'm a messy mare, always have been, always will be. Expect Blyth told you. Tea?'

Mary was and wasn't what she expected. She was bigger, stronger-looking, and not a bit like her brother.

'I was just going to put him down,' she nodded to a pram in the corner. 'But he was so comfy, didn't want to disturb him. Like a hold?' She smiled and her dark eyes glowed. 'Lovely little nipper, ain't he? Called Matthew, after me late husband and Blyth for his uncle. Get your clobber off or you won't feel the benefit.' Rosie had not expected to like Mary but she did. There was a rough honesty to her and, she suspected, a kind heart. She piled her clothes in the only clear space in one corner, then held out her arms for the baby.

Mary smiled. 'Good to meet you at last, remember you as a toddler – pretty little kid. Your Gran,' again she smiled, 'loved her I did, she was a life-saver.'

Rosie looked at Matthew Blyth. He stretched and frowned and wriggled himself awake. She smiled at him and he smiled back at her, his blue eyes achingly familiar.

'What brings you up here, today?' asked Mary, setting the kettle on the stove.

'It's Blyth.'

Mary reached down some cups from the dresser. 'What, he told you to come?'

'No, he's been posted missing.'

'Jesus Christ!' Mary sank down into a chair and gripped her hand in her teeth. She looked at Rosie, her eyes wide in alarm. 'What's that mean?'

'He was flying last night and didn't return. There's been no sighting of him.'

She gasped and struggled not to cry. 'But that's not dead,' she said eventually. 'That's what we gotta keep saying to ourselves, Rosie. What do you think?'

'If he was dead I'm sure I'd know it.'

'We gotta face it, don't look good. That's not to say we gives up.'

Rosie nodded.

'Here, fancy a crust of toast? All there is 'til Sid gets in but you're welcome to it.'

'I'm gasping for the tea but I'm not hungry thanks.'

'That's what shock does, it shuts the system down.' She blinked then smiled at Rosie. 'Least it brought you up here. Poor Blyth.' Again she chewed her hand and looked away. 'Anythink happen to him it'd break my heart. Special to me, very special.' She gasped and fought off tears. 'You let me know the minute you hears anything.'

'I promise,' she said, getting to her feet. 'Sorry I'm in a rush. My friend's brother's on the same ship, I must go and tell her.'

Mary came over and took the baby. She smiled at her. 'You'll be all right, Rosie. Got your Gran's spirit, I can tell. We both gotta believe in him, he needs that.'

Impulsively, Rosie kissed her. 'I'll come and see you again whatever happens.'

'You do,' said Mary, walking her to the door.

She was not conscious of driving back to the Wrennery or of parking the bike or even climbing the stairs to her cabin. It seemed an enormous effort to get out of her jacket and gloves and boots and trousers. Rosie sat on a chair in her jumper and knickers, too weary to think what to do.

Delia came in from the bathroom. She smiled at her. 'Hello Rosie, bad day?'

It was the kindness in her voice that did it. 'Don't know what to do,' she sobbed, 'don't know what to do.'

Delia took a blanket from her bed and wrapped it around her shoulders. 'Oh you're so cold. Here let me warm your hands. Poor girl, poor girl.' Rosie cried and cried, on and on until she could cry no more. 'Let me help you into bed, that's it hold up your arms and I'll slip your nightie on. Now lie down and I'll bring you up a hot-water bottle and some milk. It's all right, you don't have to say anything. I know. Johns told me.'

Rosie clutched at the stone. Did she really believe that Blyth was still alive or was she afraid to face reality? No, she could not give in. Second by second she had to tell herself he was somewhere out there, making his way home.

37

It would be Christmas in two days time, but Miriam had no heart for it. There had now been twenty-nine air raids. Alec was exhausted from his nights out at the ARP post, taking phone calls, checking houses and helping with rescue work – all that on top of running a pub. In the New Year there was talk of women being conscripted into war work. Goodness knows what she could offer. They talked about cutting the opening hours, but there was never time enough to make any real decisions.

Tomorrow she and Rosie were going out for last-minute shopping. She knew her daughter had no interest in buying things, but it would be good to have time together. Rosie had grown away from her. She was a woman now, with her own friends. Delia and Gwyneth were coming tonight for a Christmas drink before going home on leave. Lovely girls they were. Poor Rosie, she sighed, poor Blyth.

The day rushed on, and by the evening Miriam had worked herself into a more cheerful frame of mind. In the downstairs kitchen she wrapped a damp tea towel over the sandwiches. It was going to be a good evening. She had even had a burst of energy that afternoon and made some progress towards Christmas. All the presents were upstairs wrapped, and the turkey was down in the cellar stuffed and waiting. All that was missing was Albert. He was coming tomorrow for the rest of the Christmas. He was such an old stalwart. It would be almost as good as having Beattie with her – almost but not quite.

'Anyone at home?'

'Rosie, thought you were coming later with the girls.'

Her daughter hugged her. 'I just wanted to see you before they came.'

'Oh, love, we don't get a minute, do we? How you feeling?'

'A bit wobbly,' she said, giving her a lopsided grin, 'but I'll get there. I just have to believe Blyth's out there somewhere. Is Dad around?'

Miriam sighed. 'Just getting ready to go on duty. Worn out he is, still I've promised him a lie-in tomorrow. Connie and me will see to the cleaning.'

'Is that Rating Forrest I see?' said Dad, holding an empty toilet-roll tube to one eye.

Rosie rushed into his arms. 'Give us a cuddle you old sprucer,' she demanded.

'I don't know, ratings cuddling, never done in my day.'

She kissed them both. 'See you tomorrow, Dad.'

'That's bucked me up no end,' said Alec, picking up his knapsack.

'Me too,' said Miriam. She kissed him and handed him his gloves.

'I shall be glad to get to bed tomorrow. Bye, my love, take care.'

She and Rosie had a gin and tonic together in

451

the empty lounge bar. It was half-past six, early yet, and Bernice would call on her from the other bar, if need be.

'Which are the Christmases you remember most?' her daughter asked her.

Miriam smiled. 'Lots and lots when I look back,' she said. 'There was a special one with Daisy in the last war. You were a baby sleeping in an old banana crate. About ten months you were – a lovely stage, sitting up and taking notice. I shall never forget the moment. It was freezing cold and I was coming down the stairs with you in my arms. It was eight o'clock and I wanted to take Daisy up a cup of tea, but she was up already. She opened the door into the little kitchen and it was like fairyland.'

Rosie smiled.

'She had got these candles, everywhere in the house, and stuck them in flower-pots, jam-jars, anything she could lay her hands on. And as if by magic, all the hyacinths that were kept in the cupboard under the stairs had come into bloom. The lights and the scent of the flowers, and Daisy's face full of love and excitement, and you my new baby stretching out your hands in the wonder of it all.' Miriam's eyes filled with tears. 'You'll think this is silly, but Daisy said, "Here in the little town of Gosport, Rosie our baby is born."'

'Oh Mum,' Rosie hugged her tightly. 'I'm so glad to be home. I do love you.'

'Rosie, you're my treasure, never, never doubt it,' Miriam said. 'I should have thought last year must have been special, for you, what with getting engaged.'

'Yes, my best as a grown-up, but how about over on the Isle of Wight when we were snowed in? It was just the four of us.'

'I think you were six and Joseph a toddler.'

She was about to launch into the special moments of that Christmas when the usual gaggle of Nile widows came in, stamping their feet and grumbling at the cold.

'Evening, Miriam. Evening, Rosie,' they called, 'Happy Christmas. Set us up a rum and peppermint apiece, if you please.'

Rosie sighed. The moment was gone.

'I've just thought,' Mum said. 'I promised Garth I'd drop him round his humbugs. He's not coming in tonight. Thinks his boy might come up from Plymouth.' She bent down under the bar and came up with the bag of sweets. 'You wouldn't just run along there, would you, love?'

'Anything for you,' said Rosie slipping back into her coat.

Connie got her air-raid bag from the hook by the door and checked the contents: torch, knitting, pack of cards, latest copy of the *War Weekly*; a tube of wine-gums and the insurance policies. She'd just get the sandwiches and flask from the kitchen.

Lionel was busy finishing off the paper chains. He was dabbing the ends of the papers with glue and looping them together. Connie smiled. He was a different lad from last year. Amidst all the heartache and despair, he was her one bright spark. Mannerly, bright, and beginning to be occasionally helpful, she was proud of him. It was bringing up her twins that had given her the know-how, and Lionel had reaped the benefit. In amidst all the things that experience taught her, was the one sure-fire ingredient – praise. Kids was like furniture, they needed a good polish. A regular dusting with praise had them shining – no doubt about it.

'Auntie Connie, can I go up and get that book from the boys' room about magic tricks, to take to the shelter?'

'You be quick my boy.'

She followed after him, remembering her glasses.

The noise was like a train rushing through a tunnel: the force of it shook the fire station. Joseph was out of bed, feet pressed down into his jack-boots and trousers pulled over his legs. He and the other firemen thundered down the rickety wooden stairs, pulling up their braces as they went. Before Joseph had reached the floor, the bells were ringing. It was a full-brigade call and all the fire-engines were involved.

'Forrest, you're on the turntable with Sergeant Boyden. Something big has gone off in Nelson Street.'

Buttoning up his tunic he leapt on board the fire-engine. Nelson Street. He fought down his panic. If he thought about Mum and Dad he'd be done for. Training, that's what carried you through. Reaching Commercial Road the engine rocked over heaps of broken glass. Lights blazed out from broken windows. The debris increased to include a twisted lamp-post and an overturned lorry. It was impossible to take the direct route so they swung left and then around the dockyard wall, still rocking as they went.

'Jesus Christ Almighty!' Boyden braked hard, then backed the engine away from the edge of the crater. 'Stay here,' he commanded, as he went over to another sergeant fireman and stood talking to him.

All his training seemed redundant as Joseph took in the scene in front of him. All around buildings were collapsing, sending up clouds of plaster and brick-dust. There was the smell of gas and earth and fire. People were screaming, he could hear a dog yelping. Trails of cable littered the ground. He could not at first orientate himself. So much that he was familiar with had simply disappeared beneath his feet. Where was Nelson Street? 'Mum, Dad,' he whispered.

Boyden came back to them. 'Both mains are fractured, gas and water. The Gas Board and the turnkey are on their way. Turntable's useless tonight. We'll have to run in the lines of hose from street to street. Keep calm lads, just have to do what we can.'

Joseph ran two streets back and found a stand-pipe intact. Quickly he connected the coupling and waited while another fireman dragged the hose, full length, to where it was needed. He switched on the water and ran towards a blazing house. The force of the explosion had blown the coals out of the grate and set the hearth-rug alight. He passed a couple of men carrying a stretcher, lurching over mounds of bricks.

'I can hear a baby crying up there.' A woman pointed to a house with no front wall.

Joseph played his torch up into the remains of the front bedroom, and thought he saw the edge of a wooden cot. The staircase was still intact. Leaning into the remaining wall, he made his way up the stairs.

'Dadda, Dadda.' The baby was clinging to the bars of the cot.

Joseph grabbed the child and carried it down the stairs to safety.

Rosie was on the ground somewhere in the dark. Her head felt as if it would burst. She could hear a confused mixture of sounds: horses whinnying close by, thrashing and screaming. Sliding her hand across the floor, she tried to find her torch: instead she found a wall. Pressing her hand against it, she tried to stand. Pain shot up her leg and she slid back onto the floor. She touched her body and her legs, where were her clothes? When she touched her left leg, her hand felt sticky. Something big fell behind her with a rush of cold air.

The whinnying of horses sounded nearer and more desperate.

'Garth,' she called, 'Garth, where are you?'

Rosie began to shake and her teeth chattered.

Light flickered over her face as a torch beam swept the ground.

'Anyone there?'

'Over here,' she croaked.

'Can you stand?'

'I've hurt my leg.'

'Try, love, the building's not safe. I'll come towards you.'

The pain made her sweat and brought back the dizziness.

'Here, cop hold of me hand. That's it, you got it. Lean on your good leg.'

'I've got no clothes,' she whimpered.

'Never mind that, love. Let's get you out onto the street, what's left of it. You come with me and I'll give you me coat.'

'There's horses in there.'

Rosie leant against the warden. They swayed as he got out of his coat and wrapped it round her. As her eyes accustomed themselves to the scene before her, Rosie began to shake. She was stood on a deep crater where once Nelson Street had stood. 'Mum, Dad,' she screamed, 'they're in the Nile. You must get them out.'

The warden shone his torch across the debris and picked up a length of skirting-board. 'Here, lean on that. There's no ambulance, you'll have to make your way around to Flathouse Road and over to the Royal.'

'My Mum,' she screamed. 'My Mum, I never told her about the...'

'Look love, there's fire crews, the ARP rescue parties, the lot. They'll be here all night, digging and calling. You can't stay here, it's not safe. Do your best to get to the hospital. Follow those two in front of you.'

Rosie joined a procession of ghostly figures, staggering across the rubble towards the Royal Hospital on the other side of Commercial Road.

Lionel was frightened, it was dark and he didn't know where he was. It felt like there was a board underneath him, he couldn't make out what it was. 'Connie, Connie,' he called. 'Auntie Connie.'

There were so many different noises. People were screaming, and he thought he could hear water dripping. Then there were bangs and crashes all round him. There was a smell like when Auntie Connie forgot to turn off the oven and an earthy stink. Joe had said to him lots of times:

'Worst thing, Lionel, is to panic. Then your brain shuts down and you're lost. And when you're trapped, you gotta keep calling and calling so the rescue people know where you are.'

'Connie, Connie,' he cried. It was so hard not to panic. It was there, crouching in his stomach, waiting to come roaring out. 'Connie, Connie.'

'Aaahh!!'

The sound was coming from underneath the board. 'Connie, it's me, Lionel.'

He wriggled over the board until he found an edge. Running his fingers across, he found a knob and realised it was a door handle. Connie must be underneath. He couldn't seem to get below it but above he could feel the stairs. 'Connie, you there?'

'Ahh!!' She coughed and coughed then gasped out, 'Lionel.'

'Gonna get you out, Connie.'

'Oh Lionel, Lionel, be careful.'

Joseph was soaking wet and shivering. It was a nightmare. The houses were on their knees. Trapped in the cellars were the injured and dying.

If they were not drowned by the burst water mains, they would be burnt alive or gassed.

'Thank Christ, the gas people and the turnkey have got here,' said Boyden. 'The turntable's useless, nothing to lean against, no bloody walls. We're pulling out. The Auxiliaries have got it now and there's more engines coming.'

'Can I stay?' asked Joseph. 'My Mum's at the Nile and Dad's at the shelter in by the school.'

Boyden gripped his shoulder. 'Joe I got to give it to you straight. Not a hope in hell they're alive, now. Whole street's gone bar a couple of houses. They'll be under a ton of bricks. Sorry, lad. They'll have gone in a flash – won't have known nothing.'

'I gotta stay,' he insisted, 'just in case.'

'Joe, I'll be back later and then you're coming with me.'

He thrust Boyden's words away from him and turned back into the chaos. He swept his torch across the edge of what looked like a crater. A few feet away was a house clinging to the edge.

Inch by inch he worked his way towards it.

'Help, help!' It was a child's cry.

'Lionel,' he called. 'Lionel.'

'Joe, I'm up here on top of a door.'

He swept the torch over the sagging brickwork. The front of the house was gone but the stairwell remained. A door was wedged aslant the steps. He located Lionel clinging to the handle. He swung him free, and set him down a few feet away from him and well back from the crater.

'Connie's underneath, she's hurt bad,' Lionel whimpered.

'Connie, Connie, are you there? It's Joe.' He played the torch below the door.

'Joe, oh Joe,' her voice was faint but it was Connie all right. 'Don't you dare move an inch, Lionel,' he shouted. 'I'll get her.'

'Stretcher, anyone with a stretcher?' There was no reply. He inched his way towards her and attempted to dislodge the door. Instinct told him it was holding up the upper storey. If he yanked it free, the whole house could sweep them down into the crater. He would have to somehow drag Connie out from below.

He heard a whistle. 'Over here,' he called. 'Woman trapped under a door.'

'It's Auntie Connie,' called Lionel.

'You hold my legs,' Joe ordered the two rescue men, 'and have the stretcher ready.'

'Aah!' She screamed as he worked her free. All he could do was drag her by her feet. Too much tugging at the building would have them all buried alive.

'I got you,' he said, wriggling behind her once she was free of the house, and sliding his hands under her arms.

The rescue men let go of his legs and one of them put his coat over Connie, while the other clambered back over the rubble for his stretcher.

Joe reached back and grabbed Lionel. 'You coming back with me to the fire-engine?'

'Wants to go with Connie,' he said.

'Here you are, son. Grab hold of the edge of the stretcher and stay with us.'

'Forrest, over here.' It was Boyden. 'In that window, I heard something.'

460

Entry was simple through the empty frame. As he stepped in his boot came in contact with something soft and round. He gagged before his torch identified the object as a Christmas turkey. As he kicked it across the room a cat yowled at him. 'Anyone there?' he called. No answer. As he stepped out, Boyden pulled him towards him. The house crumpled to the ground.

'That's it Joe, we're off.'

He sat in the engine as it rocked its way back to the station. He felt numb with cold and shock. He dreaded tomorrow, he knew the pain would hit him then.

The column of walking wounded stretched down the road four deep. Coughing, crying, and hobbling over the rubble, they made their way to the Royal Hospital. In the lighted building they looked at one another. Caked in plaster, bleeding and shocked, they sat on benches waiting for the nurses to tend them.

Wrapped in the warden's coat Rosie lay across a bench and waited. Getting to hospital had used up all her strength. In the light of the clinic she could see that she was bleeding. There was a deep gash on her left shin and the bone was visible. It didn't hurt, or perhaps she was too tired to feel anything. She felt no anxiety about herself. She was consumed with fear for her mother and father. 'Let them be alive,' she prayed. 'Please God, I can't lose anyone else.'

'Her name's Connie, Connie Spooner and I'm her son Lionel.'

461

'Hello Lionel,' said the nurse. 'You sit there while the doctor looks at your Mum.'

He tugged at her apron. 'She ain't going to die, is she?'

'No love, she's badly bruised and shocked but with a bit of rest and care, she'll be fine.'

'I ain't leaving her,' he said. 'She needs me to look out for her.'

38

As daylight came, the full extent of the desolation became clear. Hundreds of houses had disappeared overnight; whole streets had gone. Yet, here and there a lone survivor clung to life. Hanging from half a wall was a bird-cage, complete with a canary. Looped across a sagging ceiling were dusty paper chains. Rescue parties and the pioneer corps cleared the rubble into trucks. Those residents who had not been injured returned to see what could be salvaged from the wreckage. Soldiers led two horses out of a battered stable.

Albert had set out that morning with such joyful expectation, and now! Looking about him, he felt his courage leak away. At eighty-seven he was too old for this – the burden too heavy. Alec and Miriam gone, it was too cruel. He leant against the bonnet of his car and wept. People passed him, crunching over the debris with prams and suitcases, desperate to salvage something. Some came back from their search empty-handed, whilst others lugged back children's toys, the old canary, and even a turkey in its tin. The old man searched out his handkerchief and dried his eyes. In the glove compartment was his silver flask filled with rum. After locating it, he sat inside and took a gulp. Closing his eyes, he let the alcohol seep into him. He longed for his wife. Beatrice, he breathed. Beatrice, lend me your lion's heart.

A tap on the window startled him. Albert's fingers fumbled to wind open the window.

'It is Joseph's granddad, isn't it? Mind if I join you?'

He nodded then leant across and opened the passenger door.

A burly fireman slid into the car beside him. 'Sergeant Boyden. Pleased to meet you.' He looked around him shaking his head. 'I was here last night. Did what we could but it was hopeless. It's beyond your worst nightmare. Wicked! Wicked!'

'My Joseph, Sergeant, how is he? Is he safe?'

'He's back at the section house. Had the worst shock of his life poor lad, but as you say, he's safe.'

'I'll go round and see him.' He stared down into the crater. 'I don't suppose his parents, Alec and Miriam are still...' Albert looked imploringly at Sergeant Boyden, as if the fireman had the power to change their fate.

He rested his hand on Albert's shoulder. 'Dead I'm afraid, and the barmaid. Joe had a sister, I believe, Rosie was it? The warden said something about her being found.'

'Oh not Rosie, I couldn't bear it.' He held his head in his hands.

'Look, Squire,' said Boyden, patting his shoulder before getting out of the car. 'I'll get one of my men to drive you over to the Royal Hospital. You come round to the passenger seat. Last thing your Joe and Rosie need is you having an accident.'

The effort of getting out again and walking around the car used all his energy. From somewhere he dredged up the words, 'Thank you, Sergeant, most grateful.'

'You leave Joe 'til later, Squire, he's probably asleep. I'll tell him you'll be round.'

He had no memory of being driven to the hospital. Startled, he looked around him as they came to a halt.

'Mr Pragnell, can I go and ask for you? Who are you looking for?' The fireman took the keys out of the ignition and handed them to him.

'Rosie Forrest, she's a Wren, she would have been in uniform.'

'You sit there, and I'll go and enquire about her at the desk.'

He prayed that Alec and Miriam had gone swiftly, without suffering. And Rosie? Please merciful Jesus, let her be spared. So immersed was he that the fireman had re-opened the door and sat beside him before Albert knew he was there.

'Mr Pragnell, it's all right, she's in Edward and Mary Ward. Here's your keys, you dropped them on the floor. That's it, put them in your pocket.'

'Thank you, you have been most kind,' he said, shaking the fireman's hand. Walking towards the stairs, he was startled by a large red-faced man in a Santa Claus costume, who pumped his hand and wished him 'Merry Christmas.'

Albert stared at him as if he were speaking a foreign language. There was no room for Christmas in a heart wracked with such anxiety. He nodded vaguely as the man strode off to the children's ward. It seemed the longest walk of his life to the door of Edward and Mary, and the greatest act of courage to tap on the ward sister's door.

'Good morning, Sister, I am Rosie Forrest's grandfather. My name is Pragnell,' he said. Telling the woman that he was not a blood relation was superfluous. No one could love her more than he did.

'Mr Pragnell, good morning to you. Miss Forrest is three beds down, on the left-hand side. She is shocked and her leg is injured, but she is as comfortable as we can make her. I'm sure seeing you will help. Please don't stay too long. She is very tired.'

Albert steeled himself for what he might find. As he reached the bed, he saw she was asleep. Looking around him he found a chair, and sat beside her. How small and pale she looked. In the bed next to her was Connie Spooner, her arm in plaster and face a mass of bruises. Sitting beside her was Lionel.

'Hello, young man,' Albert dredged up a smile. 'How are you?'

'I saved Connie,' the boy said. 'She was under a door, me and Joseph got her out.'

The little woman beckoned to him.

He bent over her bed, as she whispered, 'Can you find him somewhere, 'til I'm up to coping, Albert?'

Standing there, he felt at the end of his resources. What could he offer? Connie's physical injuries had been treated, but she would not rest until Lionel was taken care of. 'I could take him back to the farm at Romsey,' he offered. The thought of his sister-in-law Olive, and her quiet commonsense, was a balm to his spirits.

'I don't want to go. Staying here with you,' he wailed.

'You gotta be a brave soldier,' gasped Connie. 'I needs to rest, and I needs you and Albert to find out where we can go after, when I'm better.'

Albert fished in his pocket and handed him a sixpence. 'You go and get yourself some sweets, and when you come back we'll go and see Auntie Olive. Off you go.'

Connie waved her good arm to Lionel then sank back on her pillows.

Sitting beside Rosie's bed, Albert closed his eyes. Weariness engulfed him. What could he do, what would Beatrice have done? This girl was so dear to him. He was grateful that she slept. If he could just sit beside her a moment or two, he might mend his threadbare resources.

'Uncle Albert.' The voice was barely a whisper but it was enough to wake him.

'Rosie, my dear child, thank God you're safe.'

Her dark eyes swam with tears. 'I know they're gone, but they won't tell me. Just nod, please, I need to know.'

Albert took her hand and kissed it. 'It would have been so swift.' He could say no more, for there were no words adequate to the task. Being there was as much as he could manage. The day drifted away from them. In the late afternoon Delia came. Albert excused himself and went to see Joseph, promising to return later for Lionel.

A fire-boy took him over to the section house.

'Hello my boy, what a sad, sad day.'

Joseph sat on the end of his bed, his face buried

in his hands. 'They didn't do anything wrong, they were always so good to people, didn't deserve it, not them. I can't cry. I feel so fucking angry.' He glared at him, his eyes reddened by smoke and weariness. 'What are we going to do?'

'I don't know, Joseph,' Albert shook his head. 'We just have to cling together somehow. Do you want to come back to Romsey with me?'

'Can't think about that. Got to stay here and keep busy.'

'Is there anything I can get you, my boy? Anything.'

Joseph shook his head.

Defeated, Albert went back to visit Rosie and to collect Lionel.

'Oh Albert, you look so tired.'

Her solicitude made him weep. It seemed to be the only response he could offer.

'You must rest, we'll need you.'

One of the ward maids brought him a cup of tea. He realised he'd not eaten since breakfast in the woods with Towser. The thought of food sickened him, and he doubted he could swallow. Once it was finished he got to his feet. 'Goodbye my darling, sleep well.' He kissed her forehead. 'Goodbye Connie, you rest, now. Lionel come with me.'

Albert didn't know how he got home. He was too tired to speak to Lionel. Using the last shred of energy, he made his way up to the farm and knocked on the door.

'Albert, my dear, I thought you were off to Portsmouth for Christmas.' His sister-in-law Olive helped him indoors. 'Who is this young man?'

'I'm Lionel Spooner, my Mum's in hospital.

Nearly buried alive she was. I saved her.'

Albert stood there looking at her, hoping she would make up for his deficiencies.

'Sit down by the fire, my dear, I'll get you some soup.'

Towser bounded into his lap and surveyed him, his head on one side. Albert closed his eyes and passed his hand over the dog's rough coat.

Rosie didn't know how to mend herself. She had wanted to die, yet her traitorous body was healing in spite of her. The wound on her leg was too deep for stitches and had to be packed with eusol dressings, a procedure she dreaded. Even the sight of the dressing-trolley made her nerves jangle.

'You're young, Miss Forrest. It will mend, given time,' said the sister, a week later.

How will I mend my heart, she thought. All the people Rosie had loved were lost to her. All the places where she might have mourned them were gone: Lemon Street, Nelson Street, the Nile, even Gran's beach at the Round Tower was cordoned off with barbed-wire. She clung to Connie. Sleepless in the dark, they comforted one another. When she cried, Connie held her hand and, when she wept Rosie did the same for her.

Every day she was visited. After Albert had gone Delia came, on her way home to Hazlewood. She brought her handbag, washing-things, and Blyth's picture along with the one of all the family taken on Gran's beach the first day of the war.

She burst into tears and flung her arms around her friend. 'Rosie, oh Rosie, I don't know what to say. I want to wrap you up and take you home to

Mummy,' she sobbed.

'One day,' Rosie said. 'When I can walk again.'

'I'll phone the signal office every day and I'll be back as soon as I can.'

Christmas Day passed in a blur. The nurses sang carols and at the end of the ward was a tree sparkling with lights. Propped up on pillows, her leg throbbing, Rosie stared down at her dinner until the sprouts and roast potatoes congealed on the plate. It was a relief to lie down afterwards and escape into sleep.

Auntie Olive came from Romsey on Boxing Day. 'Albert sends his love my dear,' she said. 'He's exhausted, poor soul, but promises to be down on Sunday.'

Daisy came on New Year's Day, and they cried together. Joseph came. 'Can't stay here anymore,' he said. 'Joining the Royal Marines. I can live with Uncle George near the barracks. I want to get away. Feel angry all the time, just want to get stuck into the war.'

'Give me a hug,' Rosie insisted.

Tactfully, the nurse fetched the screens and put them round the bed and then her brother cried, hard racking sobs.

'We've got to help each other,' she whispered. 'You and me, we're all that's left. Oh Joe, don't go away yet. I need you.'

'I don't know what to do,' he gasped. 'I'm so tired but I can't sleep. I keep seeing everything, hearing the screams.'

'Come and see me every day, promise me.'

Wearily he nodded.

A week into the New Year Connie was ready to

be discharged. They joined Joseph at Uncle George's house in Eastney. She came to see Rosie when she had settled in.

'How's Lionel like it?' Rosie asked.

'Quite excited, 'specially as Joe's with us.' Connie smiled. 'Lionel wants me to adopt him, tells everyone I'm his mother. We'll be a mongrel bunch, made up of waifs and strays up there. It's a bit like Portsea with the beach on our doorstep. Just swap the sailors for Royal Marines. Even be room for you up in the attic.'

Rosie smiled, 'I hope to be back at the Wrennery soon, but it'll be good to have somewhere to spend my days off.'

The next week there was a mass funeral for the victims of the air-raid. The Sister was not happy at her patient attending such a taxing event, but Rosie insisted.

'I need to, Sister. My grandfather will take me and we'll be straight back.'

Delia brought her clothes from the Wrennery and insisted on pushing the wheelchair the hospital had provided. 'Your Uncle Albert won't be able to manage everything, besides your parents were good to me and I want to be there.'

At Kingston cemetery there was a large earth-covered mound with flowers heaped on top. The Mayor was there with his golden chain, so was Admiral James, and Commander Barnaby. Rosie spotted Mary in the crowd and waved to her.

'I had to come,' Mary said, coming up and kissing her. She handed her baby into Rosie's arms. 'You have a hold of him. He'll keep you warm.'

Rosie bent her head and kissed the little boy. He stared at her, his blue eyes so like Blyth's. She thought of him that sunny September afternoon, here in the graveyard, when they had smiled across Gran's coffin. But that had been a proper funeral, marking the death of one old lady who had lived a long and happy life. Now she was back to mourn her parents and Bernice and Garth and everyone else – all snatched from life too soon. She didn't know with any certainty where their bodies were.

They attempted to sing Gran's favourite hymn *'Jesus hear the prayer we offer'*.

As they got to the second verse she could almost hear her singing, too:

'Not forever by still water would we idly rest and play, But would strike the living water from the rocks upon our way.'

Rosie hugged Matthew Blyth and hoped she could be as brave as Beattie.

39

For one blessed moment she thought it was Blyth coming towards her. The pain of her disappointment took her breath away.

Justin took off his cap and laid it on the bed beside her. 'Sorry it's only me. I came as soon as I could.' He nodded to the bed cradle keeping the covers off her leg. 'I see you've been in the wars. I come bringing gifts.'

She leaned forward and kissed him. 'Thank you, Juss, that's kind of you. Get yourself a chair.'

'Ma has sent you some chocolate cake and Delia a new nightdress. There's the letter Blyth made me promise to give you in any emergency. Sorry it's taken so long.'

The sight of the familiar handwriting brought tears to her eyes. She slid the envelope under the covers for later. While Justin put the other things in her locker Rosie tried to calm herself, and think what to ask him.

'What was he like the last time you saw him? Was he extra nervous, or anything?'

Juss smiled. 'He was just Blyth, excited, keyed-up, wanting to do his job. I'd sprained my ankle and so I couldn't go with him. There was an extra fuel tank, so no room for Simmo. Dicky Bird was his observer, a very good chap.'

'D'you think it would have made any difference if you had been with him?'

'No, Rosie, Blyth is a fantastic pilot and Bird is spot-on.'

He was the only one who spoke of him as if he were still alive, except Mary, of course.

'He's out there somewhere, Rosie, I bet he is. There have been no downed planes reported, no pilots found. There are lots of little islands off the Greek coast. It's a waiting game.'

'I never was good at waiting,' she said.

'Bound to be hard in here, not able to do anything. Once you're back in the saddle it won't be so bad. Have they said when you can leave?'

'Two more days, but, as to the driving, I've got to have a medical. Delia says her date for officer training's come through, so whatever, we'll be separated. I think I'd like to get away somewhere.' She smiled at Juss. 'Wherever it is, he'll be able to find me. What about you?'

'A couple of weeks' leave, and who knows? I'd like to go back to the old *Unrivalled*, but there's talk of me going into instructing, becoming a Schoolie somewhere.'

'Would you like that?'

Juss gave a rueful smile. 'I was never the pilot that Blyth is, and Pa would not think much of it but,' he shrugged, 'that doesn't seem to matter so much as it did.'

'Will you come and see me, again? I'll be in Cromwell Road, opposite the Royal Marine Barracks.'

'Of course I will, Rosie. We're friends. I don't seem to have many left.'

'Thanks Justin, you're a jewel. Seeing you has really helped.'

He bent over and kissed her on the cheek, before taking his cap and walking back down the ward and out of the door. As soon as he disappeared through the ward door, she opened the letter.

My Darling Girl,
If you get this it means that I have got myself lost or drowned or some other daft thing. Unless my body is found shot up or I'm fished out of the drink rest assured I'm somewhere struggling to get home to you. Never doubt that.
What great times we've had my Rosie didn't we? What kindred spirits we are. Chips off the old Lemon Street block. I only realised that when we were looking at old Albert's painting up in London. It seemed to turn a key in me and say: 'These are the people that made you, this is where you're from. Keep faith with them and their values and you won't go wrong.' *I knew in those seconds that you were my one and only.*
Go and see it again for me, Rosie. Promise you will. I will be back because I'm wearing my lucky stone.
Whatever happens my Rosie I love you more than my Fairey Swordfish. All you have to do is wait.
See you in and out of your dreams.
Blyth

Oh, he knew her through and through. Rosie cried and cried, and then she put the letter back in the envelope and tucked it under her pillow. Searching in her handbag, she found the ticket to the gallery in Cork Street. She slept soundly that night.

Rosie hadn't connected the date of her leaving hospital with her birthday. Uncle Albert had to remind her.

'Happy Birthday, my darling, are you ready for the next chapter?' he asked, as he tucked a travelling-rug around her legs.

'Have you brought the flowers?' she asked him.

'Hyacinths as requested,' he said, starting up the car.

'Just right, they were special to Mum.'

'Is Joseph meeting us there?'

Rosie shook her head. 'No, but he sent this.' She fished in her pocket and brought out a blue-and-white football rosette. 'It was Dad's, he wore it the day Pompey won the cup. I've got a hair-ribbon Mum bought me when I was little.'

Albert took out his handkerchief and blew his nose.

Poor Uncle, she thought, he has had to carry all of us through this terrible mess. It has been too much to bear. She ransacked her mind for something that would encourage the pair of them.

'Gran always said, in times of trouble you had to face them, mark them and then move on. We're doing the first two, perhaps they'll carry us through to the third.'

He gave her a ghost of a smile. 'If my Beatrice said that it must be the gospel truth.'

At the crater where Nelson Street had once been, they stood looking into the depths. Rosie had not seen it in daylight, and was shocked at the extent of the damage. Her memory of that night was of shivering in the dark, of noise, confusion and pain. Then she closed her eyes, and words and pictures flitted through her head. Mum was standing on Gran's beach after she'd got the man to take their picture on the first day of the war.

'I want us to remember we were a family,' she'd said. 'If this snap comes out it's living proof of it.'

Rosie thanked God she had got a copy of the photo, and had taken it with her to the Wrennery. Then there was Dad smiling at her that day when she'd got a letter from Blyth. The same day they had received the news of Connie's men having died on the *Royal Oak*. She had felt guilty about reading it.

''Course you're sad,' he'd said, 'but you can't lie down under it. Seize all the joy and good things that come your way. Anything else is letting the enemy through the door. You go and read your letter.'

She could see Bernice in her big slippers, winking at Joseph and thumping out, 'I don't want to set the world on fire,' on the pub piano.

And then there was Garth whispering endearments to Fortune and Damson, as he fed them sugar lumps.

She held Albert's hand. 'Good bye, God bless,' she managed to choke out before throwing the flowers, the ribbon and the rosette down into the void. They paused for a moment then, hand-in-hand, a walking-stick apiece, they made their way back to the car. Rosie relished the warmth of the seat and the smell of old leather.

She realised, with a jolt, that she was on her own. The only other female relations were Lily and young Beatrice in Canada – too far to be of use to her. Whatever wit, courage and wisdom the Forrest women had possessed, she would have to carry forward into her own life and make something of herself. She could not put everything in storage on the chance that Blyth would come back to her. No, she had to live every moment. Rosie knew her life would go forward from one faltering step to another. I have been well loved, she thought, and I have a lot to give. If Blyth comes back it will be a wonderful bonus. If not, I shall savour every moment we had together.

After a while, Albert took her hand and kissed it.

'Happy birthday again, my darling, twenty-four years. We must plan a treat.'

Rosie pressed her fingers against her stone necklace. 'Well,' she said, smiling at him. 'There's this gallery in London that has an interesting picture we might take a look at. I happen to know the painter. He's a bit of an old Bohemian but it's well worth seeing.'

Albert rewarded her with a chuckle.

Rosie grinned. Somewhere in her head she could see Beattie smiling, her dark eyes full of mischief.

'That's my Rosie,' she said, 'that's the spirit.'

The publishers hope that this book has given you enjoyable reading. Large Print Books are especially designed to be as easy to see and hold as possible. If you wish a complete list of our books please ask at your local library or write directly to:

Magna Large Print Books
Magna House, Long Preston,
Skipton, North Yorkshire.
BD23 4ND

This Large Print Book for the partially sighted, who cannot read normal print, is published under the auspices of

THE ULVERSCROFT FOUNDATION